The Orphan of Pitigliano

Marina Brown

Published by:
Gilberte Publishing
5377 Paddington Drive.
Tallahassee, FL 32309

ISBN-13: 978-0-9897543-6-1

Cover Design: Robert Burke

Printed in the United States of America
First Edition March 2020

PRAISE FOR

THE ORPHAN OF PITIGLIANO

"Couldn't put this book down! Its intrigue and originality kept me turning page after page, often holding my breath to see what was about to happen to characters I'd come to love—and in some cases hate. Bonus: now I'm drawn to Etruscan artifacts…"

— Liz Jameson, Literary Editor

"An absolutely riveting book to read! A love story, set deep in the Etruscan caves and small farms in Tuscany, where the passions of young people are magnified by the fear of their Jewish identity being discovered."

— Janice Hartwell, Professor Emerita, Florida State University, Department of Art

"The superb and magical *Orphan of Pitigliano* is Marina Brown at her best. Contrasting the horrors of WWII with the beauty of Italy, this story is filled with Brown's trademark lyrical language, her sharp eye for telling details and lush descriptive passages. The story is complex and evocative, filled with conflict, sacrifice, and over all, *il malocchio*—the Evil Eye—that will impact characters for generations."

— Claire Matturro, author of *Sweetheart Deal*

"Brown paints her stunning story against the blood-stained, war-torn canvas of the Italian countryside during World War II. *The Orphan of Pitigliano* is a feast of Old World mystery and magic, betrayal and heartbreak, sin and redemption. A stunning story!"

— Donna Meredith, Associate Editor of Southern Literary Review and author of *Buried Seeds*

"In a treasure of a novel that underscores the horror of fascism in Mussolini's Italy, Marina Brown takes us on a pulse-pounding and page-turning journey from Boston to Tuscany and back again. She weaves history, mystery, religion, tradition, wisdom, suspense and even an ancient tomb into an accessible tale of hate, hunger, heroism, strength, superstition, survival, betrayal, forgiveness... and love. Read this book. In return, you'll get "the Eye." And you'll see the Holocaust through the unique and creative lens of a gifted storyteller."

— Peter Reinwald, Editor, Tallahassee Magazine; a former editor, Chicago Tribune

"Once again, Marina Brown has delivered an engrossing tale of love, betrayal, good, and true evil. Set in the Nazi-occupied Tuscan hills of Italy, Brown keeps her readers in her storytelling grip from the first page. With its intrigues and plot twists, *The Orphan of Pitigliano* adds yet more depth to her growing literary contributions and will undoubtedly draw in yet another legion of loyal readers."

— Sam Staley, Director, DeVoe L. Moore Center, Florida State University; Author of *Calusa Spirits*

"Marina Brown's spellbinding novel, *The Orphan of Pitigliano,* combines hidden identities and hidden treasures, secrets, romance, and a curse that crosses continents to claim its victims. An exciting read!"

— M.R. Street, Tallahassee Democrat, Author of *Hunter's Moon*

"A compelling and powerful tale of suspense and mystery, filled with vivid characters, love, and an ancient magic that keeps the pages turning! Glorious writing!"

— Barbara Palmer, Art Historian, Rome

"*The Orphan of Pitigliano* is a sweeping, multigenerational story of love, betrayal, and supernatural evil, set against the backdrop of Italy during the rise of fascism. Filled with thrilling action and unforgettable characters, the reader is drawn relentlessly across decades and between continents as the buried secrets of the past will not rest. A deeply engrossing page-turner for the head and heart."

— Lisa Blackwell, Senior Editor, DraftWorks

"A thrilling read! This book is full of the glories of Tuscany; the magic of Etruscan tombs, as well as the little-known lives of Italian Jews forced during WWII to conceal their identities. In language both beautiful and accurate, history buffs, lovers of Italy and those who cherish a never-ending story of love will find themselves mesmerized."

— S. K. Fielding, *Libreria Centurione*, Florence, Italy

Acknowledgements

Thanks for the careful reading and commentaries of Lisa Blackwell, Liz Jameson, Terry Lewis, Sam Staley, Jean Esposito, Janice Hartwell, Barbara Palmer, and particularly to the gracious M.R. Street. A bow to Claire Matturro for her constant support and clarity of thought.

My gratitude to the people of Pitigliano who shared with me their stories, to Professor Nancy de Grummond of Florida State University for thoughts on Etruscan archaeology, to the grave robbers I met long ago who told me their secrets. And most of all—

My affection and gratitude to Douglas Kiliman, editor par excellence, organizer supreme, potentate of punctuation, checker of facts, IT magician, my co-traveler in the Tuscan mists—and my life companion, always.

Marina Brown, 2020

Other Books by Marina Brown

Lisbeth
Airport Sketches
Land Without Mirrors
The Leaf Does Not Believe It Will Fall
Walking Alone Together, An Anthem for Caregivers

Chapter 1

Boston 1975

The room was hot. A sweet, acrid smell clung to the turned posts of the bed and lay like a fog on its linen. Outside, a church bell began a muted ring somewhere in Boston's North End.

In the candle's light, Carlo watched the shadow of Father Paolo as the elderly priest moved his hands above the woman's body. His eyes were closed as he grazed the air along her head and shoulders toward her hips and feet. At times he paused to shake his hands as if they'd become contaminated and he were shaking away what he feared. At other times he worked his fingers, massaging in midair what Carlo took to be imaginary muscles. Or were these only hocus pocus semaphores that made the air dance with dust?

The priest's lips were parted at times. At other moments his jaw was set as if he strained against a weight. Occasionally, he bent very close to the woman, his crucifix dropping down onto the fragile shell of her chest, and he whispered in her ear a ribbon of Latin syllables Carlo thought he'd once heard at a funeral.

Yet Paolo was all Carlo had. The priest may not be young, but at least he was Italian. And that alone might help. Carlo hadn't had a hard time finding a *paisan* of the cloth in Boston, though an Irishman would have been easier. But when he'd explained the situation, the first three Italian priests had gone quiet, then tried to direct Carlo to a doctor. "Find a good psychiatrist," is what they'd told him before hanging up.

Now Father Paolo wasn't being that helpful either. All Carlo had wanted was a good Italian priest to pray over his Aunt Giuliana, anoint her with holy oil, and get some of the Sacraments down her.

It was all he had left—a hollow belief that the woman's devotion to the signs and signals of the Church would, when administered by a priest of her own country, somehow let her rally. Yet here she was, not three weeks after arriving for her first visit, wasting into death, fragile as dust, while the old cleric performed like a conductor over her body.

A cadre of doctors had ruled out the usual physical ailments of age. No organ gone bad; blood and breathing as they should be. In fact, they'd been shocked at Giuliana's youthfulness. But surely if what was happening to the woman were psychological—even spiritual—the Sacraments she held so dear would get the ball rolling—would bring her out of what looked like a kind of suspended animation. At least Carlo had to hope.

Father Paolo continued to whisper to the inert woman, swirling an occasional manual flourish, but which mostly had become slow draws down the contour of her body in a way that struck Carlo as strangely sensual.

"Father. Father… I need to have a word with you."

Carlo shoved himself up from the creaking rocker he'd hauled down from the brownstone's attic. The thing had sat up there when he was a child and even though it had been sent from the old country as a gift, he was the only one who'd liked to sit in it—a little boy, rocking back and forth while someone hung wet clothes in the attic's desiccating heat. He had always associated the chair with the rural Italian farm house he'd been sent to visit. It was where Giuliana and the other diminutive women had presided, ones who'd stayed behind in Pitigliano when many young people were leaving Italy for America. Carlo remembered summers there were some of the most magical of his childhood.

Now, nearly thirty years later, Carlo expected his aunt to love the little touch of the old country he'd tucked into a corner of her room. But she'd shied from the chair like a pony from a snake.

"Look, Father, I'm sorry to interrupt you… but I don't think…"

The priest took out a handkerchief and wiped at his face. The white cotton came back a greasy brown. "No matter, young man, you can't interrupt me, because I have finished." Paolo patted Carlo on the shoulder, smiling the wrinkles around his mouth into thick leather folds.

Paolo had another look at the frail woman who seemed to alternately hold her breath, then reluctantly allow her chest to rise for a little air. Carlo had told the priest he guessed his aunt was over fifty, but in outlying Italian towns where birth records were kept by the church and churches occasionally burned down, even his aunt might be unsure of her age.

What was clear was that she had managed to remain beautiful. Yes, Carlo could actually say that about this woman entering her sixth decade. She had retained the beauty of her middle age as she prepared to enter her old.

Even now, Carlo could see Father Paolo's eyes wander along her high forehead with the thick brows and dark lashes so quiet against her cheeks. She was thin, but along with the very-non-peasant taper of her fingers, youthfulness illuminated the woman's hair as it spilled dark and lustrous across the pillow—a sleeping Medusa deep within a dream.

Carlo touched Paolo's elbow and the cleric seemed to rouse and allow himself to be escorted into the hall.

"Look, I appreciate that you are here, Father. You are in fact the only priest willing to come have a look at Zia Giuliana. But what we need is some holy water, maybe a spot of oil on her forehead. She's a great believer… really. When I stayed with her as a boy in Italy, it seemed like that's all we did—celebrate saint's days, light candles, say rosaries. But waving your hands over her like a… a huckster in carnival magic show, just isn't going to get it, Father."

Carlo was immediately sorry. After all, this priest *had* come. For that matter, his Zia would have smacked his cheek if she were aware he was talking to a man of the cloth like this.

"Ok, ok… I'm tired, Father. Excuse me. Come downstairs and let me open some Chianti. Do you have a few more minutes? Are you off for the rest of the day?"

Father Paolo laughed out loud. "Well *amico*, it's been quite a while since you've talked to a priest hasn't it." Paolo picked up his satchel and headed for the narrow stairs. "As old as I am, I don't get 'days off,' and evenings are filled with classes for the kiddies and meetings with the auxiliaries. But as for a glass of Chianti… make it a quick *grappa* and we can talk."

Carlo went back in to his aunt. He moved the pillows under her head and readjusted her crossed hands, feeling their olive parchment give beneath his own. He suddenly wished he had parents still here. Right here. In this room. Ready to take responsibility. Knowing what to do. Letting him go back to being the thirty-something broker with the stable of long-legged, upwardly-mobile ladies who appreciated his car and his curly hair and asked only to be taken to where he could show them off. Life had been a win/win. Now it had become complicated.

Then a voice reminded him it could get worse.

"Who's the 'man in black' in the hall?"

Carlo jumped as his sister materialized beside the door. Sylvie had always liked spying on people. On the occasions they'd lived together as teens, she'd been a little snitch with a knack for turning up just when the teenaged Carlo had broken some rule. God knows she broke enough of her own. But her mastery of the raised eyebrow and inclined head had gotten him into more trouble with their constantly changing foster parents than had any outright accusations. But for now, not only Zia Giuliana, but unfortunately Sylvie too, felt like his responsibility.

"The man you saw is Father Paolo," he said, anticipating a sarcastic shrug. Carlo avoided looking at her directly, but knew that his sister's mane of wavy hair probably obscured most of the pale face and jet-black eyes that made the telephone ring at all hours of the night and a series of men and boys appear at their door. For him, her looks were but another annoyance. He also knew those dark eyes to be taking in everything they saw.

"Look, Sylvie, I need to go downstairs and talk with the priest for a few minutes. You stay here with Giuliana, all right? You don't have to do anything… just sit with her. Read a book, stare at your phone… I don't care. The sitter from the agency will be here in a while, then you can go do… whatever…"

Sylvie crossed her arms. "So, let's see, she's been to see a shrink; some neuro doc; and somebody to make her eat. Then what? Oh, yeah, the recommendation to a psych ward for a few weeks. And now you expect a priest to fix everything? This is not real. Let's get the magician from the eight-year old's birthday party next door. Ohh… abracadabra…" Sylvie waved her hands over Giuliana's outstretched form much as Father Paolo had minutes before.

"Stop that!" Carlo rushed at her from the door and spun her around.

"You *will* treat your aunt with respect," he hissed. "If you've got a better idea, let me know. But I'm running out of them. I don't intend to see a wonderful woman waste away—without knowing why! And I *will* explore every way possible to make her well!"

Carlo felt the saliva accumulate in his mouth. He wanted to spit. He let Sylvie's shoulders go, and out of breath, shoved his hair back into place. He was never having kids—not without ending up in jail if this is what it was like.

"Now sit down and go to sleep or whatever the hell you want… but just stay with her." As he closed the door, he added what he knew would make Sylvie snigger and even to him sounded like sappy lines from a Hallmark card. Yet he meant them with all his heart.

"You never know when a miracle will occur, Sylvie. Just be watchful and wait."

***

Father Paolo, who knew his way around old Italians' sitting and dining rooms, leaned back into the Chesterfield's faded flowers, his feet on an ottoman somebody had needle-pointed many years before. Paolo, whose pale coloring suggested Nordic rather than

Italian roots, nevertheless had poured a grappa for himself and another for his host.

Carlo slumped into a faded, overstuffed chair, its musty aroma rising in an invisible cloud. Christ, Carlo hated the combustible taste of grappa! The vaguely greasy alcohol was usually reserved for after a meal, when your stomach could take it, when you wouldn't immediately become drunk, and when you could cram something else in your mouth to loosen the grappa's gnaw at your gut.

"Saluti" smiled Paolo, lifting one of the tiny etched glasses sent as Christmas gifts from unknown relatives in Orvieto. "It is good—good to finish this part of the day with something manly, no!"

Manly? No. Choking down gasoline wasn't manly. But trying to get to the bottom of his aunt's ailment and juggling an uncontrollable sister, a job, and what once had been a rewarding social life were taking every ounce of Carlo's macho reserves.

"Absolutely, Father. Yes… grappa. Do you drink it every day? What about limoncello? Now that always reminds me of *la campagnia* where some of my folks are from. I mean it's like drinking a lemon meringue pie! Or… or sleeping on lemon leaves!" Carlo could already feel the grappa's grip. It made his senses feel alive.

"Ha! Limoncello! Now that's a good ladies' drink. But still, yes, cold enough, limoncello can clean the palate. It always makes me want to go into the field and, like a donkey, graze on mint!" Paolo burst into laughter that bounced his gut up and down and threatened to upend the second grappa he'd poured into his glass.

Carlo took another sip. He was still grappling with the image of Paolo on all fours munching sprigs of field mint and swishing his tail against flies when the priest, who had stopped laughing, reached over and grasped Carlo's shoulder.

"But we mustn't be so light, my son. Drink your grappa, but listen to me." Paolo's voice had dropped as if someone might be listening. Carlo instinctively looked around for Sylvie leaning around a corner. But they were alone in the old, high-ceilinged room, its padded furniture absorbing even their breathing.

"The matter with your aunt, Carlo, is not medical. Nor can I, alone, do anything…"

Carlo sat forward, ready to interrupt. Of course, if not medical, then spiritual. He was not prepared to believe that his Zia had gone crazy and was purposely starving herself to death. Nor that the Church could do nothing. Giuliana would believe anything the priests said. Now they must say that she should get better!

"My boy, there are some things that don't fit into our life here… here in Boston. Here in the U.S. But they exist." He paused, searching the ceiling for the right word. "Shall we call them shadows, then? Long, dark shadows that can lay across us… *sent* by someone to lay across us… and that if not lifted can take the life." The old man was staring into his nearly empty glass, exhaustion or sadness draping him from head to foot.

"I have no idea what you're talking about, Father. Shadows? Giuliana is not eating. She's in a dead sleep. Unresponsive. What kind of shadows can do that, for god's sake?"

"The kind that are brought from the *streghe,* Carlo. *La fattucchiera.* Maybe a *jettatora* of the *malocchio.*" Paolo shook his head slowly. "I have seen it a few times, my boy. When I was a child in the old country, my neighbor, *una bella ragazza*, fell into a deep sleep. She was so young, a beautiful girl with a wedding date set to a rich man's son. But there was much jealousy for that reason. We never knew who it was. One of her friends? Her false friends, who was a secret *fattucchiera*—a sorceress skilled at throwing the evil eye? You have heard of *il malocchio*, have you not, Carlo? I have seen women and men who have received such a curse. Sometimes they never have awakened."

Carlo slammed the little glass onto an embroidered doily on the table. "This is nuts, Father. Sorry, but you're a man of God and you're sitting here telling me about witches and… what… demons? You've overdone the damned grappa!" He was standing now and looking for a place amidst the furniture to pace.

"Carlo, may I ask you a question?" The priest continued to rotate the little etched glass between his fingers. "Do you remember any little things that perplexed you when you were small and visited your Zia in Italy? Things that she did that you found strange?" Paolo took a last sip of grappa and rolled it across his tongue. "For instance, did she spit on your head? Did she tell others what an ugly little boy you were, though in private she would call you handsome?"

Carlo stopped near the door, his back to the priest. He felt as if someone had opened the ancient blue shutters that had kept the rooms of the old stone house so dark in winter. Now, as if in a flood of Tuscan sunlight, he remembered how, in the market place, his aunt or his grandmother would suddenly spit on his head when one or other of their neighbors would smile and call him… what was it… *"adorabile."* Sometimes even the neighbor would spit on his head after calling him "cute." Carlo would swipe at his head and rub the sticky gob onto his aunt's skirts as the old women laughed at Carlo's little stamping feet. Of course, his aunt, and his grandmother too had spat on his head—it was part of his childhood.

"So what? Maybe I had some dirt in my hair…" said Carlo.

"No, Carlo, it was not dirt. It was protection. Do you remember anything else the old women did? Any necklaces they wore? Any little rituals they performed? Those women are from the long-ago world… where these things were understood and respected. I am sure that Giuliana knew many ways to protect those she loved." Paolo sat back with a half-smile, slowly raising the third grappa to his lips.

Carlo came around to face him, feeling equal sensations of joy at remembering little details of his summers with his Italian family and a growing alarm at what the priest wanted him to know.

"Oh, you're right that the women had some funny ways, Father… little things that all the people did back in that village. But whatever they were, they were just superstitions. Like who hasn't knocked on wood or avoided walking under a ladder. It means nothing." Carlo slumped back into his chair, closing his eyes.

"I remember Zia Giuliana coming to kiss me good-night and always telling me to uncross my arms and legs, that it was unlucky to sleep on my back with anything crossed. Had something to do with the way you're laid in a coffin. That was weird. But no big deal. I slept on my side."

He sat up, head back, smiling now as he recalled another sun-touched day with his grandmother. "Yes, there was this sleepy bottle-gray cat who seemed to adopt me each summer. And she would always laugh and clap her hands if Gaticolo sneezed. She would tell him, '*Molto! Molto!*' She wanted more sneezes because she said they brought good fortune to the house."

Carlo shook his head and downed his own second glass of grappa. "Then I remember one time when Giuliana and I made each other so angry—the day I brought home the injured bird. She was so furious that…"

"That she threw it right out the door!" Paolo finished Carlo's sentence with a boom of laughter.

"That's right! How did you know that? She screamed at me about bringing bad luck home—'right under her roof'! I lost my temper too and spent the next several nights sleeping under the grape arbor secretly trying to nurse the little guy back to health."

"And so, you see, you were kept safe by your auntie, Carlo," said Paolo. "These little things, these little practices were like a web that had been spun by people who loved you. They did these things to catch the eye's jealous gleam. Think of her spitting and avoidance of birds as a *threat shield* if you like. What is it that America now erects against incoming missiles? Think of her spitting as countering with the moisture of life the implicit dryness of death that *il malocchio* can bring. And the bird's eyes, or the markings on the feather of a peacock—she would make you avoid them at all costs for like the evil eye itself, they may bring misfortune." Paolo swallowed several times as if his own throat had grown dry and he sucked at the last drops of grappa.

"You must remove *il malocchio*, my boy. I believe this is what has befallen your aunt. Maybe you cannot take her back to Italy to have the curses removed, but there is another way. Find some piece of her clothing, an ornament that she has worn. Ah, you could then send it back… to the old women of the village. But to whom should you send it? Are the women still there? How could you be sure it was not one of them… a jealous old lady… who had thrown the evil eye? But I could assist you in this. If you have something… perhaps an item your aunt kept in her possession. Even something small, a trinket… a piece of pottery….”

The priest sat back slightly in his chair, seeming to offer a kind of professional overview of evil that alternated with a conspiratorial urgency. “While these special old women know how to remove *il malocchio*, it is of course we priests who are schooled in such a dangerous art. Without a priest, you would have to take such an item as I have described to the village, the place where the evil eye was first cast, where this misfortune probably began. Yes, these old women see it often. But I believe that in this case, because it is an emergency, you must bring this thing to me. Having an object… an object… will help me focus the removal, will help me relieve your aunt even quicker.”

Paolo was leaning forward, his eyes suddenly red and his words rushed as if these instructions were what he had come for. “You will try to find such a thing, won’t you, young man? Yes, I sense it may be some piece of pottery, something *ceramico…*” Paolo closed his eyes, stopped, swallowed dryly, then began again.

“*Ragazzo*, such an object is used to focus the *malocchio*. It often carries the sign of the eye. Such objects are very powerful. If you find *this* thing, it is imperative that you bring it to me, and then, in the presence of your aunt, I will be able to lift the veil under which she now lies.” Carlo watched as Paolo seemed to grow agitated, his blue eyes darting toward the ceiling and the corners of the room even as his voice appeared to fade to a painful whisper.

The priest stopped once again, his hand slowly reaching down between his legs. He was staring with wide eyes into the dusk in the dining room behind Carlo’s chair. Confused, Carlo watched as the priest’s color slowly changed from the ruddy bronze of a man still used to walking outside among his parishioners to a waxy tallow. And then he began to gag.

Carlo jumped forward, kneeling before the old man who now bent over with dry, racking coughs. "Are you choking, Father! Spit! Try to spit it out!" Paolo slipped onto one knee, spasms from deep in his gut jerking him from side to side. Then with one hand between his knees, he slumped onto the faded carpet, his eyes wide open toward the dining room.

"Oh god! Help!" Carlo wasn't sure what he was supposed to do. A heart attack? Should he pound the priest's chest? Food stuck? A Heimlich? Carlo pulled the priest forward. The old man had stopped coughing now and only his chest quivered beneath Carlo's fingers. Sweat poured from Carlo's face onto the priest's collar and worn jacket. He forced open the old man's mouth, stuck in as much of his hand as he could, and felt for a bolus of something blocking the priest's airway.

"Goddamn!" Carlo quickly withdrew his hand with the sensation that a dry metal rasp had raked its skin. In fact, blood had started to well up in hundreds of tiny abrasions along Carlo's fingers and palm as if the interior of the priest's mouth were jagged pumice. Paolo was neither coughing nor struggling now, and even the hand that he had jammed between his legs had fallen limply to the floor.

"Oh god! Come on, Father, don't die. Please don't be dead... Somebody!" Carlo ripped away the white collar, searching for a pulse that must lie somewhere along the priest's neck. What he felt trembled more than beat. Carlo pulled open the purple shirt. He had never seen anyone have a heart attack. Was this what it looked like? Now he couldn't remember where to put his hands or how hard to pump.

Carlo threw his weight onto Paolo's chest several times. It was impossible to tell if the strange deep shudders were actual breaths. Finally pushing himself away, he ran to telephone an ambulance. What had happened? It was so fast. He rubbed his hand across his face while he waited for the call to ring through. Jesus, this was just what he needed. A priest checks out in the middle of his living room; his aunt in a coma upstairs; his sister... Sylvie?

"Sylvie!" Carlo aimed his voice upward toward the stairwell.

But from the darkness of the dining room, next to the parlor where the priest lay spread out on the floor, a gentle voice answered, “I’m here, Carlo. No need to shout. I’m just keeping an eye on things.”

Chapter 2

Sylvie sensed, rather than saw, that light had begun to tint the gauze curtains of the bedroom. Morning always materialized like this she thought, revealing itself like someone terribly shy, who will shortly develop a brilliant personality.

She rolled over, the simile forming in her mind. I am like this morning, she mused with her eyes still tightly shut. New, untested, a bit foggy… but somehow sure that something has changed from the darkness that preceded it.

Indeed, since the old priest's visit two weeks before, Sylvie barely recognized the sensations that traveled in and out of her mind, across her shoulders, and along her arms. It was as if she stood off to the side now, watching a new Sylvie taking shape. And one she wasn't displeased to house.

She arched her back slightly, wanting to stretch, knowing she would be stiff when she peeled herself away from the person lying beside her. But instead, she lingered, letting the nerves of her knees and hips, stomach and chest explore the outline of the tiny figure that lay so still at her side. The fact that she lay here now, that she relished the physical warmth of another made her smile—like a mother watching at the birth of another.

In her little game, as she crept to wakefulness, Sylvie decided to see how her other senses would describe the person she was curled against. Keeping her eyes closed, she turned to expose an ear from beneath her own tussle of hair. She could hear the heart beside her—like an African drum—she smiled to herself. A drum in a forest where its beat reverberates against trees and is muffled by brush—and whose drummer at this moment, sounded weary and tired. Yes, that was it. Poetic, but that is what she heard.

She rubbed her nose. There was a slight glaze of oil. Smiling at her own vanity, Sylvie wondered if her nose were as pink in sleep as when she was awake. People always liked its little rosebud tip. Now she took in a long breath, opening her nostrils, picking up the scent of the figure beside her, hesitantly waiting for something acrid, but now nourishing herself on the warmed, almond-like aroma she associated with contentment.

Without disturbing her aunt, Sylvie pushed herself up onto one elbow and looked down on the figure beside her. Here and there, sunlight dotted the flowered wallpaper, dappled the carpet, and slanted between the shades across the woman's form.

Giuliana's breathing was imperceptible, shallow, conserving the little air she took in and reluctantly let go. Yes, something had changed since the afternoon of the priest's attack in their living room. Changed for Sylvie most of all.

Sylvie let her hand pull at a few strands of the woman's hair that had drifted across her face. Instead of exasperation at Giuliana's intrusion into her life, Sylvie could now hardly leave her side, as if a tendril had reached from one to the other and now thickened, formed an impenetrable branch.

No longer pallid, Giuliana's cheeks too had taken on a crimson tint that flowed across her throat and chest. And sometimes when she wasn't in the room, Sylvie swore she could hear the woman's soft croons. While she didn't speak and didn't move, Carlo said he had the feeling that something inside of Giuliana had awakened. Of that, Sylvie was sure.

Drawing the coverlet up around the woman's chin, Sylvie padded to the bathroom and shoved the ringlets back from the face in the mirror. She must have inherited her own mountain of curls from Giuliana's side of the family. Even their eyebrows, like little birds in flight, arched in the same way.

She finished washing her face and slipped into the loose blouse and jeans that caused the local street laborers to call after her, "*Bella Contadina*!" Beautiful peasant! For the last weeks, she had resolutely refused invitations from the boys who telephoned and the junior professor who slipped poems into her backpack. Sylvie was simply content to stay beside Giuliana, sketching on a pad during the day, or cuddling against her at night—absorbing something for which Sylvie as yet had no name—yet something that she was sure had always been her own. The *Recipe Book* is how she thought of it—instructions from her aunt which she couldn't quite read, but that gathered in her mind, familiar, awaited, and sometimes frightening.

"Sylvie! Check the time!" Outside her door, Carlo dashed down the hallway working at buttoning a cuff. "We're leaving in half an hour. Traffic to Logan will be crazy!"

Sylvie barely heard him. Instead she stared from the bathroom at the rocker, where its mahogany sheen flicked back and forth in the shadows, picking up the morning sunlight as it seemed to rock serenely on its own. "Jesus," she muttered, not wanting to move.

Her eyes checked the window for drafts and then with an implausible thought, Sylvie went to her aunt. The old chair had quickened its arc. Now it made little "*rumphs*" against the carpet, tilting forward to the end of its short runners and lifting itself high onto the ones at the rear. Giuliana couldn't sit up, much less get across the room and into a chair. Yet though her eyes were closed and the coverlet undisturbed, the woman's breathing came faster and tiny orbs of perspiration were forming where the dark hair fell away from her face. It was only when Sylvie reached to take her hand that she realized her aunt's arm was rigidly held a few inches above the bed, and that the hand was extended, middle fingers curled inward, toward the bounding chair.

"Sylvie!" Carlo's voice was receding down the stairs. "I got your suitcase down from the attic. You know we're leaving for the airport at nine. Get whatever antique rags you're taking and pack! Oh, and I grabbed some of the little clay *tchotchke*s from the box of pottery shards Zia used to carry around. A priest or some old Tuscan witch may want them…." His voice disappeared into the bathroom where he continued to mutter, "… want them… and her nightgown… and her underwear for all I know…."

At the sound of Carlo's voice, Sylvie felt the old woman's hand relax and again drape itself onto the bed. In the corner, the chair began to slow. Sylvie stretched out the curled fingers one at a time, noticing how the dome of the nails was just like her own. She stood watching the chair for some moments, wondering if it would rock again by itself. How odd, she thought, I don't feel afraid. I should. I should be terrified, and I should tell Carlo—about the chair—and about the priest, the one who she heard now lay slowly recovering in a Catholic rest home—and about the evil that had emanated from him. And feeling it, how she had taken steps. Or was it that the steps had taken her?

Sylvie closed the door and sat down again beside the old lady who lay captured in her dream. She didn't want to leave Giuliana—not now. It was true that hosting her from Italy had been Carlo's idea, a romanticized effort at "getting in touch with his beginnings," he'd said. He always talked like that—"*his* beginnings"—as if their shared genes had expelled any of *her* Italian DNA. And so Sylvie had ignored his project, ignored the woman when she came with her delicate carriage and proudly-held head, and she had left the room whenever she felt Giuliana's eyes descend upon her with a combination of questioning and familiarity.

Even when this sleeping sickness had begun, Sylvie had found other things to do, if you considered slouching on used couches in a coffee house frequented by college drop-outs to be "doing something." Even there she hadn't fit in.

She reached down and took the old woman's hand, following the labyrinth of veins between the knuckles. Sylvie had drawn some impressive tattoo designs just like these curling veins which she'd sold to the clove-smoking slackers for $10 apiece, and yes, she'd let a professor feel her up a couple of times in a stinking public toilet lit by florescent lights, too. But mostly, she'd slept until two, smoked in the bathtub till five, then with deep blue shadows against her white skin, downed whatever leftovers Carlo hadn't eaten, and begun her prowl of friend's houses and basement apartments, usually ending up pissed at someone along the way. From the college educated dopers to the skinny dreamers committed to their downward spirals, Sylvie watched from the sidelines, wondering whether this was her own future, or something else she had yet to find.

Suddenly, the door to the bedroom flew open. Carlo held onto its knob, his feet planted apart, head cocked to one side and— the universal sign of exasperation—one hand jammed on his hip. Did women find that attractive, Sylvie wondered. The take-charge guy, all buffed up from the gym, and all that oiled black hair? Who's he kidding, she smirked to herself.

"Sylvie," he said, now pushing past her and shoving the old rocking chair aside. "Here's your damned empty suitcase. You can buy another pair of ragged jeans in Italy. The nurse is here, the cab is waiting and… we've got what we need," he said, indicating the pottery vase he plucked from a box of broken shards his aunt had liked to finger. "We'll get rid of the broken remnants when we get back. Now, for God's sake, give Giuliana a kiss and let's just, for the sheer novelty of it, *not miss the plane*."

Carlo quickly wrapped his aunt's wrinkled cotton nightgown around the little pot, a dot or two of its black paint flaking into the folds. And stuffing the bundle into a plastic bag, he extended his watch threateningly toward Sylvie, punctuating his message with a menacing arched brow.

It was only as Sylvie was giving Giuliana a final embrace that she felt them, the tiny fingers pressing against her leg, like a spider's claws when it knows it will fall. And then the old lady's whispered words, cracked and ragged, in a broken dialect that Sylvie shouldn't have understood, *"Segui gli anelli nelle palme, amore... e stai attenti..."*

"I will," Sylvie whispered back as the nurse entered the room. "I will be careful." But she had no idea what was meant by the "rings in the palms" her aunt wished her "to follow"— these *anelli*—if they were gold or sparkling with stones. Was she to bring Giuliana back a gift? Perhaps put a beautiful ring on her hand, a way to tell this woman she had only now fallen in love with, that she was as Italian as Carlo and that she would follow the old lady's *Recipe Book*, the one that seemed to be writing itself in her head?

The cabbie punched his horn in the street downstairs, Carlo shouted an expletive, and with a final hug, Sylvie kissed the dark curls of the woman, whispering, "Ti amo, Zia. Don't worry… I'll look for the rings and other things. I'll bring one back, or make it tell me its secret!"

***

The woman shivered slightly after the girl had left, after the nurse had bathed her and straightened the bed, after the shades were tilted to let in some filtered sun and the sitter herself had floated into an upright nap beside the bed. Giuliana shivered though she was warm, shivered beneath the quilt and the crocheted blanket. But this chill was from a long-ago damp—the one only the soil can bring, but where in the gloom, her memories were burning bright.

Chapter 3

Italy 1938

Giuliana could smell the earth. She could smell the people who huddled against it like worms hoping to find a soft patch in which to burrow.

Without lights, she could smell their breath and tell which of her relatives had eaten a morsel of bread and which ones saved their own hunger to give a few crumbs to the little ones.

In the darkness, she would let her fingers trace the buttons and hems of their clothes, the course stitching of seams, their knitted shawls made from the wool of sheep grazed on this very Italian soil. And though here, you couldn't tell they were yellow, she could also feel the rough edges of stars sewn onto the clothes of everyone inside the cave, and in spite of the cold, they made her feel happy.

"Giuliana." Her cousin's thirteen-year-old fingers pattered against Giuliana's coat. "Is that you?" she whispered. "I am so cold, and now I can't find my mittens. Can I wear yours for a little while? Mine must be someplace in the dirt."

Giuliana reached down and pulled her hand out of one knitted mitten, stretching the cord that ran along her back and down her other arm to the mitten on her left hand. Her mother knew all about girls, even teenage girls, losing gloves. "I'll share one with you, Rebekah. Just wiggle closer and put your other hand in my pocket."

At home in Firenze, friends said the cousins were like two sides of the same apple, one turned toward the sun, the other in shadow. Though one leg had always made walking difficult, Rebekah was already a beauty, blonde, with bright eyes that seemed to glitter in the light. Giuliana was dark with velvety skin and tumbling curls. Her father said she was more a beautiful plum than an apple.

But from time to time as children, Giuliana had broken off play with her angelic-looking cousin. You didn't want to display a doll Rebekah might have wished to have, or later, wear a dress that Rebekah would admire, for to be sure, within the hour, the doll would be cracked and the dress stained or ripped. They were just coincidences, her mother would tell her, something to be ignored.

"Shh," somebody said in the dark. Someone else coughed, a low, rumbling volcano of a cough that suggested a sickness coming on. With some discreet shuffling and adjustment of limbs, Giuliana's mother moved nearer and wrapped her arm around both girls' shoulders. Giuliana knew her mother had taken pains to wash away her lovely perfume, the "smell of a garden at twilight." But even after walking more than 100 miles and huddling in barns and caves, and now this ancient tomb, the trace of it lingered at her temples and rose subtly from her throat.

"We must be very, very quiet now, children," she breathed. "Soon, the lady who will take us to safety will come. But the men are listening for her special signal. We do not want to confuse it with anybody else passing in this part of the land."

"Where is my brother?" asked Rebekah.

"Your mother and father and Simon are all together near the entrance. They're fine. Now be very quiet and I will pass you some cheese and olives."

After the girls had eaten, and later grown frustrated tapping letter codes into each other's palms, they slumped into one another and drifted in and out of sleepy thoughts that were interrupted only by the occasional clump of the tomb's tufa wall sloughing onto their heads.

No matter that they were "on the run," as her father called it, Giuliana was happy to be with her cousin. Though their fathers were brothers, Giuliana's papa, a Professor of Archaeology at the University of Firenze and Rebekah's, a lieutenant in the *Esercito d'Italia*, the Army of Italy, due to their frenetic schedules, the family gathered together only on the High Holy Days, the occasional Seder, and the thrilling bar mitzvahs that still took place inside Firenze's old Jewish quarter.

But now it seemed everything had gone wrong. Giuliana's father said that Italy was returning to the bad old days—the days before Italy had even been a country—the days when men who wore beards like his and the silky white prayer shawl she loved to touch—would no longer be welcome. Now somebody was making him leave his job at the university and had forced Rebekah's father to leave his job in the Army as well. Her father said that it was only going to get worse.

"But why, Papa?" Giuliana had wailed. "Why can't we stay here? This is our house! I don't want to go!" But her usually gentle papa had been firm. He had even explained that on their secret run from Firenze she wouldn't be allowed to take her miniature circus with the real canvas tent she'd had since she was small, nor the collection of tiny porcelain ladies whose painted black hair she'd occasionally polished with Vaseline. "Only yourself and what clothes you can carry in a pillowcase, Piccolina."

"I am *not* little," she'd countered at his pet nickname. "I am already 14…15 in months!" Yet she vowed to at least take her ancient teddy, Ottavio, worn and dirty, already an artifact of her childhood, and like the rest of the family, sporting a crudely stitched yellow star on his chest.

Giuliana drifted up from thoughts of that last day in Firenze to hear her mother's voice, sharp and annoyed in the darkness. It was aimed at her father she thought; and in response, as always, his voice came back filled with patience that flowed like warm jelly on a holiday latke.

"You are making too much noise, Nathan. It will go up through the stone to the forest floor."

"Just a few more scrapes. I can feel the outline… elegant handle… not too large…"

"We are *escaping*, Nathan…" her voice was tense, bridled in the tight quarters. "The University days are behind us. No more Etruscan pots, no more urns, no more…"

"Be still!" Enrico Ferrero sounded like the gunnery Lieutenant that he was. Younger than Giuliana's father, Enrico wasted no time in coaxing or explaining to his brother. He believed in expedience and quick thinking. "You must be more decisive, Nathan," he had always said. "Professors die in thought; soldiers live to think about life." Enrico was tall and muscular, a pencil-moustache dashed across his lip, and the one upon whose plan the two families in the cave now depended.

In spite of his often harsh manner, Giuliana was glad he was their leader; he seemed to know things others did not. Things moved fast when Zio Enrico was with you. And his presence kept his son, Simon, in check.

Giuliana was grateful that after the families had scaled the steep rock outcrop, sidestepping the deep tufa paths the ancient Etruscans had carved for their flocks, her final collapse into this ancient tomb had not been beside Simon. Even here in the dark, she pictured him sitting upright beside his father, as if closeness to authority might rub off.

Simon was tall, even for 17, with long arms and shoulders that had taken on a new breadth. He now used them to shove people, to pin them into corners—to try to lift their skirt.

As the eldest child, Simon had always taken charge. In charge of games, of toys, in charge of children who came to his house. Between the adults who played cards at a felt-covered table and the children who ran up and down stairs, sat on bedroom floors, and explored the garden's edge, there was a kind of no-man's land. Safe within the family, the two sets of parents barely lifted their heads at the squeals that emanated from one room or another. Even the silences weren't worrisome—those times when Simon had closed the door. That was why Papa hadn't understood Giuliana's sudden insistence on playing in the parlor among the grown-ups, far from Simon. Nor later did she tell her father of her cousin's taking her to the wooded area behind the garden and demanding that she take off her panties. He had gripped her hands that day and tried to remove them himself. But when Mama had called from the house, Simon had let go, and Giuliana had said that her tear-stained face was from a fall in the garden. All she knew was that Simon was tall and strong, beloved by the whole family—and that he frightened her.

"I've got it!" Nathan barely exhaled the words, but his excitement was a shout. "Look here, Piccolina!" Giuliana heard him blow dust from the pot he had just extracted from the soft tufa, then she felt him reach in the dark for her pocketed hand. "If only I could see this piece, I would guess it is black with… maybe a delicate red and yellow vine design around a central medallion. But put your hand here, my dear. Though it is tiny, you can feel that it has two beautiful arched handles. If so, it is very rare. Vessels of this kind are often only found in tombs where there are other even more valuable artifacts." Giuliana carefully stroked the little vessel. It almost felt as if it warmed her hand.

"Nathan." Enrico crawled over his wife and son to his brother's family. "What the hell are you doing?"

"Listen, Rico, where did you find this place? I don't think it's been excavated… at least not very well. Probably a few grave robbers over the centuries. But, my God, Brother, just a little digging and this exquisite Etruscan bucchero practically leapt out of the dirt. Why, if there are more…"

"Not now! I heard the old woman's signal. She'll be here in minutes. Make sure everyone is quiet and that they take everything out with them. We will go single-file. The last time I was here was as a new recruit. I don't remember it well, but my comrade's mother was born here… in some village just under the mountain of Pitigliano. She says there is an entrance, a tunneled cave into and up through the mountain. We can then make our way from there to the protection of the city's ghetto." Enrico patted Nathan for encouragement. "But there are Nazi sympathizers here as well, Brother. We do not want to be seen seeking refuge. It's good that you shaved your beard. We must not let our appearances draw attention to us if we should be observed. Each of us must look out for ourselves. And don't forget," he added, "Rip off the stars."

Giuliana heard the men embrace and Enrico clamber back over the stretched legs of the two families.

"Where is your sack, Giuliana?" whispered her father. "Give me some of your clothes. Should we be stopped, you must say nothing about this thing that I am wrapping in your… wrapping in your pajamas." She heard her papa chuckle. Even without his beard, even in the dark, she knew he looked handsome when he laughed.

"We have a secret now, don't we, Piccolina. And if I should forget, you must remember this place, make a little map in your mind of this… this shed for sheep… and the tunnels that run from it. There are treasures here for the future."

Only Enrico heard the old woman's knock, but when the crude wooden door was shoved open, everyone felt the rush of icy air. With no more than a shoved finger into a shoulder, the family told each other it was time to go, and ahead of her, Giuliana saw the humped silhouettes of her family as they crawled out on all fours, lumbering camels, against an indigo sky.

No one spoke. They were good soldiers, following orders, as shoes slipped on mossy rock and hands reached for leafy handholds that were but shadows. Giuliana saw her mother fall to her knees once, and Papa silently reach forward and haul her up. But even Mama, so ready with complaints, said nothing.

At first, they had walked downward into a low valley, then the land rose upward through a thick forest with jagged outcrops of tufa that in the eons of exposure to the elements, had hardened and now cut at their legs.

Giuliana marched behind Rebekah, who from time to time was partially carried by her mother. Then came Mama, with Papa in the rear. Sleep and fatigue made her only dimly aware of her surroundings, but as per Papa's directive, she forced herself to take note. She also hugged the little pillow sack protecting his precious vase and Ottavio, the grizzled teddy bear who was following orders and like her, keeping perfectly still. Yet Giuliana could not suppress a gasp when the family suddenly emerged from the forested trail and stopped to catch their breath below the towering mass that was Pitigliano.

If she were to lie on her back and look up, she was sure the dark hulk that was part mountain and part enormous city would still cover half of the velvety sky. It looked impenetrable. A city that had always been there, from ancient peoples of the East to Etruscans to Romans to the Medieval Medici lords, built on a platform of stone where six and seven story buildings, towers and turrets, fountains and crenelated walls roughly clawed at the sky. An aqueduct seemed airborne across the tufa crag, holding two parts of the city together with a series of elegant arches, and nowhere could Giuliana see an entrance or a gate.

There was whispering between the bent form of their guide and Enrico. Then her uncle came toward them and gathered the family together.

"We must be very careful here," he said nervously. "The old woman says there was a rally... something... last night in the square in the city. Now the leaders are staying around here before they return north."

"What was the reason for their rally?" asked Mama.

"They are... they are the Fascist Youth, the *Balilla*, the same as in Firenze. But she says these are from Milano, well-trained, like military men—and excitable."

Giuliana felt Papa's hand tighten. And then the old woman was moving ahead and they all fell into a line behind her.

The climbing was harder now. They were exposed against the pale tufa as the crumbling path lifted, then plunged into thick brush where Etruscan excavations had slashed leafy fjords. Though it was but a half moon, against the rock their shadows threaded together in a blue echo of their sweating chain. They had been climbing for a half hour when suddenly, only steps in front of Giuliana, Rebekah, who had tried hobbling on her crippled leg, dropped to her knees with a scream of shock and pain.

"A snake! Mama!" Everyone had been warned about the hatching season for vipers in the Tuscan hills. Rebekah had careened off the path, hitting her head, and now lay on the ground gripping her calf. Enrico was instantly beside her, "Quiet, girl. Stop!" He placed his hand across her mouth, rocked her back and forth, and tried to pull away her hand to see the injury. Everyone had frozen. A snake nearby. Fascists on the slope. And it was impossible to see. Enrico asked his wife to bend low and light a match. Just as quickly, he snuffed it out. "Rebekah, you are all right. Look, I'm putting your "snake" in your hand. It was only a thorn. Just a drop of blood—a scrape on your leg and your head. Now, be still… or…"

The burst of light from the metal torch seemed to explode in their faces.

"And what do we have here?" It was only a voice, but the shift of boots on rocks said there were others waiting nearby. There was also the sound of women's muffled surprise and a scurrying in the underbrush.

"State your names and present your papers. What is the reason for your trespassing on these slopes in the middle of the night?" The orders tumbled from someone only recently out of adolescence. Giuliana smelled something foul on his breath.

Suddenly the voice behind the light was screaming. "You are in the presence of the Armed Vigilance Corps of the Fascist Youth! Do you understand? We expect immediate compliance with this order!" Then, as if intuiting something, his tone began to drip with sarcasm. "Or are you gypsies? Are you mentally stupid? Are you… Jews?"

No one spoke. Realizing the risk of their exit from Firenze, each family had burned their identity papers before they'd set out. They'd been assured that in Pitigliano they would receive new documents that showed they had been inhabitants of the city for generations. Now, beside their thoughts, only Rebekah's whimpers punctuated the silence that shrouded Pitigliano's crags.

Without an answer, the flashlight began to play on each member of the group. Enrico, holding his daughter, her dirty forehead oozing blood; his wife, who knelt over the child; Giuliana, gently stroking her cousin's back; and Nathan, standing apart, tall and formidable, his wife peering from behind.

But it was cousin Simon who spoke. "Thank God, you have come," he addressed the voice.

The light swerved to Simon, standing blonde and pale in its glare. "You are right, Sir. We didn't think they would let us live. They *are* Jews and they tried to rob us when we became lost after visiting my sick brother.... They've even struck my little sister." Simon went to Rebekah, knelt down with one arm around Enrico and the other pointed toward Nathan's family. "Thank God for you, Sirs. These... these Jews might have killed us," A slight tremor lent pathos to Simon's voice. No one in the little group moved as they stared like stricken animals into the light.

The one flashlight increased to four, and all of them now swerved to play on Nathan and his wife and daughter. "What is your name, Jew?"

"I am called Ferrero," said Nathan in a voice his daughter had never heard.

"And your first name?"

There was a hesitation. "Adolfo," replied Nathan, this time Giuliana recognized the tone her father used when he'd told the punch line to a joke.

"Are you a Jew, Ferrero? A Jew out to thieve from good Italians and to hit their children?"

"No."

"Ah... I believe the answer is "yes" to at least one question. I see one half of a tanned face, and one half of a face where very recently there grew a beard. I believe you should have answered that you *are* a Jew, *Jew!* I believe you are lying to me. Empty your pockets. And you too!" The flashlight lit the face of Giuliana's mother.

Nathan pulled out the insides of his jacket pockets, then the pockets of his coat. Only a rumpled handkerchief fell to the ground. The flashlight directed Giuliana's mother to do the same. She slowly pulled out the white interior of her right coat pocket. But her hand lingered in her left.

"Pull it out! What are you hiding?" The man screamed as he suddenly advanced on her. From behind the flashlight, a black-shirted arm darted and grabbed the woman's clenched fist from her pocket.

"Open your hand, Jewish whore!" Both girls burst into tears as Rebekah's mother whispered to be still. In the next instant, the man swung his flashlight, holding it with two hands like a club, he brought it squarely into the face of Giuliana's mother. She collapsed, her skull opened, dead, even before she fell. The flashlight searched belligerently for a moment in the dry leaves, and there in the dirt, her fingers still curled around them, were the two yellow stars she had snipped from Nathan's coat and her own.

The tall Fascist didn't have time to turn toward Nathan, nor was there time to spit the insults he saved for arrogant Jews, when, from behind, the professor brought down the huge rock directly against the youth's tightly-shorn temple. Not yet twenty, he too was dead, hatred leaking into the dirt. But death was in the air. The shot that killed Nathan came anonymously from the darkness. "A Fascist victory over a Jewish dog," a chestnut-haired youth would later say. What he would forget to mention, was that not so very long before, he had called a man named Levi, "grandpa."

For seconds after Nathan had fallen onto the body of his wife's killer, his own murderer and the other young Fascists remained motionless, captured in a tableau that might have signaled the end of a play, the moment when the curtain falls. The bullet's echo bounced from tree to tree until the valley swallowed it and for a time it seemed even a sullen moon had stopped to observe the sordid scene. But a shout from Pitigliano's parapet caused each of them to look up, then quickly retract into a shadow.

"The Commandant's not going to like this…" whispered one of the young Italians. "And not with the way your breath smells. What'd you drink… a liter of grappa?"

"Shut up," said another voice. "We neutralized a couple of Jewish vermin who were trying to pass messages to the ghetto. You got that?"

"And you saved us!" A higher-pitched voice, but no less intense, was accompanied by the sound of Simon pushing himself toward the men. "The Jews… the dirty Jews… they had kidnapped us. And now we must come with you!"

There was silence for a moment, while the young Fascists tried to process the layers of complication they had plunged into.

"Where are you from? Where are your parents?" asked the emerging leader of the band.

"We come from L'Aquila, to the east," said Simon, apparently pulling on the geography he learned at school. "My father is here. He is on leave from the Army while we visit our relatives in… in… Castellalcino." Every village had a castle, guessed Simon quickly, one hamlet like any other—why not a Castellalcino? "But we are very frightened," he whimpered. "… those Jews…. Will you give us protection, Sir? Perhaps my father can even help…."

The leader seemed to come to life with this new possibility. A trophy, a little military expertise, something to assuage official ire from the group's impromptu, and deadly, foray outside the walls of Pitigliano.

"All right, Benadetto, you and Matteo take the body of Lorenzo. What is your name, boy? Gather your father… and your family and follow us quickly." Another shout came from above, but closer this time. The now nervous group coalesced out of the dirt and leaves, and heaving the body of their comrade between them, crashed noisily toward the parapets. Among them were the dark outlines of Enrico and his wife, bent beneath the weight of the now silent Rebekah.

But Simon had run back. He had an errand. He removed the gold watch and ring from his uncle's hand and the cached pearls from his aunt's undergarment. He kicked the yellow stars he had taken from his own mother's pocket into a crevice where they would soon disintegrate, leaving those of his aunt spread in the dirt as evidence of their crime of birth. But the star sewn onto Giuliana's little coat wasn't among them. Nor was she. In the end, of course, since Simon had decided to leave his Jewishness behind, it really didn't matter, and as far as he could tell, neither did she. Let her little yellow star go out, he thought. He had chosen the winning side and would proudly take his family with him. Being Jewish had never helped anyone.

***

The old woman's hand lying across Giuliana's mouth hadn't moved from the moment Nathan had been shot. And now as they heard in the distance the militants' voices receding, Giuliana could feel the old fingers' slight release.

"You cannot go into the city now..." It was difficult to understand the woman's country dialect, but the meaning was clear. "We must leave here immediately. They will come back to search for money on your...." The old woman went silent again as a branch snapped in the woods nearby.

Then she took Giuliana's tear-streaked face in her hands and whispered again, "You cannot go to the ghetto. There will be problems tonight there. The Germans and Fascists will go in through its iron gates. There will be big problems. But I will take you, child. Do not be frightened of all that comes."

She took Giuliana's hand and wrapping her other arm around the girl's back, led her deeper into the woods, down a ravine, and then another, descending ever lower, away from the looming walls and her parents' finished lives.

"Tomorrow we will double you," said the old woman as the woods thinned and the first lines of scarlet fingered the sky. "Tomorrow you will stay a little Jewish girl—but in secret. And we will make a copy of you as a Catholic. Two Giulianas. Won't that be nice? And I have always wanted a little granddaughter… a little fish I did not expect to come swim in my pond." The old woman sadly squeezed the smooth hand she held between her two wrinkled ones.

"Piccolina," Giuliana thought she heard her father say. "My little Piccolina. Remember us."

Chapter 4

With each shuffling step on the rough tufa upon which medieval Pitigliano was perched, Simon had felt the existential shift. As his family and its cadre of Fascist youth felt their way up the winding donkey path toward the outer gate and the inner arch of the city, Simon knew everything had changed. A right-angle turn to their life of before. By his choice. By his power. He tried to keep himself from smiling, but in the end, in the dark, he didn't resist.

For now, he would follow these blundering Fascists, but Simon had no doubt that though he was young, he could out-think them. No doubt that with just a few words twisted, he could turn a moment to his will. There was electricity running through him as ahead he saw the looming curve of a wall twenty feet thick and the arch that penetrated it. But instead of entering triumphantly, proud to have "rescued" innocents, the black-shirted men skirted the grand opening, and hauled their dead comrade down a smaller, obscured path that allowed them to enter the walled-city's far end, where stones laid down in the 1400s met those of Etruscans' from the 7th century B.C. Like tiny capillaries, shoulder-wide alleys, *vicoli,* led into the heart of Pitigliano, that though impressive from afar, was still hardly larger than a compacted village. Simon had only seen the town from below. With its grand palace, what looked like a cathedral, and most astounding, a soaring aqueduct stretching across the top of the city's promontory, he guessed that the Medici mass would have seemed awe-inspiring to ancient challengers.

As the band struggled through the underbrush, Simon had moved from behind his parents and sister to alongside the black-shirt called Gianni at the head of the line. The young man wore a military-style kepi cap which Simon knew was typically reserved for officers. He wasn't sure Gianni was actually in the Army, but he knew authority when he saw it, and though his father was also an officer, Simon knew who would hold sway on this dark night. He had always prided himself on his scent for where power lay. The boy also had seen the look on his father's face as he moved past him. "The look of a beaten dog," thought Simon. "The look of a Jew."

"Stop here," whispered Gianni, turning back to those laboring under the weight of the dead youth. They were steps from a small opening at the base of the 300-foot wall. "We're going to bury him."

Grunts came from Matteo and Benadetto as they lowered their comrade's body into a heap beside them. "Lorenzo can't just disappear, Gianni. We can't go back to Milan like he didn't exist."

"And we can't exactly explain that while we were fucking milkmaids on the hillside a Jew bashed in his head. No, Lorenzo was always a little different, right? So he goes AWOL. He decides he likes country life. He wants to own a goat. I don't care. It doesn't matter. Lorenzo is not coming back and nobody saw him go."

There was sullen silence from the two recruits. Kicking at leaves and scratching their crotches, they each nervously evaluated covering up a tragedy versus their own fantasized futures. At last, self-preservation triumphed and Matteo reluctantly murmured, "*Va bene*." With that page of their adolescent lives seemingly turned, they dragged their dispatched friend and their own consciences toward a shallow ravine where they both would be buried. Then Benadetto asked, "… so how did we acquire four strangers and two dead Jews?"

Gianni himself went silent for a moment while he struggled for something believable to report to the leader of the Milanese Fascist Youth Corps.

"I might be able to help, Sir." Simon's voice was higher than he wanted it to be, but nerves or not, he'd already taken a chance tonight and so far, he liked the result. Stealing a glance at his parents, he noted how his mother's head hung in exhaustion against his father's shoulder, while Enrico, who seemed to have added a dozen years, attempted to quiet the whimpering of Rebekah. It was as if the two of them had grown old and unsure in the last few hours. And Simon felt disgusted.

Drawing closer to Gianni, Simon dropped his voice into the range of a peer. "Sir, I think that you must have heard our cries for help… even from above. My family had been kidnapped and was being viciously attacked by those Jews. My little sister… well, who knows what might have happened to her if you had not arrived. Everyone knows that Hebrew's rituals call for Christian blood… and the younger and fresher the better. I think you are heroes for your intervention. If possible, Sir, I would like to repeat our thanks to your superior."

Gianni stepped back and looked at the youth, a slight smile beginning to flicker at his lips. Simon wondered if perhaps even to someone eager for an alibi, the story of an Army officer and a strong youth being overcome by a middle-aged man and his wife was a bit of a stretch.

"So, the Jews were attacking your family. And why was your little family wandering about these country hills?" Gianni seemed as much interested in hearing the rest of Simon's story as he was in knowing if it were actually true.

"My family was on holiday in… Castel… Castellmont… and we became lost after…."

"Stop! Where are you from? You don't even know! Matteo, shine a light on his face. Maybe there is another Jew right here, breathing his fetid breath into my face!" Matteo knelt down to find his light. "Should we pull down his pants and see?"

"Sir! There is more!" Simon knew that a light on his face would show him drenched with panic. "The Jews… uh… they stole something… something very valuable in particular. We had just purchased it from a dealer in Firenze and were bringing it to our relatives in… in Castellalcino!" The town he'd chosen suddenly had come back. "It is an urn… priceless, I understand. And… it is in the hands of a Jewish child, the daughter of the thief you so bravely dispatched, Sir."

Gianni and Matteo had forgotten about the light. Now, better not to have it. Even Milanese had heard about the rich buried Etruscan treasures found in these parts. The countryside was riddled with underground tombs, each filled with urns and gold. "There was another Jew of that family? And she has this urn?"

Gianni began to laugh and then threw his arm around Simon's shoulder. "And you would know this Jew child who escaped? You would know this urn?"

Simon felt something swift and red sweep through him. He recognized it as the same thrill he felt when after doing something illicit, he had not been caught. The pocketed wallet of a friend's grandfather, the chemistry exam answers lifted from his teacher's satchel, the fondling of a major's wife at a military reception— even as his father was having a ribbon pinned onto his chest by her husband.

"I think I would recognize this Jew child," said Simon with wide honest eyes. "I will help in any way I can. And Sir, if one day you might even recommend me to join with you… to join your important party organization, I would make myself useful to you… in every way… in any way at all."

Chapter 5

"Giuliana! Are you ready? Do you know the time?" Rosetta Portini's grey hair had been twisted into the knot atop her head, just the way she'd done every day since long before The War to End All Wars, when the young *contadina* had shifted from maiden to married woman. Now, her husband long dead, she relied on transient farm workers and harvesters to help her with the 20 hectares from which she managed to scrape a life from the soil, and on her son, who lived in the village of Sovana nearby, but who had other ways of helping his mother survive.

As the light slid from the late afternoon sky, Giuliana had only to glance through a tiny window in Rosetta's house to see the mighty silhouette of Pitigliano in the near distance. Like a volcano from which the widow's stone house had flowed, Pitigliano sat at the center of dozens of scattered farmlets, small plots where everyone from early pagans to devoted Christians had prayed, lived, and died. And in each case, their cemeteries and tombs abounded in the soft tufa stone.

Giuliana swayed a little as she stood. She had had nothing to eat since a little bread and broth before sunrise and now her thoughts seemed to fill her limbs with enough sorrow to make each movement the effort of ten. "I am ready, Nonna."

In so many ways it seemed the past year had evaporated like the morning mists that surrounded the mount of Pitigliano—tiny particles of water, or of life, that changed substance before her very eyes. One year ago, Giuliana had been a young girl just beginning her life, adored by her father, sometimes chastened by her mother, comforted by a teddy bear, and quietly following the path of a religious tradition that to many, seemed as ignominious in its way as was she. But on the night, one year ago today, in which she had seen both of the pillars of her life killed before her eyes, Giuliana felt that she too had been sacrificed. How many times had she wondered what lessons her parents had yet to teach her? What was she to believe in? Whom was she to trust? Which things in life was she to value above others? There were hints. But they were few.

Giuliana opened the little box of candles that she kept in the basket alongside her clothes. Beside it was the yellow star she had worn, and the tiny urn, still wrapped in the pajamas her father had placed it in, ones that now smelt of the soil. Carefully, she pulled out only one small wax taper from the box. The rabbi said it would do. That was one of the lessons she thought would please her parents—her continued efforts with the rituals and mitzvahs she hoped she was performing correctly.

Giuliana had been *bat mitzvahed* at twelve in Firenze, a day of quiet celebration and pride, but a day that now she could barely remember. And now tonight, the *yahrzeit*, the one-year anniversary of her parents' death which she would commemorate with only Rosetta and a woman who had come down from Pitigliano's ghetto beside her, filled her with a realization of the hazardous and hapless state of being human. A circumstance that could be extinguished as quickly as the candle in her hand.

"Come, my child," called Rosetta. "It is eighteen minutes before sunset."

Over the last year, the old woman had made a place for Giuliana in the small stone house, a place for the "granddaughter" whose appearance didn't surprise rural farmers. The *contadini* were always taking in a child whose parents had died or who had too many others to care for. Anyway, another mouth was usually a small price to pay for two busy hands. But Rosetta hadn't wanted to pour this child into a ready-made mold. The old woman believed in keeping her the way she was and adding perhaps a little Catholic frosting on top for protection. And so it was that each Friday night Giuliana had lit the Sabbath candles, and that, many Saturdays, she was secreted across the fields to the base of Pitigliano and up the winding stone tunnel leading into the ghetto and its brilliantly illuminated synagogue. And it had been on each and every Sunday in the church that she draped her head with a kerchief and with Rosetta, knelt, crossed herself, and played with a ringlet of beads while her lips opened and closed in a monotone of vowels she only vaguely understood.

"Giuliana? It is time."

But for a moment, Giuliana laid down the candle and regarded the outline of the little vase. She hadn't unwrapped it since the night her father had secured it in cloth in the dark of the tomb. It was the last thing he had touched, she thought. And it occurred to her that some of Nathan's warmth, his wishes, his scent might lie along its body and curved arms. She shook her head, feeling suddenly unsteady, and wondered if she should have had some tea. Yet the vase, no bigger than a cobble, seemed to want to throw off its wrappings. She lifted it from its nest in the basket and nearly dropped it back into the pile. The swathed urn was as heavy as iron. Carefully, she pulled back the tiny cotton stripes of her night clothes, dusting away the crumbling tufa that rolled in pieces from the interior. She had never looked at the ceramic vessel before—only felt it. Now, she reached her bare fingers to touch the radiant blacks and reds, ochres and whites of the vase. It was as her father had guessed in the darkness of their hiding place—graced with leafy designs—but also covered in details: figures, lines that appeared to be letters; symbols that when she looked at them askance, seemed to be moving quietly against the sheen of black— and emanating a kind heat that made Giuliana close her eyes with a sharp gasp.

"My dear, you should come now. Are you all right?" Rosetta's voice was near the door and sounded worried.

"I am coming, Nonna," Giuliana said huskily as she re-covered the treasure in the basket. "I am fine. I am strong now."

On most nights in the twelve months since her parents had died, Giuliana had recited the Kaddish prayer for the dead. Several of the widows in the ghetto had come to view Giuliana as a goddaughter whose religious instruction had been tragically suspended, and they waited for her each Sabbath in its dank tunnel, escorting her to the balcony in the synagogue and showing her the ghetto's cave-like interior—the ovens where matzos and challah were baked, the *mikveh*, the ritual bath where wives would bathe when their menstrual periods and a seven-day purity period were complete. It was these "aunties" who had given Giuliana the proper words for *kaddish*, a prayer of mourning, that she said every day.

One of these grey-haired *anzianas* had been brought by Rosetta's grandson to assist at the *yahrzeit*, the first anniversary of Giuliana's parents' deaths. The girl watched her, understanding what it was to mean. She knew it was the time when mourners are to turn from death and loss and the emptiness that when she wasn't busy with animals or inside chores would steal over Giuliana like ghosts that carved at her soul. The old women told her it was time to replace the past and all that was gone with life and a future in which she must be brave. But at not yet sixteen, Giuliana felt like a sculpture whose maker had run out of clay; she didn't know how to make herself into a finished vessel, or from what substance she would be constructed. But the old ladies were willing to help.

The room was chilly in Rosetta's house, just as it had been one year ago. Small candles flickered in niches, and the shutters were closed against any observance of what would have seemed an oddly un-Catholic scene.

The old woman pulled a shawl over her head and quietly began to croon. She sat at the head of a small table, her eyes closed, her fingertips touching one another as she rocked back and forth gently. In a tuneless chant she intoned the ancient *niggun*, "*Ner adonai nishmat adam…the human soul is the lamp of God. We light this candle in remembrance of you. May it be a source of comfort, blessing, and light…*"

She asked Giuliana to tell her something about her parents, the way they looked, what they liked to do, something sweet they had said to her that touched her, how they had comforted her as a child. She asked the girl to think what they might say to her now, what they might want for her as she grew. And though walking back into the rooms of her childhood in the presence of this kindly old woman and Rosetta felt as if they were enfolding her in a warm blanket in the middle of a frigid plain, the future, its road, the outlines of the woman she would grow into were for Giuliana ephemeral. She was living inside a body that grew and laughed and labored and wept, but its central piece seemed to have disappeared.

The old woman rocked slightly as she sang, Giuliana's body picking up its rhythm. Then slowly opening her eyes, she asked the girl to hold her hands over a bowl. The old woman poured a pitcher of water over Giuliana's hands, reminding her that with the cleansing water, she could again look to life, remembering always her losses, but trusting that life was awakening again; that her period of deep mourning was over. And with that, Rosetta brought out the food, a part of both Italian and Jewish life—as much a part of ritual transition as a blessing from a priest or the Hebrew toast to life, "*L'chaim.*"

Chapter 6

Livorno 1940

"No! No, it won't happen! As long as I live, it will not happen." Enrico slammed his hand against the stone sill. "I do not have a son. Do you understand this? And neither have you given birth to one!"

Enrico, now known as Captain Enrico Ponti, stared out from their flat toward the Ligurian Sea and one of the canals that brought ships and their cargo to the bustling port of Livorno. His hand reached for his stomach and the burn that wouldn't go away. A year, no, longer—and the lie he'd swallowed was like the open ulcer that churned beneath his belt; the lie he lived, a cancer. Nothing remained from before, thought Enrico. The honest soldier willing to fight for right, the loyal brother, the son of the House of David—all gone. Even the new pure Italian name, "Ponti," which he had chosen to be called in exchange for the one that identified him as "*Ibraica*," humiliated him on an hourly basis. No, for the last year, nothing seemed real. He did not belong here—here, with the pubescent "true believers," the Fascist brats who goose-stepped up and down before the city's massive pentagram-shaped Vecchia Fortezza, jutting out their stubbly chins like scrawny Mussolinis. Was it worth what he'd become? Now he played the part of a "headmaster" to these boys, who as they strutted up and down the pavement, played at versions of the Romans they had seen in the newsreels, versions of Il Duce, the histrionic cartoon whom Enrico was sure Hitler saw simply as a convenient fool.

He should have said, "no, thank you." No, better, "shove your goy identity papers up your asses" when the Milanese boys in Pitigliano had pushed him forward. All they'd wanted was an excuse, a little prize in the form of his "military consultancy" to divert attention from their crime. And now, in self-loathing, he profited from their cowardice and his own, denying in a hundred different ways who he was.

Enrico didn't want to command the troop of narcissistic adolescents nor hear them spout the xenophobic slogans that had grown ever-stronger over the last year. What he wanted was to be back in Firenze; to be a soldier again, training to lob a few cannon balls at Ethiopians or Greeks if he were called to by Italy, but not mustering a militia of children who hated Jews and others with the ferocity that only corrupted youth can muster.

It sickened him that he now pretended he didn't have a brother who had died being braver than he or a son who had delivered up his own heritage.

"Rico, he is our son." His wife, Talia, stood beside him, whispering as she always did when they mentioned Simon. For Enrico, she could have been a continent away.

"Simon has saved our lives… no, it is sure. What would have happened to us that night? You know the truth. There was death walking outside that wall of Pitigliano. If not for Simon…."

Enrico knew that Talia didn't approach him as she might have a year before, and he knew too that he didn't invite her to—to run her fingers along his back or touch his calloused fingers as had been their special language. He kept his distance now, silent, somehow lost and needing to be, his surety of purpose given way to slumped shoulders or unpredictable rages. A man who seemed to no longer belong to himself. Now, as he had grown used to doing, he simply turned his head from her, and her voice disappeared.

The small apartment they had been assigned overlooking Livorno's tropical waterfront might have made them happy under other circumstances, in another time. Livorno's wide boulevards lined with palm trees that swayed against Wedgewood-blue skies most of the year would seem a billet most military men dreamed of. But for Enrico, it was the evidence of his cowardice. He heard Talia speaking, something about Livorno now, and he forced himself to listen. He should try, though it was even harder recently when the accusatory words in his head drowned out those of others.

"And besides, it is a bit safer here, Rico. Jews…." She dropped her voice even lower, though the flat's stone walls were five hundred years old and two feet thick. "Jews are treated better here. I wish we had come here in the first place. Perhaps your brother… Nathan… Teresa… perhaps they would not have…."

Enrico turned on her, unable to control what he mentally directed at those for whom he now worked. "Jews are hated everywhere! Don't be stupid. You only think we're accepted. You only think they don't laugh about us… our noses, how we smell, how we pray, the devils, the medieval devils they think we conjure. Oh, and of course, our money!" Sweat gave Enrico's face a crimson glaze. "I see it daily, Talia. From the inside, I hear what they say, I see the jealousy… yes, jealousy because we are more learned, or because Jewish merchants have made fortunes in commerce. And while for now they silently hate us in public, they thumb their noses behind our backs. They think I am one of them, a hater of the "kikes." And they don't hold back, Talia! I tell you, soon it will be worse. Open your eyes. Do not think Livorno is any different from Firenze, or tiny Pitigliano, or Rome."

She stood staring at him, the letter from Simon she had wanted to show him still dangling in her hand. "And I, Talia," he continued, "I live the life of a hypocrite, of a cheat, of an imposter who laughs along with them at the Jew jokes, who makes the little gestures of money counting or of a circumcision's 'clip.' Thanks to your son, I have become one of them. It would have been better to die honestly in the forest." He slumped into a chair. "Nathan was a braver man than I, and Simon is a still greater traitor."

The two of them listened to the silence hardening between them, the years of marital telepathy now a chasm where a sad loneliness welled up.

"He is your son, Rico. And we must protect him. It is the other one… your daughter… *La Jettatura*... whom we must fear!" She said nothing more, but dropped the letter on the table beside Enrico and left to join the Christian women from her neighborhood on their way to the church to pray. And to offer prayers of protection for Simon and for her own protection from the crippled child who lived in her home.

Dear Father,

I hope that you are well.

Enrico hadn't been able to resist the letter's pull. A mistake to even have let his eyes turn its way.

I hope that you can in your heart welcome me again. Our parting was not what I had wanted, but it seemed that our very survival depended on such extremes. These times are dangerous for everyone, yet I had no idea that there would be bloodshed that night. I say prayers for Zio Nathan and Zia Teresa. Do you know what happened to Giuliana?

I learned that you are now serving our Fascist cause in a military capacity in Livorno. I am very happy that you and our family are safe. Unfortunately, for me, there has been a bit of trouble. I will speak carefully at this time, but it has become necessary for me to leave Milan and find a more secure place. The Youth Militia unit with which I was associated did not work out well. And so, dear Father, I have decided to join the church. I believe you will agree that in these coming times, it is a good place for me. You have your place, and I will have mine.

Only two things. I will need some money to travel from Milan back to Pitigliano, where I plan to enter the seminary. And also, any information you may have on Giuliana's whereabouts. I would of course, like to become a good cousin to her, poor girl, if as an orphan, she is somewhere still in that area.

Please send as much as you are able, Father, to the Albergo San Gimignano in Vicarra. They are allowing me to stay in their stable for now.

Your loving son,

Simon (you need only use my first name)

***

Though no letter accompanied it, a packet of money addressed to "Simon" was dropped off at the Albergo San Gimignano's front desk a week later by Georgio, the traveling postal clerk who brought the rare letter to Vicarra and several other mostly illiterate rural communities. But the following day, he was back, though no one expected him for a month. This time he peddled his bicycle furiously from tiny post office to post office with flyers that had come to the police station in Cimona. It was the same flyer that had been initiated in Milan. The same one sent by the police command center in Pavia. And now the ones that would be distributed to each small village all the way to Florence. On stiff white paper, its thick letters read:

WANTED

BE ON THE LOOKOUT FOR JEW OF 17-19 YEARS.
BLONDE HAIR, BLUE EYES, STRONG BUILD
ANSWERS TO NAME: "SIMON"
WANTED FOR MURDER IN MILAN

Mounting his bicycle to head toward the next village, Giorgio stood nodding his head at the postal clerk of the *albergo* that handled the mail. "Can't be too careful, even out here in the country, can we?" He waited a beat. It was all he could manage before launching into the crime's details that had been passed from police station to police station and from post master to postal clerk for four hundred miles.

"You won't believe it, but the Jew got caught passing himself off as a regular Christian Italian. It seems he'd even joined the Fascist Youth Militia in Milan, helped with the roundups of other Jews and closing down of "yid" shops... when, get this... while trying to niggle some boy in the shower, the other kid notices the Jew's *cazzo* is circumcised. So, the boy begins to shout, "Hey Jew, you're cut… or something like that. That's what some people say he was yelling. And then the kid goes silent." Giorgio could hardly get the story out fast enough, perhaps adding a few details along the way when he noticed other *albergo* guests stopping to listen.

"So, when they finally break into the shower, what do they find? This pale little skinny kid lying in the water, shower still going, and his neck is snapped. That's right, the big Jew somehow broke his neck—that's what they're saying. And the Jew kid is gone. Can you imagine? Jews are supposed to be lightweights, only got big fingers for countin' money! But this one, don't want to mess with him, I guess. They think he's heading south toward us."

The clerk of the albergo looked again at the Militia ID photo printed below the "wanted" words on the poster. Then he pronounced very slowly the word, "Simon." The clerk of the albergo was short and delicately built, a full-head smaller than the postman, but he looked into the distance, drew himself up an inch or two, swallowed hard, then went out toward the stable. There, feeling at the same time as brave and as nauseated as he ever had, he washed down the stable walls, changed the hay that had recently been a human bed, and carefully locked the door behind him. The clerk of the albergo felt very lucky to be alive with such a Jew on the loose.

Chapter 7

Five or six figures were scattered along the road that connected Pitigliano, Sorano, Elmo, Sovana and other hamlets spread across the Tuscan plain. From the shed's vantage point atop the little *collina* on which the milking lean-to sat, the figures were still hazy, but Giuliana knew the moving black spots were old ladies, middle-aged farm women, and the occasional young matron, each of them paying a solitary visit to Rosetta as they did every week. Once or twice a man had come alone just after dark when families were preparing to eat or bedding down their flocks and when it was likely he wouldn't be noticed in the shadows along Rosetta's lane.

For the last year and a half Giuliana had slipped into the mostly anonymous guise of the quiet granddaughter of a hardworking widow, and the girl now knew the routines of the animals and the people in this part of the rural *campagnia*. She knew the day washing was done at the river; when the bees were smoked so their honey could be taken; when the grapes were plucked and stomped; and the grey-green olive trees shaken of their ubiquitous treasure. She also knew how to balance a bundle of dried kindling and brush atop her head and when not to walk in the woods lest a hunter mistake you for a *cinghale*, the razor-backed, mightily-tusked wild boar of Toscana's thick forests.

It was only a few hours past dawn, and today the ground fog still lay in streaks of lavender across the fields, too wet to be lifted by a sleepy sun and sent skyward to make a cloud. Watching the ribbon of visitors who appeared to slowly slalom between the tall cypress trees that lined the road had become a ritual as normal to Giuliana as was the milking of ewes or the feeding of their lambs. She had come to know that each Friday would produce this slow-motion cavalcade of supplicants, at least that is what they seemed. All Giuliana knew for sure was that each Saturday, Rosetta had a larger bag of coins beneath her apron than the day before. What Giuliana didn't know was what went on inside the old stone farmhouse when the shutters were closed and where the soft sound of the old woman's voice undulating in a rhythmical drone was certainly not a part of everyday farm life. *Farm life*. How strange it was that it was her life now.

For a moment, Giuliana had a vision of herself as she pulled at the ewe's teats, sending the aroma of fat and grass and animal essence into an enveloping cloud while spurts of milk rattled against the metal can. She was a city girl, after all. She'd been proud that her mother had called her a "reader and a writer." She could play the piano and she could reference verses of the Torah that had even made her father proud. Yet here she was gripping a sheep's buttocks between her knees, unable to find a book to read other than the Christian Bible in what she thought was Latin, and wondering, as was everyone in Italy now, if war would come to Tuscany too as it had in the provinces of Poland and Czechoslovakia the year before. Everything seemed unhinged and easily lost. Nothing could be counted on for long… especially for an orphaned girl who pretended at being Catholic, but who lit the Sabbath candles each Friday in a Christian home. Giuliana's original life, the secret one Rosetta helped her lead, seemed as easily lost as the fog lying across the valley.

Indeed, from small things to large, nothing seemed certain; everything had become a question. When she thought about it, there were even an intriguing few about Rosetta's grandson, the young man who had only recently come to stay with his father in the neighboring town of Sovana. Yes, thinking about the tall boy with his dark brows and curly hair was better than trying to sort out the possibility of war or odd chants behind closed doors by old ladies in black. Giuliana would just let her mind settle on the breadth of this boy's shoulders and a dimple she'd seen when he laughed. That should be enough to push the war news from her head.

Just then the ewe that Giuliana held between her knees bucked to indicate that her little teats had emptied the last of their thick, warm milk—richer and more nutritious than anything made by a cow, Rosetta said. Giuliana dipped a rag in the soapy water beside her, ran it over the pink udder and teats, and sent the impatient sheep off to her friends, perhaps to wonder about what had happened to the little lamb twins she had dropped the week before. Giuliana would feed those eager babies from a bottle again within the hour, but right now her curiosity had overcome her as she saw not an old woman in black round the corner into the side yard, but a large car with a woman she knew at its wheel.

Rosetta seemed to have heard the motor of the big black car as it belched toward the entrance, scattering chickens and setting the sentinel dogs into a panic. And unlike her usual Friday habit, she came out the front door of the low farmhouse to investigate the fuss.

Built from the soft stone harvested from the land and chinked with smaller stones and straw-filled mortar, a red-tiled roof stretched over both the house and the side barn where the cow was kept. The whole place had the pastoral look of stability and protection. Yet Giuliana watched as Rosetta hung back behind the fig trees arching over the door. Bandits were not unknown in the countryside; Mafiosi from the south had recently been making forays into Italy's mid-section; and the Fascist cadres had begun to consider the business of even small farmers and merchants theirs as well.

But rather than a black-shirted party member, a middle-aged woman in a light jacket swung her legs halfway out of the driver's seat. She looked unsure, referring to something she held in her hand and looking from the road below to the hills beyond as if calculating distance. Then she turned to someone else in the car and said, "I think this is it."

Talia (now) Ponti stepped out of the car. Adjusting her purse on her arm, she directed the person in the passenger seat to, "Stay here," then slowly crunched her way toward the farm's front door, nervously eyeing the dogs who were behaving like centurion guards.

"*Buon giorno*," said Rosetta from the shadows, stepping forward only as far as the top step.

Talia stopped with a gasp of surprise. "*Ah, scusa, scusa*, Signora." She raised her hands as much as if she were confronted by police as by an old woman in a black cotton dress. "Scusa. I am not sure I am in the right place, but may I ask you if you are Signora Rosetta Portini, the… the…." Talia seemed unable to find the words she wanted.

"What is it you have come for, Madame?" asked Rosetta, kindly, but giving nothing away.

"Well, it is about my… about a family member… maybe two family members…." Talia dug in her pocket for the paper on which may have been not only directions, but perhaps a description of the purpose for which she had come to see Rosetta.

"Can you tell me what is the problem with your family member? I will tell you if I can help. There is no need for my services if I cannot…."

Giuliana suddenly realized the bucket of sheep milk at her feet was being lapped at by the two lambs who had pushed through their little barricade at the back of the shed. But she couldn't move without revealing her presence to the woman she now clearly recognized as her aunt.

Talia cleared her throat. She seemed embarrassed and prepared to leap into the car for a getaway if the old woman became angry or began to laugh. "I… well, my daughter… has begun to… well, things seem to have begun to… uh… happen." Talia opened her palms in frustration and took a breath. "Forgive me. I am very nervous. We have come from quite far away… your reputation…." Rosetta took a step from the shadows that seemed to give Talia some confidence, and she began again.

"My daughter is very young, only just-turned fifteen and very innocent I am sure…. And yet, sometimes… odd things happen… when she is in a room. Bad things… to people with whom she is angry. She can make… Well, it seems that sometimes, she… she can make things move. That she can… punish people." Talia's head dropped and she let her fingertips tap at her forehead as if to settle her thoughts back into place.

"I have been told that the woman who lives here is a *maga*... a magician, capable of helping my daughter. I hope that you are she." Talia seemed humiliated to be speaking of magic and the supernatural even as she stood in her sophisticated jacket near a large, modern car. Yet her voice was desperate. "I hope, I hope that if you are this woman, that you can bring back the girl of before…." Talia's palms were now pressed together, shaking in hope toward Rosetta.

Suddenly, two figs dropped onto Rosetta's head. Then three. Eight more hard green figs fell onto her shoulders, then a dozen seemed to fly from higher in the tree, each one striking Rosetta's face and chest. The old woman retreated within the entrance, rubbing her head. And the figs stopped falling. Slowly, Talia turned to face the car. Rebekah leaned on a cane against the side of the sedan playing aimlessly with the hem of her dress, but looking pointedly at her mother. "I think I'd like to go now, Mother," she said. "I have things I want to do." And then Rebekah shifted the golden strands that drifted in the breeze around her head and lifted her gaze toward the shed, where curtained in shadows within its stand of trees, Giuliana stood without breathing.

"But I hope to see my cousin again," she smiled. "I think I will. Don't you, Mother?"

Chapter 8

The old cleric had met Simon where the two dusty roads joined. One led onward to Sovana; the other serpent-like, wound upward and into Pitigliano. As the departing bus roiled a yellow cloud behind it, Simon picked up the roll of clothes he'd salvaged on his run from the Youth Militia's headquarters in Milan and assumed what he hoped would be a look of innocence beaming from a Christian youth bent on a spiritually-devoted vocation. The journey south had probably strained that guise, he guessed. After all, you don't eat without money, and you don't have shelter without it either. Without lira, you call attention to yourself. You make a tall, muscular youth with no job, no family, and no papers, suspect—perhaps even *a suspect*, he thought.

Simon didn't know how fast news traveled to the tiny rural villages where often the spoken Italian was so filled with dialect that inhabitants couldn't understand those from another village twenty miles away. He especially didn't know how fast news of the murder of a young *Balilla* member in Milan would have carried. Therefore, the lifting of a few lira from a sleeping vagrant, appropriating the purse of an elderly widow, and the outright grabbing of two schoolboys' lunch boxes which had left them sprawled in the street and sobbing, seemed perfectly reasonable. One does what one must, thought Simon.

The cleric, having shaken the newcomer's hand and picked up his roll of clothes, now walked Simon to the far side of the car. "It is a climb to the top," he said. "Might as well do this part in comfort."

Simon had seen the monastery when he'd left Pitigliano with the Youth Militia, and he had laughed along with Gianni and his new friends at the tonsured brothers sitting like "fat, brown frogs" eating cheese beneath a tree. Now some of that cheese, and an identity-obscuring brown robe were exactly what Simon wanted. It also might give him a chance at something else he wanted—to know the whereabouts of Giuliana—and the little treasure so neatly folded in her clothes.

***

The bus from the North may have just let someone out at the crossroads at the base of Pitigliano, but Giuliana, as usual on this Saturday morning, would be on foot. Just as she had since she'd come to live with Rosetta, Giuliana prepared for the surreptitious trek to Pitigliano's synagogue that lay deep within its ghetto and behind its massive walls. It was as if the two of them, the old Catholic woman and the young Jewish girl, nevertheless had a common mandate from an authority greater than a militaristic government that had laid down harsh rules. Theirs seemed to come from a better place.

Certainly, the Racial Laws had become more restrictive in the last six months. Giuliana had heard that Mussolini was under more pressure from Germany to follow their model of seizing Jewish property and expelling Jews from any profession where they came in contact with non-Jews. Perhaps all professions would soon become illegal to those who wore the yellow star, she thought. There were even rumors that in Poland and Czechoslovakia, which the Germans now held, Jews were being taken from their homes and apartments and placed in some kind of holding camps. Giuliana was sure this couldn't be true. Restricting of a profession was cruel and unfair. But the Germans couldn't just take you from your home. No one would put up with that.

Perhaps such wrongs were why Rosetta had determined that Giuliana would not lose her own identity. "Yours is a tradition of ancient holiness," the old woman had said. "If not for yours, mine would not exist." Rosetta had friends within the Jewish quarter of Pitigliano; old ladies who, like Rosetta, were without husbands or extended family nearby. Many of them had sent their children to larger cities to find work, and some of those children had returned, ousted from their well-paying jobs because of identity cards which now bore a large "E" for *Ebraico*—Jew. Most of them, as well as some families, would not return to the restrictive ghetto if they could help it. Instead, they loaned themselves out to farmers like Rosetta, hoping to be submerged into the landscape, grateful for the time being that Italians seemed to be less Jew-hating than elsewhere in Europe.

And yet Rosetta told Giuliana she needed to be very careful. "Nineteen forty, this new decade, full of war… is not about to bring good things, child. Adults do not always make decisions that help. Mussolini, our Prime Minister, has signed a pact with the madman Hitler. He has promised that Italy will fight on the side of Germany—a Pact of Steel, he calls it. Germany has gobbled up Austria, Poland, and Czechoslovakia with barely a whimper, and now this Nazi country with its gaping maw seems that it will likely invade the rest of Europe… yes, Denmark, Norway…. Holland is close. There is talk that France will soon fall, that Hitler will walk the streets of Paris. I sometimes lay awake at night and fear I hear their tanks coming over the Alps to us, or at least forcing us all to behave as Nazis… angry devils who wish to rule the earth. I do not think that will happen, my dear. And yet, we should all be careful. I am old, but you are young, and you have… this secret. The secret of your birth, one that you must protect and deny at the same moment." Rosetta laughed quietly. "Of course, there are many secrets afoot. I hear them all the time." She turned to roll the pasta dough that would soon hang in tongue-like strips from a broom handle across her cupboard doors.

Giuliana stared at Rosetta, her head now filled with pictures of marching men in boots. Posters of their muscled ranks were layered onto the walls in Pitigliano—men with their arms thrust in the air, angry looking men, some youth. She could remember such men in the dark of a night over two years ago that she tried to forget. She couldn't recall those shadowy faces, but she could mentally paste the poster's grimaces into their place.

There had once been pretty movie stars or happy men with accordions on the papered ads. They'd made her stare with excitement at the gaudy walls of Firenze's central square. Now she paid little attention to whether these angry faces were Italian or, as Rosetta suggested, German. All she knew was that being Jewish represented a threat from them. But like the night outside Pitigliano's wall, she wasn't sure from which direction it would come.

"Rosetta…" Giuliana wanted to change the subject, and the old woman would be a while in the kitchen, rolling and cutting the sticky dough. Time to shove the thugs and their jutting jaws from her mind. Giuliana came close to her, and having grown in the last two years, now looked Rosetta steadily in the eye. This woman had taken her in, had held her hand as she struggled to learn how to be something she was not, had cradled Giuliana's shaking shoulders as she wept and raged against the impossibility of what had happened that night at the base of Pitigliano's walls. Rosetta was what a grandmother should be, thought Giuliana. A woman who teaches from a distance of years, who can unravel confusions and unlock secrets, who can teach mysteries' solutions. Giuliana had many questions, some too embarrassing to ask even Rosetta, though she was sure she knew the answers. But there was one that came to her now. Another mystery. One that somehow was associated with the people who came along the road to visit—and the special visitors she had seen—her cousin and her aunt.

"Rosetta, what is it that happens when the women come to you and the shutters are closed and the door is locked? What are the words that I hear you saying?" Giuliana had never looked in the big chest where Rosetta kept her few clothes. She had never glanced at the contents of the worn leather pouch where the old woman kept her stack of enormous paper lira. And now she felt she was asking about something much more private. But she wanted to know. In some way, it seemed important to know.

Rosetta slowly put down her rolling pin and wiped her hands along the bib of her apron. Her eyes were red-rimmed from years of sunlight in the fields and from the wood smoke whose aroma even now drifted from the rafters and walls of the small stone house.

"You have noticed that I have… visitors? My friends who come to tell me… to tell me things." Rosetta's head was cocked to one side, its ball of grey hair tilting gently to one side. She sat down, regarded Giuliana, appraised her growth and the steady gaze the girl now fixed upon the old woman. Then with a small smile playing at her lips, Rosetta rose with the help of the table. Her knees were stiff as always, but taking Giuliana's hand, she led her to a small wooden icon of the Virgin Mary attached to the plaster wall beside the fireplace.

"Yes, you should know. Why not? You hear through the door. You see the sad people or the frightened people. And sometimes you see them return; sometimes they are changed, are they not? Somehow, they are relieved, or perhaps happy, or perhaps they have found justice."

Rosetta looked more closely at Giuliana, then took her face in both of her hands, each old paw bearing the wrinkled tan of the peasant and as creased as her sagging cheeks. "I have no daughters, nor a granddaughter of my own," she said. "Why should I not show you… perhaps teach you a little?" She seemed to be speaking out loud her inner conversation.

Taking a key from the pouch beneath her apron, Rosetta swung the hinged Virgin away from the wall and inserted the key into a blackened lock. Then, with an ever-broadening smile hovering about her lips as if she were about to show a fine gem to a potential buyer, she carefully pulled a wooden box from the cache in the wall and placed it on the oak credenza where the few good dishes were kept. On its surface was painted a serpent, its head rearing. Then Rosetta slowly lifted the box's lid, saying, "In the name of the Father, the Son, and the Holy Spirit."

In the dark of the little room, Giuliana saw only a collection of common items arranged around the bottom of the box, none of which seemed worthy of an invocation of deities. A jar. A glass bowl. A small pitcher containing a yellow liquid. A number of small containers which seemed to store powders and held bunches of green herbs. An iron key. Some matches and a knife were among the scattered items in the box. "What is it?" she asked.

Rosetta raised her eyebrows, her thick peasant hands closing the lid of the box and replacing it in the niche in the wall. "It is the means of restoring tranquility, my child," she said. "It is the power of Christ to remove *il malocchio*, the curse of the Evil Eye." She sat down and looked at Giuliana. "Not everyone can do it… this work I do," she said. "I could teach you some things, some words. But it is really the Spirit that must do the miracles. Still, those who can lift the *malata* that comes from the Eye, are different."

Giuliana didn't understand. Her father was a scientist and though she knew that country people were superstitious, he had dealt in facts. Facts about people from long ago with their own strange beliefs. Suddenly, Giuliana found herself remembering a book from the pile on her father's desk, one she had thumbed through as a child and which had been quickly removed from her hand. "Don't ever touch such a book, child," her father had said. "Its contents could be dangerous…." There was nothing more, except that the book had had pictures of eyes—painted eyes, staring eyes. Ones that even then had made her uncomfortable.

"Il malocchio can be placed upon anyone by a bad person, a jealous person… a person who was simply born with such an eye," Rosetta was saying. "And yes, the curse may even fall upon a Jew. It is good that you at least learn how to protect yourself… maybe one day even to dispel it." She paused a moment, gazing again at Giuliana. "And *grazie a Dio*, some of us have other gifts as well. Perhaps you have been sent to help me."

Suddenly, the sound of the horn came from somewhere along the cypress-lined lane leading to Rosetta's little *fattoria* farmlet. A moving cloud of dust could be seen bucking its way toward the house. Inside the swirling flume, Giuliana knew that the ancient bulb trumpet attached to a World War I vintage Fiat was meant to hilariously announce the arrival of Sergio; Sergio, Rosetta's grandson, who with his good humor and jokes, his brawn and bravado could make the old woman double over with laughter, covering her mouth with her hands and making little squeals that sounded like a girl's.

Rosetta quickly closed the door-like icon on the wall and ran out to greet the young man, taking Giuliana's hand and pulling her along.

"Ah, you have brought a brass band, *bambino*! Such a noisy boy! The spirits are holding their ears in their graves!"

Sergio was three years older than Giuliana, tall and newly grown into his limbs. He drew his arms and legs out of the tiny car, a broad smile shadowed by a spill of dark curls across his forehead. Now he pulled out of the car something that resembled a baby in a coarse cloth, bound with a leather thong.

"You insult this warrior, Nonna! This *cacciatore* of dangerous beasts. Like a centurion, I have speared this one from fifty meters… maybe a hundred!" Sergio strode to the steps, lifting the wrapped boar haunch above his head. "You will eat well in the winter, my lady! Then all the old farmers will come calling, winking at you for tea and *cinghale*... when what they want," he said, nuzzling her wispy bun, "is something else better tasting!" Rosetta lovingly swatted his face, then grasped it with both hands and kissed his curls.

"Come inside, *nipote*, I have bread that will be hot and sweet berry marmalade." Giuliana hung back, watching the two from the arbor's shadow with a mixture of envy and delight. Family love, built on food and feeding—the kind she saw in nests and in lamb's suckle. She could now remember only faintly the challah her mother had prepared and the matzos of Seders.

"Nonna, I cannot stay, but I do have a favor to ask of you." Sergio glanced briefly toward the arbor. "I was wondering if I could ask Giuliana for her help…."

Giuliana saw Rosetta take a step backward, raising her hands as if in warning. "This is not wise, my boy," she said quietly. "She knows nothing about this." She turned, but Giuliana heard her say, "I am here to protect her…." Then Sergio put his arm around the old woman and walked her toward the well nestled beneath an arbor of grapes where they sat together, heads nearly touching, the strong old woman and the strong young man. Giuliana decided Sergio's charm had a certain intoxicant quality to it, like the new wine she had tried last fall, because when the pair returned to the arbor, Rosetta had said, "Sergio has something he would like you to help him with."

And just like his grandmother, Giuliana had finally said, "yes."

Chapter 9

Giuliana had not ridden in an automobile since she'd come to live with Rosetta two years before. Her father and mother had owned a large green Lancia in Firenze that doubled as a kind of holiday chariot for family outings. It also became a mobile repository for dusty shards and broken vessels which, like crockery crosswords, Nathan later pieced together at the university. But here, Rosetta rode her donkey or hitched it to a small wooden cart. Giuliana loved the little pram even though the old donkey seemed to take longer getting anywhere than she would have walking alone. Today would be her first day riding with Sergio—her first day riding in an automobile alone with someone who was not her father. And for an instant she felt herself gently release Nathan's hand, the one that she knew protected her.

Rosetta came to the side of the car, her arms filled with a cloth wrapped around bread and fruit and hard-boiled eggs. "You must have something to throw to the hungry wolves if they come to eat you!" she laughed. She deposited the food in the back seat, then took Giuliana's shoulders and pulled them forward, bowing the girl's head. "In the name of the Father and the Son and the Holy Spirit…." A string of incomprehensible blessings poured over Giuliana's head, weaving what felt like a wreath of invulnerability. Then the old woman lifted the girl's face and kissed her forehead and both cheeks. "You must follow Sergio's instructions, my child. He was taught by my son who was taught by his father and the other fathers before them. But you must be careful. The men of the earth, the spirits from beneath the earth, and the crumbling earth itself, each offer a different danger. Follow what Sergio says and all will be well." She kissed Giuliana again and stepped back from the car.

***

"*E' bello oggi, no*?" Giuliana glanced at the youth beside her who wrestled the steering wheel of the elderly sedan back and forth along the road. Sergio's voice didn't seem to go with his body, she thought. He was tall, with hands and arms that were strong, and powerful shoulders that stretched the rumpled shirt of a farmer. But his voice had the operatic timbre of a tenor. Highish, melodic, a surprise, but not unpleasant.

"Yes, it is beautiful today," she said shyly, embarrassed that after this offering she would not know what next to say. Yet she wanted to say more. She would like to tell Rosetta's grandson that she was grateful to step outside of the confines of anonymity of the little stone house; that the soft summer air lifting her hair in tiny gyros was making her want to laugh out loud; and that at 16, she felt ready for whatever adventure he was taking her to in this ancient countryside of Toscana.

"*Pane*. Is there some bread… and butter in the basket?" Sergio was smiling as he glanced toward the back seat. "Nonna's bread and the butter of the goats will give us strength… and keep us warm below." All at once, he interrupted himself, pointing excitedly toward what appeared to be a ridge crenelated by towering cypress trees that jabbed black fingers in a distance far away. "This is where we are going. You can just see the beginning of the forest now."

Giuliana turned back toward the road, a knife and the warm bread in her hands. Beyond, the land was striated with fields and hills and rows of iconic cypress along the undulations of ochre *strade* that wound across the land. She scanned the vista for the particular ridge that excited Sergio. A small village sat crookedly with crimson roofs along one side of a low valley, quilts of green and yellow and iris-purple stretched upwards in all directions. Beyond, an outcrop of low mountains looked neither far nor near. Giuliana knew that kilometers were merely illusory through the haze of sun-saturated air. But Sergio's gaze was on a promontory that erupted at the end of the downward slope and which seemed pockmarked at its base by dark purple eyes.

"Is that where we're going?" she asked, excitement lifting her own voice an octave or two. "We are going to the woods? Are we going for kindling? Mushrooms! Perhaps it is mushrooms that grow in little valleys!" Giuliana bounced back in her seat, feeling herself flush like a child at the prospect of a secret's unveiling. Rosetta had said nothing about their "mission," only that her grandson was to be trusted. And yet Sergio had said, the word "below." His grandmother had spoken of the dangers within the earth. Now Giuliana looked at him squarely. They were not going for wood or for mushrooms. "Exactly what are we to do in this place, then?" she asked, suddenly feeling an uneasiness crawl along her shoulders. Then he turned to her and held up one of his hands, the palm turned toward her.

"This may tell you," he laughed, then put his hand back on the steering wheel, nonchalantly looking out the driver's window. With a sudden flood of dread, Giuliana grabbed his hand back, turning it over as if it now belonged to her to examine. The palm was rough, like all agricultural laborers' in Toscana, but in the middle of the palm were deep red circles; circles on top of circles that covered life lines and heart lines from fingers to thumb. "What are these? These *anelli*?" she demanded. "What are they supposed to tell me?"

She was 16, but she was not stupid. Nor, she knew, was she knowledgeable of all the things that went on in these primitive communities where, as she had begun to see it, superstition and old magic existed alongside bona fide religions she at least thought she understood.

Sergio gave her a bemused glance from beneath his cap, withdrew his hand wrist first and shook it dramatically as if her touch had offended him. "We all must live, you know," he shrugged, lurching the front wheels abruptly to avoid a rut. "Let's have a bite of bread then…."

"No. I will not be buttering your bread until you say what it is that I am to do to help you." Even as she crossed her arms and assumed the universal position of pout, she realized that some of what she did was directly lifted from a movie her parents had taken her to before the war and before the current inauthentic version of her life had begun. She realized that she was at once frightened, angry, and flirting like the woman in the film, and that she missed her parents all the more for finding herself unable to interpret what these opposing emotions were supposed to mean. Then she burst into tears that were very real.

Sergio bounced the car off the track they had turned on and came to a stop beneath a grove of beech trees that stood like sentinels guarding the leafy forest beyond. He turned off the engine and with a sigh, shifted to face Giuliana. He bore the look of a professor about to elucidate a theorem to a particularly dim student.

"But you must stop crying before I can explain anything to you," he said with another sigh. "Sniffling sounds will make you unable to hear." Giuliana felt another layer of irritation descend. Being treated like a naughty child didn't at all fit with the image of the woman in the film. Then, Sergio dug his hand deep into his pocket and pulled out a bundle made of a dirty piece of cloth.

"Do you see this?" he asked. It was unclear if he really wanted an answer. "This belongs to us. To us who live on this land. It is our patrimony. It lies beneath us like an ancestor." Sergio held the soiled packet cradled in the palm with the red circles. "From the dust of which we are all made, from the soil which nourishes us, our fathers created beauty. It lives beneath our feet even now. Our ancestors show to us their lives in these beautiful things. From their births, their celebrations, their wars, their feasts… and their deaths… they have left these tokens to us so that we will not forget them. They live on, just in a different way than before."

The morning mists had retreated into the forest, and now Sergio sat before a backdrop of saturated siennas and lavenders, his face darkly focused toward Giuliana. Still, she did not understand. Then he slowly began to unwrap the package.

Just as she had in her room when she undid the swaddle of nightclothes from the tiny urn her father discovered in the cave, now

Sergio carefully pulled away the cloth from another delicate object, one he seemed to revere. “It is beautiful, is it not? It is small, but it is perfect—a bronze horse. Look, its hooves are as delicate as twigs. And its mane, like tiny eyelashes….” Sergio hovered over the small, blackened pony like a vigilant father.

Giuliana looked up at him. “Yes, it is truly beautiful. But what has this to do with us here now? Why do your hands have red circles that are to tell me a story?”

Sergio furrowed his brow even as his lips began a smile. “But don’t you see, oh young girl from the city… Jewish girl without a name… Catholic girl without belief. You are going to become, like me, a preserver of the past, a custodian of antiquity… someone for whom this war may be very good. You are going to become a robber of Etruscan graves.”

Chapter 10

Livorno 1941

Another wave rolled in, and another, this one different, sweeter, thick, a jasmine-honey that clung to the nostrils and the hair. As each woman passed, a new fragrance, lemons from Tuscany, musk from Libya, fortified lavender from the South of France, settled in a kind of olfactory parfait on the room. Yet layer after layer, the stacked fragrances became sour, pounding Rebekah's frontal lobe and setting her sinuses afire. And yet, she couldn't move. Not now. Her mother had seen to that. No embarrassments today.

With her daughter's cane carefully cached, Rebekah's mother, Talia Ponti moved gracefully about the salon, her newly blonde hair a perfect cloche as she bent for air kisses and face-averted hugs. The women, a dozen of Livorno's most well-positioned doyens, as well as the new northern additions, knew their part of the choreography as well. Slouching, smoking, fingering strands of pearls whose original owners may not have given them up willingly, the women assayed each other's bounty and the likely power that their respective husbands held. Of course, there were a few sidelong glances Rebekah's way as the women surveyed the room. A crippled girl, even one of the now-preferred Aryan coloration, was not something you displayed if you didn't have to. It was only because now *Captain* Enrico Ponti had put his foot down, that Talia had bitterly let her daughter make an appearance at all.

"And who is this?" A particularly thin woman in a cream-colored dress stood at an angle above Rebekah, gazing at her over her shoulder, as if a frontal view would give too much credence to the girl's existence. Rebekah knew the woman's Italian was shabby, but her superior tone made clear no mention would be made of it.

"Yes, this is Rebekah," said her mother, looking to see if she were being called elsewhere in the room, omitting any familial connection.

"Well…" The woman pronounced it, "Vell." "Hers is a very pretty dress. I cannot obtain this kind of silk in Germany at the moment." As if Rebekah were a plaster mannequin, the woman reached down to finger the fabric of the girl's skirt. A cascade of *Shalimar,* rose and vanilla, spilled from the German and threatened at Rebekah's gullet. "Perhaps I can buy it from you," the woman said to Talia. "I will even take it with me today," she said more quietly. In times of war, words are spoken, shoulders are rubbed, understandings occur and deals are made that would never have happened at another time.

For Talia, to have this many wives and consorts of Fascist and German officers in her apartment, to know that she fit in here, shed of her rough coat, anklets, and thick shoes in favor of smooth gabardine suits, silk stockings, and shoes with delicate straps, was perhaps more than any plain-born, Jewish woman could have dreamed of. And to do it when others like her were being rounded up into ghettos or worse, allowed the unreality of the moment to take on a theatrical vibration. Barely grounded in reality, because all that had before been true was now upended, Talia might have believed herself both actress and playwright, speaking words once intended for the lips of another, but which now were handled perfectly by the understudy. "Of course, dear Vera," she said. "I will have Rebekah change and you may take it home today."

Talia took Vera by the elbow and steered her toward a group of laughing women, overcome with enough hilarity that ashes were jolted from the tips of their cigarettes. "Do you suppose he straps it on?" one burst out. "If he doesn't catch something on the streets of Paris first!" another joined in.

Rebekah sat perfectly still. It was unclear to her what these women with their highly rouged cheeks found so humorous. Ever since their family had come to Livorno, adults gathering in groups along the street or in the ever-more thinly-stocked markets had grown more tense. Stiffly downing espressos they didn't seem to want or drinking wine with distracted looks, everyone now quietly discussed the war news that found Italian troops grimly battling in the mountains of France, as well as on the North African front. Only six months before, German soldiers had triumphantly marched down the Champs Elysees when, like Denmark and Norway, France had fallen. For a time, Rebekah thought Italians seemed proud to be German allies. But recently anxiety had settled over everyone with the feared entry of the United States into the conflict. Still, Rebekah heard only yesterday a drunken street vendor shout, "We're on the winning side! The Furher! Il Duce!" Pumping a black and red swastika in the air, he had slobbered, "Sieg Heil! Sieg Heil!" until his face was crimson, while people near him had noiselessly backed away.

To Rebekah, the women here in her apartment, in their silky blouses and sheer stockings seemed to be working very hard to ignore whatever news turned the rest of the thinking *Livornese* nervously grim-faced. Even the wife of another officer had whispered of the bombing of London by planes of the German Luftwaffe and that many had died including children her own age.

Rebekah watched her mother, now leaning against the piano, a wrist draped across the arm of her new German friend, Vera, and wondered if the woman who had carried her out of the murderous cave in Pitigliano, today would have cared about dead children. Or even one of her own.

Rebekah closed her eyes, feeling a familiar movement along her shoulders. It was one she'd sometimes felt as a child, a wave of fever that quickly passed, something her mother blamed on a "tantrum." Not really a shudder, it was as if the sputtering of a failing electrical wire were attached to her spine, seeking to close its circuit in an arc along her fingers. And yet, when this feeling occurred, she was the Generator. Both detached and alert, Rebekah was the Force. Rebekah the conduit. Her thoughts the Prescriptor for things she only sensed; for a floating hatred that as she'd grown, seemed too large to hold—an ancient Awareness that when it found her, she could not contain.

Suddenly the German woman gasped, grabbed at her arm and pulled away from Talia with a frantic shriek. "Let me go! Stop! Let go! Are you crazy! Stop!" Vera shook her arm up and down, now cursing in German as blood flew onto her ivory blouse. Pulling at Talia's fingers which had embedded themselves deep into the German's arm, Vera sank to her knees, begging for help from the stunned women watching the spectacle, their prosecco flutes lifted higher now to avoid the spray of blood. At last, wrenching Talia's fingers from her wound like dripping talons, Vera staggered to her feet, unsteady and terrified.

And then it was over. With only Vera's sobs above the silence, Rebekah slowly opened her eyes and pushed a strand of hair behind her ear. The room was in confusion. Picking up her stunted left leg, the one that refused to work as it should, she crossed it daintily across the right, shoving herself slightly forward to better see the result of the social catastrophe.

Vera's arm was wrapped in table napkins. Wailing, she was being escorted by a quartet of women toward the door. Food had been knocked to the ground and the piano bench turned over. Other women were gathering their jackets and purses, and as if they were fleeing a dangerous animal, inched their way toward the door.

Only Talia sat perfectly still. With her once delicately manicured hand now wet with blood in her lap, her gaze was fixed fast on Rebekah.

"Oh, Momma," said her daughter, when the last woman had left, "The thin lady, the one who couldn't speak Italian properly… she forgot to take my dress for her daughter in Germany. Do you think she will she be coming back for it soon?"

Chapter 11

Simon awakened with a gasp, as though water were running down his throat, as though it spilled from a baptismal fountain overhead, threatening to drown him with celestial liquid. He sat up, still coughing dream-water, though he was in fact dry except for the perspiration laying in tiny beads along his cheeks. At least he hadn't awakened the light-sleeping brother with whom he shared the tiny cell he'd been assigned. There was no one to wearily intrude and politely ask what the dream had been about.

But in fact, since coming to the Abbey of Sant'Angelo, so serene on its jutting cliff, dreamily afloat above its morning cloud, Simon had had few uninterrupted periods of sleep. He felt exhausted, and it wasn't just the occasional referential nightmare. It was the prayers that were doing it. Endless sessions during the days— and masochistic repeats at night. At least Jews took time to sleep.

Matins in the morning at 6; Third Hour Prayer at 9; the Noon Prayers; the Ninth Hour Prayer at 3; Vespers at 6; the Midnight Prayer; and just when Simon would drift into his deepest sleep, the 3AM Vigil Prayers. But tired or not, he knew he was likely safe here. Here, conversation was limited to shy nods. Here, heads were lowered and gazes not held. No one wanted to know a family's lineage. And no one forced you to shower naked in sight of others. In this hilltop hermitage, safety alone might be enough for now and privacy a bonus blessing. Yet, Simon speculated on how many secrets would come spilling out if everyone were forced to drink some holy truth serum, or the liquid sacrament's celebration lasted too long or the quaffs were too deep. He occasionally wondered if any of the other monks had ever killed someone.

A bell rang from far off. With a sigh of exasperation, Simon knew too well what that 2:45 ring meant. The Abbey was huge, sprawled over the top of a precipice and built from the sandy tufa that though soft when carved, time-hardened on the outside to withstand even the occasional earth tremors of the region. In the candlelight that always burned between them, Simon glanced at Brother Luigi, the octogenarian who shared his cell. He'd learned that the old man would not rouse unless shaken, and tonight before bed he had whispered to be left to sleep until Matins at 6AM. Usually two monks said the Vigil prayers at the same time, but let the ailing monk rest, Simon thought. What did it matter? Everybody always slept through the droning middle-of-the-night Psalms anyway—at least he did.

Yet Simon was grateful to the creaking Luigi who now snored in tea kettle snorts beside him. He had been endlessly patient, teaching Simon the rudiments of monastic life, never once showing surprise at how little the young initiate knew of Catholic belief or ritual. The rustic old monk must have racked it up to how spiritually corrupt the outside Catholic world had become with bright young men like Simon not even knowing how to properly cross themselves. How surprised he would have been to discover that this particular monk had never been in a church before he came to the Abbey of Sant'Angelo.

In the darkness, like a windup toy, Luigi's breathing slowly stalled, hovered, then stopped for the 30 seconds that Simon always found himself counting. He shoved the old man to make him turn over, then forced himself up and out of his own bed, wishing at first to plead illness as Luigi likely would by morning. Instead, Simon reminded himself that the small hours always brought their own benefits, if you looked for them. And he thought that tonight there might be one—an opportunity to privately examine the Abbey's altar a little more carefully—perhaps even see if the reliquary had been left open. After all, it always paid to know your environment, your territory, what surrounded you. He hadn't been taught this by Enrico, the military tactician. It was something Simon had always known—situational awareness, the ability to choose options when others felt uncertain. He also knew that Catholics liked their gold, even if it came in candlesticks and crosses, and that the reliquary might hold even more. Always a good thing to know, he chuckled to himself—a very good thing to know.

Simon tugged tight the cincture around his waist. Made of cord, he could loosen it when he slept, though the rules of the Benedictines stipulated sleeping fully clothed, but "without a knife at your side." Perhaps there had been killers in the ancient St. Benedict's midst, Simon mused. Still, summer had been miserable in the thick woolen robe. He pulled the additional scapular over his head forming a kind of work apron and added a hood. Only his feet felt unfettered. Simon had often watched his uncle Nathan as he prepared for Jewish services. The *kippah*, the *tallit*, the *kittel*, and the *tefillin*, all accoutrements a man wore when he simply wanted to speak to God. How bizarre to have to dress up in medieval layers as he did now, or in layers of shawls with tiny boxes strapped to your head to perform rituals of magical beliefs and what Simon thought were outright scams. Again, he reminded himself why he believed in no God—but just in himself. Just what he could control.

Glancing at the cell's only adornment, a crucifix hanging like a threat between the beds, he crossed himself in case Luigi were peeking through half-closed lids. Then taking a small walking stick from the corner to handle the terrain, Simon slipped silently out the door.

The way to the sanctuary of the church from the Abbey was treacherous in the near dark. Tiptoeing down the gallery where the cells were aligned, through the wooden gate of the cloister, and along an open garden that looked out over the valley, Simon had a clear view of stars and the occasional light that remained on in one of the houses below. He also had a view toward the rocky hills that surged toward where the sun would come up hours from now. Then it was up a winding path to the church and in through its side door near the altar.

But tonight, something caught his eye. As he crossed the garden, leaning for a moment on the low wall overlooking the valley and the forest on its other side, he could make out a tiny cluster of lights through the trees. Moving forward and back, like fireflies confined in a jar, the lights shifted this way and that, disappeared, reemerged, and showed startling activity for the wee hours before dawn. Though sound would carry across the valley, he heard no voices to identify the bustling dots, only, he thought, the faint scrape of metal on stone. And then, just as he turned toward the sacristy, one distant muffled shout.

"*Ce l'ho*!" I have it.

Chapter 12

Livorno

Talia had refused to be in a car with Rebekah following the ruin of her ladies' afternoon. Basically, refused to be anywhere in the apartment that the girl might be found. "I have made the arrangements in Pitigliano," she told Enrico. "But you must take her there. That child hates me and wants to destroy me." She lit a cigarette and ran the ruby tips of her fingers through her hair. "With the damage she's done, I might as well retire to oblivion myself."

Enrico knew all women exaggerated. He saw them laugh too loud in the bars that were becoming more commonplace in Livorno. He saw them swoon if it were too hot, tremble if it were too cold, weep if a puppy were lost, and take to their beds with the afternoon headaches that Italian women had turned into art. Yet he wasn't sure Talia was exaggerating what had happened at her soiree. Even members of his own department seemed oddly quiet when he neared lately, their little bands disbursing, conversations melting away. There was no outright hostility yet, but men listen to women, and Italian women could be insistent.

Yet to ascribe the superstitions of old ladies to the behavior of his daughter was absurd. Hysterical women come from all countries, he internally smirked. An Italian diva or a Germanic Valkyrie crying foul was sure to get attention. Maybe this "Marlene Dietrich" had scratched herself! More worrisome was Talia—the plain Talia, the one he loved, the one who as the wife of a military man on his way up, had known how to behave.

Indeed, she had changed since coming to Livorno. But then so had everything, hadn't it? Draping her Jewishness in flamboyant goy clothing with daring necklines, and a sudden interest in Wagner may have made Talia feel invulnerable among the other fashionable women, but Enrico sensed that the greater dangers for their family and himself lay with Mussolini's recent choice. The dictator had just announced that Italy would become part of the Axis alliance binding Italy to Germany and to Japan. With the decision, Germany's aims would be supported by Italy and Enrico guessed that though he masqueraded as a non-Jew, he would find it harder to pass himself off as a patriot of the German cause.

The room overlooking the harbor had grown quiet. Talia stood, her arms crossed, looking out at the enormous warships that moved like great grey beetles across the water, hiding their future homicide within.

"So, you want to be without children then. Both of them gone, is that it?" Enrico slumped in a chair, rubbing his fingers across his eyes. He hadn't been home in 48 hours, and a familial crisis was not something he felt up to at the moment. At the base, hundreds of Italian youth who had already opted for Hitleresque haircuts were arriving, eager to enlist, eager to shove their skinny arms skyward and seek the glory Il Duce was screaming over the radio every night. How to train these witless boys into fighting men, how to remove their consciences and their home-taught morals and replace those with reflexes toward murder and subjugation would be Enrico's duty. Watching those boys spill out of buses, he had stood at his office window and for a moment thought he watched a line of ghosts, skulls bouncing atop skeletons, buoyed by songs of patriotism that Enrico heard as the dirges bereaved parents would shortly sing.

"I want Rebekah to go," Talia said softly. "I didn't want it for Simon." Enrico looked at her. Beneath the powder and the rouged lips, he saw a tired woman, a mother who knew she was failing both children she had borne. She probably knew she was failing herself.

"I am frightened," she said, letting the cigarette continue its solitary burn in the ashtray beside her. "We must live, Enrico. We must live as we can now. Change ourselves to survive. Become other people. And yet…" Talia fumbled for another cigarette. "Do you remember when we were young once, Rico? The day you took me sailing. The Gulf of Taranto… a September day. And the wind, do you remember it?" Enrico was so tired he could barely follow her to this distant subject. They'd been talking about children, problem children.

"Do you remember the boat? How it was tilted so hard to the side, and everything was wet from spray and the wind. That wind out of nowhere that was so strong… so sudden…." Talia's voice was both remote and present, her eyes wide in the twilight. "You had looked away for a moment. And the line broke… and then the line broke…" she repeated. "And… suddenly, I was in the sea. It swallowed me. It held me down, Rico. It blew the boat away from me. It had chosen me to take…." Talia stared out across the harbor, rubbing her arms with her hands, the new cigarette now burning low beside the other's ember.

"I didn't tell you why I lived that day," she said quietly. "Why I was allowed to live…." She turned to face her husband, who watched her silhouette against the harbor lights coming on behind her. "Do you know about *dybbuks*, Enrico?" Talia said. "Do you believe in ghosts?"

Enrico caught his breath, shook his head and forcing himself to laugh, came toward Talia with both arms out. This war, this life was driving everyone mad. "My dear, my dear girl. Let's get out of here. Let us go for gelato…. Better, let us drink wine before dinner together. Come…." Enrico was still smiling when Talia's slap snapped his head back.

"Foolish man. So little you know of things besides war and parades." Talia stepped back, rubbing her hand, unapologetic, eyes closed and her head turning from side to side. "They are there, you know," she said finally, glancing up at him. "Things don't get forgotten in that world. Their memories are long… and they find ways to… to use you. To know when you are weak." Talia sat down, her back straight, as if she still needed to be on guard—in case. But she smiled up at Enrico, seeming to take a different tack, and with a little pat on the cushion asked him to sit beside her.

"My parents, you know, were very devout, very simple Jews—Polish village people." She glanced at Enrico, whose face had gone white in the dusk. "It seems that my father was engaged, "betrothed," to a rabbi's daughter in that village. But then he met my mother. Oh, it was a scandal. A betrothal is a contract— a business between families." Talia was breathing more easily now. "But my mother said they couldn't help themselves. It was a true love of the heart, and… together they ran away. To here, to Italy. Later, the rabbi's daughter, the one who had been abandoned, died… without ever marrying." Talia seemed more in control, but still sat oddly erect, while Enrico assayed her face, looking for pathology.

"My mother says that through the years she would see this woman in her dreams. Sometimes, my father would see her too when he slept. And in their dreams, this angry and betrayed woman would promise that my parents' forthcoming family, the one she believed should have been hers, would pay the price for his betrayal. And yet, nothing happened to them. They had but one child, me… but nothing befell them. And then the day in September, Enrico… the day of our September sail came."

Talia stood up and found the cigarettes again. Enrico came to her, lit one for each of them, and led her back to the sofa. "What happened that day?" he asked gently.

Enrico watched silently as tears spilled onto her lap, seeming to fall from the tips of her lashes from some silent source. "I was in the water…" said Talia. "And the boat was blowing away… away from me, the water covering me." she whispered. "You would never find me in the waves. You would never know how I had sunk into the sea and swallowed its water and couldn't breathe. Our future… had stopped in that instant."

Enrico held both of her hands, his mind still looking for causes, rational explanations for the near-calamity so long ago, and then Talia said, "But the *dubbyk* offered me back my life. In that water, in between death and life, she held me as a hostage. She got her revenge, Rico… got what she wanted all along." Talia was nodding earnestly, looking into the darkness as if the strange apparition danced in the shadows.

Enrico put his arms around her shaking shoulders, unsure what to whisper to calm her despair. But she wanted to complete her story and turned to face him.

"She made me an offer… this woman who had loved my father. It was very simple, really. She wanted… she wanted my family. The children I would bear. She told me I would have three. One of them she would keep, she said, and the others she would have sometimes, to use them, to bring pain, to make the living feel as she did. And always she would exact revenge for the mother she would never be. But in return, she would let me live that day." Talia let her head fall onto his shoulder.

"And I agreed," she whispered after a while. "I gave to her what was to have been ours… to save myself. Our baby, the first one who died, is hers. And Simon… and Rebekah…. She makes use of them, works through them when she wants. I feel this is true, Enrico. I allowed it that day when I relinquished them… to live myself."

And even as Enrico embraced her, he wondered how to tell Talia that her pet dachshund had been brought to him by the maid—somehow caught in the washing machine's spinning paddles and minus its soft brown head.

Rebekah had never liked that little dog… but then again, he told himself, neither had he.

Chapter 13

"Simon, my son, come in here, won't you?" The old abbot was standing just outside his tiny office, looking this way and that along the brick gallery of the monastery. He motioned to Simon who was on his way for morning porridge in the communal refectory.

"My boy, there is a guest, a man—an officer, actually, inside," he nodded toward the open door. "He is from the North. Maybe Milan? With an accent I can barely understand… and he speaks too quietly for these old ears. Come inside and help me a little, if you would." The abbot may have been handsome once, thought Simon, but here in a place so tranquil even the seasons seemed loath to change, time and forced solitude seemed to have exacted penance on the body of the bent old cleric. Now, eyes clouded, taste gone, hearing minimal, perhaps his life existed only in the fragments of scripture forever running through his mind. For a moment, the sensation of sinking into the cement of the abbey overwhelmed Simon, but then he spied the high leather boots on the man seated inside the abbot's study. And both fear and the thought of opportunity leapt inside his chest.

"Please, please allow me to introduce you to my… to this young assistant," stumbled the abbot as they entered his study. "Sometimes I am unable to hear all that I should." He slumped down into a chair carved from the ancient cypress whose offspring now lined the lane to the monastery. "Please go ahead. Or if you would be so kind, go back a bit to tell me how we may be of service to you."

Until now, Simon had kept his head down, his eyes on the octagonal tiles of the study. Humility, duty, silence, keep your head low and your ears open, and even as you blended into the background, especially when you did—avenues would be opened, others would be revealed. That was his operative mantra.

The officer cleared his throat and with barely concealed impatience began again. “As I was saying, Father, we are not, all of us, strictly military folk, you see. No, no, even though our own heritage is an example of the magnificent evolution of the human species, many of us are aware and appreciate the contributions of others… especially, of the ancients, you see.” Without asking, the man in the uniform pulled out a cigarette case, lit a long, tapered cylinder and in one exhalation encircled his head in a wispy grey cloud.

Simon immediately realized why the old abbot couldn’t understand the officer. It wasn’t a “Milanese” accent, nor the priest’s ears; it was a clumsy Italian learned in a German classroom, and one that here, combined with its pomposity, was barely comprehensible.

The German stood up, pulling at the apron of his jacket and staring studiously into the tip of his burning cigarette. “We have heard that there are some extraordinary items that lie near to us… here in these Tuscan regions,” he said, glancing in the direction of the hills outside. “That buried in tombs that are perhaps beneath our very feet, there are antiquities that lie without identification, forgotten by the ignorant peasants who, of course, would not recognize their value or importance.”

Simon, who had grown used to hearing the visiting German accents of the “trainers” who came to the barracks of his militia, was himself finding it difficult to follow the guttural glottal stops that permeated the supposed Italian. Yet one thing was immediately clear: this man, like himself, saw opportunity when it was near. Simon translated into the Tuscan dialect for the abbot and watched as the old man warily began to understand as well.

The abbot cleared his throat. “Ah yes, there are such tombs in our region. And of course, of them, we are very proud.” He paused for a moment to gaze at the white wooden body of Christ mounted on a cross over the door. “And any that are found are, of course, extremely valuable… very valuable, indeed." The abbot glanced at Simon with knitted brows, the old man's nearly hairless head nodding gently up and down. "Italian patrimony lies deep in the heart of each of us here."

The officer had come to the end of his cigarette and clearly wanted another, but having stubbed the first out on his boot, he now sat holding the stinking butt in his hand with no place for it to go.

"May I take that, Sir?" offered Simon, with a low bow and a quick smile of understanding at the officer. He was a Colonel and likely one of the higher-ranking Germans in the middle of Tuscany, Simon guessed. He would perhaps be good to know.

"Yes, yes, we are all proud of our heritage," said the officer with a sigh as he extracted another cigarette. "But these are turbulent times, are they not, Father? War and conflict are near. And for those of us who hope to cooperate together, we must help one another. Mutual benefit. Is this not right? We must together protect that which is precious. Here, here in Italia, should fighting come—should unscrupulous others seek to enrich themselves in times of trouble by the sale of, as you say, "patrimony," we, your allies in Germany, are here to assure you that you will not be taken advantage of. Indeed, we can offer protection to abbeys that might otherwise become pawns during wartime. We can provide financial resources for the religious who live there—for their simple needs, of course—to buy prayer candles and beads and the like."

Simon almost laughed out loud. The exploration to "do business," the quid pro quo was blatant. But the old abbot was probably too naïve to understand what had just been proposed. Simon translated, making sure the Colonel's intent was clear.

Then the priest asked quietly, but pointedly, "Exactly which kinds of pieces are you most interested in?" Simon's head swung to the old man in disbelief. "The older, the more valuable, you understand."

Even the Colonel was caught off-guard. He obviously had thought the process of garnering ancient stolen antiquities would require more finesse, even a little seasoning with a veiled threat or two, but not dealing with a vendor in a cassock who seemed to suggest an inventory of precious old pots and statues.

The officer inhaled some smoke the wrong way and spent a minute hacking and swallowing while he decided how to respond to the priest. Simon poured some water for him and hesitated for a moment, looking into the man's eyes as he handed him the glass. "Is there anything more I can do for you, Sir?" he asked, innocently. This time the Colonel looked directly at him. That was all Simon wanted for now—to be seen. To be recognized when he would approach the smoke-sodden officer later.

Just then the bells announcing the call to the day's third round of prayers began to sound. "Do you have a card, Colonel?" asked the abbot rising from his chair. "A place where you are staying that I may contact you… should I need to. What is the word… your 'billet,' is that it?"

The officer smiled, "Of course, Father, my 'billet', as you say, is the *albergo* in Pitigliano. Soon we will need a larger space. The old palace I think will accommodate our growing numbers here. One of your brothers can find me at the hotel for the present, however." He glanced at Simon as he was handed his gloves. Then, "I am sure that protecting the antiquities of Etruria can become a collaborative effort between us, Father, something that can bring our two countries close… in what we may one day call brotherly love…"

Simon felt the light graze along his hand and humbly bent his head as the Colonel fairly strutted out the door.

Chapter 14

The weather had shifted over the last week, putting the countryside on notice that fall and soon, the shrieking winter winds would not be long in coming. Giuliana's face was still sun-blushed from Rosetta's summer garden, from lazy hours tending to the sheep, and from the now frequent afternoon walks when a handsome young man came calling.

Yet, besides the weather, things were changing. Last month when she had sat selling cabbages beside the fountain in Pitigliano's square, beneath the soaring aqueducts stretched above her, she also sat beneath dual flags nailed to its arches. One flag bore a golden eagle clutching an ancient Roman *fasces,* a bundle of rods with an embedded axe, and now the Italian Fascist party's symbol of authority. The other flag above her head was the one now flying over much of Europe—the white circle on a red field with the virulent-looking Nazi swastika at its center.

But it was more recently that she had become truly frightened. Rounding the corner near the ghetto's fenced entrance, Giuliana had come upon three old women. The trio stood silent, staring at one another, two seeming to dare the third to move. Giuliana was partially hidden by the huge bundle of cooking reeds she carried on her shoulders, still she backed away. Then one of the black-garbed widows began to shout, *"Strega! Strega Ebraica! Puttana del diavolo!"* The other old woman spat at the third who cowered against the elaborate barricade, crying for help. Then the first woman threw a bottle of the fine olive oil made in the ghetto and so prized in the region directly at the sobbing Jewess. It struck her and slowly her pale shawl turned a greasy black, her oily fingers covering her face. "The Jewish Witch, the Devil's Whore" didn't fight back, only turned her back in shame as the widows cursed her, as they pummeled her with her "sins" against God and Jesus and all the merchants she had tried to cheat and all the babies she'd managed to eat. And she was only saved when a dozen women from inside the gates unlocked its door and pulled her in and down into the protective recesses of what Giuliana knew to be the communal kitchen. It was a place that she knew well. The place this very woman had taught her to make lamb matzos and a nut torte for Seder.

"Are you cold?" It was the only thing Sergio had whispered in the last 40 minutes, and at first Giuliana hadn't heard him through the weeping of the Jewess in her thoughts. But though it was dark and the flashlight was turned on only fitfully as the terrain changed on the forested mountain, Giuliana knew he was watching out for her. Indeed, watching her. She had come to sense it now, just as she sensed the slight shifts in the humus as it gave beneath her feet. Just as without seeing the *spillono,* the probing pipe, sink into the dark earth beneath Sergio's ringed palm, she could tell by its tone whether beneath it there would lie a hollow chamber. He had taught her these things in the summer months and she had become an eager student. During the soft nights of summer, Giuliana's senses, from her toes to her fingertips, seemed to have grown special antennae especially suited for these nighttime places where, like a forest animal, it paid to be alert to subtle shifts in the wind or the soil, or even the intentions of other animals nearby. Perhaps along with Sergio, she had begun to hope for a room holding a wealthy Etruscan's best acquisitions, those the ancient had planned on carrying with him to his new life on the other side.

"Are you cold?" Sergio asked again. How her father would have viewed his daughter now, hair drawn back beneath a dark scarf, another ready to pull across her face should they meet others in the forest, she couldn't surmise. But in some small way, she guessed he might be jealous. After all, Nathan, like Sergio, loved beautiful things, loved their history. The difference was that Sergio wanted them not only from under the ground, but for himself, to decide their fate and their disposition.

Giuliana glanced at the young man beside her, his eyes shining toward her from beneath his woolen cap. Bent forward with the tools of his trade on his back, Sergio carried a large reed basket filled with trowels and brushes, cloth padding, small chisels, and hammers and picks, along with his long metal pipe. She liked looking at him even as from time to time his form disappeared into the foliage like the forest satyrs she had seen on photos of Grecian pots. Giuliana's own shoulders were pulled forward balancing a basket of rope and wooden winches, extra flashlights, and a large clock to remind them of the time to leave—before early morning hunters might find one of them suspended above an open grave.

The woods they tromped through tonight, Sergio had said, suggested something extraordinary. With a homemade site map he and his father had developed over the years, Sergio showed Giuliana dozens of little red dots scattered like blood drops where statues, excavated sarcophagi, and man-sized urns had been found. Now, after days of walking the land in daylight, observing its contours as it ebbed and fell in waves of packed soil, Sergio seemed ready. The rotted forests, collapsed rock and oddly growing trees, coupled with the archaeology texts and geology books littering the old farmhouse Sergio shared with his father, had made the young robber think he was onto something—something that would have been evident to any scholar who'd observed his other "finds." "I think we are sitting on a prince's house, Giuliana," he'd said. "A palazzo… made for the other world, but as rich as the one the noble once lived in here."

"We must be close now," came the hoarse whisper from behind them. It was the first time Sergio's father had come with them into this part of the woods. Of course, he knew to stay silent; it was probably second nature to the man who had been taught this craft by his own forebearers and had taught it to Sergio in course. But Giuliana guessed he was observing other things in the dark like the deer or boars that might be standing stock still nearby. Rosetta's son, unlike her grandson, Sergio, was certainly a man of these woods, but had also acquired a certain cityfied sophistication. Giuliana noticed he didn't often look at her when he spoke and that he used Italian rather than the local dialect. Nor did he take the same delight in touching and holding the artifacts dug from the ground the way his son so lovingly did. But he too bore the circular red stigmata of the *spilloni*, a credential which for Giuliana, made him worthy of respect.

By swinging the basket down from his back within the next fifty meters, Sergio silently answered his father's implied question. He waved a finger toward a rounded mound protruding in the flashlight's glow from a stand of oddly under-sized trees and hauled out the long metal pipe. Sergio had surreptitiously brought huge flasks of water into the woods over the last days, pouring them into this section of soil to soften it for tonight's exploration. Now, Sergio's father took his own pipe, and together, the men began to crisscross the mound, pounding on the pipes' ends, listening like surgeons to the sounds of a heart or like dolphins for echolocation as evidence of a subterranean chamber where there slept a peaceful Etruscan about to be jarred awake.

While the two men began to dig over the spot where the *spilloni* had scraped against stone, Giuliana sat huddled near the baskets of tools, arms holding her shoulders as the men grew warmer and she felt the heat leaving her body. Yet she had on layers of wool. The last months of working beside Sergio had taught her that shimmying into caverns, tombs carved from the tufa and buried beneath a mountain of soil were places she could stay for only short periods before she would begin to shudder and to fear her stiffened fingers would drop a vase or a statue. She wondered what tonight's tomb might be like. All of the others she had entered had been mined before, many of their artifacts now only in shards, or already removed by Sergio or perhaps robbers before him.

Remembering her first visit to Sergio's "collection" near his home, she thought of how she'd laughed with delight when she saw his accumulated loot. In a storage cave others might have used for sheep fodder, a vegetable cellar, or garage for a car, Sergio had built shelves on which he placed the tomb's smaller artifacts and larger "pens" where he, his father, and a cousin or two had unloaded a few massive sarcophagi.

She loved the rows of plaster and clay figurines; loved the oddly Asian look of their exaggerated eyes, heavy with liner, and the "finger curls" painted on their snow-white shoulders. She thought the Etruscans looked fun-loving, most wearing big smiles so different from stodgy Roman grimaces she saw in Sergio's accumulation of references. And their pottery, especially the prized black and red pieces—one of which she had wrapped in her own pajamas—gave her a particular thrill, as if even touching one was an instant transport to the extinguished kingdom. On Sergio's shelves she had not seen anything like the artifact her father had given her, but she would look tonight. And look for a match for the small metal bird so prized by Sergio.

Sometimes Giuliana wondered if she should not have felt guilty. Any court would likely describe their nighttime activities and removals as rank theft. But she had come to believe that Sergio's motives were not merely rationalizations, not simply self-deceptions that left him blameless. She, like him, had come to feel their explorations were, in fact, homage to these ancients—an offering of a gift of preservation.

And tonight, indeed, Sergio believed would be extraordinary. Giuliana would be the first person to enter a space where the last living person had left nearly three thousand years before. In this unopened tomb, she would be the first to breathe the air last exhaled by royals and warriors and artists and priests. And she couldn't wait to strap on the ropes; couldn't wait to see what they had left her to view; to see if the place felt magic.

The men had finished their preparations, and now Sergio stood above her.

"You will need an extra torch tonight, a headlamp..." he whispered. "Here, let me tie it to your hat. And the string, don't forget it. The code… if you pull it tight and pluck 1-2-3 three times, I will feel it and know that we must pull you back and up. The *dromos* passageway into the tomb is narrow. I am not sure if we have dug into it or into the main room… so be careful, don't let yourself go into a place that is too tight. We will find another way. I will have the hose down there beside you. Air will always be coming down. Do not be afraid… do not panic… I am always here…."

Giuliana felt the tension through Sergio's coat, through his fingers as they skirted her face. He was frightened for her, though she wasn't sure why. This exploration was special, it was true, but she had climbed into many cold, dark places since summer began. She knew how to wrap a sculpture or a vase in one of the flour sacks she carried down and to place it in a basket that Sergio then hauled up through the opening. It was time consuming, even boring as she waited for the basket to return, but tonight would be exhilarating if Sergio and his father were right. Instead of the frequently empty tombs, "pre-robbed" by others through the centuries, possibly tonight might yield an untouched family tomb, or that of a noble who had liked gold.

"Here, put this in your pocket," whispered Sergio, pulling her near and turning his back toward his father who was preparing the pulley to drop her below. "It will protect you. And this… this in your other pocket… to remind you of me." Giuliana covered her mouth with her gloved hand, giggling into the felt. "What is it?" she whispered back.

"Here is an apotropaic," he said, putting his hand on her right side. "Just a mirror. Should there be Eyes in the tomb, pull out the little mirror and hold it up to them. Then they will not see you. It will keep you safe." Giuliana squinted at him as the forest's blue shadows played across his face. This was Rosetta's grandson, she mused to herself, still feeling unafraid. Perhaps he had learned some superstitious magic from her. "And what is in my other pocket?" she smiled, trying not to pay attention to the question now forming as to why she should need anything to keep her safe—besides, of course, the very sturdy rope.

"It is a bird. A dove. She is called Turan, the Etruscan goddess of… of the way I feel about you. Whatever is below will be made gentle if Turan is near."

"Stop this noise." Sergio's father sounded more distracted than angry. "Sergio, go over the ropes one more time. Then we must begin. And girl, let us make sure… which do you bring up first, bucchero or impasto? Black bucchero or red and black first? Thin or heavy? Would you choose a vessel covered in tin or of clay?"

Before she could answer, Sergio tugged at the ropes fastened around her shoulders and hips, and his father nodded and pushed her gently toward the tiny opening from which Sergio had removed the protective boards and dirt. And Giuliana descended into another world. Not Jewish. Not really Italian. But somehow a place where spirits resided together—without the earth blowing up.

The smell of earth, of clay, of organisms that had become their own tombs swirled humid and pungent as she was lowered feet-first down the opening. Giuliana breathed deeply as the air grew stale. Suspended here, waiting for the men to lower her, inches at a time, down the narrow hole that extended for nearly ten meters, was the first time that panic had threatened to overcome her. Sometimes this part, carefully pulling herself downward through stone, soil and roots, would last only minutes, other times, in narrow passages, much more. But what was to follow tonight Sergio had told her would, with luck, be worth the discomfort.

And in less than a half hour, now shivering with both cold and excitement as the men lowered her into the top of the fractured tomb, Giuliana's light flashed across the arc of the ceiling. She could see where Sergio's augur had broken into several places in the painted roof of the tomb, where the fragments of brilliantly frescoed birds and a smiling satyr had fallen to the tomb's floor, and where Sergio had inadvertently fractured a particularly beautiful bucchero pot next to stone shelves holding dozens of other exquisite pieces For the rest, the sweeping torch showed what appeared to be a dusty, but magnificently decorated house— a place where party-goers cavorted along the walls with chalices held high and two toga-draped invitees seemed to drunkenly wrestle each other to the ground. The tomb, its walls covered in astonishingly vibrant reds, blues, and yellows, was nothing but gaiety and abandon. And yet, as she touched her feet into the soft powder of the floor and undid the rope around her waist, Giuliana reached into her pocket to make sure the little protective mirror was still there.

***

Across the valley, a fox shifted in its nest of leaves; an anonymous star left a tiny scratch against the sky; and binoculars were set silently on a table. Only the dulled stroke of a pencil noting the time several tiny lights had flickered into dark broke the silence of the refectory. After all, details were important in tracking rodents or robbers. Patterns would give power.

And it was in the returning silence that the two men shook hands, then lifted their right arms skyward, and parting, their understanding was as clear as it was ignoble.

***

Giuliana stood for a long time without moving. She remembered the feeling. The new child entering the classroom, hearing your name from a circle of laughing friends, others realizing you were a Jew. The outsider. The one looking through the glass or from behind the curtain. She did not belong in this place, this mausoleum of frantic joy and idealized death. It wasn't fear, but that the people whose bones lie here, whose lives danced along the walls didn't need her. Wouldn't want to know her. Their lives had been completed, for better or for worse, with joy and tragedy and guile and giving, and they had come to terms with the consequences. And in one moment, Giuliana could see her own life's end, the horizon-line to a tiny sputter. The trajectory of events that raged above her head, the smallness of the war which she knew was one of many, the losing of someone you love only to have love arrive in another form, the spent blood and the weeping, and the tiny hopes that will fail, even as new ones poke their green-tipped heads from the latest misery. This would be her life. Like the people here entombed. The same. Pathetic. Perhaps, heroic. A wink in this darkness that in the end, would enclose her as well.

She stood shivering in the middle of the "foyer," sensing that from all sides, the painted figures had taken time from their revelries to examine her, to curiously guess why she had come. She didn't feel proud of why, and for several minutes she thought of strumming the tiny strings to signal Sergio to pull her out of this place.

And then she became aware of it. Low and steady. A kind of muffled tattoo. Giuliana turned the light along the base of the walls searching for an animal, and then higher, looking for a crack whose slow give would be her end. And finally, she simply laughed. "My heart!" she said out loud, her voice ricocheting back and forth and finally dwindling away before silence fell again.

Silence. How different here, she thought. It is thick, through which I can walk, but which closes behind me. My heart's beat is all I have for company. And then Giuliana laughed out loud again. She was surrounded by feasters, wrestlers, a couple in the corner who seemed to be undressing one another. "If I can hear my heart… maybe if I listen, listen in a new way… I can hear them too!" And in a way she didn't understand, she felt as if an invitation had been extended from the walls.

She pulled on the soft gloves Sergio had given her to wear when touching the items from the tombs, and laid out the burlap bags and rags. "Don't worry," she said, solemnly addressing herself to the figures around her. "We will take very good care of your beautiful things. Those who see them above will be jealous of your fine wares. You will be proud." And thus, for the next hour Giuliana wrapped bucchero vases and fat iron pots, sending them through the vertical chute to her accomplices above, not even noticing the little mirror that had slipped from her pocket into the dirt. Nor feel the painted eyes that watched from the wall.

Chapter 15

"Wait. Wait.... It is so heavy...." From the other side of the weathered oak door, barely visible behind vines and the tufa that seemed to envelope it on all sides, a scratchy voice strained as the portal inched inwards. A week after Giuliana's descent into the newly opened tomb, she and Rosetta found themselves pushing from the outside against an ancient opening in Pitigliano's wall until at last the caked dirt gave way and the ancient hinges ground the door ajar.

"Madonna! the old thing is nearly swollen shut!" whispered Rosetta, laughing as she embraced the elderly Lia, who was already shoving her shoulder against the door's close. "This tells you that the girl needs to come to the ghetto more often," cackled Lia back.

Ever since Giuliana had begun to accompany Sergio and his father, and the occasional helper on their late-night explorations, she had been occupied with the artifacts' extraction or their careful cataloging at Sergio's side on Friday Sabbaths. Yet she missed helping the women of the synagogue baking bread and matzos in the ghetto's communal oven. For almost a year, she had joined them on Friday afternoons, rolling the dough in her hands, forming the fat challah into braided balls, or the matzos into flattened circles. And once a month, while the bread baked, she would step into the cool waters of the *mikvah* next door.

Rosetta had been right, Giuliana thought, I can say the rosary and properly cross myself from left to right now, but there is something that feels like home when the old ladies with their covered heads and ready kisses welcome me into the ghetto.

But things were changing. Rosetta had told her so and she had seen it with her own eyes. It seemed she barely saw Rosetta herself these days. Where once the grandmotherly old woman had seemed content to groom goats and lambs and minister to the anxious files of people who came asking for protection from myriad curses, now she would often take her wagon early in the morning and not return until evening. Sergio would only shrug and throw an arm around Giuliana when she expressed alarm. "You do not yet know the ways of country people, little city girl. Nature needs a lot of attention." Even Sergio seemed preoccupied.

"Come now, child, welcome, welcome," Lia affectionally stroked Giuliana's cheek, then turned to lead the way up the stone steps hacked into the gut of Pitigliano's mountain. "Stay this evening, Rosetta?" she called back over her shoulder. "I would like to talk a while before the service…."

"Only if your bread is fresh and the tea is hot," Rosetta called back. "But then I must leave…. Sergio will come to get Giuliana." Ahead of her, Giuliana saw the old woman turn slightly with a glance at the impropriety.

The stairs wound upward into the earth beneath the ghetto, twisting through the stones until, as if coming up for air, they burst into the bustling security of the ghetto's hive-like complex—the school, the kitchen, the mikveh, the rooms for bottling the kosher olive oil and wine, and the beautiful cream-colored synagogue where Giuliana would ascend into the balcony to join the other women as they prayed.

"Go wash now, my child," said Lia. "The ladies are still in the kitchen. I will bring Rosetta to say goodbye before the sun is set and the Sabbath begins."

Giuliana passed the ghetto's butcher shop, where men wearing black *yarmulkes* and blood-stained aprons were chopping legs and hanging entrails, and the rabbi stood nearby with his kosher blessing for the meat. She passed the youth brigade, their hair shiny clean, the curled *payots* swinging beside their ears as they pushed a staved barrel of wine up a cobbled path. And she followed the vaguely burnt waft of matzos coming from the kitchen and the din of women's voices that made the ten women sound like fifty. Her mother would have loved this camaraderie, Giuliana thought, loved the laughter, the shoving shoulders at a shared joke, the joy of doing good works as part of serving each other. As she pushed open the kitchen door and descended its steps, she vowed to honor her mother in this most basic of godly tasks.

"Ach! There you are, *tesora.*" It was the same woman Giuliana had seen outside the ghetto's gates weeks before, covered in oil and humiliated at the hands of Pitigliano's village women. Her cheeks, now the color of two summer geraniums, were glistening with perspiration. "I am so glad to see you! Now take this cloth and wrap your hair, and you can help me at the tables with the matzos!" The kitchen was a no-nonsense production line, and whatever had taken place outside its enclave of bee-like activity would, by this woman, be thought about another day.

Giuliana pulled an apron over her head, tied its strings and covered her head with a soft white cloth. Then she washed her hands to above the elbows. Cleanliness was considered a blessing. She knew that some women were even now soaking in the pool of water of the mikveh, the spring fed bath created in a cave below the ghetto. After menses, before marriage, and after childbirth, they would immerse themselves, covering every hair with cleansing water and presenting themselves purely to their husbands. Lia had taken Giuliana several times at the end of her period, and, as with all of the rituals of her faith, she had found deep solace and a longing to no longer lie about her birth. And yet, the reasons to do so were becoming even more obvious.

"Here, here, my dear!" The woman was waving an arm toward a long table where the matzos were being rolled and pounded. "Work fast… don't stop touching it… we have only 18 minutes and it must not rise!" Each woman was rolling the dough into thin, flat, plate-sized discs and quickly draping then over the long metal rod that would be thrust into the arched oven in an adjoining room. "Ah, yes! Perfect!" she said as the crispy-edged bread was extracted from the glowing floor of the oven. "Don't slow down…. The rabbi will be here very soon."

And then Giuliana stopped. Glancing up as she wiped a droplet of sweat from her forehead, she found herself staring across the table at a face which she had last seen two years before, one which then had left her trembling in unexplained fear. It was a face that even here in surroundings so unlike any she had previously known, she would have hoped would have brought a wave of joy, of reunion, a sensation that perhaps Giuliana's skewed world had at last found a familial anchor. Instead, it produced only a kind of physical revulsion. Closing her eyes, then reopening them to assure herself of the truth, Giuliana put her flour-covered fingers to her temples and spoke out the confusion of a dozen emotions—the one word, the simple name, "Rebekah."

***

The two old ladies sat together in Lia's tiny house, built into other houses that together seemed congealed into a once-flowing pastiche of ancient stones and roofs, never certain where one began and another stopped. Only a door or a set of stairs delineated where a ghetto dweller's property line might be drawn. But Lia had been born in this house, as had her father and his father before him. Rosetta knew that it represented all of the world her friend wanted to know—except for the occasional gossip brought in by people from the outside world, the several *goyim* who shrugged at old Jew-devil tales and at the terrifying new ones afoot.

"Is it true, Rosetta, our paper has printed a rumor that Italy has invaded Egypt… and Kenya and Sudan and Somaliland? And now Greece? How is this? We won Ethiopia in 1935, though no one is sure why we needed it. And so, we go back to Africa now in 1940? And Greece? What do we have against Greece? What is it they have that we want?" The old woman pushed some agitated hairs back into their bun. "Is this to impress the madman, Hitler? To show that we are warriors? That we are not afraid to spill Italian blood in lands not our own?" Lia's hands alternated between the arms of the wooden chair and a prayer-like plea that seemed to throb through her fingers.

"Ah, Hitler! Our little paper says that he has now flattered Mussolini into believing that together our two countries can defeat France and England. Can this stupidity be true? Is Italy at war now with the two most powerful countries in Europe, England and France?"

Lia sat still for a moment, searching the face of her friend, both of them remembering the Great War of 1914, the "war to end all wars," the one that had taken their husbands, and five years later, the Fascists rise that had finally taken their hopes. "May this hatred be short-lived," said Lia at last. "May your farm be spared should fighting come here. May the Jews survive if it should… hiding in plain sight, forgotten about."

Rosetta took the hand of her friend, feeling the skin slide along its bones. All that Lia said was true. Again, men were about to die seeking glory, or power, or retribution. Perhaps simply because men, like rabid animals, must make an enemy to best. It had happened before. Yet for her, and for her friend, it was too much war for one lifetime. They had played together as children during a time when Pitigliano didn't note differences in its residents, when Rosetta knew the inside of the synagogue, just as Lia had touched the toes of a carved catholic saint. Now, like burrowing animals, they needed to crawl through a mountain to say hello or to help one another. God knows, we will need help, she thought.

"How is the girl doing?" asked Rosetta after a time. She wondered if that was the real reason Lia had wanted to speak with her. It was certainly more relevant to her friend's daily life than the carnage in Ethiopia in 1935.

"Ah, yes, the girl." Lia poured a bit of tea into each of their cups and yet she remained quiet for a time. "You had told me that she is different. And I see that she is different from the country girls near here. Different from other Jewish girls in the ghetto. Different from Giuliana." Lia sighed heavily. "She is pretty, and I am sorry for her infirmity, but she is… unusual." Lia looked at her friend from beneath still dark brows.

Rosetta pulled her rough shawl tighter as a shiver rolled along her shoulders. She already felt guilty for bringing Rebekah here to the ghetto. Perhaps, guilty too for promising more than she could accomplish. But the mother's anguish had been acute when she had come the second time with the girl, this time chauffeured by a man Rosetta had guessed was the child's father. She hadn't been sure what would become of the blonde spirit with the withered leg if left in the care of this distraught woman, a mother who, collapsed in tears, wept that she feared one of them would be harmed… by her very own hand.

"But she cannot stay here with me," Rosetta had said to Talia. "I already watch over one child. But I will take your daughter to the ghetto where she will blend in and not be seen, and I will go there to see if… if I am able to help her in the way that I do others."

And minutes later, the elegant socialite from Livorno had fled Rosetta's courtyard without a backward glance at the delicate angel who stared menacingly at the departing car.

What else could she have done, thought Rosetta. This family were Jews masquerading in a city filled with Fascists and Nazis. She would do what she could.

But even as she had asked Lia to allow the girl to stay with her, Rosetta had been aware of a power that came and went, a kind of pulse that emanated from the child, the same force that had been present when the rock-like figs had rained down on her at their first meeting. Of the potential of that power, she felt sure Rebekah was unaware. Yet, it came stronger when the girl's glance lingered, and fell as she turned away. And it frightened the old woman. A *jettatora,* she knew, could be powerful without meaning to—a lightning rod along which harm could spontaneously flow. Once those powers were harnessed and given intention, great danger would ensue.

"Yes, she a bit different," Rosetta said warily. "In what way? Has anything happened?"

"I don't know, exactly," said Lia. "I blame no one, of course. It's just that…."

"What happened, my friend?"

"My old cat, the one who slept at my feet all day," said Lia, "Rebekah asked to hold it. She seemed to like the old girl, always kneeling down to stroke it, and so I placed it in her lap. She petted it, whispering a little to it. She seemed to like that old cat, really. And then she held it up to look it directly in the face, and… and… the cat died there… there and then. It just died, without a sound. Yes, the old girl was ancient," said Lia. "But not the two strays I used to feed. The ones whose little bodies were found by my neighbor just below my window. But their heads…. Their heads were at the bottom of the great wall."

In her lap, in involuntary response, Rosetta found her middle two fingers curling inward and the outer two stretching into horns. Protection, she thought, from forces she didn't understand—from the ones with tanks in Milan and Berlin—and from those here, near those she loved. She wasn't sure the little implements behind the Virgin Mary's door would be enough.

Chapter 16

The women in the kosher kitchen had hurried to complete the baking by the time they would hear the voices of men entering the synagogue. They wanted to have already climbed the narrow stairs that took them to a screened balcony overlooking the men's pews. Though hidden from the upward gaze of men who might have been distracted from their prayers, women could look out at a round stained glass window, the raised *bema* from which the rabbi spoke, and toward the blue-draped ark behind which the Torah dwelt. While Pitigliano had always been the seat of the Dukes of the Orsini family, the home of wealthy bankers, and profitable commerce, the opulence of the synagogue's interior was also palatial. Twelve gilded twelve-armed chandeliers dropped from the ceiling. Here, polished walnut pews and dramatic checkerboard marble floors were a reminder that in this part of Italy, Jews had not always been objects of scorn.

In the communal kitchen, the cousins had found themselves separated by the sweating cooks at the matzos table as the flat discs were whisked this way and that, but Giuliana managed to steal glances at Rebekah and to sit near her during the Shabbat service. The appearance of the cousin of her childhood, the crippled girl she'd both "mothered" and mistrusted when they'd played; the child marched away with her terrified family in the middle of a murderous night; and her frightening reemergence with a transformed mother at Rosetta's door had left Giuliana's head spinning. Nothing was as it was left. Nothing was as it should be. It seemed unknowable if this was how adulthood was to be, or if this was a sign of the times in which trusting in what you saw or believed was taking a risk.

Yet, how beautiful Rebekah had become, thought Giuliana. The skinny arms had filled out and though she seemed fragile still, there was something about Rebekah's gaze that seemed knowing—as if one looked into an ancient glacier where events were trapped, where latent power lay. But there wasn't time to know more. As the Shabbat service ended, all the women moved in one large body toward the narrow exit leading down and out their own door.

Old Lia had sat beside Giuliana and kept track of the time. Now, after twists and turns in the ghetto's narrow passages, arm in arm, they hurried into the tiny *vicola* that, like a rain chute spilling out its contents to the freedom of the night, would lead first to the heavy door of the outer wall, and beyond it, Sergio's escorting hand. The sounds of Sabbath greetings had now grown dim as Lia and Giuliana wound their way toward the passage.

"May I come too?" The two spun around at the sudden sound of a voice that seemed too close. In silhouette, a halo of hair glowed champagne from the light behind Rebekah. She seemed to shimmer in the passageway. The old woman seemed stricken for a moment.

"But… but we are going nowhere. We… you should go back to the house…."

Rebekah came forward, reached around Lia, and took Giuliana's hand. "Dear Signora Lia, you do not understand. This girl… Giuliana…. We are sisters. Like sisters. We are cousins. I have missed my Giuliana so much." Rebekah put both arms around the older girl, little sobs coming from beneath her blonde hair.

Giuliana, like Lia, didn't move, a perfect ambivalence paralyzing even an embrace, the struggle of a blood fealty against the churning feel of danger.

"I am so alone, *Cugina*," murmured Rebekah near Giuliana's ear. "My mother has abandoned me. And my father as well. This place is a refuge, but I cannot stay. I cannot stay for long…."

"Child, you must go back to the house. Come, now… it is time for Giuliana to leave." Lia was pulling at Rebekah's shoulders when from down the passageway, the sound of crunching stones was heard, faint at first, then accompanied by a low curse as someone had tripped and stumbled. The women didn't move or breathe, held by the dancing light from a hand torch that traced back and forth below them, it scalloped first along an outcrop of crumbling stone, and then skittered into the earth.

"Hello?" There was a pause as the speaker evaluated the darkness for movement or sound. Then, "Giuliana?"

"Ah… it is Sergio!" Giuliana cried with relief, releasing herself from Rebekah and running as carefully as she could down the slippery passage. "I am here…."

Not sure why, she threw her arms around the black outline filling the tunnel and kissed him full on the mouth. It was a sensation she had often thought about but never allowed. Now, in this one second, this one graze of warmth, the flood of his aroma, the give of his flesh, the awareness of muscles that if needed, would protect her, Giuliana stepped away from childhood, ready to partake of a potion of which she was frightened, but wanted to drink.

"You were late," he said into her hair, his voice deeper than usual. "I was worried. The door was hard to open, but unlocked." He pulled her face next to his, "You are precious. You must be careful. We…."

"Why, cousin, you have an escort."

Rebekah's voice danced against the stone. "A strong man has come for a dangerous journey?"

Sergio swung the torch around to flood her face with light. Rebekah didn't flinch. Her eyes seemed transparent and her skin liquid in the humid air. She was a seraph. An angel. And it seemed she saw through the light and through the darkness, perhaps further, into flesh.

"I would like to know such a strong man," Rebekah said in the lilting voice of a child, but with her gaze focused on Giuliana. And again, she whispered, "I would like to know such a…"

Then suddenly from behind her, women's voices, distressed, growing louder came echoing down the stones. "Lia? Lia!" "Oh my God! Help her!" "Has she fallen?" "She is injured!" "Where is the girl!"

Hearing the voices, Rebekah limped toward Sergio—a fragile waif, needing protection—from a strong man.

Chapter 17

Simon was deciding whether it would be more appropriate for him to assume a slight stoop, a posture that would suggest humility and a willingness to comply with the wishes of an admired superior. He then tried pulling himself straighter. Or, if a taller, more assured demeanor, one that would project a certain assertiveness, the smooth calm of someone who could be relied on for covert assistance—would work better in these circumstances. For in truth, Simon had never imagined himself in such a situation.

Dressed in a monk's coarse brown cassock, he was being escorted by an officer wearing leather boots and a snug fitting military jacket across Renaissance tiles that were still glossy after four hundred years. The Orsini palace, the central jewel of Pitigliano, overlooked the entire countryside, a vista that included the massive aqueduct and a straight vantage point to Livorno, two hours away. Its fortress-like architecture, with parapets, ramparts and a half-dozen internal courtyards, had been home to the progressive Orsini family since the 1500s, a time when the economics of a vibrant Jewish merchant class made sense to the ruling family and enabled the Pitigliano ghetto to thrive. Now, the palace's ruling residents were intent on wiping out that enclave.

"Wait here," snapped the SS officer as he retreated along the Orsini's gallery. "You will be called."

Simon decided on a neutral persona for the moment, choosing a chair in the waiting vestibule that seemed nondescript, but sitting in it with an erect back and his hands confidently on its arms. The room around him, though but a prelude to the reception hall, was adorned with intricate frescos circling the top third of the room. Deep coffers crisscrossing the ceiling held glimpses of gold angels and warriors in battle with whom the Orsini, a family on par with the Medici, had identified. Even the doors through which he would pass to meet the palace commander were taller than the arches of his abbey's gothic entrance. Yes, he decided, he would stand erect. Always accommodate to your surroundings, his instinctual mantra told him. If power is admired, project it—understand the moment's coloration and assume it.

"Enter," came the command of the officer who now held the massive door ajar. And with that, Simon marched in to meet the man he hoped would become his mentor—in what métier he was yet to decide.

"Ah, welcome, young man. Come in and sit down." The Colonel remained seated, but his eyes glanced toward a nearby chair. His voice sounded almost faint in the high-ceilinged room where two ornate fireplaces and a bank of arched windows seemed to eat up his words with their magnificence.

"Sit in this chair," he said pointing not to the one before the gilded desk, the one reserved for formal visits or punishments to be received, but to another smaller one beside him.

Simon was glad he had avoided the abbey's barber this time around, the tonsurer who might have removed most of his wavy, blonde hair. When he, the Abbot and the Colonel had met briefly in the dark the second time at the abbey, Simon had worn the cassock's hood over his head. Now, he tilted his head in acquiescence toward the officer and with a compliant smile moved around to the chair, moving it ever-so-subtly, toward the other chair. A shift not unnoticed by the older man.

"Ah, it is good that we meet… in the daylight. But yet we have not formally met, have we?" The Colonel was thin, with a powerful jaw that suggested he expected getting what he wanted, though what that might be was not yet clear. His hair, like many of the Nazis seen in photos, and now on the streets, was combed closely to the razored side.

"I will begin," he smiled amicably. "My name is Colonel Dieter Hansbach. I command this region of Toscana, from here to the sea, from here to Orvieto and Grosseto. The Orsini palace seemed a good place for such a command, is it not? I assume you have not been in a palace before? It suits me more than the temporary *albergo*." He lit a cigarette, inhaled deeply looking at Simon, then still examining him, offered him a cigarette and a light from his gold lighter.

"What is your name, my boy?"

"I am called Brother Federico" said Simon, inhaling with a depth that suggested this was not his first cigarette.

"And you are adept at knowing things, are you? You see things in places that others may not? In forests? In the dark…." Hansbach's eyes were half-closed, as if he were examining a painting he wished to buy—or a bucchero pot.

"I try to know my surroundings, Sir." Simon could feel his humble smile want to curl into one of ironic superiority.

"And you do not feel… anger or distrust in sharing some of your knowledge with people like me? You would not find it easy to tell us falsehoods or half-truths if we should come to… do business together?" The Colonel's eyes were calm, his voice almost lulling.

"Of course, I would uphold any part of an arrangement that your Excellency and I should agree to. I am Italian, but I admire what Germany has brought to the world, its power, its view of history. I am but a very small monk in a small place. It would be an honor to assist you." Simon let his eyes fall, silently calculating the effect of his words. He had included the things he'd mentally practiced should this very moment arrive. Now he would let them fall through the air in the hall of power and see if his delivery had been worthy of applause.

Hansbach was quiet for a full minute, allowing Simon to realize that the Colonel too had risks to consider before he proceeded. "Then let us shake hands, Federico. I believe that together, we may find that our crossed paths will have benefit." He reached forward and took Simon's hand, allowing his fingertips to explore the contours of its palm. Simon sensed a standing ovation.

"You will go out to where the lights were hiding in the trees, where the robbers were extracting the treasures beneath the earth.

Meet with them, begin to help them if you can. Find out what lies there in that grave and in others in this region. Buy pieces like the ones whose pictures are here in this book, but only these, these will be the best. There is a market for such items in these times. There is money to be made here, and all that I need is a brave man like you to assist me… and to share in the rewards."

"I will do what is required, Your Excellency," said Simon standing as Hansbach rose.

"Come here, Federico, let us seal our understanding with an embrace. It is a custom of our country before men go out on important missions. It binds them together." Hansbach pulled Simon's hand close and down beneath his own jacket, where it remained as the fabric drew tight and hard.

And after some time, their released hands slowly rose in a salute that was filled with the requisite Fascist zeal as well as their shared collusion.

Chapter 18

Rosetta was quietly inconsolable for several weeks following the incident in the tunnel and the injury to her friend, who now lay recovering somewhere in the ghetto. Speaking little, washing the same cup and saucer again and again, ignoring the few sheep that hadn't been sold, and fingering the box from behind the Virgin Mary without lifting its lid, Rosetta seemed lost.

"I am to blame," she muttered frequently as she gazed across the fields toward the aqueduct of Pitigliano. "To blame for my friend and for having taken the girl there. Too old for war on both fronts. Too weak, too weak to help." She had turned away the visitors who traveled down the road to her little house, saying her powers were diminished, telling them to simply pray for their desires to be granted. And baffled, they turned to Giuliana, who patted the old people's hands telling them to come again in a week. That it was a temporary malaise that afflicted her grandmother. "Wait and see, she will be herself soon," all the while wondering what would become of them—of her—if not for Rosetta's clever filtering of the world.

Even as that Sabbath evening had left Rosetta filled with regret that she had not been there to somehow protect her elderly friend, it had terrified Giuliana, who, like Rosetta, examined again and again its events.

"Where is the girl?" had come the old women's voices that night. From down the passageway that served as an escape route from the ghetto, Giuliana had heard one anxious exclamation, "Lia is hurt… I saw the blonde girl near her…. What has happened?" Searching for help and for Rebekah, the neighbors came down the passageway. Yet, seeing Sergio's light, the women had gone quickly silent, even as, with backs against the wall, several had tentatively advanced toward what seemed to be shadowy intruders.

"Oh dear! Oh dear.... Auntie Lia.... Hurt?" Rebekah had cried out dramatically. Her voice seemed distressed with surprise—almost theatrical, thought Giuliana.

"What could have happened?" Rebekah turned from Giuliana and Sergio and quickly headed back up the steps toward the anxious knot, her voice dropping as she reached them. Sergio pulled Giuliana as quickly as they could maneuver over the steps and out the thick door. "I must not be seen here," he had whispered. "And I think your welcome may be at an end as well."

Later, out and huddled in a nearby barn, he bundled her jacket around her chin, and kissed her lightly. "At least the blonde girl was brave," he said. "Brave to think so quickly and stop the women. If not for her, this goy might have faced the wrath of a hundred angry Jews. People kept in pens have short tempers, you know." Then he added more seriously after a pause, "But it is the Fascists who would shoot us. Us so-called 'Aryans' who would frequent a 'vermin's lair'."

***

The winter had come early in 1942. Autumn's usual explosion of color had turned overnight to withered brown. The harvests had been meager, and worse, government officials were demanding farmers appropriate a percentage of their crops to feed the Italian troops who were currently being crushed by the Allies in the north of the country. Everyone seemed hungry, everyone on edge as German soldiers began to be seen in camouflage-painted vehicles along even rural roads.

And ever since the episode in the ghetto when the old woman, Lia, had been injured, Giuliana had herself felt ill—a constant headache and an inflamed rash that ringed her neck. Without an explanation, it made her wonder as to the safety of her nightly descents into the earth.

Still, Giuliana and Sergio, his father, and one or two revolving helpers continued to work the tomb in the forest. By day, Sergio stayed out of sight, avoiding the green-shirted Fascist patrols that were rounding up able-bodied men to fight either in North Africa or in the fields of Belgium and France. By night, the little cadre would wrap themselves in wool and labor beautiful pieces from beneath the earth, careful to rebuild the forest's floor before dawn, secreting their fragile artifacts in bushels of mushrooms or a haunch of boar as they exited near the road.

For Giuliana's part, the nighttime excursions were an escape to an exotic world whose physical dangers seemed less worrisome than those above ground. Word had drifted from the ghetto that Rebekah, "the blonde girl who had been brought to live with Lia" had, after the old woman's accident, disappeared. Some thought she had been rounded up by one of the Fascist bands; others guessed she was a spy. Giuliana only knew that the quiet cousin of her childhood had been replaced by a now beautiful young woman who frightened her. Rebekah's appearance in the tunnel and her strange approach to Sergio had made Giuliana think of the times her favorite toys had ended up in the possession of her cousin, when Rebekah's infirmity had been turned to some imperious advantage, when her cousin's charm left Giuliana feeling a grey bystander beside a luminous power. If she were honest, Giuliana knew she wished Rebekah would remain missing—safe somewhere, but far. Besides, there were other things that weighed on everyone's mind.

Though even farm life, where the ability to provide for oneself with crops and hunted game was becoming more difficult, Rosetta still insisted on taking some small rations of their flour or even eggs to the ghetto's door. The Jews inside were being systematically starved, she said, relying only on provisions its thrifty dwellers had laid up over the years. Giuliana had become expert at finding wild turnips and leeks from the forest to boil and eat, and she would sometimes trade her ability to write letters for the illiterate farmers for a chicken she would add to Rosetta's donation. Though Giuliana didn't go into the ghetto any longer, she knew that she could easily have been one of those held in what was becoming a prison. She wondered how many Jews had used the very tunnel through which she had come and gone to evaporate into the countryside, to live a kind of *sub rosa* life in an anonymous holding pattern where one huddled, waiting for the world to come to its senses.

It seemed that for her, there was really only one place that, despite its dangers, had come to feel comfortable. A refuge. A place where the future was not to be feared—for it had already played itself out. For Giuliana, being below ground was now equated with security, though in truth, each time she entered the tomb, she looked again for the small mirror that had fallen from her pocket many months before. Passing convoys of Fascist troops who hollered sexual taunts, or the German officers who with salacious smiles asked for directions along the labyrinthine rural paths, made her wonder if the little mirror's protective powers would extend above ground as well.

Sergio had remained pleased with the artifacts that they were extracting, though he told her even better ones were sure to come. There was much discussion between Sergio and his father as to expanding the vertical shaft so that others could descend and extract the pieces more quickly, but Sergio had prevailed so far, insisting that discovery was assured if a gaping hole was discovered by hunters, or an animal fell in to ruin the treasures.

And this suited Giuliana. The tomb had become her own world now, a place where in the flickering light, the painted figures seemed to welcome her arrival with smiles. She had worked her way from the *dromos* from where she had sent dozens of black and red bucchero pots toward the surface, to now, deep within a narrow passage leading to one of the two main rooms at the back of the tomb, she had begun to find new artifacts of metal and polished stone. Sergio told her that it was in the internal rooms that the personal items associated with the deceased would be found. Weeks before, in his storage space, he had shown her examples of elaborate wigs of braided human hair; fibulas, that resembled large safety pins to hold draped togas; boxes made of woven metal where jewelry was kept; and heavy earrings and bracelets that a departed noblewoman could not live without when she left her earthly home. Giuliana was reminded of the feeling she'd had when her mother had let her examine the contents of her velvet jewelry box—a scramble of pretty things she wished were hers to wear.

"I am worried," he mumbled aloud, as if his thought had inadvertently escaped its own mental cave.

In the dark, Sergio sat with both hands on the wheel of the aging Fiat that was again taking them toward the woods and their nightly work. Looking more like a tentative novice than the confident chauffeur who usually by now had pulled Giuliana next to him and managed the curving roads with one arm, he seemed preoccupied and anxious.

"What?" asked Giuliana, caught off guard. Sergio was never worried. He took action. He made her feel safe, in part because he never seemed to worry even as food became scarce and their clothes were slowly turning to patched rags.

"Things are changing too quickly," he said, responding to his own thoughts. Giuliana had been telling him about Rosetta's decision to sell their last sheep and how despite her headaches and feeling hungry much of the day with the war and the bad harvest, she didn't want the little animal to go. How thinking about the beautiful contents of the tomb made her happy enough to stave away the pangs of hunger.

"Are you talking about the war?" she asked. "Yes, I know. And there are reports that Italy is not doing well. That there is fighting all over North Africa and that Hitler has suddenly directed us to go battle in Russia. Also, other things about the… the…." Here she stopped herself, not wanting to say the word, "Jews" out loud. As if, like the name of Yahweh himself, to say the name of her own people at this time might bring down another curse on the cursed people. And yet, the thought was there. The whispered knowledge that across Europe, whole neighborhoods were being emptied. Now Giuliana looked stiffly out the window.

But Sergio's thoughts hadn't traveled with hers. "No, my dear. Not the war… exactly. But something strange. The pots…. The buccheros, the small figurines… are being removed from the storage cave. They are the best ones."

"But it is only you and me… and your father who go there, isn't it?"

Sergio didn't answer for a moment as if the disturbance in his well-executed plans had hijacked his tongue. Then, as if to himself, "Yes… but my father has found a new buyer, one with what he calls, 'museum-tastes.' And when I am not there, or when we are in the forest, the artifacts are being removed. This has not happened before. My father and I always know a buyer very well before we even show him something… even in these hard times." Sergio glanced in the darkness at Giuliana. "Besides, as you know, I do not sell the best pieces. One day, when peace returns, they will go in our museum for everyone to see."

He smiled at her. It was the first time he had included Giuliana as part of his future dream. It would be their museum, he was saying. She squeezed his hand. One tiny word to build on, she thought. To build a world on. But in this moment, Sergio's "scaffolding" for that future was somehow at risk.

"I don't understand," she said. "Your father has given no other explanation? He is selling the things you… and I… have worked so hard to extract, but did not consult you? Does he give you money for these?"

"I have refused to take the money. I don't know this buyer. There are dangerous people who traffic in artifacts, and I do not wish to have personal contact with him. But I do have a plan." He pulled the car to the side of the road, flicked off the lights and turned to face Giuliana.

"It is risky, but perhaps, perhaps it will solve this problem and another you do not know of." Sergio's voice resonated in the tiny car that without lights could have been the subterranean mausoleum itself.

"I propose to dig another shaft. When my father is not there, when he is in Sovana. I will dig a separate entrance."

"No, Sergio. Why? This is too dangerous. The earth will collapse. Alone you cannot…." Giuliana felt her head throbbing.

"Yes, yes, my dear, alone it will not be easy. I will be careful. But this will enable us… you and me… to get out what I believe to be the most beautiful, the most precious pieces in the two main rooms. They will be stored elsewhere. They will not be sold. Italy, for all its troubles now, will not lose them."

"I don't know…. This is too dangerous, you said so yourself. I could not bear if…."

"And there is something else." He put his finger gently against her lips. "We will use it to store guns."

Guns. The word didn't belong in the car. Guns, terrible, harmful, exploding with loss and loneliness, carriers of tragedies, orphans, and carnage. Guns were the means to fill tombs, not to be stored there. Guns were not to pollute the party that she attended beneath the soil each night. She wished peace for her quiet friends, not this modern plague of death shot from a metal pipe.

"What are you talking about?" she said, anger darkening her voice.

"I am a partisan, Giuliana. I am against what Hitler stands for. I am against what the tyrant Mussolini has brought down on this country ever since I was a child. There are those of us who can no longer watch men dragged from their impoverished farms to fight foreign wars or to eat the shit that Hitler tries to sell to Italy as great deeds. This country is complicit with the dictators now—a partner in the crimes that are waged against other countries who do not expose their necks. And we partisans, lovers of Italy… we will fight."

She could feel the sweat running along his neck. She could feel the passion of someone whose beliefs would direct his courage and his flesh. She didn't fully understand, but she sensed the same resolve she had seen the night her father lost his life trying to save her mother.

Sergio said nothing more. He let his words linger between them, let them settle into Giuliana's consciousness, let their fertility find root in her youth and their aspirations and the righteousness of such a cause.

Giuliana could feel another layer of the life she believed she would lead peel away. The studious Jewish girl, now the peasant girl who had come to love this quiet, pastoral life, even the mysterious underground hours—she felt them all ready to now be scoured down, to be replaced by some desperate imperative dictated by a war she didn't understand.

And yet, as she looked at Sergio and felt the surge of justice and of his brave heart, after a long pause, Giuliana whispered, "I will help you. I will do what I can."

Chapter 19

It was two weeks since Lia's fall in the narrow passageway of the ghetto. For Giuliana, Rebekah's sudden appearance inside Pitigliano's Jewish quarter had been confusing and frightening. Her cousin's approach to Sergio, irritating. Worse was Giuliana's growing sense that Rebekah had had something to do with the injury to the old woman who had cared for her. But since Rosetta's recent despondency and withdrawal into herself, there had come no word from the women within the ghetto. In fact, aside from the rumble of military vehicles, Pitigliano's commerce and trade, gossip, and rumor all seemed to have withered into silence. The only things Giuliana knew for sure were that the war raged, she felt herself falling in love with Sergio, and that her head throbbed and her throat ached ever since the night she left the ghetto after seeing Rebekah.

Now, having stabled the donkey she'd used to make the rounds of farmers with hopes to barter a little salt for a bag of flour, to Giuliana's surprise she found Rosetta out of her room and stirring the fire they'd taken to keeping low since cut wood had become so hard to find. The old woman was animated. Hair tidily combed into a tight bun, her apron in place beneath a heavy shawl, Rosetta seemed to have thrown off the blanket of guilt she'd worn since Lia's accident and appeared ready for some kind of action. Giuliana stood in the doorway trying to read what.

"Come, child. I have been waiting for you," said Rosetta, smiling as she lifted a heavy pot from the fire. "Close the door and come sit with me." Rosetta poured crockery mugs of coffee for each of them, then moved to help Giuliana take off her own winter shawl and pull on an indoor sweater. As Rosetta drew Giuliana to the table, the winter's light had all but gone, and away from the fire, the chill that seeks bone was settling into the room.

"I have been thinking of you. And of me," said Rosetta kindly. "And it is time that I come out of this sad sleep I permitted myself. To step into my grave before it is dug is not in God's plan. Perhaps, in his graciousness, he has allowed me a few more mistakes before that final time. For know this, child, even age does not, and my powers do not mean that I cannot make a mistake in judgement. Today I heard that Lia is growing strong again and holds no anger towards me. That knowledge now gives me strength. And so, let me speak to you of things I had not planned to do so soon, but which in these times may help you—things that may be the twig that causes the tree to fall to your right or to your left while you only smell the passing fragrance of its blooms."

Nearby, on one end of a low bench sat the box that had been removed from behind the Virgin's image. It was opened and the implements inside were now arranged in a circle around a bowl with water on the table. Rosetta's face was a deep sienna in the firelight, her black shawl now pulled tightly around her shoulders and her hair loosened into a white halo about her head. She seemed to be a disembodied spirit, Giuliana thought, with an intensity that had vaporized the despondent old lady she had been earlier in the day.

"How is your headache, child?" Rosetta reached out to touch the swollen ring of red that circled Giuliana's throat. "And this?"

Giuliana moved closer and put both hands to her temples, almost sensing the throb in her fingertips. The pain had been there for the last weeks. "It is the same. It never leaves," she said, untying the twist of hair at the base of her neck. "And here. Sometimes I find I cannot swallow even the water that Sergio sends down into the grave. It burns. I… I don't know what is wrong with me."

"We must be sure," said Rosetta, taking her hand. "Come and sit with me here."

Rosetta slipped a thin, woolen shawl around Giuliana's shoulders and sat facing her. Then she lifted the small bowl of water above the girl's head, saying, "In the name of the Father, the Son, and the Holy Spirit."

Giuliana looked alarmed. "What are you doing, Rosetta? I am so tired. I have a headache and a rash. It will go. I have not asked for a special favor like the people who come here…"

Rosetta lifted her hand. "I have had news. I have heard that you met the girl Rebekah in the ghetto. You had not told me. And now you have grown ill. Be still now, child, while we learn what has happened." Rosetta put her hand on Giuliana's arm, pressing it gently away. And with that, Rosetta dipped her right thumb into a small glass of olive oil, and three times shook the drops into the water.

Only their faces seemed alive in the firelight, Rosetta's head covered now by a black scarf, Giuliana's with a veil of dark hair. The oil fell into the water and immediately broke into a galaxy of tiny globules that floated across the surface.

Rosetta's head rocked back and forth, "It is as I had expected. The oil does not hold. When *il malocchio* has befallen someone, the oil is unbalanced, power has been stolen. Tell me, Giuliana, did Rebekah look directly at you?"

Giuliana's head seemed filled with a dozen nails, each a spike from which she couldn't run, and she felt her throat tighten. A wave of heat rolled across her, the same feeling from the sweltering ovens in the ghetto, across the table where she had first turned to look directly into the eyes of Rebekah. "Yes," she said simply, "Our eyes have met."

Rosetta, nodded, seeming to gain strength from the ritual she proceeded to perform. From her box she extracted a fresh herb, a fern-like sprig of evergreen rue, dipped it in a vessel of pure water and made the sign of the cross along Giuliana's head, chest and limbs. Then she pulled two sewing needles and a pair of scissors near.

Lifting them, she began to incant, *"I thread these needles through the eye,"* inserting the tip of one into the eye of the other and holding the attached needles above the bowl. *"Occhi contro occhi, perticelli negli occhi. La gelosia si spezza e gli occhi esploderanno." (jealousy cracks and eyes will burst.)*

She pricked each of the scattered oil bubbles with the tip of the "threaded" needle, then dropped the needles into the bowl. Then repeating the incantation, she held the scissors over the bowl and stabbed them into the water three times, whispering, *"I trample upon the eye as a duck tramples on the lake; I trample upon the eye as a swan tramples upon the sea; I trample upon the eye as a horse upon the plain. I have the power of the wind over it, the power of wrath over it, the power of fire and thunder and lightning and nether stars... and the power of other worlds over it...."* Rosetta was gasping as she lowered the scissors beside the bowl. Her eyes were closed tightly and her old, dry skin was covered in perspiration as she whispered, "In the name of the Father, the Son and the Holy Spirit." And between them, all of the small circles of oil had come together in one serene disk in the center of the water.

Giuliana, who too found herself bathed in sweat, touched her head and felt her throat and realized that for the first time in weeks, she wanted to dance.

It was some time before the two of them spoke, holding one another's hands and reaching into the faraway space of religion and superstition and good and evil that from time to time is visited upon humble people like themselves, marveling at how sometimes, the unknowable can be harnessed.

"And all of this I will teach you," said Rosetta, pushing herself up and with a weary smile, turning into the darkness. "… teach you to know of the evil eye's bewitchment, to protect yourself from it, and if necessary… to cast its power yourself."

Chapter 20

"Is that the last of them?" The old cleric straightened up from his final cursory feel inside the pannier. The patient donkey eyed him with a distinct look of relief and gratitude. This was, after all the second haul of the week the grizzled animal had carried for Simon and the abbot. Now the freezing stable of the abbey was beginning to fill not with animals and their fodder, but instead, with earth-covered implements three thousand years old.

"That is all for now, I think," said Simon, leading the donkey toward a trough of hay. "I understand these to be good pieces, but I have the feeling the old man is saving some back—waiting for the demand to increase." Simon made himself sound like a seasoned merchant, tossing in some professional commentary on the state of business, when in fact, he had never in his life traded anything, much less traded in stolen Etruscan artifacts.

"I think the demand is already high," said the abbot, scratching some dirt from a glazed pot. "Italians never would pay what the Germans are willing to. And there's another thing—if the fighting comes into this valley, it will be impossible to get the pieces out. Out of the earth, if they're still working a grave, and out of Italy. We need to get more items while the German is still here." He came near to Simon in the thin moonlight of the stable. "Ever thought about joining their little enterprise?" Simon almost laughed. First the commander at the palace and now the humble abbot with a mercenary streak, both wanting Simon to "go undercover."

The abbot could have been a caricature of all the benign, clueless clerics whose brains had been numbed with Bible verses and ecclesiastical wine. But the bespectacled old man was an opportunist's template. "If you help to load the pieces from wherever they are kept, you can see their "inventory." If you go with them, underground… so much the better. 'First pick,' as it were." The old man's lips pulled back along cracked, yellowed teeth, a dry laugh pointing out that he had just made a joke. "Yes, yes… you can pick them up first. See what I mean? You can pick up the prize before anyone else gets it—first pick! See what I mean?"

Simon nodded and turned away, rolling his eyes at the abbot's comedic efforts, but elated to have found himself in this curiously protected position—the middleman between a man who seemed to be the leader of a band of expert grave robbers and the trusted supplier of the artifacts to the commanding officer of the Orsini palace. Not only that, thought Simon, but as a side benefit the midnight prayer sessions wouldn't include him if he were "on assignment" in the forest—"doing the Lord's work," while only getting his hands just a little dirty.

"Oh, one other thing," called the abbot as he pulled the long woolen stole around his shoulders. "A farmer found a girl hiding in his barn. Not from around here. I don't know her story, but we need to get her to the convent. Girls without families are like acorns to squirrels these days. A soldier, or soldiers… will pick her up, hide her away, and partake at their leisure if we don't get her to the nuns. You'll take care of it won't you, Simon. She's in the gardener's shed."

And because entrepreneurs must be always ready, Simon wondered if he could take her on a side trip to visit the palace. Likely someone there would want to buy.

Chapter 21

Livorno 1943

Captain Enrico Ponti stood looking out over the harbor at Livorno. It was filled now with supply ships and boats transporting troops plucked from Italy's interior toward both the north and south of the country. With these innocent youth, the united German and Italian armies were hoping to fragment the Allies, who, despite their air power, as yet seemed uncoordinated and committed only to defensive moves.

But Enrico knew not to believe the screamed patriotic harangues of Mussolini. He could see the poorly-trained Italians as they shuffled onto the boats; he knew the poverty from which they'd come and the lack of real allegiance to an Italy that had only in their parents' lifetime been united as a country. And he could read the reports that, though heavily redacted even for military consumption, showed the Allied incursions across the Axis' heavily fortified lines. Germany had been taking nightly bombings for a year and was returning the favor with a vicious Blitz on London. Czechoslovakia, Romania, and Poland's capitals were already in ruins. Enrico doubted that Hitler's tenuous friendship with Mussolini would extend to a committed defense of Italy while the Fuehrer battled the Soviets, British, French—indeed, all of Europe and North Africa as well. Even the Italians seemed fed up with the jut-jawed strutter, and there were rumors that Mussolini's days as "Il Duce" were numbered.

Enrico looked around the spacious apartment and its relative safety and toward the room where Talia spent most of her day, sleeping or pretending to—a place he only entered when it was dark and a forced conversation could be avoided. Soon all of this would go, he thought, just as their old life, their family had become only memories.

And each day the charade they lived here seemed more fragile. He could see the groups of Jews being rounded up from the neighborhoods surrounding Livorno's magnificent synagogue, their frightened faces, and the arrogant backs of the Nazis loading them into lorries. He had witnessed a rabbi's attempt to intervene with a woman being beaten by black-shirted youth, and in front of Enrico, paying with his life. No… conversations with his own Jewish conscience and its recriminations were far harsher than Talia's depression.

Now, this telegram that had just been delivered to the apartment, the one with his reassignment, the one that would at least allow him to be behind a weapon and to replace with action the racial hatred and class snobbery in which he'd been steeping since he offered up his own soul to stay alive—now what was inside the wire might just save him.

Enrico slowly pulled up the seal. Would it be to command an Italian tank unit in France? Perhaps gun positions along the southern coast toward Sicily? He stretched out the manila paper, adapting to the oddly formed letters of the teletype machine.

"*Captain Enrico Ponti*" danced across the top of the page.

Duty Assignment:
Report December 8, 1943 to Colonel Dieter Hansbach, Commanding Officer Orsini Palace, Pitigliano, Italy
Subject:
Force intervention of Italian partisan bands.
Object:
Destroy militia groups active in mid-Toscana region. Intercept arms accumulations and storage. Destroy militia groups in area that harass and fire on Fascist and German forces."

Enrico's legs began to give and he let himself fall into a chair. Why there? Why Pitigliano and not Libya? Why not the Russian front? Pitigliano had not only failed to be the place of salvation he had sought for his and his brother's family; rather, it had been the site of their murder. The old *Pitigliana*, the woman to whom they had taken Rebekah, had ceased to communicate about a daughter who was lost in a thousand ways. And it was somewhere near Pitigliano that Simon, the son who had brought them all to this point, was in hiding.

Enrico sat for a long time in the darkening room, his hand on his pistol, cocked in his lap. The dark ghosts of lost possibilities seemed at ease here, cloying seducers, plying him with recrimination. Why not? they seemed to say. Why not now, rather than wait through a few years of horrors, followed by more to be endured. What value did he still have to any of the people he had loved, and in a way that was filled with anger and remorse, loved still? Probably none, he thought. No one cares. He sat for an hour absorbing that knowledge. The lists of people he had known, hated, cared for, fought for, and abandoned scrolled through his memory, and Enrico understood at last that none of it meant a thing. None of them felt love, even tenderness toward him. None of them would care if he lived or were extinguished. None of it mattered at all.

And with that realization, Enrico felt his head clear, as if a curved knife had reamed his skull of culpability. "I am empty," he thought. "I belong to no one."

He put his pistol away and standing, glanced at the closed bedroom door, and began to pack his bags.

Chapter 22

Giuliana sat in the near dark, no longer cold beneath the blanket, but shivering with anticipation as the thin beam of light sputtered in a circle along the ceiling. Roots could be seen intruding through the rock and the fine layer of smoothed clay the Etruscans had laid down for their canvas. The brilliant colors of frescoed coffers and faux garlands turned the tomb's roof into something resembling the bower of a spring garden, which even now on a frigid New Year's Eve seemed a promise of good things to come.

Around her was a scattering of broken vases, but in this interior room, lined with sarcophagi topped by sculpted figures reclining on their sides, each holding a goblet of wine or plate of ancient delicacies, it seemed the banquet that had begun millennia ago was still in full swing. She had not been into the tomb, nor into this, its heart, in weeks. But it seemed clear that the nearly life-sized statues of men in togas and woman in transparent drapes meant to extend their party, no matter an intruder's presence.

For the past month, Sergio had worked alone in the cold earth above this room. His father and the occasional helpers didn't extract in winter when the earth was frozen and pottery more brittle than usual. Instead, they made the rounds of purchasers in cities where in the past, the market for antiquities had been thriving. It was in the winter months that they reduced their inventory and added to their wealth; for though arduous, grave robbing was nothing if not lucrative. But wartime had changed everything. Many buyers had dried up. Food or passage on a boat out of Europe was more important than an original urn. Except for those who couldn't leave. Particularly for a well-placed German occupier whose accumulated artifacts, once nicely camouflaged, would be secreted out of Italy and find their way to a secluded basement in a Swiss chalet in the Alps.

Now, in these last weeks, sometimes in the morning, dirty and smelling of work in a way that aroused even as it confused her, Sergio would arrive at his grandmother's small house, his hands scratched and raw, his demeanor preoccupied. He sometimes brought wood for Rosetta that filled the trunk of the old Fiat he parked near the barn. Wood that the old woman insisted on moving herself while Giuliana bathed Sergio's hands or warmed his feet in a basin of water.

"I don't understand," Giuliana had said, waiting for him to add an explanation to the mysterious absences which lasted until dawn. "Are you really digging all night? How many shafts must you have tunneled? Perhaps you're taking diamonds and rubies in fat bags and leaving only pottery shards behind." But Sergio had only smiled, stretched an arm about her, stroked her hair as he might a kitten, and bending her gently against a kitchen counter, kissed her like a man whose thirst had left him parched and only Giuliana's lips could refresh.

Suddenly, inside the tomb, Giuliana found her reverie interrupted as the plaster above her head began to crack. The scrapes of Sergio's shovel or the pick he was using to fracture the tufa, the sounds that had been a kind of mesmerizing metronome to her thoughts, stopped for a moment and seconds later she heard his muffled call to "Stand away!"

Scrambling onto the narrow banquette that lined the tomb's walls, Giuliana watched as large chunks of rock, plaster and roots collapsed onto the floor of the mausoleum. Dust flooded the room along with the smell of earth and worms, of burrows' interiors, of roots' organic fingers and toes that clung to the soil and fed the foliage above. And then, Sergio's voice, a kind of whispered cough as he hung by ropes in the tunnel, "Giuliana! Giuliana! Tell me you are all right!"

In minutes he had used the come-along to lower himself onto the pile of rubble, and with his own torch, find her laughing behind one of the couched figures, herself draped in a blanket that covered her head and shoulders.

"Sergio! I didn't know you were so close! How you dug through all of it! You are a machine! I had thought you would be hours! You are a beautiful big rat in a tunnel!" she laughed. She clasped her arms around him, pulling the blanket around his shoulders, even though he was wet with sweat. And they stayed that way, inhaling the dark fragrance that drifted from the earth and along their skin, glad that the powder of this ancient soil covered them and that they tasted it even as they longed to taste each other, feeling as if its fractured mortar had bound them.

Slowly, she took his fingers, stiff from the cold, and brought them inside her jacket, then found his lips, chapped, rough, dry until she moistened them with her own. They were no longer cold in the dark, his warmth spilling out and across her opened blouse and in the semi-darkness, he found Giuliana's breasts, their hardened tips like alabaster as he kissed them, sweeping a flood of arousal across his thighs. And watched over by statues who along the walls of their tomb proclaimed the magnificence of their own carnal delight, Sergio introduced Giuliana to what these ancient witnesses had perhaps hoped to enjoy all along.

***

Across the valley, wrapped in a shawl, Simon had watched the dots of light that from the monastery's passage had become a kind of beacon—a glow that suggested that his supplier would soon have more product to sell. But not now, he reasoned. Not in winter. The older man, who with his son worked the tomb, had shut it when the weather turned cold and the earth froze. The small point of light Simon now saw between the trees signaled someone else was busy in a place they shouldn't be.

After watching the little glow move here and there for a half hour, and with curses of annoyance, a kind of proprietary imperative, and overwhelming curiosity, Simon now reluctantly dragged on his cloak and boots and set out toward the tiny speck of light across the valley. He guessed that either a thief was cheating his supplier, or that perhaps he and the Colonel were being deprived of pieces so valuable the old man and his son were extracting them for better prices elsewhere. Secure that his own humble brown cassock was a protective excuse, Simon pulled its hood low on his brow. The religious were always doing something involving self-punishment, he knew—why not an hour's trek in the freezing cold.

It had taken Simon longer than he'd expected to cross the valley and make his way into the rocky forest. Even from a distance, he had heard the sounds of scraping. Yet by the time he reached from where he guessed they'd emanated, all had grown quiet. Now he approached quietly, waiting moments between each carefully placed next step. Any sign of a hand torch illuminating the forest floor was gone, but surprised, Simon now saw that the earth itself seemed to be glowing.

From beneath the ground, a faint aura seemed to be warming the soil. Soft voices and an occasional intimate laugh were not what Simon had expected. He looked around to assure himself the robbers had not stationed sentries near, and then kneeling in the darkness, he peered into a narrow opening in the earth. Simon had presumed to find competing thieves plundering an already pilfered site. Instead, with the fresh baskets of soil and rock at the entrance hole, he found that a new tunnel had been excavated and that beneath the frigid earth—a young man's voice was responding to a woman's softly rhythmic moans with the repeated croon of one word, the name, "Giuliana."

Chapter 23

"Put them in the stable!" "No! No! Not with the horses, you idiot! Baldino! Show him where the sheep go!" The men coming down Rosetta's crumbling path led three sheep who seemed as confused as their owners.

"Armando, move the cow outside for the moment. Yes, yes, a bigger crowd of animals! Authenticity, compatriots!"

The man waving his arms like a policeman for The Ark was as weathered as the stone tiles atop the old barn. Around him in the late April afternoon sun were a dozen men, young and old, in worn caps, threadbare jackets, and shoes some had taken to packing with straw for lack of a firm leather sole. Each of them had been asked to bring whatever animal was left on their small plots of land. It seemed that an animal fair was about to break out. To a curious Nazi eye, it might have seemed in its innocence that these boney animals and their equally gaunt owners were holding a sale—a kind of "close-out" market to fill their pots for a mighty last supper before the final battles would begin. Yet privately, even the staunchest German occupier had begun to question the war's final outcome.

There had been discussion before the gathering as to whether so many animals in one place would in fact draw the gustatory envy of the Fascists and German troops who now patrolled even remote parts of impoverished Toscana on the lookout for their own food supplies. But the cows and sheep were only shills, audaciously meant to camouflage the men who accompanied them. Men, intent not so much on ultimately butchering the four-legged animals as they were on dispatching those with two legs in shiny jackboots.

As she stepped out of her house, Rosetta's hair was pulled into a tighter bun than usual. With a long shawl about her shoulders against the early spring's chill, she carried a basket of bread morsels which she tossed sporadically to the few chickens grumpily clucking at the intruders churning about their yard. Occasionally, one of the gathered men would come to her, doff his hat as he exchanged a few words, then seemingly himself pocket a piece of bread—one that later, in the dark of a tunnel or a shielded roadway, would be found to house a detonator capable of initiating the explosion of a train or truck of oblivious Germans.

Inside the barn, Sergio, his father, and ten other men gathered around *Il Buio*, the Dark One, the leader of the partisan groups that gathered tonight. Slowly, over half of the region's men had been divided into squadrons, platoons and companies that were harassing Germans at every turn. Recently, forced to transfer all supplies to trucks after the railway was blown up in Grosseto, Germans had become even more infuriated when the flattening of the ammunition depot in Siena had forced a whole battalion to withdraw simply to have enough arms to defend itself from the "brigands" in the countryside.

"A half squad, the three of you… Renato, Dino, and Sergio… will take enough rifles with you to supply the rest of the company to the south. Hide them. Where is it you keep them, Sergio… in an old cave… a tomb? We will need them in the next week. We will begin assassinations of opportunity. You can feel free to do it. Germans on motorcycles. Germans taking a piss. Wherever you will have cover and a quick strike and escape. They will become unnerved. They will hate leaving the shelter of Pitigliano's walls. Later, in a few weeks, we will begin the mining. There is but one road into the city. We will blow it to pieces and cut off their ability to reinforce themselves."

The men nodded, glancing at each other with sidelong leathery smiles. Baldino began pulling away a mound of straw covering a blanket and then the blanket under which were orange cylinders of dynamite wrapped with twine. "Now those of you with detonators, take five bundles each," said Il Buio. "Be careful to keep them dry. We will let you know when we will begin the placement." The leader was small, but authoritative as he went on to explain the movement and plans of other platoons and companies of partisans who plowed fields in daytime and became snipers after dark. He told of how Jews were being rounded up in city after city in Italy per orders of the now occupying Nazi forces and how the local partisan bands and farmers were caching those wearing yellow stars in caves and hiding them in barns. The diminutive Il Buio told the men they should all be proud of the stand they had taken. Then he looked around, shaking his head as if he had forgotten something he should have asked earlier, what with all of the other things on his mind. “Is anyone else here?” he asked. “Anyone new? If so, who stands up for him?”

There was a rustling in the dark at the back of the barn, and pulling another man forward, Sergio’s father simply said, “This is The Monk. He sometimes works with me. He wishes to join us.”

Il Buio flashed a light at Simon’s face, oddly sweaty in the evening’s chill. “A monk? A man of God wants to fight? Where do you live, monk?”

Simon lifted his head. Another lie? Oh well, why not the truth? Well, of course, not the whole truth. Besides, the abbot was already compromised, and Colonel Hansbach would likely later be pleased. No, the pseudo-truth—that he was a man of the cloth as well as an Italian patriot— would further his credibility with these Italian bumpkins.

“I live at the Abbey Sant’Angelo,” said Simon. “I can come and go at many hours without questions or query.” The men twisted toward him, looked at each other and nodded. A good catch they seemed to say.

“Very well,” said Il Buio. “Both of you are responsible for him,” he said nodding toward Sergio and his father. “He is part of your squad.”

The commander took a swig of grappa from his flask. “Now, anyone else?”

“Yes,” said Sergio, turning toward one of the internal stables where Rosetta kept the donkey. “This is my trusted friend. Brave and loyal, a good lookout, to be relied on.”

"And the name?" asked Il Buio.

"You can call her "Etrusca," said Sergio, proudly pulling the figure from behind the animal. Giuliana couldn't move as the flashlight played across her face. Nor could she think or run. It wasn't timidity, nor reluctance, nor apprehension in a room full of men. Rather, her eyes were riveted toward the back of the barn, in the shadows where she knew that Simon stood. Here was the boy-grown-to-man who, if he were the same as he had shown himself to be the night her parents died, now held all of their fates in his hands.

Chapter 24

"Child… child…." Rosetta tried knocking again and put her hand on the door's handle, withdrew it, wiped it on her apron, then knocked again. "Giuliana, we must talk together, child."

It had been three days since the meeting of partisans. The barn was now empty except for the old donkey, a half-grown lamb and the chickens. Il Buio had assigned Sergio and his father to a *squadra* that would recruit bands of partisans in the rural Apennine mountains two days away. And from the darkened and confused barnyard meeting, with only a kiss blown from the car, Sergio had been whisked on assignment with the departing *resistanzi* without learning that the Monk, who had been introduced into their midst, was as dangerous as a time bomb.

Since then, Giuliana had sequestered herself in the tiny room beside the kitchen. "You must eat now, my dear. Just a little something. If you are sick, we must find out why to make you better."

At last, Rosetta said, "Giuliana, my dear, I am opening the door."

Though outside, the weather was crisp, the darkened room felt thick, filled with a dank fog like a garden after a summer rain. Only a pale spatter of ochre light shone through a gnarl of vines covering the window. Across the room, Giuliana, a soft silhouette, sat with her back to the door, but facing the piece of furniture that dominated the tiny room, an old dressing table with a blackening mirror.

"What are you doing? Giuliana?" asked Rosetta, her eyes adjusting to the gloom. "Giuliana? Turn to me…"

And slowly the girl swung herself toward the figure in the door, stretching her arm out with something in her hand.

"What do you have, child?" Rosetta came toward Giuliana, noticing the girl's face, swollen and reflecting a line of fresh tears. She cupped Giuliana's hand in her own and saw that she held a small dark object with something illuminated on its surface in her palm. Looking more carefully, Rosetta detected it to be a delicate-appearing vase… and that it was glowing.

"What is this?" she asked, feeling suddenly cautious. "What is this thing?"

"I have had it for a long time," Giuliana said softly. "I have had it since I came to you."

Rosetta sat down beside her, turning Giuliana's hand toward her to examine what it held. The small vase was dark against the paleness of the girl's palm, but circling the bead of light that seemed to come from the pottery's interior, were the distinct outlines of blue and yellow and red that formed around the light a dramatically painted eye. The effect was of an unwavering stare with a luminous power projected from within.

With a gasp, Rosetta clasped her hand over the vase, snuffing the strange glow from the room. With her other arm, she pulled Giuliana to her and lay her cheek against the girl's hair. She didn't speak for a long time. Then, "This is from a tomb, is it not? This vase… this power… perhaps this amulet of your protection."

Giuliana pulled herself up to look directly at Rosetta. "It is something my father gave to me the night he was killed. He found it in the tomb we hid in that night… and he asked me to keep it, to always remember where it was found."

Rosetta gazed toward the girl, the darkness now obscuring her face. "So, this, this vase was found before your father died. It… was present when the murders, the duplicity of your cousin… when it all happened?"

"Yes, all of it." Giuliana gently lifted Rosetta's hand and together, they could see that the glow from the little vessel had diminished, and as they watched, it slowly faded into darkness.

After a while, Giuliana began to whisper. "Something happened in the barn the other night, Rosetta. Sergio does not know, nor his father, I think. But the one who betrayed my parents, the one whose deceit denied his own blood… my cousin, has returned. He was at this farm, pretending to be a patriotic Catholic brother, and he has joined with the men here, calling himself a partisan." Her voice rose bitterly. "But I know it is Simon… the Jew… the one who betrayed us to the Nazi youth. Simon, a Jew like me," she wept.

Rosetta rocked the girl in the darkness, stroking her hair again and again, herself feeling a shudder of fear travel along her shoulders. But Giuliana had more to say.

"I am afraid of many things, Rosetta. Of the depth of the tombs, of the possibility of death in this war, of losing you or Sergio… and of certain people." She sat up and her voice grew stronger. "When I returned here from the barn, I… I did what I sometimes do when I am sad or frightened, I held the little bundle I carried when I came here, the one with my old teddy bear and the yellow star… and my pajamas in which I keep wrapped this vase from my father. But this time…." Giuliana pressed the tiny vase to her chest.

"This time, it felt different. It felt alive, heavy. It is ridiculous, I know, that I say it. But it was warm through the cloth. Its markings were… they seemed to throb. And its eye began to glow as I thought about my fear of Simon… and of his sister Rebekah."

Here Rosetta dropped her hands, and in the dark stared toward Giuliana. "His sister? The girl you met in the ghetto kitchen is the sister of Simon who pretends at being a monk?" Rosetta hadn't been able to see the children well the night of the deaths at Pitigliano's wall. Now her head reeled as she grasped that the frightened woman who had dropped off the girl with malevolent powers at her doorstep, the child placed inside the ghetto for protection, must have also been the mother of the betrayer of his own family.

"Ah, my dear, my dear," crooned Rosetta thinking of her friend Lia who told her of the death of cats and her own unexplained fall when Rebekah had been near. "Let me look again at your tiny vase," said Rosetta.

The little black urn was cool in her hand, the outline of the eye impossible to see. "Do you remember when I told you that I would teach you to protect yourself from *il malocchio*? When your throat was painful, the rash ringing your throat?" Rosetta felt Giuliana nodding in the dark.

"This I will do. I will teach you signs to counter the eye. And I will also teach you how to throw it, if you must. You have described great evil within these two, a brother and a sister who do not bear you good will… who have no conscience that keeps them from inflicting suffering. Their powers may be from the Dark One, or from an absence of Heaven, but you must learn to protect yourself. In your grasp, my child, I think may be something more powerful than the magic I know." Rosetta opened Giuliana's fingers. "Take the vase in your hand."

Rosetta first turned Giuliana toward the blank wall and away from the mirror that still reflected slight images of their two forms. "Close your eyes and do not open them until I tell you. Now, child, I want you to picture Simon, the one who betrayed your family, and beside him, his sister, who has powers to bring chaos down on those of whom she is jealous. You must concentrate. You must picture their faces as you face the wall. Remember the harm they have done. Convey your fear and your anger to the vase in your hand and command from it protection. Ask it to protect you with its eye… to turn the evil of others back upon the sender."

Giuliana said nothing, yet with her hand on the girl's shoulder, Rosetta could feel her grow warm. Giuliana began to rock slightly, her breathing increasing to a kind of rhythmic croon, and between her fingers, Rosetta saw the trembling vase begin to glow.

***

Afterwards, the old woman carefully wrapped the little vase in the nightclothes where it had lain in a box in a drawer since Giuliana brought it to the farm. Rosetta was careful now not to disturb the girl who had finally sipped some soup and succumbed to a deep sleep. Together they had watched something powerful evoked from the small ceramic vessel that left each of them exhausted. It was only after Rosetta had pulled a blanket over Giuliana and drawn the curtains against the morning light that she noticed the marks on the plaster. She touched them gingerly, running her fingertips around the singed perimeters—two blackened circles burnt deeply into the wall. The two points where Giuliana had focused the power of the vase's eye.

Chapter 25

The backs of the two men were stiff as they lifted and hoisted their wares, wrapped them in coarse feed sacks and straw and deposited them on the waiting cart. Yet the stiffness wasn't from exertion, it was the kind that set the jaw hard and caused things that shouldn't be slammed, to instead land with thuds. Even the air about the two felt tight, strained and pocked with sidelong glances that threatened to erupt into confrontation.

Sergio and his father had only arrived back at their storage cave that morning. It had been easy to gather new volunteers for the cause. Yet, despite the presence of others, the tension between the two men had threatened to erupt more than once.

Sergio's father's cap was pulled low over his brow, his shirt wet and yellow beneath his arms. His forearms bulged with the effort of lifting things for which he ordinarily would have asked for help. Sergio himself seemed to position himself as far from the older man as possible, climbing on shelving high into the storage cavern and struggling down with each artifact instead of passing it easily to his father.

"This should not be sold," said Sergio, avoiding his father's face and placing a large, elegant urn higher on the scaffold.

"Bring it down," stated the older man roughly. "There's a buyer."

"The best ones are mine. Forget it," said Sergio, ignoring the direct order. "I'm the one fetching them. I decide."

"*Che diavolo fai!*" The hell you do! came the response followed by a large chunk of tufa that hit squarely on Sergio's back. Sergio, infuriated that his father would risk smashing any of the artifacts that surrounded them in quadruple layers, turned slowly as he clung to an outcrop high on the wall.

"*Che cazzo!* Do you think you're going to be the capo forever! Do you think I give respect to one who risks these treasures! Or to one who sells to unvetted buyers! Or to one who brings into our midst a "monk." A monk! A monk from where? A monk with an accent not from here, I tell you."

Sergio's father grabbed at his son's ankles and with a powerful jerk pulled the younger man down causing dozens of smaller pots and small funerary vessels to tumble down atop the two, fracturing as they fell against the wood and walls.

"Eh!!You don't like the Monk! Well, you had better like him, better kiss his sandals… and his ass! Where do you think we've been getting buyers all this winter? In wartime, who wants old pots and dusty bones, eh?" Sergio's father pushed his son hard against the wall. "The Monk knows people—people with money. Oh yes, Signore Sergio, you who fancy yourself the brave *partigiano* fighting for freedom against all of Hitler's troops. It is with the money from the Monk that we are buying your precious guns."

Sergio pushed his father away, turned and began to pick up shards that were scattered all over the dirt floor. His thoughts tumbled over one another. Every instinct of the poor rural farmer, the discriminated-against peddler, the clandestine grave robber had taught his people to be cautious of outsiders. But it seemed that greed had somehow trumped his father's basic instincts, the inherent rules of the subsistence life, the ones that warned against interlopers and unfamiliar faces. And now, Sergio felt trapped; guns didn't come for free.

"The Monk is going with you," said his father.

"Going where?" Sergio stopped with a handful of fragments.

"You're going to the coast to pick up one hundred rifles. I got word from Il Buio's man yesterday. Dino and I will go South with one delivery. You and the monk to the coast to pick up more."

"I'll go with Dino. You take your precious 'holy man.'" Sergio threw the shards in a basket, for the moment uncaring where they landed.

"A monk is the perfect cover. The roads are more dangerous to the west, he will be a benefit. Look, with the missions that are planned, we need more men. Not everyone will be known to us. Do your duty. Protect the Monk. Bring back the guns.... Besides, we could use another set of hands to dig your storage tomb larger." He blew his nose *ala naturale*. Then after a silence, he sniffed, *"Che diavolo...* we farmers can show a monk who's used to tiny prayer beads what it means to wear a callous!" Sergio's father smiled down at him, pulled his son up and threw his arms around the young man. Sergio slowly slipped his arms around his father's dusty back as well, each gently patting the shoulder of the other. *Famiglia,* family— always the bedrock of Italian life.

"Ah, one more thing," said his father as he headed for the door. "Take the extra bushel of artichokes and the baskets of quince we picked last week to the convent. Good for their bellies and stars in our crown." Then he added as he shoved a shred of rumpled paper to Sergio with the contact for the seaside guns, "Use the truck Il Buio has sent and pick up the monk outside the convent, he'll be waiting for you there."

Chapter 26

Early the next morning, Sergio hoisted the vegetables and a half dozen baskets of fruit into the truck Il Buio had provided and headed first for his grandmother's house. Giuliana was on his mind and he wanted to make sure he was on hers. The hungry nuns could wait.

As Sergio bounced the lorry into the barnyard, he found the chickens walking in circles in "full-cluck." They even ringed his legs as he stepped out, as if he were the grocery boy arrived to fill their empty stomachs. The donkey was braying in the annoying voice of a petulant teen. The curtains were drawn on the house, and it was clear that the hungry beasts had been ignored. Sergio, filled with alarm, ran toward the cottage and began beating on the door. An old woman and a young woman alone in these times suddenly to him seemed like dangling bait.

It was minutes with his fists against each of the windows before Sergio heard his grandmother's call to be patient, that she was coming. And with a look of early morning surprise Sergio had never seen on her face, she opened the door with a groggy smile and her usual kiss.

"I slept too long!" she exclaimed. "Nothing done. No coffee to give you. No bread even…."

"Don't worry, I'm not hungry," he said. "Why are you not awake? Where is Giuliana? The animals are going crazy out there."

Rosetta patted his shoulder, gave him a kiss on each cheek, and watched him carefully as she shuffled to the kitchen,

"Everyone is all right," she said tentatively. "We were up late." Then turning to Sergio with her hands flat on the table and her neck stretched toward him, said, "Giuliana has important things to tell you when she wakes. Things that…."

Sergio couldn't wait on proprieties. "Then let me see her now. I want to talk to her before I head to the coast." He didn't wait for Rosetta's approval, but went to the poorly hung door of the room where the girl slept and knocking lightly, pushed it open.

Giuliana lay beneath a coarse blanket on an iron bed only wide enough for her alone. Hair undone, it covered the pillow with what looked like tendrils from some underwater anemone. Sergio saw that her eyes were not yet open and that her breathing was deep and sighing. He knelt beside her bed and laid his head against her shoulder. "Are you awake?" he whispered.

The question, repeated with his lips against her forehead brought a sleepy laugh and Giuliana's little fist against jaw. "No, I am asleep and in the middle of a wonderful dream. Don't disturb me, you brute." She rolled toward him and offered her lips for a kiss. "It was about you," she laughed. And with the kiss reciprocated, she shoved herself onto one elbow and fully examined Sergio's face, struggling to bring herself from the depth of her dream.

"What *are* you doing here at this hour? What time is it?"

"It is early, but I must go to the coast to pick up… what we will need for the coming mission. But… but I had to see you before I left. I somehow thought you were not well. Was I wrong? I had sensed that something… something was wrong."

Giuliana was now fully awake. "My love, come here," she said, sitting up and pushing her hair from her face. "I must tell you something." She put her hands on Sergio's shoulders, alert now and desperately serious. "Yes, something is very, very wrong. I am frightened… and you must know this quickly… this danger from someone who had passed himself off as…."

Suddenly, from the kitchen, there was a crash of metal, the sound of the kettle tumbling to the floor. "My God!" came the panicked call from Rosetta. "There are Germans in the yard!"

From the bedroom, Sergio and Giuliana grasped each other's hands, and now heard the squeak of brakes of an over-powered vehicle and the sound of feet hitting the ground and heading for the house. Deep guttural voices were yelling orders.

Rosetta called something in the Tuscan dialect that Giuliana didn't understand, but immediately Sergio pulled her from the bed, wrapped a sheet around her and nearly dragged her to the narrow wardrobe by the window.

"You must hide," he gasped. "There is a bounty on the heads of Jews now. And you are a woman…." But instead of opening the wardrobe, Sergio, pushed it aside, and beneath it, pulled up on an iron hoop attached to a door in the floor. "Go down there, say nothing. It is cold, but safe. I played there as a child. Quickly!" Sergio fairly lifted her off her feet and dropped her onto the roughly descending steps, his hand protecting her head as he lowered the trapdoor.

Giuliana clambered down the few dirt steps into the dark, heard the door above her closed and the wardrobe shoved back into place. Immediately came the voices of the men.

"*Aufstehen! Du fauler Lummel*!" Get up, you lazy lout!" Giuliana could hear two voices whose language she didn't understand, and she guessed there were others in the house. *"Hier ist ein Jude! Ein illegaler Jude!"* She recognized the last word. The one the voices spit out with particular disdain. They were searching for an "illegal Jew."

"I am just waking up," she heard Sergio slur sleepily, as the boots entered her room. "What do you want with a Jew. We have no Jews here."

She could hear them rattling through her drawers, opening the doors of the wardrobe above her head, and the yells that came when it was obvious its contents were not those of the man in the bed. There was a crash on the floor above her, and she heard the air rush from Sergio's lungs as he hit the wooden boards. Then came Rosetta's voice, not hysterical or even anxious, but with a lilt and even a laugh.

"Madonna! What a mess you have made. Boy, stand up." she sounded like a bemused grandmother with four or five naughty children. "These are my things, of course. See, my nightie, my hat. My grandson has slept here to help me start the morning fire after a checkers game that lasted far, far too late last night."

The men probably understood little or nothing. But Rosetta's demeanor suggested nothing covert could ever have happened at her farm. Instead, Giuliana heard her saying, "No Juden here.... Instead, I can offer you some coffee to take away the chill."

Soon, apparently without drinking the proffered drink, the heavy boots were marching into the yard and the powerful engine began to turn over. Leaving without a quarry, the Germans seemed even angrier than when they'd arrived. Then one last German voice very close to the house yelled, "*Geh zuruck zu dir nach Hause, dummen jungen*!" And again, this time shrieked in Italian, "Go back to your own house, stupid boy. Next time we will find a Jew! Or maybe take you instead!"

Sergio gathered his clothes and as he pushed aside the wardrobe and opened the trapdoor, he whispered, "I love you, Giuliana. Be safe and very cautious! I will be home in a few days." Her desperate calls warning of the monk were lost in the dust as Sergio sprinted toward the truck.

***

No one was waiting outside the convent as the truck turned through the rows of vertical cypress sentinels. Perhaps, guessed Sergio, the monk had had second thoughts about joining him on the trip to the coast. A sense of relief flooded over him. For Sergio, the unknown youth whose only credentials were that he wore a cassock, inspired only distrust. And though his father found it the perfect opportunity, this stranger's ties to someone powerful enough to buy the numbers of stolen tomb treasures they were selling him, made the monk a dangerous unknown. Yes, moving 100 weapons alone was going to be exhausting and was likely to take more than one trip. But alone was better than with a pallid stranger who perhaps already knew too much.

Sergio drew up to the little convent, its ruddy sandstone blocks glowing in the morning sun. Behind the large wooden door, he could hear sheep baaing in their human voices and women's voices laughing as they engaged the animals in "conversation." He climbed out, hoisted one of the baskets of quince to his shoulder and tucked the other beneath his arm. Then he pulled the old grey rope protruding from the wall to ring the convent's bell.

As the sheep scattered about the little courtyard, an old nun gingerly opened a tiny, hinged window that was shielded by a carved iron grid. "Yes?"

"I have brought some fruit and some artichokes for the nuns," said Sergio, smiling. He knew this old sister and she welcomed the occasional gifts from Sergio and his father and the other farmers nearby.

"Come in, my son," she said. "We are grateful."

He stepped through the smaller door built into the larger wooden barricade, knowing to keep his eyes down and to turn his back to the convent building as he placed the boxes and baskets in a little group by the door.

"I will get someone to help you transfer this kind gift," said the nun, disappearing toward the structure's gallery.

Sergio had just set down the last of the containers from the truck when he heard a youthful voice behind him coming from the direction of the convent. "I know you!" said the speaker. "Ah… I didn't think I would see you again!"

Sergio spun around and for an instant was confused. There were two nuns coming toward him, and between them, someone who very clearly was not. Instead, he might have thought himself gazing at an angel, who with a slight limp, appeared a fragile seraph.

Rebekah wore a simple white shift. Her hair was free, waving in ringlets about her head in the sun; her cheeks seemed burnished from the inside, and as she approached, he thought he had never seen eyes so pale or so luminous. There was a sense of recognition, but he was too stunned at being addressed by this radiant creature flanked by two black-clad nuns, to be able to think.

"We have met," she said. "Do you remember? In Pitigliano?"

Sergio felt tongue-tied, turning his head from side to side, embarrassed and smiling sheepishly. "I only go there sometimes," he said.

"This was not in the city," she said taking a step toward him. "We met in the tunnel of the ghetto," she said. "By the gate... at night."

The nuns had transferred most of the artichokes and quince into their own baskets, ignoring or paying no attention to the interaction between the two—until Rebekah's last words—"at night." Then they glanced at each other and headed back toward the convent, hurrying with their baskets of fruit.

Rebekah turned to see them go, then stepped even closer to Sergio. "I must leave here," she said. "I know you to be a good person. I can feel it. I am here against my will. I was brought here against my will. I ask you, Sergio.... That is your name, isn't it? Sergio, come back for me. Help me to leave this place. Perhaps you will even take me to my cousin... to Giuliana."

Rebekah's hand was cool against his arm. He felt its lavender shadow mount his shoulder and his desire to move dissolve. But mostly, it was her face, the translucent eyes with the centers of jet black that held him, fixing his gaze to hers. Now he remembered the night in Pitigliano's passage, how the girl had come close to him in the darkness of the tunnel, how her presence had unnerved him and, he had to admit, thrilled him at the same time.

"Are you in danger here?" he asked glancing toward the building where he saw four nuns advancing toward the gate.

"I may be..." whispered Rebekah, never shifting her eyes from his. "Come for me, Sergio... in eight days from today as the sun sets. I will wait at the bottom of the hill."

The four sisters positioned themselves beside Rebekah and solemn-faced, shooed Sergio from the convent compound toward the gate. Once he was on its other side, the oldest nun underlined the rasp of the huge key's turn with a shove to the barricade to demonstrate its invulnerability.

Sergio wasn't sure what had happened inside the convent walls in the last minutes, nor, as he readjusted his shirt and vest, what was happening to him. All he knew for sure was that he needed to cover a surprising arousal as he walked stiffly back to the truck.

"In eight days' time," she had said. "As the sun sets." It was as if a dainty princess from a lost kingdom had begged for his help—and it was only he who could save her.

Chapter 27

Sergio had no more than pulled away from the convent when he saw Simon trudging up the road. His hopes that the monk had changed his mind or had been detained at the abbey for some holy task were immediately dashed. Simon even wore the round-topped, broad-brimmed hat that friars around the world seemed to fancy. On the youthful monk, it looked an ill-chosen masquerade.

Simon smiled brightly at Sergio as he climbed in and the truck accelerated. Perhaps observing Sergio's glance at the long voluminous robes, the monk cocked his head and chirped, "I could have changed into regular clothes, but I think clerical clothes are best at this time, don't you? But you mustn't worry, these vestments won't stop me from doing heavy lifting or loading." Simon was amicable as he fidgeted with his cassock and settled in the car. To Sergio, it seemed his companion was regarding the next days as little more than an extended holiday picnic—with guns.

Sergio had made up his mind to have as little to do with the monk as he could during their drive to pick up the small arms needed for the partisan's attack. Sergio felt as if his thoughts had become tiny people running from one side of the swirling silo in his head to the other. The unwillingness to share any of those thoughts with someone he didn't trust was best handled by silence. Those darting thoughts—the orders from Il Buio giving him new responsibilities to prepare for the coming fight, the arrival of Germans at Rosetta's farm only hours before and the danger to Giuliana should they return, and now the strange intrusion into his mind of a shimmering apparition who would, she said, be waiting for him at the convent when he returned—put Sergio in no mood to make small talk with someone he wished to know as little as possible.

"The brothers think that I am traveling to bring food to a farmer and his family," said Simon to no one in particular. "The man is dying, and very likely one child who has caught his same lung disease will die too." He began to rifle through a basket on his lap as his stream of consciousness ramble continued. "It is too bad that such things happen in wartime. Diseases, though can occur even without fighting." He pulled out a small round of cheese and a tube of salami, slicing several pieces in his hand. "Famine they say will come by spring. No one left to tend the farms. Animals gone…." Simon took two of the pieces of cheese and crammed them in his mouth. "… fallow fields with nothing planted to grow. Young men like you off at war…." He bit into a round of salami, then handed a little cheese and meat "sandwich" to Sergio.

Sergio had eaten nothing since midday the day before and though it felt like capitulation to Simon's mindless patter, he took the food and quickly downed it, following it with swig from an old bottle of wine in its woven carrier. Silent and hoping Simon would remain so, Sergio gestured to Simon that he could drink too if he liked, and in turn, accepted more salami, cheese, and dried figs from the "monk," all the while hoping to God that this wasn't the food intended for the family of a dying man.

The rolling hills in the province of Pitigliano were beginning to only slightly flatten as the little lorry wound its way west on the road toward Livorno. Sergio was worried they would encounter more Germans and more checkpoints as they came closer to the entry point of supplies whose harbor was beginning to take daily Allied bombings. Livorno's town was a new favorite target for strafing fighters, and Sergio briefly wondered what it was like to try to live in a place used for target practice by winged devils that materialized from the sky.

Luckily, the arms they would transport back had been smuggled out of Livorno and now were in the basement of a bicycle shop in tiny Sassetta, about 50 kilometers southeast of the harbor. Il Buio had even had the name of a nonexistent bicycle company painted on the side of the truck. The words, "*Ruote Volanti,*"

"Flying Wheels," in red letters a foot high, paired with a blonde monk in a round hat, made Sergio shake his head doubting that the German or Fascist soldiers would find the pair "invisible." Instead, they might be fascinating.

Sergio took another long drink from the jug of wine. It tasted much better than it had when it was new. The cheese was salty and good, and the chestnut-lined road was straight. He found himself studying the monk who was now concentrating on finishing off the figs and the last of the bread.

"So, where do you come from? Your accent says not here," said Sergio casually.

Simon didn't look up. "No, you are right. My accent is different, is it not. Sometimes I cannot understand you rural Tuscans at all." He glanced at Sergio. "I am from everywhere it seems. My parents were traveling merchants and we moved about in a lorry much like this one… all over Italy and to other parts of Europe too."

Sergio said, "Really? I would have guessed closer to home. And so, did they "give" you to the church to become a monk? Get some indulgences for you to keep them out of prison on this side of heaven?" Sergio wasn't usually sarcastic, especially not to those of the church, but with this suspicious monk, he didn't feel the need for respect. Besides, the wine seemed to have dissolved a layer of polite caution.

Simon looked at Sergio quietly. "No, they were burnt alive trying to save a group of little schoolboys when the gas they'd poured on a campfire exploded. I was sent to the abbey as an orphan." His voice broke as he whispered the last word.

"I am sorry, Monk," said Sergio. "I am sorry. I should not have said that." Sergio took another draught from the bottle and passed it to Simon, who declined, wiping at his face.

They drove in silence for a long time, and then with the need to make amends for his remark and also because it was central to the reason he did not trust Simon, Sergio asked a question that implied facts he at this moment only suspected.

“So, do you have an interest in the pieces that you buy, or is it only for a patron that the Etruschi potteries have appeal?” Sergio and his father had not found anyone nearby with the very, very good taste of the secret purchaser, but Sergio knew from his father that Simon was somehow involved—and that alone was worrisome. Sergio guessed the church was hoarding antiquities to sell at a later date.

However, Simon seemed to perk up at being invited to speak about the riches of the tombs. “Ever since I was a child, I have loved the work of these ancient peoples,” he said. “I have only been able to look at the artifacts in books until now. My dream is to one day descend into an Etruscan tomb… as you do and your father. In some way, you are heroes. You are revealing these beautiful things to a world in which they will at last be revered and protected.”

Sergio’s head was spinning with both a mix of the wine and what Simon had just said. The words from Simon’s mouth were ones he might have spoken. Could it be that he had misjudged a lonely, orphaned man who had discovered a shaft of light from the underworld shining into the paucity of his religious life?

He looked at Simon, still distrustful. “But perhaps you have come to know others who appreciate these items as much as you do… others who are not circumscribed by the poverty of a monastery?”

“Yes, yes, it is true. But the person’s name cannot be told,” said Simon, smiling as if he were sharing a secret with a dear friend. “The buyer is also a monk who, unlike most of us, has great family wealth. He is well schooled in the pieces that he wishes to obtain, and one day, when the war is finished, he will display them for all to share—for Italy to see.”

Sergio felt himself sighing a great breath of relief. If this were true, the pieces his father was selling to the monk were to be saved; were being collected all together—they were being cherished in the same reverential way he did.

“I am happy to hear that,” Sergio said simply and smiled at Simon who was now digging in a cloth satchel between his knees.

"In this book are examples of unusual pieces which this cleric wishes to obtain if possible," said Simon. "He has circled several of them as being of the kind that are most beautiful. Look at this one… it is so big! Here is another of a color he says he admires." Simon flipped through pages of the book. "There is one here… where is that one… one that he likes most especially. Says it is not pretty, but unique in some way I do not know… magical, he says. Supposed to glow," he giggled.

Sergio glanced at the glossy pictures in the book, yellowed, stained, and captioned in German. He mentally shrugged that most good scientific books were published in Germany and momentarily wished he had paid more attention to the German teacher who had spent a summer working on their Italian farm.

"Here it is!" said Simon, pointing to a nondescript little bucchero with odd markings. "Supposedly, one other was found near Pitigliano many years ago. It was destroyed during the First War. Superstitious people said it had powers…." Simon laughed out loud. "Pottery power!" He grew serious. "But if you ever see one like it, please do make it available. There is somebody desirous of owning it. Someone very, very rich who would cherish it." Simon was still staring intently at the little photograph when Sergio abruptly put on the brakes and zigzagged to the side of the road.

"Che cazzo!" Sergio yelled out the window at a knot of thin women who were standing in the middle of the lonely *strada.* They only waited a moment before coming toward the lorry on both sides. They were dirty, dresses and blouses in near rags. Several of them smiled, others simply looked vacantly through the windows at Sergio and the monk. The one closest to Sergio put one foot on the running board and with her two hands, suddenly pulled open her blouse. She then reached down, tossed her skirt high and showed him a cavernous pelvis above a mound of straggly hair. "Twenty lira…" she said. "Right now."

Sergio began to roll up the window. Simon was looking at the hood of the truck where another woman was sitting on the bumper, her dress open while she squeezed and pulled her breasts from side to side as he stared. The woman at his side was trying to reach through the window to touch him, saying, "We are hungry. Give us food and we will give you a suck. Give us money and we will fuck you good."

Sergio had stalled the engine, but now it was started again and he backed up quickly, knocking the starving woman on the hood to the ground and scattering the rest. "*Stronzo!! Testa di merda! Vaffanculo*!" they screamed as the rocks flew after the truck. Huddling in the road, the strays, abandoned and turned feral, would bite.

Sergio and Simon were quiet for miles after encountering the women who were willing to sell themselves for something to eat. The war—the war had changed humanity into something neither of them had ever seen.

"Do you have a woman?" asked Simon, knowing the answer, but finding that to his surprise, he would be able to ask about Giuliana in a natural way.

"Ah, I don't even like to think of her with the vision of those poor souls in my mind," said Sergio. "But yes, I think I do." He smiled at Simon.

"And does she like your work below the ground… does she find it is too dangerous?"

"As a matter of fact, she goes there herself," said Sergio proudly. "She even knows something about the pieces now. She is a quick learner. She has a little Etruscan vase of her own."

Simon looked out the window. And then, after many minutes, Sergio said, "Let me have another look at that picture in your book… the one you said was special…."

They had stayed silent for the last hour, each man's thoughts filled alternately with pottery, war, and women's bodies. Then the lorry turned toward little Sassetta, oddly hilly even though closer to Livorno's plains than Pitigliano. Along the way, they had seen groups of German vehicles, positioned like guard dogs at the entrance to tiny hamlets. And as if they were stencils atop the rolling ridges, numerous medieval forts and castles seemed to serve as lookouts to herald the approach of an ancient neighbor's mounted army.

But at the peak of the crag in front of them was something mesmerizing. Silhouetted black against the afternoon sun, the 13th century castle at the mountain's apex resembled nothing so much as a giant sky-pointing nipple. Alert and filled with promise, Sassetta's mammarian grandeur forced both men to laugh out loud. After a final swig of wine, Sergio handed the last of the bottle to Simon, both of them wiping their mouths on their arms in sputtering guffaws.

"Have you ever had a woman?" asked Sergio, relaxing as the end of the journey was almost here. "I mean before you joined the monastery… or after. I mean, after probably happens too." He stole a glance at Simon who was only smiling a smile that told him nothing.

"No. No, I have not." There was silence. "But I have thought of it. I have thought about what it would be like."

"Hmm," said Sergio with a philosophical nod. "It is something beautiful. Something…. I don't know how to say it to someone who has never done this thing…. It is a step into another world. For one excruciating moment… the world in a glorious flood of… of…"

"Do you do this with your woman?" asked Simon almost shyly.

"I do sometimes," answered Sergio, amazed that he was having this conversation with someone he had feared and distrusted only hours before.

There was silence for a long time. And then Simon said, "Do you know where I could find such a woman? I would need to… to be taught…."

Sergio had never heard such a question. This kind of thing happened naturally where he lived. Living with animals, living in tiny houses. It was not something for which one needed schooling. And yet, this man, like him, but so different, had asked a question that softened Sergio's resolve to keep him at arm's length.

"There is a woman… who would inspire you. But I think if you came to know her and if you came together… you would be the one to teach her. I do not know this woman well, this girl really, but I am sure she is innocent…" said Sergio almost reluctantly. "She is beautiful, like an angel of light. She is fragile. She is alone and… and she is very, very desirable. Any man would find her…" his voice trailed off.

Because it was his business to notice each nuance within his environment, Simon saw the slight adjustment of cloth of Sergio's trousers and how his fingers turned pale against the steering wheel, and he read Sergio's thoughts. And in the animal kingdom where he lived, Simon intended to have her first. And if the timing were right, Giuliana too.

Chapter 28

Though Sassetta was tiny, it had become a quiet locus of resistance activity. As a market town, wagons that came and went were not unusual; slaughtered animals, some of whose entrails covered caches of explosives, slipped by unsuspecting Germans who always regarded the locals as unschooled illiterates and barely human anyway. They were right on only one count.

At their arrival, Sergio and Simon had been pressed into service almost immediately by the *resistanzi*, directed into a kind of quarry from which mining tunnels fanned beneath the mountains.

They had first been taught by a pair of Italian Army deserters how to properly take apart and clean the stolen rifles lining the subterranean caverns beneath the "nipple" castle overhead. The arms would be doled out as the men from surrounding towns mysteriously appeared, then disappeared along with their caches.

Then, Sergio and Simon, along with a dozen other partisans, spent several days dividing ammunition into small circles of cartridges, tightly wound and ready to be secreted inside a loaf of bread or around a swaddled baby's waist. The various combinations of subterfuge and innovation bound the men and gave them confidence. Laughing and sweating in the underground caves, they never noticed the careful counts one of them was making of how many rifles were heading to fighters in the north, or how many pounds of explosives were heading south.

Yet while the ordinary volunteers perspired in unison and lifted flasks of grappa when needed, the capos were more secretive. In private huddles the wary commandos, who would somehow materialize in one town, only to be gone the following day, maintained an overview of where the Germans were and which squad or platoon of partisans should be called upon to ruin the Nazi and Italian Fascist operations. From them, Sergio learned that 1944 had seen the tide of the war turn. The Nazi Axis no longer seemed destined to rule Italy or Europe, nor for that matter, with the Americans' entry into the fight, the German homeland. But, said one sinewy capo, "A dog who is maimed will bite all the harder." It was happening now with the Nazi occupiers, he'd said and recited atrocities that neither Sergio nor Simon could comprehend.

"There are massacres on the streets in Palermo; Jews are gunned down or beaten in the bright of day. Twenty thousand were lined up along the river in front of the Parliament building in Budapest. They were shot, one by one, and their bodies rolled into the water—babies and toddlers among them. Italians who resist are treated the same. Priests, nuns, the old, the young who cannot work, those who are mentally or physically disabled, of course the Jews… all taken away or shot because it is easier."

Sergio pictured Giuliana as the capo detailed the horrors—and his grandmother who seemed afraid of nothing. They would both be easy targets, and he was eager to return to Pitigliano.

Sergio and Simon stayed three days in Sassetta. Much of it, Sergio had spent at the feet of the wary capos learning techniques for surprise and ways to wire explosives. Now, nearing home again, the lorry filled with bicycles—and guns—he would send Simon back to the abbey until he would be called to take his place inside the walls of the town. The attack would begin sometime after dawn in a few days. Il Buio would tell him the hour. For now, it was Sergio's responsibility to distribute the rifles and powder to the local resisters and assign them their fighting posts. And then he would find Giuliana.

Chapter 29

Giuliana heard the squeals of the last adolescent sheep. Even from her hiding place beneath the armoire in Rosetta's house, the animal's shrieks were as if it already knew what the soldier had in mind. Now would follow the roar of the German's truck, the shouting that always accompanied their departure, and at last, the grunts of an old woman as Rosetta struggled to shove aside the cabinet and allow Giuliana's subterranean escape.

Giuliana had spent most of the last three days in the dank shaft of the basement, where now a small pile of rugs made a nest on the steps to keep her warm. After the German's first eruption into the courtyard only to have discovered Sergio, the Nazis had returned every day, once or twice, at different hours, each time more angry than before. Each time they took something belonging to Rosetta, queried her about Jews, shoved aside tidy shelves to pocket preserves of fruit and last year's legumes. They obsessed about the young man they'd discovered in her bed, and seemed annoyed they had let him go. Today one had yanked down Rosetta's grey knot of hair accusing her of trying to hide golden coins. And each time Rosetta countered with an actress's performance.

But with the Nazi confiscation of the last of their farm animals, it seemed to the old woman that the only quarry left might be Rosetta herself, and in only a matter of time, something below the armoire would be discovered—something that the lonely German men would prize much more than a lamb.

"We must leave." Rosetta said it to herself, as if it were the repetition of an internal litany and had only now found voice. "We must leave, my child." Rosetta lowered herself down onto the first step of Giuliana's underground repository. "They will be back. If not all of them at once, then one or two will come in the night to steal the last of our cheese. The last crumbs of bread. Us. We are not safe from the Huns nor from the others roaming the countryside—the Fascists, the Communists. The world is upside down…."

Rosetta sat staring in the dark into the deeper darkness below. "We must take what we can carry." She said it absently, stroking Giuliana's hair. "And we must go in opposite directions."

"But what will happen when Sergio returns?" whispered Giuliana. "And I pray that he returns…. He is with Simon now. He doesn't know the danger, not to himself nor to the *partisani* and the plans. Somehow he must be told before Simon…."

"Sergio is not here." Rosetta's voice had a hard edge now. "It is up to us to protect ourselves at this moment, child." She sounded suddenly strong with exasperation at their plight. She shoved her hands on her knees and pulled herself from the passageway. "Gather only clothes for warmth. If you have written something… anything that speaks of your past life, or of this one, quickly burn it." Rosetta was becoming unrecognizable with resolve as she moved around the tiny kitchen, her back straighter, her step powerful.

"The only things that we will carry with us are my box from behind the Virgin and your father's tiny vase. It must never leave your hands, you understand. Never. It must be protected."

For the next hour, the two women went through their clothes and Rosetta's belongings, examining them with the eyes of enemies looking for traces of prey. When they had burnt the scraps of a diary Giuliana had begun and buried two photos Rosetta had kept of her long-dead husband and parents, they sat together on the stable's stoop.

"Eat this before we depart, my child." Rosetta knocked a glass crock Giuliana had never seen against the stile. It was a kind of thick country pâté, made from boiled lamb and meant for perhaps a Christmas feast.

"I will go to the storage shed in the communal garden near Sovana, the one which is kept by my son, the place holding so many of the treasures of the tombs. I can stay there safely for a time."

Rosetta dug into the little crock with her bare hands and passed it to Giuliana.

"You know about this place?" asked Giuliana. "… where the shelves are full… where…."

"Of course, my dear. This… work… is not new to us. In a poor land, one must learn to live from the land. Most do not treasure it as does Sergio, of course." And then Rosetta said, "But you will not go there. You must climb to the new tomb. It is where Sergio will likely go when he returns. It is safer in the woods, more hidden—perhaps a place where you will be protected."

She glanced at Giuliana. "Protected not only by the spirits that reside beneath the soil, but it is where the guns are." She looked carefully at Giuliana's wide eyes in the fading light. "Yes, I too am a partisan, child. An old woman with panniers of rifles beneath fagots of wood is not as conspicuous as someone who would seem to be more foolhardy."

"And one more thing, beautiful Giuliana. Before we go, come here." And with that, Rosetta pulled a pair of long scissors from her pack, grasped the dark flow of hair that lay along Giuliana's shoulders, and cut into it. Shearing away the waves and the little ringlets that circled the girl's face, the old woman removed the thick corona that had made Giuliana a kind of exotic shepherdess who would let her white-coated charges nuzzle her own mane of hair. And in minutes it was gone.

"Put these clothes on. They are Sergio's. You will know from their scent. Do not be angry," she said, her arm around Giuliana's shoulders that shivered with grief. "It is better to have no sex. It is better to leave your beauty for a time and hide in the skin of another. And yet your beauty grows, child. In another way."

Chapter 30

"And did you find him, my son?" asked the old abbot. "The sick die quickly during times of war. Did he at least have that last meal? Even a little cheese and salami can be of comfort." The monastery was chilly at this hour, the thick morning fog rising from below its precipice causing a cloud to circle its base. The abbey seemed to be floating.

"No, I did not find him… alive," sighed Simon, lifting a wooden bowl of porridge to his lips, as much to drink as to hide the exasperation he always felt around the naïve cleric. "But though the old man was gone, I am humbly grateful for your allowing me to try to seek him. I said a prayer with his wife for his soul." Simon shook his head disconsolately, then looked up. "Yet I did accomplish one thing in Livorno. At my worship at the Cathedral, I received a small note from the Monsignor there. It is for the priest here at the Cathedral in Pitigliano. I would ask permission to go there to present it to him, if I may."

The abbot had Simon repeat his request since half of every conversation was lost to what sounded like nervous insects in his head. But of course, the young monk, whose abilities assisting with the underground artifacts that were so helpful to the abbey's finances, would go in to Pitigliano. He really hadn't needed to ask.

Using the monastery's wagon, Simon wound his way toward the massive pile of Pitigliano's buttressed walls, the cathedral's towers seeming to push out the top like sprouts in a summer garden. He wouldn't go to the church, of course. His destination was much more grand—the Orsini Palace. And he knew his welcome would be much more profitable to all concerned.

Yet as the old horse advanced in its cadenced plod, Simon couldn't help but notice that these were the same forests and rolling hills his and his uncle's family had struggled across that night so long ago—the night he had been reinvented—the night when, it seemed, he had united with his true self. Then he had known nothing about the Catholic church, about Nazis really, nothing about the value of artifacts that lay beneath the ground. And now he had become adept at manipulating all of them. It was near here that his Uncle Nathan had found the little vase, the one he had only glimpsed in the darkness, but which had seemed to carry its own light. Simon wondered if he could find that cave again, wondered if there were other treasures sitting right before his eyes. It was a secret desire he wouldn't share.

Four uniformed German soldiers stood at either end of the bridge as Simon crossed it. Six patrolled the roadway leading in double and triple curves toward the city's *barbacane,* the massive gate that within it held an iron portcullis for barring medieval enemies. Reaching the city itself, a second arched opening punched into walls 15 feet thick and was fronted by a new German guard house surrounded by stony-faced blondes who alternately looked angry or bored. Simon was tempted to try his charm on one, but decided to save such spontaneity for someone of greater value, and only steps away. In fact, the Colonel should be waiting for him now.

Simon was no longer impressed with elaborate military rituals inside the palazzo—the frantic heel clicking and parade-ground turns. He now entered Hansbach's suites as he would the abbot's office, fully in control, knowing the script, sometimes, he thought, even writing it. But today the entire palace felt on edge.

Ordinarily, Simon's official audiences with Dieter Hansbach were punctuated with their mutual flattery and the double *entendres* that they fancied were private communiques. But today Hansbach didn't get up from his desk. Smiling distractedly at Simon, the Colonel simply held the monk's hand for a second too long, then asked for the "information." "Show me what the resistance have up their sleeves," he said. "And I'll know how to crush them...."

Without being invited, Simon came around the desk, laying the sketches in tiny lines and the carefully written lists in front of Hansbach. Drawn on coarse, caramel-colored paper used to line the monastery's cupboards, Simon had translated everything he had learned in the caves at Livorno. Helping to hold down the rolled papers, Simon allowed his other arm to graze the Colonel's shoulder, knowing that hard news can be made so much better with a tactile nuance.

Dieter muttered below his breath as he read every word and examined every drawing.

"My God, boy, these are excellent! Names. Numbers of guns we should expect. The plan of their attack! You are like a *Geist,* a spirit who has taken over their bodies and minds! This is excellent work."

With a sigh, moving from the desk, Hansbach motioned Simon to join him on a quilted sofa whose silk had begun to fray where the Colonel now daily threw himself in frustration. Once he would never have let himself be seen without his tight-fitting jacket and golden epaulettes. Now it constrained him, as for hours he peered at charts and maps, each showing another attack, a mined convoy, a gun-strafed outpost, a lost skirmish in these cave-filled Tuscan hills that continually surprised his dispirited Nazi conscripts.

"I have been sent a Captain," said Hansbach inviting Simon to join him. "What's his name... Italian... Yes, Ponti. An Italian sent from Livorno to dispatch these thugs, these farmers and pathetic merchant resisters who seem to believe they can win against the whole German army. This Captain is a joke. And here, a gentle monk, a beautiful youth who joins our cause has done so much! I know you ask nothing, Federico, but I want to do something for you. Come here, sit closer beside me again... the way we did the night at the abbey. Oh, and close the shutters, won't you, the sunlight is so bright. Everything good happens in shadows, does it not?" he smiled. "And take off your cloak, my boy, we want to be comfortable. Give me some peace now before I must plan how we will destroy these rebels."

Later that afternoon, the old horse gratefully marched into its own stall within the abbey compound. And like the horse, that folded its legs and stretched onto the hay, Simon found in his cell the little haven he needed—the bed, the rough blanket, the moveable brick beneath his pallet where he hid the growing bundle of lira still warm from the Colonel's trousers, and where he could collect his thoughts for what to do about the German-allied Captain from Livorno, the Fascist called Ponti—once a Jew—whose pathetic indecision in a cave had given Simon the chance to demonstrate how one turns events to his own cause.

Simon knew that in the next hours, Colonel Dieter Hansbach would reveal the partisans' arms cache locations and plan for attack to this newly arrived, so-called patriot whose job was to destroy Pitigliano's resistance. Certainly, should Enrico Ponti be successful at crushing the partisan attack before it began, his value would rise in the eyes of Hansbach. For now, it was only Simon who occupied that elite position. Yes, he sighed to himself, his was a position that was more than procurer of information, more than procurer of ancient treasures for the German commander. Hansbach had spoken of a time beyond the war for the two of them, the kind of climb Simon knew he could make if he weren't interrupted by a past that could betray him—in the form of a Captain from Livorno—of Jewish descent.

Ah, and one more thing, he thought before he drifted off. There was something else he wanted to decide. A little issue more personal than a rifle or an Etruscan pot. When would he collect what he'd only toyed with until now, "the blonde angel," the "very desirable" girl Sergio had so obviously wanted himself? Simon guessed it was only a matter of time until Sergio gave in to his desire for Rebekah. And by God, he laughed to himself, the peasant would find that someone had been there first.

Chapter 31

Sergio had abandoned plans to drive the arms-filled truck to farms and forest "depots." He would instead direct the *resistanzi* to come in themselves to collect the pilfered rifles and mines. For now, the squadrons and larger platoons didn't know the details Sergio carried, but he must wait first for the higher partisan commanders to specify times and exact locales.

But things were changing rapidly. Since his departure for Livorno, Sergio had warily noted that the roads had become dotted with German vehicles. Even approaching Pitigliano, trucks carrying what looked like troops could be seen rumbling along rutted, narrow roads toward the citadel. The build-up of Nazis had begun in the spring, but there was a marked escalation in the days he had been gone.

Sergio turned the truck onto a small lane several miles from the roadblock he could see in the valley below. Better to head for the abandoned sheep shelter on the edge of a woods high over the valley—a good place to sequester the lorry. Then perhaps a cumbersome bicycle from inside would come in handy after all.

It was dark by the time Sergio rolled the thick-tired bike into the perimeter of his destination, Saralo, barely more than a cluster of houses clumped around a marble memorial to the dead of another war. He hid his bicycle, and in the shadows, walked to the door of a platoon leader in whose window he could see a candle flickering. At the sound of his tapped code, the door carefully opened, then closed quickly as Sergio dissolved inside.

Immediately, Aldo, the local capo, laid out some changes to their plans made in the last few hours. "What is happening all over Italy is now here. I don't know how many Jews are left in the ghetto in the city. I hear that they are taken in dozens in trucks to… places from which they are not likely to return. I know of two farmers only yesterday who were shot and their families taken because the Germans thought they hid Jews. They even shot one man's horses. The Germans had learned that the farmer rode a white horse to the fields by the hiding-caves when the 'coast was clear' and a black animal when Germans were near."

Aldo sat bent over, looking exhausted from the news. Yet, Sergio knew it was only the beginning. He gave Aldo the detailed plans for the assault that had been devised by Il Buio and were to be disbursed to each of the squads below him. He told him where the trove of arms was hidden on the hill and of the imperative to move quickly to gather and place the mines and allot time for the fighters to enter Pitigliano before the attack. Most importantly, Sergio described the collaborative bombing raids from Allied planes after the bridge was blown. But it would be up to the partisans to actually bring it down.

Aldo was what Sergio admired most—a strong and honest peasant, whose Italian spirit could be heroic. And with a confident embrace and a *"buon correggio,"* Sergio was on to the next hamlet and its partisan leader, peddling, or often carrying the bicycle through woods and over the rocky terrain. At each stop during the night, he didn't fail to ask his comrades to look for Giuliana and his grandmother and to tell them to leave the farm and not to return.

It was behind a barn as he whispered this last sentence to Renzo, a smart youth who often acted as runner among the resistance fighters, that he heard that Giuliana and Rosetta had already left the little plot of land the old woman had called home for fifty years. They had been buying bread from the boy's aunt near Sovana said Renzo. It was understood that they were going to split up and that Giuliana was going into the hills above the valley. "You know, the high forest hills, across the valley from the monastery."

Sergio knew them well, of course. The tomb was the obvious place she would flee—unknown to most, filled with guns from which partisans would be taking their stocks, and the place of their first touches beneath the eyes of ancient dwellers they both felt were benevolent friends.

"I must continue, Renzo. I have only this day to prepare everyone in the area for what will be a major blow into this occupation by enemies. You must take the information I have given you immediately to the responsible men. Do not stop. Hide, yes. Be clever. But no matter what, get the information through. I will do the same. But if you hear of her, if someone is going to the place where Giuliana is… give them this for her. Tell her, *"Ti amo"* and that I will come as soon as I can." Sergio pressed a little effigy into Renzo's hand, another image of Turan, like the one he had given her before her first descent into the tomb—his small talisman of love.

Chapter 32

Enrico glanced down at his uniform's lapel. Something caught his eye amid the insignias, the regimental patches—the medals that came without his really having done anything, simply because Italians liked the pretty colors upon which the bits of bronze were hung.

The splash of color that caught Enrico's eye was not for valor, however, but from a tiny bolus of spaghetti sauce that had escaped during his earlier desultory meal. And there it sat on his chest, waiting just as he was, to be carefully examined by Colonel Dieter Hansbach.

Enrico hated what had become the daily interrogations and upbraidings by the Nazi. Palatially ensconced in the Orsini grandeur even as the great German conceit was collapsing, Hansbach nevertheless managed to incorporate every hackneyed cliché of the "Teutonic brute."

For most of the last year, the supposed collaboration between the Italian Army and the Nazi occupiers had become a farce, and as he cooled his heels in the echoing waiting hall, Enrico knew he actually didn't give a damn what the Colonel thought. What peeved him with frustration however, was that he, as an officer who'd been assigned a mission, couldn't find, much less interrupt the partisans who were blowing up military outposts and assassinating anyone wearing a uniform.

For Enrico, it was all about the game now. Mice running from his cats they were— disappearing down holes or into thin air. As a point of pride, Enrico wanted to win a few tails. Privately, as an Italian, he wished victory for these resourceful rodents.

"You will enter now." The officer was already leading the way into the receiving room where in the distance Enrico could see that

Hansbach was pacing in front of the gilded desk. His rage was audible from the door.

"Unacceptable! Unacceptable to the German High Command!" Hansbach eyed Enrico like a howitzer gauging its range. "This is how the Italians fight? This is all you have to offer? Excuses. Blame!" Hansbach jerked at the tight belt cinching his middle; it had taken increased abuse over the last months.

"Oh… let me read from your pathetic communiques. "Lying *contadine…* the farmers will not admit to hiding partisans." "Shop keepers who will not tell…." "The children seem to have seen nothing!" Hansbach slammed his hand onto the delicate desk, bouncing papers, the inkwell, and the last of his coffee into the air. "How weak you are, Ponti. You have done nothing since you arrived!" Enrico felt himself rising to the bait, felt the anger surging from beneath his stained jacket.

"Sir, you see that in the report I have also detailed the interception of a cache of arms on the outskirts of Sovana, stolen Berettas straight from the factory. Also, that four Communist resistance fighters were discovered hiding in the basement of the mayor's office in the town of Sovana. All of them were arrested…."

At this, Hansbach flew from behind the desk as if he would lift Enrico from the ground. "You arrested them? Arrested them! They should have been shot on the spot—and their families as well! Pitigliano and all around it is crawling with such pigs. Do you think I am an idiot… sitting here with no resources? Is that what you think, Italian?" Enrico heard a muffled cough in the anteroom outside and wondered if the duty officer were taking notes.

"Something is going to happen soon. My source has reported that the plans have been made. There are arms disappearing from the armory below this very palace daily, guns come in from the outside. They are infiltrating everywhere, Italian. Maybe you are one of them? Is that possible? Could you too be a filthy traitor?" Hansbach came very close to Enrico.

"Because that is what I must assume if you do not present me with ALL of the *resistanzi*! I want them ALL! And if you do not do this… then both you… and of course, your family members… in Livorno, isn't it… who were complicit with you, you, whose cowardice has infected them as well… you will all face the same fate as the other vermin of your kind!"

Enrico ran his fingers gently along the outline of his gun, feeling its cold turned to warmth against his body, thinking for a moment to shoot the Colonel, thinking how the spaghetti on his jacket would mingle with great bursts of Nazi blood, how the liquids would form an artistic abstract, how in the seconds after he himself would be shot, he might find his way back to the self that had once been a proud man of a noble heritage. Yet, what would any of it really matter now.

Those who had tried to assassinate Hitler had failed. Maybe little Enrico Ponti, the denying Jew, wouldn't fail, but in the end, to live or die, even to live or die in the thousands… what did any of it matter. "Simply play the game," he mentally shrugged. "Without judgement, without conscience, without a soul."

With that, Colonel Hansbach threw down the folder containing Simon's now organized script of the partisan attack. Outlining the secreted snipers, mined bridges, and scores of guerilla skirmishes that were planned, the task of foiling such a desperate operation was nothing if not daunting.

Then Hansbach stepped back and gave Enrico the overwrought, straight-armed salute. "You will report to me in one week that the partisans of the region are exterminated. There will be no more excuses. No more excuses from our little Italian "girl" playing at being soldier!" He turned his back on Enrico, shouting over his shoulder as he retreated to his gilded desk, "And one thousand *lira* fine for that smear of garbage on your uniform. So Italian! So, so Italian!"

"Heil Hitler," responded Enrico by way of a curse. And clicking his heels the way Hitler and the disgraced Mussolini liked, he headed for his car.

Later that day Enrico assembled nearly one hundred men under his command. Like a bemused automaton, he reiterated their mission to search every cave, cavern system, any hole in the ground that would hold arms for the resilient ghosts who seemed to materialize to blow things up, kill, then vanish into thin air. Any sound, any smell, any shallow indentation in the soil was to be approached carefully, he said—gunpowder and explosive devices were easily set off.

And even as he spoke, Enrico found himself wishing he were one of the illiterate shepherds and farmers and tailors and wine-sellers and starving men who belonged to this earth and believed in their right to defend it. It all amounted to having something to believe in, didn't it? And he knew with certainty, that he did not.

Chapter 33

Rebekah had slept only hours a night since being brought to the convent—a place she felt to be more like a prison than a place of refuge for those seeking protection. Only one day out of seven was she allowed into the open to exercise in the yard because the nuns feared raids from the German patrols. But on that eighth day, Rebekah believed that Sergio would come for her. A month after seeing him in the ghetto's tunnel, five days after their serendipitous meeting over a basket of fruit in the convent's yard, Rebekah wondered if something had changed.

For the first time, most of the powerful sensations that flooded her thoughts seemed to have fallen silent. For the first time, something she could only describe as "gentleness" had settled about her. She wondered if this were how other girls felt, this freedom from a desire to have what belonged to another. For now, it seemed that Rebekah would "get" what she wanted. She believed Sergio was coming for her—not Giuliana, but for her.

Yet it was as she thought of him, his dark curls, the strength of his shoulders, the caress she had heard in his voice as he'd held Giuliana, that into the picture there would intrude the rest of the tableau from the tunnel. It was then that the old thoughts returned—the feeling of white-hot lava that coursed along her veins and frightened her with its imminent eruption. The embrace. The reciprocal kiss. The sight of her cousin in the arms of a man she believed could be hers. No, while she preferred the new tranquility, in this matter, she must follow her… inclinations.

It was on the seventh day, the one before Rebekah hoped Sergio would arrive, that the old abbot drew up in his belching car at the convent's gate. It was the day when all of the convent's nuns, as well as its non-religious staff and guests, Gentile and Jew alike, were led into the sanctuary to say their confessions and receive Holy Communion. The old man was always accompanied by another monk who helped the abbot with the Host and Wine. Today, the younger cleric appeared to hang back, to be less than delighted to be helping with the convent's required confessional responsibilities. Staring out the window of the convent toward the rolling tufa hills, the assistant seemed like a student wishing for a break from school.

From the sanctuary, one by one the nuns entered the narrow confessional box where the abbot waited with his hand cupped around the better of his two nearly-deaf ears. The other communicants, in scooted paroxysms, inched their bottoms in unison along the wooden pews and were then escorted, one by one, from the sacristy into a small anteroom next to the confessional booth. In the waiting room, they were asked to think over their sins of the last week and mull over ways they could repair their behaviors to please God.

But each confession was taking longer than the first, likely because the old abbot had nearly succumbed of boredom during the nuns' repetitious lists of menial failings, and he was now drifting into REM sleep as he listened to the narrow lives and good behaviors of the "guests."

Then it was Rebekah's turn. She would be the last to confess, but now the young person ahead of her seemed to be keeping the old priest fascinated with some interestingly novel variation on sin. A half hour passed, yet instead of the hooded young monk who ushered people back and forth becoming more sullen, he had grown animated.

He came near Rebekah's place in the pew and motioned for her to follow. Dutifully, she got up and limped behind the hooded figure to the "waiting room." Continually looking behind him to be sure she followed, he abruptly turned into an anteroom adjacent to the one where the others had waited their turn. Furnished only with a desk and a straight chair, the room was barely illuminated by a small, high window that faced a wall.

The monk at first hovered near when Rebekah sat down at the desk. For a moment, she wondered if he were watching her from within the hood. Then in a muffled voice, he suggested, then directed her toward another chair, a small rocker in a corner. Reluctantly, she shifted toward the new seat, just as the monk closed the door and locked it.

It took no time at all. Simon grabbed her arm and heaving his robes above his thighs, seemed to squat down onto the chair, pulling Rebekah's legs apart and forcing her into his lap. His hand was across her mouth and her delicate wrists were now pinned behind her back by his other hand as he thrust himself between her legs—and the wooden chair began to rock.

She felt the warm blood run along her thighs. She felt him, some part of him like a bludgeon that thundered into her gut and her stomach again and again. And she felt his hand where it pressed across her nose and her mouth, forced her down, stinking of incense even as her breath was cut off, even as her scream was trapped in her throat, even as the rocking chair became the pounding hammer to the stake that was ripping her apart.

In the convent's bell tower, a series of low chimes had begun—vespers, the call for the nuns to return quickly to their cells and prepare for evening prayer. The monk had finished with Rebekah. He lifted her off his thighs and pushed her casually to the floor. Not harshly, simply as a piece of used cloth or an unworthy piece of meat that had fallen onto his lap at dinner. He didn't speak. In the darkened chamber, what light there was seemed to float in stria of dust, and she only saw the man's outline as he smoothed his cassock into place and readjusted his hood.

Yet, as he closed the door behind him, she knew who it was. The same "monk" who had brought her here to this alien place. The same "monk" who had tiptoed into her bed when she was a child and put his fingers into places that hurt. The same one who then as now, caused the cascade of red feelings, the sensation of lightning along her arms, the overwhelming will to sin.

Chapter 34

In the past week, across Toscana, men in steel helmets seemed to be everywhere. Since Rosetta's decision that she and Giuliana should leave the tiny *casa*, the rumble of heavy equipment along the rural roads suggested that Nazi reinforcements had been called in to supplement the "local" occupiers. Rosetta had said that the Germans didn't seem to know which enemy to take on first— Italian Fascists who had split from Hitler, Communists who saw an opportunity to gather the political spoils that lay scattered across Italy, or partisans whose skills at ambush and assassination sparked frank fear in soldiers who before were used only to provoking it. And even though the coming days terrified her, Giuliana felt a rush of pride that Sergio and the resistance were worthy foes to these Northern invaders who had originally come sounding like brothers.

Yet so much of what would happen in the next days with the partisans near Pitigliano would depend on the operation's surprise. Giuliana was sure Sergio would have returned by now from the west and would no doubt be rushing to inform the comrades before the beginning of the attack that Il Buio was orchestrating. But Sergio didn't know yet about Simon and the danger he posed. If Simon were privy to the partisans' plans, Giuliana guessed that, as he always had, he would be turning that information to his own devices. Even if she must ignore Rosetta's instructions, Giuliana decided that her best chance of warning Sergio of the danger of her cousin lay in staying near the house. And leaving Rosetta near the village of Sovana, she had crept back to wait for Sergio.

And there was something else. An odd kind of masculine independence had swept over Giuliana as Rosetta sheared away her hair. "So, this is what it feels like…" she'd said to herself, with hat pulled low and one of Sergio's vests over a loose shirt and pair of trousers. "It's as if I am invisible, yet more powerful." She smiled, suddenly aware why men would be loath to give up this "secret power." And with just a few rearrangements, Giuliana felt she'd entered their private club.

It was late afternoon and Giuliana had drifted into a light sleep back in Rosetta's barn. She was surprised to feel a kind of contentment as she settled with her pack beneath old straw that even in its sourness reminded her of the playful lambs that had once warmed this part of their enclosure. She wasn't sure of a plan, only that she would try to intercept Sergio here.

But through the ragged edge of her sleep, Giuliana was suddenly aware of a kind of interrupted scratching, as if something were being dragged haltingly or secretively. And whatever it was, was just outside the long wall of the barn. Feeling her stomach fall, Giuliana guessed that just as Rosetta had said, the Germans had indeed returned.

"*Posso farlo... posso farlo.*" There was the sound of high-pitched breathing attached to the dragging, and with what sounded like childlike efforts, someone was telling themselves, "I can do it."

Giuliana crept through the straw to where an old shutter tried to meet its window without success. From there, she would have a view of who was pulling and who or what was being pulled. "*Non e' molto piu lontano....*" She could hear now that the dragger was young. And he was feeling tired, encouraging himself as he measured his distance. Feeling a little safer, she lifted her cropped head just in time to see another head closely resembling hers attached to a youth's body that was laboring a heavy leather pouch up the hill beside the barn.

She ran to the door, peered out, then with delight called, "Renzo! Renzo! What on earth are you doing here?" The teenager who had often carried messages between Sergio and Giuliana, and partisans as well, stood straight up as if an electric current coursed through his body. He looked in Giuliana's direction, but seemed incapable of either moving or responding to his name.

Giuliana ran toward him, relieved to have found someone she knew; perhaps someone who knew where Sergio was at this moment, perhaps even someone with food. But Renzo, finding his feet, turned and began running, suspicious of a strange boy hiding in Rosetta's barn—one who knew his name.

It was only after a ridiculous game of cat and mouse in the woods beside the farm that Renzo allowed Giuliana close enough to prove what she'd been yelling for minutes, that she was indeed the same girl who lived with Rosetta—but with different hair.

Tired from their adrenalin-fueled chase, the two collapsed onto an old trunk covered with furry lichens. "You look so different," he said, shaking his head, looking saddened by the whole prospect. "We could be brothers."

"No, no, Renzo, we could not be brothers. We could be friends… and we are. But tell me why you are here on Rosetta's farm? Why are you not with your family… safe… or better, hiding? I think the Germans may see you as a plum to pick… send you to go polish their tanks or something."

"Ah ha! I think it is I who found a plum!" Renzo stood up and wiped the sweat from his forehead. "A heavy pannier fell off the side of a German motorcycle. It was just lying in the road, nobody near it. Nobody owning it! I found it, and now… it's mine!" The youth laughed in his naïveté, and began walking toward the barn where the pannier was left in the grass.

Giuliana stood up. "Wait, Renzo. This is dangerous to have. You must drag it back. The German will come looking for it. Renzo. Renzo, what about Sergio? Is he back?" she called.

Renzo turned around. "Yes, he's back… but… organizing…." Even here with no one around, the boy didn't yell about the "plans of the resistance."

"Oh, yes. Wait. I forgot. He wants you to go to the place in the hills, across from the monastery. He said you would know the place, that he would go there. And also that…" Renzo suddenly dug his hand into his pocket. "I almost forgot this too," he said running back toward Giuliana. "Here is this tiny figure," he said pressing the tiny

Turan into her hand. "And he told me to give you this as well...." And with that Renzo stretched up to give Giuliana an embarrassed kiss on the cheek. "He also said to tell you, "*Ti amo*!" Then Renzo turned again toward the barn and began to skip from the woods toward the worn leather pouch with the swastika branded on its side, his anticipation turning his steps into dance.

Renzo was only feet from opening his "present," what a poor country boy might have thought was a gift from some saint who had disliked motorcycle travel, when the shot rang out. Renzo stood for a moment staring at the German beside the barn. And then he slowly sank, his knees collapsing beneath him, his head falling to the side, and finally his weight dropping onto his "gift," never opened, never really his.

The German motorcyclist strode from the barn toward the body that, as it lay draped across the pannier, seemed to have melted into little more than cloth. He kicked at Renzo twice, finally grabbing a leg and pulling the boy off and away as if the limb were that of a dead deer he'd shot on a hunt. Then, glancing around, the German sat down beside the packet, lit a cigarette and reaching inside, pulled a large square of bread and a fat brown *wurst* from the motorcycle bag. Giuliana could hear him belch as he dragged at a bottle of beer—heard him spit phlegm in the direction of the body only feet away. And she felt Nathan's little Etruscan vase which she wore wrapped in cloth from a string around her neck grow warm.

As she ran through the woods, Giuliana turned around only once to look back. Rosetta's barn and the motorcycle were now the size of child's toys in the valley below. The only thing that spoiled the vista was the wavering plume of black smoke that rose from the barnyard where the German had sat—where he had looked up to find a pretty boy staring at him, a delicate boy, who, as he grasped something around his neck, had leveled his gaze like a rifle finding its mark—and found it. There had been nothing more. Only the slight aroma of burning cloth and flesh.

Chapter 35

Giuliana had stayed in the woods all that night, watching images of Renzo's death that like paper dolls layered themselves one upon the other, his body falling in a hundred different directions—but not once getting up. She thought that perhaps she had eaten. Bread crumbs were scattered in the folds of her vest—only she didn't want to think from whom the bread might have come, nor of the bread's baking, nor of fire. For this moment, shuddering alone in a countryside that still felt alien, Giuliana only wanted the warmth of Sergio or the quiet hand of Rosetta, or better still, the solitude of her tiny room in Firenze and the sound of her father's prayers and her mother's kitchen kettle. All of it so long ago, lifetimes really. She mentally smiled at a girl she no longer knew who had carried a teddy bear and could proudly recite the Torah. Would that little girl want to know the one who now could both make a man happy in a dank underground tomb and immolate another in a field? Giuliana wasn't sure she would want to know such a one herself. And fingering the little vase that hung between her breasts, she wondered if when her father had given it to her, he could have guessed at its power or of the use she had just made.

Shivering beneath the leaves she had piled around herself, she awaited the dawn when she would begin the trek to the tomb where Rosetta had told her to go—where she should have gone. Perhaps Sergio was called back to Livorno. Perhaps he had been diverted elsewhere by Il Buio. Perhaps, like the German in the barnyard, he wasn't coming back. Remaining near the farm didn't make sense now. She should have listened. In wartime, Giuliana was finding, nothing was certain. Promises, pledges, plans—life—even the person you'd been before could be lost along the way. She pulled her jacket tighter and waited alone until the forest stirred.

***

It would be necessary to pass near a tiny hamlet on her way to the tomb, and her hunger made Giuliana consider a careful stop at the home of one of the partisans for whom she had carried a few messages following the big meeting in the barn. Surely, Aldo would spare her something to eat along the way.

The route to his house carried her from the forest itself through one of the deep trenches dug by the Etruscans that Sergio told her had linked an ancient necropolis to the surrounding towns of Sovana, Sorano and Pitigliano. He said no one knew how the miles and miles of subterranean roads had been carved or if the passages dug deep into the tufa had simply been worn down by ancient wheels, which as they were "resurfaced," were deepened yet again. All Giuliana knew was that as she stood in the middle of one of the trenches' paths, she could touch each wet, moss-covered wall with her hands and that sixty feet above her loomed two flat faces of rock that would let in light for only minutes a day. It felt like a descent into a long, primordial trap. It would not be good to meet an adversary here. There was nowhere to flee.

Yet, this would be the only way to the tomb. Having descended eroded notches that once were steps, Giuliana had passed what might have been an ancient altar, and further down, entered the towering fjords of stone. Keeping as close to one wall as she could, Giuliana inhaled the decaying vegetation and began walking through what seemed to be hanging veils of fragrance, one column of air giving way to another in the chartreuse light. After an hour of tracing the topography of the rock with her hand, the indentations from erosion had begun to feel musical. Bass notes where the stone was shallow and sharp chasms where treble notes would linger—all of it undulating in a kind of craggy rhythm. Immersed, nearly dreaming, Giuliana felt herself surrender to the litho-melodies, so that when the rock wall suddenly ceased, she found herself falling forward onto her knees. Yet though she didn't utter a sound—someone else did.

"*Shtil*!" A voice nearby hissed the Yiddish word, "Silence." Or was it German? Knowing it could be either, Giuliana lay prone on the path and tried to assess what had just happened. And then, after many minutes, "*Lozn aundz helfn*..." This time the words were clear—Yiddish words that offered her help, and Giuliana raised her head.

A hand extended from the darkness, and then another. In a mixture of Italian and Yiddish she understood that a family running from Sovana was in hiding here in one of the carved caves that dotted the route. Sergio had explained that medieval hermits had spent their days deep in these crevasses and that people felt them to be at once holy and aligned with the devil. These people, Giuliana thought, were neither, simply another set of humans turned to troglodytes by the disruption of war.

The elderly grandfather explained he was trying to make his way to Pitigliano where he thought he would find safety in the ghetto. But Giuliana warned that Pitigliano was no longer a haven for Jews... that he must find another place to hide. "I will take you to someone who can help you. He will know somewhere safer than here. Here you can neither come nor go without the possibility of meeting someone who... will stop you." The old man and his wife had charge of two young children, and now he sat rocking in the darkness, unsure of any choice. "It will be by the will of God," he crooned. "We wander in the wilderness. We look for a sign."

The old man would need someone more persuasive than she, decided Giuliana. Then she said, "Ah, old father, I have such a sign as you need." She pulled out the little bird that had come to her from Sergio through Renzo and she placed the talisman in the old man's hand. "Keep this. This is a sign from Yahweh that when a man who shall be called "Aldo, the ancient one," comes to you, he is your guide and your guardian. His body is young, but his soul is blessed with wisdom by God, and you must follow him to safety." Giuliana surprised herself with her "prophetic" pronouncement. Yet it was just what the old Orthodox Jew needed.

"Bless you, my boy. You are the herald that has been provided. We will wait. We will trust this amulet and the One who comes from Yahweh." He placed his hand on Giuliana's shorn head and whispered a Hebrew prayer, and then she hurried again along the pathway toward the house of God's new messenger where, as the sky slowly lightened, "Aldo, The Ancient One," was slopping the skinny pig and skeletal chickens that resided in his garden—and reviewing the plans to blow up a bridge.

Aldo sent his eldest son to gather the old Jews and their frightened charges and secret them through the forest to a cattle shed with an underground cellar for keeping field vegetables fresh. Inside the deserted cellar, now lived two other families of frightened refugees from the small ghetto in Sorano. They welcomed the children and old couple. But for Aldo, it was Giuliana's arrival that was welcome. Sergio had told him of her lack of fear beneath the earth and her skill at delicate tasks under difficult conditions. Such a "boy" was just what the partisan now needed to complete the intricate wiring that would be laced through the interior stanchions of the bridge that joined Pitigliano's rocky mount to the rest of the countryside. Once the bridge was down, Il Buio had explained, the Germans would be "sitting ducks" for the American bombs.

After a porridge of turnips, two eggs, and a piece of old sweet bread that for Giuliana, tasted like the manna the Hebrews had gathered from the undersides of desert leaves, she agreed to help Aldo. "Sergio would want it," the partisan told her. "He runs everywhere now, his mind only on the success of our attack. You will be helping him to undertake this. What good is it to hide in a tomb when you can help Italy… and make Sergio proud."

***

Sergio squatted on the floor of a tiny bell tower alongside the church in the crumbling village of Raggioni. A long rope hung from the rafters where it was attached to a bell that the gangly teenage partisan beside him tolled every Sunday. Today it only served as the focal point around which Sergio's detachment of 15 men and boys circled, each of them gazing intently at the plans their leader had spread out on several dirty pieces of canvas.

"I know most of you from our school days," said Sergio. "I trust each of you like a brother… and I believe your trust comes to me as well. I am no better than any of you, but for the next days, you must do as I tell you. My orders come from Il Buio and his lieutenants who understand the ways of this enemy. But we are men. And we know the region. And we are brave Italians. As your leader, I will hear your advice, but you will do as I say. Do we agree?" The men acknowledged their willingness. Sergio crossed himself as he asked for the Virgin's blessing, then stood up and embraced each of them. This is what made the resistance strong and resilient, he knew. The camaraderie of brothers and the "back stories" that bound them to this portion of the Italian soil and each other.

His father had been assigned one Pitigliano platoon, Sergio the other. And though these men could neither read nor write, he knew their innate grasp of how to negotiate the terrain, their expertise with rifles, and of their cleverness at trickery when needed. One relief was that the monk had been assigned to his father. Though their trip to Sassetta had not been unpleasant as he'd expected, there was something that troubled him about the monk, something which, as yet, he couldn't identify. Sergio didn't want to have to rely on the unvetted holy man as the operation neared its final readiness.

"The call will come in the next hours, perhaps dawn of the day after tomorrow," said Sergio. "It is only the last, and most dangerous thing that we have yet to do. I now ask for volunteers to infiltrate the walls of Pitigliano, lay the mines around the palace, and place the explosives at the city gate." Sergio held up his hand and shook his head as every man's hand shot in the air.

"Ah… I knew you would all salute with your lives," laughed Sergio. "But it must be the smallest of you. The youngest maybe. And the oldest of you… whoever will not draw attention. Pietro? Will you do it?"

A dark-skinned boy who had a twisted back, but an intelligent face, gave a determined nod. "I too will volunteer," said Arturo, a grizzled old man whose clothes were in tatters. "I fought in the first war, and explosives were what I did best."

Sergio surveyed the other tall, healthy-looking men. Finally, one man at the back said, "I know of one who is an expert at this! I saw him today with Aldo. He used him to crawl under the bridge, stringing wires in and out of the bridge's supports. The boy was fearless, dangling above the gorge by a small rope. I will get him."

"Very good," said Sergio. "I will put you in charge of the placement of interior mines. Here are the precise locations—the palazzo, the interior of the gate, the guard houses at the secondary gates. Arturo, take Pietro and when Aldo's boy arrives, take him too. Go into the city, pretend to sell cabbages, I don't care. Make changes as you need, but if the boy is small, let him pretend to play, let him pretend to deliver bread. It doesn't matter, but keep him busy until each of the explosives is placed and the wires well hidden." Sergio himself would be meeting with the regional commanders and via the partisans' secret communications links would get them certainty of when the attack would begin within the next hours.

He would also make a trip to Rosetta's farm to verify his grandmother was not there and another to the tomb on the hill to see Giuliana whom he desperately hoped was well hidden in their odd "Etruscan home." Giuliana, whose face danced before him in each moment of stillness. Giuliana, whose whispered words were the only peace now to be found.

Chapter 36

Riding a horse given to the partisans by a local *contadino* who no longer needed it to plow his fallow fields, Sergio traveled back roads and woods for most of the next day to check on the local capos. Assuring himself that they understood that when the word came, they were to immediately gather in the vicinity of Pitigliano, he also checked that the distributed arms actually had adequate ammunition, that those needing codes had memorized them, and that the few radios shared among the fighters had batteries that worked.

"I think we are ready, my son," said Sergio's father as they huddled for a moment beneath a tree, each of them on a horse going in a different direction. "Il Buio himself has inspected the bridge and the placement of the explosives. The dynamite from the British is packed in hollow trees and old logs at the base of the stanchions. There are only three detonators that must be connected before the bridge can be brought down and those will be done in the hours before we begin. A master box will be on the ridge. I have just come from Aldo who says the same youth who strung the wires on the bridge has completed the task inside the gate and around the palace… *un bravo ragazzo*, if you ask me! When the Germans lie in pieces, we should give him a medal!"

There was a moment of silence between the two as each of them stared into the fog-filled valley, a metaphor for the past and the future which were at the moment indiscernible. How quickly childhood had passed. How quickly middle age had come. How unnoticed could be their end in the next hours.

Then Sergio's father reached out and grasped his son's hand, handing him a pouch of apples and bread. "Be safe, my boy. Take no chances." And unable to resist, he pulled Sergio toward him and kissed his forehead as he would a child's, then pulled the horse away and toward the distant path.

"Papa," called Sergio in a hoarse whisper, "Have you seen Giuliana? And where is the Monk?"

His father reined in his horse and backed him up a few feet. "I have not seen the girl… girls do not show themselves in the last days. And the Monk will join us tomorrow night. He wishes not to carry a firearm, but he is willing to run messages between the squadrons during the attack. He is a brave young man…very alert." Somehow that was the very thing that worried Sergio.

And for a long time, he watched his father recede down the winding path into the valley, the fog eventually enveloping the now tiny figure. And Sergio found himself glad that he had been kissed.

***

Sergio wasn't sure whether Rosetta's house or the tomb where he hoped she had gone would offer the best chance of finding Giuliana. But his father had only recently been to the excavation to gather arms for his squadron and hadn't seen her, so perhaps she had stayed at the farm even though nothing about it provided safety. Still, Sergio had been in the saddle all day and perhaps his grandmother's soft bed was the best place for him too before the battle that would soon come.

When he arrived, he found that though Rosetta's door was locked, the cellar door was only lightly closed. The rock-hewn store room below, where generations of garden tools, tinned vegetables and old dishes were aligned on rickety shelves, became the perfect vestibule to gain entry through the kitchen's trapdoor.

Sergio did a quick appraisal of the house, aware that Germans might have come looking for him there. And though the rooms were not ransacked, it was clear his grandmother and Giuliana had left quickly. Closed drawers had been emptied, but certain cupboards, usually locked, were now ajar. However, Rosetta's quilt, the big one she had worked on since he was a child was still there, folded as if waiting for him, and Sergio couldn't resist. He lay down on Rosetta's bed and pulled the blanket's stripes to his neck, letting their colors wrap him like rainbows, hoping their brilliance would let him sleep.

It wasn't until the sun was slipping away that Sergio woke. Damp with perspiration, he jumped from the bed, fully awake and frantically aware that he had forgotten something. As if a life hung in the balance, he stood for minutes, breathing heavily, staring through the window as the sky darkened into slashes of scarlet, when he remembered—at sunset, he would "come for her." "On the eighth day" he had promised, he would come to help the beautiful girl in the convent to leave the place that so distressed her. He had made that pledge, and now that he was awake, it was as if something powerful were drawing him there. It would be for Giuliana too, he said to himself, wondering why he felt the need to justify his impulse to reach the convent. Yet all he knew was that he must hurry.

The horizon had transitioned to purple as Sergio led the horse in the grass beside the road. A few fuchsia striae remained, but the stars now were busy arranging themselves, seeming to vie like divas for some tiny square of heaven.

At first, the convent appeared dark, but through the gate Sergio could see the faint glow of candles in what was likely the refectory. Otherwise, except for the occasional bleat of a sleepy sheep, the Romanesque building itself seemed to slumber. And then, almost as if a cobweb had brushed against him, he felt her hand against his leg.

Rebekah stood gazing up at Sergio, her pale skin seemed to be made of the moon, radiating softly white against the woods' umber.

"You are here!" whispered Sergio, stating the obvious, but with such delight that Rebekah laughed lightly, "And you are as well!" She grasped his leg and leaned into it. "You did not forget me."

Sergio reached down and helped Rebekah to climb behind him. She had only a small cloth sack with her, but it and her clothes had the freshness of bergamot, a scent that mingled with the night air to create a hypnotic that cloaked them as Sergio turned the horse into the woods.

The girl's warmth behind him, the strands of her hair that now lay along his shoulders, and the delicate exhalations of air she made when the horse stumbled were disconcerting, intoxicating in a way he didn't understand, making his tasks for the dawn hours before battle seem very far away. Sergio still didn't understand why she wished to leave the convent, a place probably safer than any other for her. But feeling this luminous creature's arms about his waist, feeling her utter dependence upon him, gave him a feeling of manliness that was hard to interpret.

Staying only on small animal paths along the lines of fields, Sergio had decided against taking Rebekah to Rosetta's house. Instead, it would be safest if he transported her to an abandoned farm not far from his grandmother's own. Only a week before, its owners had been dragged from their beds, and both they and the family they sheltered shot. Sergio believed it would be safe there for now. The Germans had cleared out the "vermin" and wouldn't be back for a time, especially not with what would be happening to them in the next hours.

As he expected, the house was dark. Set in a circle of cypress pillars, the cottage was hidden from its own path by a leafy grape arbor whose clustered fruit glistened in the moonlight. Sergio took Rebekah by the hand and led her inside the house, leaving her at the door as he felt for the candles that all farm houses kept on their dining tables. Then he pulled the curtains, and lit one small candle from the table.

When he moved to the next room, Rebekah followed, clinging to Sergio as he went from the simple living room to a kitchen alcove and to the two small bedrooms where the candle's flicker made the ceiling dance. "We are making sure no one else had opted for this safe house too," he said, smiling as he would to assure a child.

With the candle held high, Sergio spied one of the old-fashioned cold-boxes farmers often kept, the kind whose designation was usually incorrect. Yet inside, he found a bit of hard bread and stiff cheese, both of which, as the two of them tore and bit into the little trove, they found delicious. Sergio said he would find someone to bring her more food tomorrow, but that for now, this would have to do as her feast.

They continued exploring the family's abandoned rooms, finding a light blanket that he wrapped around Rebekah's shoulders and a soft deer skin that would keep her warm tonight. But instead of following him further, she suddenly sat down on a bed and began to silently weep.

Sergio lowered himself beside her, unclear what had come over this strange girl. He felt her shuddering as he touched her shoulder and believed that he too was trembling.

"Do you think that you can be nostalgic for a place you have never been?" Rebekah whispered the words to the darkened room. "Or miss something that you never had?" She turned to face Sergio. "Do you think you can lose what was never yours?" He couldn't see her clearly, only that her cheeks were flushed and that the candle illuminated their tears. And that her suffering wounded him too.

"I don't understand," said Sergio. "These times have brought great losses… perhaps your parents… your home…." Sergio put an arm around her, not knowing what to say. "But whatever you have lost, some can be regained…."

"It is something different," she said sadly. "Whatever I have wanted from life, it has been had by someone else. The yearning for it… the knowledge that it will never be freely given… wholly mine, brings suffering."

As Sergio stroked her hair, felt the weight of her head against his shoulder, he struggled to understand the losses, the disappointments of this exotic fairy whose origin he couldn't fathom.

"Is there not some law of the world that would make things equal," she said. "Some great punisher who would diminish the many gifts that come so naturally to some?" Rebekah closed her eyes, seeming to dream of such an Equalizer.

"Sometimes, I think there is. Sometimes, I feel it." She turned to him and placed his fingertips against her eyes. "Sometimes, I even help it." And then, standing up and turning to gaze at Sergio, she said cryptically, "But not like some. Not like those who steal from your body and leave their poison inside." Her voice had lost its softness and had become narrow and bitter. In the half-light, Sergio could see a ruddy surge begin to color her arms and then rise toward her throat. Her eyes seemed to glow the color of ice. And then she turned away, weeping.

How defenseless she is, he thought, embracing her from behind. How people must hurt her when they speak of her leg… this waif, this pale… tendril whose beauty is marred. Or perhaps it is that the others find her delicate skin so different in this land of dark people. Sergio turned her to look at him, "You should have the world," he said. "They have only hurt you from spite." He didn't know the details, but he added them, filling out Rebekah's story, finding a role in it for himself.

And then he took her in his arms like a father or older brother, inhaling the green notes of forest in her hair, excited by the warmth of her slender fingers as they curled along his neck and the way her body fit so well against his own.

"I am so tired…. Can we lie down for a while, dear Sergio," she asked. "I know you cannot stay with me, but it would bring me comfort…."

Chapter 37

For Rosetta, the last terrifying days had become a series of improvisations. Like Giuliana, she too had not followed the plans the two had made when they left her farmhouse—though she had tried.

Hobbling with another old woman for anonymity, Rosetta had headed first for Sovana, where Sergio had a repository for some of the family's stolen artifacts. But it was too far, and instead, she would go to another closer one, one of a series of shabbily boarded caves that punctuated the tufa surrounding the communal gardens outside Pitigliano's walls. Here, farmers kept hoes and harnesses, broken axles and crooked wooden wheels. These rustic storage caves, once used as dwellings by everyone from Etruscans to impoverished Tuscans, were now rarely visited except during harvest or spring. It was inside one of them that Sergio and his father had dug their largest "storage museum," and where Rosetta planned to find safety from the marauding German patrols, who, she surmised, wouldn't have known of these ancient cubicles.

She and her shuffling friend entered the lower garden, taking note that some farmer had hidden a sheep beneath a shallow overhang. It was perhaps one of the last walking pieces of meat in Toscana, she smiled. But then she saw that something was terribly wrong. The earth at the side of the garden was rutted with deep gouges, the corrugated impressions Italians had come to fear. Instead of low hand-plowed berms with remnants of potatoes or squash, these dark striations were from heavy trucks with heavy loads. And as the two women came from behind a stand of trees, Rosetta saw why.

Pulling down on her companion, the pair quickly dropped to their knees in the dirt, pretending to vigorously pull at tubers, something the rest of Toscana was doing—eating up the very roots which would have sprung to life in Spring.

The rumble of the truck vibrated through the dirt and into Rosetta's fingers. From the base of the stony promontory and from behind a thin stand of trees, the Germans in a thick-wheeled lorry only glanced at the babushka-wearing women as the convoy rumbled by, heading away from Pitigliano and across the bridge.

But to Rosetta, it was suddenly clear what was happening. Kneeling only a few meters from the very cave which Sergio, her son, and his father before him had used for three generations, she could see other German soldiers hauling from it enormous vases and boxes of pottery and struggling under the weight of massive carved sarcophagi. Just as offensive to Rosetta, the laughing Germans ogled and stroked the statues of half-clothed Etruscan women, who three thousand years after their make-up was applied, could still provoke a reaction. Sergio's museum was being gutted.

Rosetta's hands were covered in dirt and the face of her friend was dark with smudges from pretending to eat the clawed-up, rotting roots. Yet from inside the cave, now came such an unlikely pair that the rustic old woman who dug in the dirt beside Rosetta sat back on her heels and stared. Was it a general? Perhaps a colonel? Neither woman would know such things—only that a German military officer in a shapely tunic and a youthful monk at his side were laughing as if they were brothers. Holding some particularly interesting artifact to the light, the officer patted the monk affectionately on the bum. And Rosetta and the other old woman, sensing great danger, rose, carefully folded their aprons over handfuls of useless grass, and tottered away from the robbery of a robber's cave that was going on in full view.

Could this be the monk Giuliana had spoken of? Surely not one who so brazenly paraded with a Nazi. Sergio would know what to do when he returns, she thought. He would know whom to trust.

***

After that, Rosetta had spent another night at the farm of a friend, but the pallet made for her was taken when the woman's young family arrived, fleeing the daily kidnappings that had begun to occur all over Italy as Germans sent Italians to labor camps in the North.

She had thought to go to the ghetto, but she knew that her chances of being taken for one of the solitary Jews who still hid there would likely end with a rifle butt or a bullet. But there was one place she had forgotten about. And with the food and a few necessities she carried beneath a bundle of firewood, Rosetta guessed she could survive in such an obscure place for a while.

As she walked through the fields, back toward the great mass of Pitigliano, passing others who were displaced, homeless, frightened, abandoned, or lost, she felt an eerie sense of freedom. Surely, she would not live much longer, even without the war. Hardship, years of poor harvests—old widowed women from this part of Tuscany didn't live much beyond 60, if that. Even then, they were likely burdensome and silently wished by others into their graves. Now, Rosetta need only fulfill the destiny that had been written for her; it shouldn't take much longer. She was tired. She had read the futures of others, struggled against their evils and incantations, confronted powers that she feared, and now alone on this road with strangers, Rosetta could honestly say that she was at peace. Somehow, the rest had fallen away. She was ready for her own future to find its conclusion. War, loss of treasures, loss of loved ones and their dreams—even the desire to see how their stories would play out no longer seemed important. She would not rush things, of course. But for the first time, she was ready, as if she could see a destination ahead.

It was hard to find at first. For Rosetta, it seemed a lifetime had passed since she had entered the cave at the base of Pitigliano, the place where six years before, in a few deadly minutes so much had occurred that had changed so many lives. These were some of the oldest caves associated with the city, she had been told. These were the "hives" where the earliest Etruscans had burrowed to have a sweeping vista of the surrounding countryside; a vantage point that left the ancient priests and soothsayers close to their gods.

Rosetta had played here as a child, but had been warned by her father of the place's danger. She had never understood if it was from vipers or magic that she had been warned away. Now, as it was on the tragic night six years before when Giuliana had become an orphan, it would be her own refuge for a while—if God willed it.

It took her nearly an hour of climbing, but at last Rosetta found the cave's entry, thick with vines, the underbrush woven into knotted, woody plaits. Only vaguely could she see the weathered door that collapsed inward. New trees and tall grass made climbing near the entrance a struggle.

Rosetta took out the tiny lantern she had brought from her house and lit its candle. She had never entered more than a dozen yards into the darkness, even as a child—nor on *that* night. Now she sensed from the echoes her scraping feet made that the cavern was long and deep. When she stopped, the sounds of scurrying and the distant crumble of falling tufa suggested she would not be entirely alone. And despite the remembrance of the tragedy that happened here, with its entry facing the very wall of the towering city above, Rosetta felt safe, glad that she was here, sequestered, protected by the earth.

She prayed that Giuliana was also safe, secreted in the tomb in the hills where Rosetta knew Sergio and his father were digging. She was proud of this adopted girl and of her own son and grandson who had shown themselves to be honorable, willing to protect their land and what lay beneath it. That was it, wasn't it? Honor, righteousness, the courage to love and to protect what is truly important—the ability to know when you have found it.

Now she held the lantern high. The smell of humus, of petrified droppings, of millions of microbes feasting on dead organic matter made the air feel wet. Stepping slowly deeper into the cave, Rosetta found detritus everywhere and scraped herself a kind of cushion from the brush and blown-in leaves. She covered her little mound with her head scarf and began to feel as she had as a child fifty years before when she would make a make-believe house from twigs. A strange elation washed over her. Oddly, she didn't feel tired. And despite the long walk and climb to the tomb, Rosetta experienced a feeling of adventure rising. She thought she should lie down and perhaps sleep a while, but instead, she took her candle and stacking her small pack against a wall, began to explore deeper into the cave.

In the flickering light, she could see piles of bone, small rodents and birds who had been feasted on by wily mammals with sharp teeth. She saw some shards of crockery pots, uncertain if they were of modern or ancient origin—either would not be unusual. And then she saw something odd, something out of place amidst the browns and blacks. It was yellow. Touching what seemed to be fabric scraps, now mostly covered in dirt, the mustard-colored cloth threatened to disintegrate in her hand. As she picked the pieces up, Rosetta realized by their crude shapes that these were the yellow stars that must have been ripped off by some of the fleeing families—Giuliana's family—the very night of the murders. Rosetta felt her head reeling. Of course, the stars would be someplace here. She lifted the lantern and looked warily into the corners to see if anything else remained. Had the Germans come back to bury Giuliana's parents? For now, she could see nothing else.

Yet, this must have been the place that Giuliana's father had found the vessel, the vase that held a power unlike anything she had known.

Rosetta sat down near the yellow stars, in an area where the shadows stretched their shapes into what seemed an enlarged circle. If she held the lantern high, she could see small niches in the walls, and if closer, the fragmenting frescoes that had been made into a kind of gallery of faces—portraits, spotted by mold, that gazed into the center of the circle like witnesses making careful observations. A shiver came over Rosetta, and her hand went to the two talismans she carried, a Christian cross and a small bronze mirror. It was the one given to her by Giuliana when they parted, one the girl said she had lost on her first descent into a tomb, refound, but which she now believed she was meant to give away.

As she sat, joining the faces of Etruscan gods in their focused interest in the center of the circle, Rosetta began to see that there once had been a kind of mound in the middle of the room. Now crumbling, she saw the remains of a smoothed, worked surface, what might have been a kind of raised centerpiece and lying near, another fractured form that, as she examined it, took on a basin-like shape.

Rosetta picked up her lantern and placing it on the low, flat "altar," gently began to move some of the dirt away from the other ill-defined structure. Her breathing was coming rapidly though she wasn't exerting herself, when slowly, she felt her head begin to pound and a flush of fever wash over her. The candle wavered dangerously, threatening to go out as she looked around for signs of someone entering or her own route to escape blocked. What she saw instead, was the audience of faces in the tufa, animated now, eyes angry, wordless, willing her to leave.

But Rosetta decided to stay. Perhaps this was to be her destiny, she thought. And she felt no fear. With a crucifix in one hand and the mirror in the other, she stood and lifted her amulets. Turning in a circle, she began to chant the familiar incantations to forestall the evil eye. Deflecting the stares, the penetrating gazes from the walls with the mirror, she turned the eyes' malevolence back on themselves, all the while invoking the powers of the Father, Son and Holy Spirit.

Slowly, as Rosetta's head whirled, she began to feel a retreat of the anger within the room. She sensed that these guardians of the ceremonies that must have occurred here, were mollified. And finally, she sat down in the sacred dirt beside what seemed to be an altar.

As she laid down the cross, and pushed her hair from her wet brow, her hand touched something that had not been visible in the wavering light of the candle. It was cold, nearly buried in the dirt, with scoring that, as she touched it, was deep and defined. Rosetta glanced at the faces around the room. They had faded into the murky browns and blacks of the cave. But with the candle held aloft, she saw now that the hard artifact in the dirt, as long as a foot or a large man's hand, was a carved metal disk with an irregular form.

It took little to extract it and dust the powder and earth away. Its surface was divided into sixteen parts, she counted, with scratched letters she couldn't read in each of the segments. Its contours were familiar to people like her, farmers who slaughtered and handled the organs of their animals. And in one breathtaking revelation, it came to Rosetta that she might have found what Sergio always described as the most sought-after artifact of collectors. And one of the most sacred pieces of Etruscan magic.

If so, she now understood the basin near the altar—the divining trough where the liver of a sacrificed sheep would be examined by high priests. Sergio had told her of this artifact and how it was believed the Etruscans could read the future, tell of battles' outcome, predict from where danger would flow from the regions in the sky which corresponded to regions of their known world. All could be told from the story told in the liver. And this metal disk was the template for priests to follow—a kind of Bible for divination.

Rosetta looked around again at the faces, not knowing who they were to represent, but believing that they nevertheless had acted as guardians to this sacred place and protectors of the liver that had perhaps predicted their own demise.

She asked them for permission to use it now; to take it with her tomorrow. She vowed to protect it. And vowed to honor the traditions and deities she would invoke. She begged for intervention as she would read the liver of the now-living sheep in the garden below. Praying that her loved ones would find safety in the battle to come and protection from the evil that was circling near, Rosetta planned to read the future.

Chapter 38

Aldo's wife had stood beside Giuliana, holding a blanket for privacy as the girl climbed into a tub of water recently boiled on the stove. It was the first bath she had had in days, and one that her muscles reacted to first with spasms and then with a lovely ache that seemed to slowly wash away along with the grime.

Draping a cloth around Giuliana's shoulders, Aldo's wife continued in the kitchen making small packets of sausages that she would give to the *partigiani* when the attack was over. Her laughter and chatter and the packets themselves drifted into the background, but her optimism spread a lovely warmth around the little room.

Drifting in and out of sleep, Giuliana looked down at her hands as they floated beneath the water. The past few days seemed to have belonged to someone else. She had never before touched electrical wires. She barely understood now the process whereby small explosions would lead to larger ones. All she knew was that by her actions, dangling in a harness much like the one she wore when she descended into a tomb, she had helped the cause that for Sergio and Rosetta and resistance fighters who took risks for Jews, she had done her part. She wondered if Sergio knew.

"Here, *ragazza,* let me wash your back." Aldo's wife had finished a basket full of packets, and was simply getting on with another task. "I didn't know you to be a girl when Aldo brought you in here. You were asleep… do you remember? Your hair… did you do this on purpose?"

Giuliana was too tired to say much, only that it had been a precaution. But as the woman scrubbed and chatted, she did sit up straight in the tub when the woman began to examine the little vase around her neck. "Ah… this is a flask? I thought it was to hold Holy Water… but…."

Giuliana smiled at the woman and wrapping the cloth around her, reluctantly pushed herself out of the water. "It is only an old gift. I sometimes wear it for luck. It is nothing. Nothing of value," she said, the motorcyclist's last look of shock flashing across her mind. Then smiling her gratitude, Giuliana accepted a worn but clean blouse from the woman and pulled on the only other clothes she had—too big, but having once been Sergio's, feeling like an embrace.

"I must now go. You and Aldo have been very kind. But I cannot stay." Aldo had tried to insist that Giuliana stay with his wife, or that he take her to Rosetta. But Giuliana had insisted. "He will be waiting for me… I should have been there days ago. That is where Sergio expects me to go. Yes, the attack will come soon, but I know he will want me with him before."

Aldo had finally agreed to take her at nightfall as far as the base of the hills. He himself had dug in the graves in this region, but found little. He said he was glad that it was Sergio and his father who had discovered a productive site.

"I hope that you find the boy there, Giuliana. I cannot guarantee it. I do not expect it. In the last hours I have learned that the attack will come tomorrow. The comrades will take their positions at first light. Sergio will be commanding a group of them. He will be very…." He shrugged and averted his eyes.

"He will be very busy, I know," said Giuliana. "But he will come to find me."

***

Struggling up the ridge and through the underbrush in the dark, Giuliana would need her memory more than her eyes to find the excavation. Tonight, it seemed that the forest was in a welcoming mood, no roots reaching out for her ankles, no vines tearing at her clothes. Still, the worked tomb was not meant to be found.

She had expected to come upon one of the partisans somewhere near, standing guard over the second entrance whose underground cavern had become a cache for resistance guns. But there was no one when she finally attained the ridge where the excavation had been camouflaged.

A wave of fear washed over her for the first time. The kind of terrible loneliness that used to well up in the days after her parents had been killed. She had come to find Sergio, to warn him. Perhaps, if there were time, to love him. Surely, he would be looking for her as well.

Giuliana let herself sink into the damp leaves, a profound exhaustion threatening to overtake her. With a tiny flashlight that Aldo had given her, she let it play along the forest floor, trying to read its dirt, a disturbance of its leaves, looking for the fake forest floor with which grave robbers cover their secrets. And then she saw it—the way the humus lifted in a kind of half circle and scattered dirt lay atop the leaves. It was barely a change from the rest of the forest topography, something an animal could have made, but for Giuliana, her heart leapt that below, this beloved "animal" had come to wait for her.

Crawling closer, she could see that the opening into the tomb had only been hidden from one side. Now indeed, the aperture was apparent, and even the dark outline of the ladder leading to the first level could be seen.

Leaning over the opening, Giuliana discerned the slight movement of light, reflected shifts as it diffused and bounced from wall to wall in the dark labyrinths below. And a deep relief swept over her. This had been their plan, to meet here—this place, their first place—where Sergio felt she would be safe. And he waited for her even now on the eve of the attack. She would warn him herself of trouble Simon could cause and make him proud of her own assistance to the cause. She would remind him of why he must stay alive.

"Sergio…" she softly called into the opening. "Sergio…." There was silence at first, then a scraping against the rock and a slight movement of the light. And then a muffled, "*Mi amore… veni qui.*"

Smiling, Giuliana tucked the little light into her vest and prepared to crawl down onto the ladder and into the sanctum from where Sergio's voice had come, when she heard an indistinct sound—from which direction, she couldn't tell—if up or down or deep within the woods. She stopped, her head now below the level of the forest floor, waiting for another noise or movement. But nothing came. And then, from inside the tomb, "*Mi amore....*" an echoing sound, further away than before, the voice like the light, playing spatial tricks with the rock.

Giuliana slowly resumed her careful descent, stopping from time to time, listening, softly calling the word, "Sergio," not knowing if he were close. And with each lowered foot, she took stock of the tomb, as always, sensing the "activity" that for her, had come to mean the presence of friends. With both feet at last on the hard tufa floor, she resisted the desire to immediately follow Sergio's voice, and stopped for a moment to shine her light along the walls, to say "hello" to the figures whom she had most recently left—servants carrying plates of food to the banqueteers, dancers who pranced to reed flutes, hunters who were still bringing hares to be roasted, and nobles in flimsy togas who lounged with fat bellies, double chins, and flirtatious painted eyes. Sometimes she had thought she heard the flutes and the plucked hand harps. She had hummed with them when she was alone in the tomb, even danced in circles pretending she was one of the guests. But tonight, there was no music.

Giuliana backed up against the wall, playing the flashlight back and forth, running it along the bowered ceilings and down a hall that turned. She thought she caught the movement of a hand. And from another direction a head turned in her direction. She looked more carefully at the musicians. The flutes were not held to their mouths, and instead of a panpipe, one of them was painted with a dagger.

And from deep in the tomb, came her name, "Giuliana." The narrow passageways distorted the sound, but very clearly, she was being called. She lowered the flashlight and began to make her way toward the voice in the near dark, when just beside her she heard the sound of breathing, heaving breaths that were joined by others' respirations. A barely audible keening, a mournful lament arose from the walls, rising and falling, enjoining others in a pitiful eulogistic chorus.

Giuliana found tears spilling down her cheeks, unsure what was happening as a great sadness poured from the figures who were mere shadows on the walls. Only their eyes seemed softly illuminated, glances passing one to the other, as if they shared a secret that had silenced them.

And then, "*Veni... veni...*" "Come," came the call again from down the passage, from the chambers only recently opened, where only she and Sergio went, where the most valuable treasures had been found, the guns kept, where she had been initiated to the joys the Etruscans here trumpeted.

Giuliana called, "I am coming, Sergio," and keeping her eyes down, she focused not on the sounds that were all around her, but on the dim light ahead. As she turned the corner and entered the low stone room, the sense of dread that seemed to have spread along her limbs was suddenly lifted.

"Sergio!" He lay on his back, a deeply shadowed silhouette on one of the stone banquettes that had held a noble's rotund form. Relaxed, with his arms open and one leg against the wall, Sergio had perhaps been sleeping when he heard her call. Now he held his arms wide for her as she ran to join him on the cushioned stone bed.

Giuliana crawled against him, finding the crook of his shoulder, her hands along his chest, her lips against his cheek. Like an animal whose senses investigate clan or foe, she inhaled Sergio's scent, the smell from his hair and skin, his work, his desire. And she sat up with a terror so great that no sound was made. Only the great pounding in her ears and the awareness that the man beside her was no longer alive. That he was a man she didn't know.

In the next moment, from behind, Simon looped the gag across Giuliana's mouth forcing down her head with his knee while he tied her hands behind her. Suddenly she realized that even "Sergio's" voice had been wrong. That her wish to believe he was here had deceived her.

Simon pulled her up from the inert body on the banquette. "Cousin! Cousin Giuliana. What a surprise! It has been too long! How long I have been trying to find you…." Masked by the dark, Simon shoved Giuliana against a wall and sitting down, played a flashlight along her figure.

"You have changed over these years, yes… but not for the better, I think. Your hair… it is not a good look. Way too short. You won't be found attractive." He laughed quietly and seemed to shrug, now running the light around the interior of the tomb. "But you and I discovering each other here inside an ancient grave, a treasure-hunter's tomb…. Well, we have come a very long way, have we not? Both of us poor, wretched Jews… on our way to gas chambers very likely, if not for me. You know this, don't you? If not for me, you would be a pile of cinders. If not for me… my parents, too. Oh, yes, and precious lily-skinned Rebekah. You know about Rebekah? Rebekah, the little sorceress. She'll never go to the ovens, far too clever. Has powers…. Has sex appeal. Gets her way… most of the time." Here Simon bent over double with laughter. "Other times, someone else has his way. And oh, yes, did you know she knows Sergio too? Probably as well as you do…."

At this Giuliana ran toward him, as if she were a car or truck or a bullet, but Simon merely held her off with straightened arms, that as she hit him, crumpled her to the stone floor. He lifted her up and backed her toward the banquette, roughly shoving the body of the man onto the floor.

"Like this *paisan* in the dirt, you are here at the wrong time, Cousin. Let me see, Rafaelo, his name was. A *partigiano*, I guess, a good one… here in the forest guarding the guns. But I don't need guns, do I. Not my kind of treasure. I am a monk, a man of the cloth, you see. No, I like the treasure from the other world… the kind these greedy old ancients thought they'd buried and hidden away."

With his flashlight, Simon pointed to the pile of priceless artifacts, sculptures, funerary wear, pottery, and small amulets that were all heaped together in one corner as if in preparation for removal in the sacks that lay nearby. "While the partisans play, this monk will take things that pay…" he laughed. And then he came toward Giuliana, whispering, "And whatever else suits his fancy… other little treasures." Pushing her roughly against a flat sarcophagus, he reached down and forced his hand between her legs and with his other hand tore open her blouse. Then suddenly, Simon stopped.

"And what have we here?" Simon let his fingers trace the outline of the vase around Giuliana's neck. He was silent as he mentally matched the curves of this piece to that of another one—one he had studied for hours. "This is it, isn't it? This is the vase from the night Nathan gave it to you. The one I have been seeking. It has powers, does it not? Special powers. My God, it is glowing! This is the one then… the one from the book." He jerked at the string which even as it snapped, cut a shallow curve into Giuliana's throat. Simon picked up his flashlight to examine the piece, shaking his head with his serendipitous theft. He was bending low over the little specimen when Giuliana's foot caught his jaw and the tiny ampule flew high into the darkness, end over end, coming down somewhere near only to join the other shards of debris that lined the floor of the tomb. For a moment he didn't move, and then as she watched him lift his cassock and undo his belt, Giuliana felt the sanctum fill with his silent fury.

The voices that had accompanied her to this room now rose to a cacophonous choir, rising and falling in overtones that created a piercing harmonic that seemed destined to bring down the stone slabs above. Leaving her body behind, Giuliana rose up and joined them, drifting to the walls, smiling with the moribund revelers who wept as they drank and drank to forget. Joining those who had ceased to mourn their old bodies, preferring those that could no longer be violated or hurt.

It was then that she was approached not by form, but by a presence. Lying on her back, Giuliana watched from both above and below as the reds and blues and ochres of a hunt scene began to dance. The powerful frescoed stag stood on his hind legs and before him a fearless goddess, a warrior, held him impotent with her fixed stare. Giuliana felt this Essence enter; felt her own power come into focus, felt her own eyes beginning to blaze. And even as her father's powerful vase lay in pieces beside her, her gaze narrowed to a thin stream of hatred that when Simon lifted his face to glory in his conquest, his eyes were met with Giuliana's own, a fiery curse melting his flesh.

Simon fell backwards, stunned, screaming invectives, reaching for Giuliana, a blinded bull whose forehead still smoked, when from someplace above them came a shout.

Even Simon, demented with pain and anger silenced himself. Wiping curls of burned flesh from his face, he silently reached for his gun, and before Giuliana could gather a breath, clamped his hand across her mouth.

The shout was now followed by a second from above their heads, this time slightly louder and with urgency. "Captain, look here! The underground cavern.... Somebody has been here. We need enforcements, sir!"

"Go on, get them," said a second, older voice. And the sound of running, perhaps the sound of someone falling in the underbrush, diminished overhead. There was silence in the forest for a time and beneath the ground. Giuliana could make no sound and the man who pinned her down responded to the intruders with only the quietest click of his gun. And then after many minutes, they heard someone slowly descending into the tomb.

With each step along the ladder, Giuliana knew that that someone was coming closer to the end of his earthly life; with each footfall into the soft tufa powder, he was nearer to the dead all around him than to the life he'd left only feet above his head.

There were no more shouts, but the footsteps continued forward, stopped occasionally, and a voice mumbled once or twice. Slowly, a long, powerful stream of light began to turn the walls garish where they illuminated the passages' broken plaster and missing garlands.

Then suddenly, it seemed the intruder, as Giuliana before him, identified the hidden room which was the source of the faint glow. But instead of entering, he waited in the vestibule of the burial chamber, apparently overcome with the brilliance of these untouched frescoes, as vibrant now as the day they were painted. As if his breath alone carried his words, the man from above whispered to himself, "Ah, Nathan, my brother, you would have found this a paradise…."

Giuliana felt the physical response in the hand that laid across her face and the slight intake of breath as Simon heard his father's voice. Yet it was only as the light from Enrico's torch moved from the corridor and began to crawl across the floor of the darkened room that Simon stood to meet it.

At first, Enrico's light swept along the honed paving stones of the floor, gauging the perimeters of the space. Then it climbed the walls with their fuchsias and blues. The light stopped momentarily when Enrico seemed to observe the mound of artifacts, plucked from their original placements and now very obviously ready for transit. And then the light swung to examine the recesses, the shadows behind stone seats and massive sarcophagi, and without a halt to its movement, the shoes, robe, and finally, face of the monk who stood holding a gun.

"Do you not recognize me, Father?" said Simon as the light ghoulishly illuminated his face. "It is I, the religious, Federico. I come from the abbey." He paused, then with a facetious sigh, he sadly went on. "Ah, you don't, do you. You perhaps remember, "Simon, the Jew?" Yes, yes you would. Living in the past, aren't we? Well, Jews as a group are very passé now. You need to get on with the times, Father," laughed Simon, sarcastically.

"But wait, you have, haven't you? You turned in your Jew card too… to become Captain Ponti, water boy for Nazis in Livorno. Nice apartment, no ovens to worry over. But whatever are you doing here? Back here where you let your soul be sold. That's what you think isn't it? Here you are, marching around a wet forest in the middle of the night, giving orders to capture nice little Italian boys who only want to eat their pasta and play with their goats and puny guns. Do you not feel ashamed, Father?"

Simon slowly began to walk toward Enrico. "But I helped you once, didn't I, Captain Ponti. And because we share the same blood, I may do so again. It only requires a little compromise… what for you, I'd call a little moral slumber. You noted, I see, that I have some items ready for transport, unimportant detritus destined for dusty antique shops. But we poor monks, well, we need to do what we must do. And besides, your commander… and my friend… Colonel Hansbach, would very much appreciate your understanding and help." Simon stopped feet from his father. Enrico didn't move.

"Or perhaps you are now taking your job oh, so seriously, Papa? Planning on a heroic wipe up of the Italian boys with their pitiful guns? Then a cozy back-slap from a grateful Colonel? Well, well, you never know what could happen, do you. You might just get shot in the line of heroism. You might just get shot trying to rob a grave."

From within the black silhouette that was Enrico Ponti, the orange flash of the pistol's fire danced back and forth in the little room, its sound waves reverberating against the stone walls of passage after passage, only to begin their return.

As Simon fell to his knees, light glanced across the ceiling and arced along the walls while Giuliana, statue-like, willed herself invisible in the shadows. "You are under arrest," said Enrico, his tone flat. "You are only grazed. Kneel with your head on the floor and do not tempt death… for it is close."

He flashed his light in a circle around Simon, looking for the gun the Machiavellian "monk" had held moments before, but who now cradled his arm, moaning softly.

With his weapon pointed, Enrico ordered Simon to stand and expose the gun's location. Simon struggled to his feet, the brown robes falling in folds as he pushed himself into a standing position. He towered over Enrico, seeming to envelop him in shadows. Then turning slightly, Simon looked directly into Enrico's eyes and fired into the medals aligned along his father's chest. The one shot became many as again the vibrations traveled round and round the room. Yet Enrico did not fall.

A silence descended for moments in the tomb as if layers of ancient powder whipped aloft by human intrusion needed to settle.

And then, “You are my son,” declared Enrico softly, straining against the blood that surged into his chest. “And because of it, I will not repudiate you. Nor forgive you.”

And with that, Enrico lifted his own gun to his temple and fired.

Chapter 39

Sergio had left Rebekah by midnight, his head reeling, a sensation of revulsion at what he had done mixing with the memory of the most overwhelming physical experience of his life. It was as if he swam in a white-hot caldera, its liquid slowly flooding his limbs and core until he had erupted in a way that wasn't just physical. He wanted it not to have happened; he wanted to fight for his country, to gather beautiful artifacts from the ancients, to one day marry Giuliana, the cousin of this *magicianne* whose scent now covered his body, and who, it seemed, threatened every other of his life's desires. Yet all he wanted at this moment was to have her again. "Stay here for one more day," he had told her as he strapped on his bandolier of bullets and pulled a blanket to her chin. "I will send for you… find a way to come and get you. I came before and I will again."

***

Sergio had ridden for an hour along the tiny path that in the hours after midnight seemed light despite the lack of moon. Ahead, at the appointed outcrop of boulders, he could see a knot of sappers squatting in the grass around a tiny fire shielded from sight by the rocks. Sharing their last swigs of red wine before a few hours' sleep, one of the group separated himself stiffly from the little circle to give Sergio the latest status of preparations.

"Sergio, hail, oh Chief!" the youth laughed in the hoarse dialect of the Tuscan hills. "You are late, Maestro. I had to take the report myself." Shoving his head against Sergio's shoulder, he added, "Mmm, you have the victorious smell of a rutting bull. Happy cow, happy bull, I'd wager." Sergio shoved him away and with a dirty look, sat down beside him. "Is everything in place?"

"The charges are all planted, and the wires strung from the last of them to the box that Il Buio wishes you to press at six tomorrow morning. He says you know where it is hidden." The young sapper then handed Sergio a note, which though he couldn't read, he examined carefully before handing it to Sergio.

Sergio scanned it by the light of a flickering match. Nothing had changed from the movements Il Buio announced at Livorno. Once the bridge was exploded and escape from Pitigliano denied to the Germans, partisans would open fire from the walls into the palazzo at the panicking Germans. At Il Buio's radio signal to the Americans, the partisans were to abandon the walls, allowing the Allied planes to sweep down on the remaining Germans trapped between the city and the fallen bridge.

"You are brave men," said Sergio to the group of fighters who had stretched themselves close to the fire. "We are all brave! Soon we will cauterize this sore on our land. Burn it out! So, sleep well and deep. Let the Virgin watch over you. We wake in two hours."

Sergio propped himself near his men, watching the stars slip through the trees, fearing that sleep might bring a somnolent recrimination worse than what he now experienced. Yet sleep would only diminish the still pulsing memory of what he had felt an hour before. And if he were honest, he would relive his tryst with an angel a dozen times before dawn and the battle whose end he hoped to survive.

Chapter 40

The risen moon seemed little more than a fingernail scratch in the night sky as Rosetta, draped in her black shawl, stepped from the entrance of what she now thought of as a temple—the most sacred space she had ever been, including the great cathedral of Pitigliano whose murky shadow loomed above her.

With the metal plate in the shape of an animal's organ strapped across her back, Rosetta fully realized that though she had long dealt in what some called "magic," she would this time abandon its foundation in Christian ritual and the powers of Christ and the Virgin for something far older. Potentially, far more powerful.

As she made her way from the base of Pitigliano's wall toward the lower storage caves and garden, she felt her heart pounding, not with fear nor fatigue, but rather like a clock whose seconds piled one on another, valuable moments passing, lost opportunities to intercede in something important. Rosetta didn't yet know what impelled her, but with each step she felt her strength grow.

The garden was snarled with vines, the rutted gullies of the lorries, and upended stumps. But in the near darkness, she knew exactly where she was headed—to the secreted treasure she had seen the day before. Following the little stomps and a wet bleat, as if the lamb had only awoken from a baby's dream, Rosetta felt in the darkness for the stony indentation, the shallow cavern where some optimistic farmer had hidden the little animal.

Running her hands around the perimeter, she felt the rope that tied the sheep to a crude metal ring; felt its head, the size of its chest, its weight. There was no question as to what she would do. It was as if she had been commissioned in the "temple" above to act out this rite—one that through blood would help exact both revenge for one civilization's violation and perhaps save the lives of another.

Rosetta sat down in the small cave, pulled the lamb's body between her legs, its head extended backwards against her shoulder, and with her knife and a whispered prayer, forcefully and quickly, slit its throat. The sound of air escaping the animal's lungs and gullet were all she heard. It collapsed gently into her lap, warm blood pouring across her chest and legs, its head reclining in the crook of her elbow like a child's. "In the name of the Father and the Son and the Holy Spirit—and other gods whose power I will serve, I commend your soul to heaven," she said, wishing only that by morning the flesh would not have spoilt and someone could survive on the animal's sacrifice.

Now, she wasted no time. Banking some soil against the lantern's glow, Rosetta proceeded to open the lamb's gut and run her fingers along the wet organs, the firmly coiled intestines, the tiny spleen and pancreas, lungs which still fluttered, the heart, and finally, the liver. She cut it out and laid the deep red organ atop the lamb's back, spreading it into the same configuration as the metal plate she now took from her backpack and laid beside it.

Overhead, the night sky had become even darker as thick clouds now rolled up from behind Pitigliano and lightning began to stab a kind of jagged course from the northwest. Rosetta could see that there was something wrong with the lamb's liver. By the candlelight, she saw that the upper left was swollen and appeared to have hemorrhaged at some earlier time. She had listened to Sergio's long explanations of Etruscan practices and understood their belief that evil emanated from the northwest quadrant of the sky—just as the storm that descended upon her now. Here in the garden, beneath the shallow overhang, continuous thunderbolts left her cowering in her blood-wet clothes; yet she had no desire to flee. Rosetta closed her eyes, one hand on the lamb's soft flesh and the other on its metal replica, forming a kind of conduit between the two. She sensed the electricity in the air around her, the feeling of anticipation, a reciprocity from her right hand to her left, from the lightning overhead to the darkness of her cave, from an ancient time to this.

And in that moment, the sky exploded. Sizzling flesh, the pain of hot metal that coursed along her arm, across her chest and into the body of the lamb—then threw Rosetta forward and onto the floor of the cavern. The lightning bolt left the air and stone and grass burning around her. Rosetta lay quiet, her hair singed, her arms scorched and smoking. And there she dreamed.

The woman smiled at her, oddly gentle for a woman dressed in ancient fighting clothes. And yet, she helped Rosetta to her feet and with fragrant water, washed the dirt and blood and pain from the old woman, and embraced her. "You will come with me," seemed to come not as words, but as knowledge to Rosetta. "I will show you the way. Save those who must live. Offer death to others. You will know the difference and the way." And with that, the dream faded and Rosetta awoke to beating rain against her forehead and the realization that she had much to do.

Chapter 41

Simon had waited only moments after Enrico's self-inflicted fatal shot before he himself had fled. He had swept the tomb with torchlight, screaming for Giuliana. "Come out! Come out, whore!" Plunging among the statuary, stepping into the pile of antiquities now scattered across the floor, kicking the legs of his father from his route, Simon was desperate to leave. "They will blame you! You'll be a murderer! Come out now, Jewish bitch!" But Giuliana was already gone.

The small aperture in a tufa wall and her memorized geography of the mausoleum's twists and turns allowed Giuliana to already be breathing the wet night air, filled now with electrical calligraphy and growling thunder rumbling in from the northwest. In the near distance she guessed the storm was already over Pitigliano.

Scrambling as fast as she could, Giuliana stumbled down the rocky forest's scrub toward the only place she might find Sergio—the site where earlier that day she had helped connect the final explosive charges to the black box he would use to blow Pitigliano's bridge. She took nothing with her from the tomb, except for a handful of shards quickly scratched from the debris-strewn floor, shards which she prayed contained the remnants of her father's gift to her—the powerful vase Simon had ripped from around her throat. Now, perhaps only a keepsake, Giuliana wondered if she would even need it.

***

Though Giuliana had been the first to leave, for Simon too, the way out of the tomb and the forest had been treacherous as he slipped and staggered from tree to tree, relying on the lightning to show the path, even as he feared the saplings he grasped with his damaged hand would be the conduit of his destruction. Still a few hours away, dawn would be put off by the storm that raged across the farmland near Pitigliano and its surrounding hills. And even as he painfully careened down the drenched terrain, he knew his patron could use the time to advantage.

***

"Captain Enrico Ponti was pronounced dead of a self-inflicted military weapon wound to the head inside an excavated tomb in the region of Pitigliano in Toscana. Motivation for fatality is not known. No other survivors or witnesses have been identified.
The tomb is one of many in the area that over the centuries have been used by professional robbers and at present, by resistance fighters hiding illegal arms. It is believed that Captain Ponti was involved in such illegal sales of antiquities and movement of illegal weapons.

Colonel Dieter Hansbach folded the copy of the report on the Italian officer's death that he had just ordered teletyped to Berlin. He handed a glass of wine to Simon, who, stepping from the bath, winced at the wound along his hand. Yet he was smiling broadly now, the stench of tomb and forest safely swirling down the drain.

"I would love to offer you a massage before taking you to bed" said Hansbach, stroking the youthful shoulder. "You have had quite a night. But the evacuation must begin within the next hour." He poured himself another goblet. "Let them blow up the bridge. We will have left through the tunnels… and it is all thanks to you."

Simon sipped his wine as Hansbach played his fingers through Simon's wet hair. "Yes, my golden boy, you have supplied me with the highest quality artifacts even as you show one of my own officers to be a fool. And more, you have exposed the puerile plans of these bloody farmers! What a treasure you are!"

For the next moments, Simon relaxed into the arms of Hansbach, proud of his cleverness, yet promising himself that one day the fragments of "magic" that lay broken within the tomb would be his and glow only for him. The only possible obstacle, was the remaining matter of Giuliana.

Chapter 42

Rosetta's knuckles were torn from the pounding. She had climbed from the public garden back up the rocky path toward the "temple" from which she had taken the sacred metallic artifact, the one she believed had enabled her to receive instructions which she barely understood. But she hadn't entered the cave. Instead, she continued past it to the hidden entrance shielding the tunnel into the Jewish ghetto. She knew it well—it was the heavy wooden door that over the years she had entered to bring food and friendship to her Jewish peers and the "drop off" location for Giuliana on her way to Friday services. But now it was past the middle of the night, with only hours until dawn—and a night filled with thunder and pounding rain. Rosetta knew that few Jews, mostly elderly faithful and the rabbi, remained in the ghetto. And yet, somehow, she also knew that this was her commandment; an ancient directive she had no will to oppose. She resumed her pounding.

Suddenly, the perimeter of the door began to glow. The thin outline of space on the other side warmed to a candle's yellow, and Rosetta yelled above the thunder her own name and need to enter. Slowly, deliberately slow, the door pulled back. A hunched silhouette no taller than a child stood at the entrance holding a candle cradled by a withered hand.

"It is me, Rosetta…" she said to the shadow, fairly pushing herself inside. "I need help! I will try to save you! Let me in… we must have others! Let me in!" The frail figure with the candle stepped back, muttering the word, "Rosetta? Rosetta!" But Rosetta was already half way up the tunnel, making her way to the home of the rabbi, hoping he was not one of the ones already taken from the ghetto and sent to a destination of no return.

Like the old woman who had let her in, the sleepy rabbi had watched the removal of two-thirds of the Jewish population of the city by Nazi intruders whose spittle had landed on most every Pitigliano Jew. By nature, he was stoic and reserved, and over the years had been more prone to acquiesce to first Italian, then German demands than to opt for confrontation. But, on his own, he had recently come to the conclusion that there now seemed little to lose. Pitigliano's Jews were being systematically "disappeared," and what little was left of the community's way of life dangled, dismembered, like an artifact from the kosher butcher's hook. "What do you ask us to do? What plan are you offering?" he asked Rosetta.

Her response surprised them both. Speaking slowly in words that seemed preformed, she simply said, "Burn the ghetto."

***

At 3 AM, the interior of the Orsini Palace was frigid, its four-foot thick walls offering no insulation against either heat or cold. At this hour, even seasoned military men were draped in brown blankets, randomly stomping their feet as they groggily listened to Colonel Hansbach and his protégé.

"They plan to blow the bridge at first light—though with the storm, perhaps it comes a bit later," said Simon to the gathered German officers. They huddled around Simon, who sat like a Biblical prodigy in a candlelit Renaissance painting, his finger pointing at the vulnerable bridge.

"Gather all papers of importance, all weapons and communication devices that you can carry. Bring with you bivouac tents, food, and maps—important are the maps if you have them," ordered Hansbach. "Anything else, destroy here in the palazzo. We will depart at 5 AM. Gather at the entrance to the ghetto. There is an old, unused tunnel system through the Jewish quarter that will lead everyone out below the bridge. By the time the bridge is blown and the American bombers execute their impotent sorties, we will have established ourselves to the northwest and be calling in our own planes to rout out the so-called partisans from the town."

Chapter 43

"Sir, I do not think I should do this.... Not now...." The teen was red-faced even by the last light of the wispy fire. "It is far. Maybe she is no longer there...."

Sergio stood over the boy, his authority masking his guilt. "I say that you go now. We try to save all innocent Italians. The Germans who will be left will ravage the countryside in anger—and here is one to save. Go, now! Do not speak another word," he ordered, avoiding the boy's eyes.

The boy pulled a thin blanket over his head and shoulders and mounted the exhausted horse Sergio held for him. "Gather her and be back here in one hour. I will wait. Her name is Rebekah."

***

Throughout the night, Aldo and several others had remained near the explosives' primary detonator hidden only two hundred yards from the bridge. Since Giuliana's final connection of the wires to the dynamite hidden around the expanse's base, Aldo would remain on guard until Sergio arrived. No one wanted a premature explosion. The rain had in fact caused Aldo and another farmer to crawl down to inspect that the explosives were protected. But he hadn't expected the new arrival at the detonator site when he returned.

"Giuliana!" he whispered with surprise upon seeing the dirty, exhausted girl hunched and shivering between two older partisans. "I thought you were at the tomb... or with Sergio." Then with alarm, "Where is he?"

A faint moon glow occasionally flickered between still-towering black clouds as the storm receded. But Aldo could see the dark circles beneath Giuliana's eyes, their whites filled with a fearful resolve.

"I do not know where he is…." She trembled uncontrollably and the man beside her gave her a cigarette which she left off after a few futile puffs. "Aldo, come close. I am very afraid. There is something that may go terribly wrong here." Giuliana's words were shaking. "It is about the… the 'Monk'… the man who calls himself a monk and knows of our plans." Now she stood up and looked wildly toward the hills and the tomb from where she'd just come. "But he is not a religious man. He is tied to the Germans. He will inform them of our plans."

Aldo stood straight up. "How do you know this?"

"He was in the tomb when I went to find Sergio. He is capable of… anything. And he is friends with the Germans in the palazzo. Where is Sergio? Is he not here? He must know this." Giuliana struggled to mount a nearby rock as if Sergio could be seen from a higher vantage point.

"Not yet here," said Aldo with obvious and mounting worry. He looked at a watch he pulled from his pocket and at the scattering of men now grouped around the girl.

"When do the partisans positioned in the city mount the parapets?" asked one of them. It would be their job to fire on the German troops penned inside Pitigliano when the bridge was blown. He looked at his own watch and at the faint glow now beginning along the eastern horizon.

Aldo had just started to say that they should be climbing the city walls even now, when suddenly a muffled, but powerful noise seemed to shake the rocks at Pitigliano's base. Aldo pulled binoculars to his eyes, frantically scanning back and forth at the feet of the bridge, imagining a misfire and the bridge falling before it should. But the bridge was intact. With his glasses, he followed its route toward the city gate, which remained closed. Then to the massive aqueduct overhead, which still stood. And finally, to the rocks below the gate. And then he gasped. He didn't understand what he was seeing, but it wasn't anything he could have expected.

Chapter 44

"Burn the ghetto?" The old rabbi had sat incredulous in his sleeping cap and ragged night robe. "What are you saying?"

Rosetta looked at him, at his wife who had joined them, and at the three or four others who had been awakened by her desperate knocking on the tunnel's door.

"The goal of life is to live, Rabbi. It is not to preserve this, a rocky grave. It is not a willingness to sacrifice God-given existence through stubbornness. Life is also not about permitting killers to kill us—you and me and this community—because we are too filled with sanctimoniousness—or simply cowardice." Rosetta's words spilled from her mouth in a prophesy-like torrent that mesmerized the rabbi and those around him. Like Joan of Arc or an angelic Jewish *malakim* exhorting callow followers to take up arms, Rosetta changed as she spoke. To those who heard her, her words seemed to come with a powerful command.

"From this house, from this humble grouping of houses, this ghetto set apart through hatred, tonight we may offer appeasement to God for injustice. We will honor the Righteous who have died at the hands of the unjust who occupy our town and carry away those we love. Tonight we will dispense the punishment God has placed in our hands to use. And as from the Burning Bush from which God gave the Commandments, from Jacob who wrestled with the prince of fire, from the Passover Candles that burn in remembrance, and the rededication of the Temple as Hanukkah fires burn never-extinguished, I exhort you to offer up justice tonight to the occupiers who have killed my loved ones and yours—and to do it with fire. We will live, even as evil is vanquished. This ghetto may perish, but God's Will will be done."

And it seemed that everyone who heard Rosetta's words believed something that hours before they would never have contemplated. Each of them felt something at once ancient and new propelling them back to their houses to gather a few cherished mementos and all of the cooking fuel and gasoline they had.

The rabbi went into the sanctuary and from the closed ark removed the Torah covered in its elaborate mantle. His wife took the *yad* for following Torah text and the previously hidden silver crowns that had capped the Torah scrolls. He also gathered the Hebrew Scriptures, the *Tanakh*, and several books of the *Talmud* on Jewish law. And he carried with him the *ner tamid* from above the altar, in which burned the eternal flame symbolizing God's never-ending presence.

Just as Jews had gone out in an exodus so often, this, another diaspora, seemed familiar to each of the ghetto's inhabitants who now, at Rosetta's direction, dragged their furniture to the tunnel's rocky entrance and inundated it with flammable liquids—cooking oils—and flour that would explode like gunpowder as the heat and oxygen of the tunnel mixed.

One by one, the old Jews slipped past the pile of furniture, bedding, and books they had struggled into the narrow passageway. Exhausted, they sat down on the far side of the blockage. There were many yards between them and the outer door to the fresh air of the valley. Once the conflagration was begun, they would need to run for its exit. But for now, Rosetta told them they must wait here. That the moment when God's commandment would be executed was near. And their wait would not be long.

Yet in the minutes before, it was old Lia who had come to her friend with a final sacrifice. "I will wait outside the ghetto gate in the town," she said. "...and I will lock it behind the Nazis once they have entered. You have been a friend to the Jews, Rosetta. I will now do my part and meet you... at the other gate... in heaven."

Just after 5 AM, the ghetto began to ring with sounds of Nazis near the iron fence, shouting for the Jews to open their enclosure.

The shouts were accompanied by what sounded like an assault on the barricade. It didn't take long before the noise of marching feet and men screaming orders told the gathered Jews that the ghetto itself was entered. And within minutes, the tumult of the invasion echoed down the tunnel. The rabbi waited, trembling, as he heard the passage fill and knew Lia to have locked the ghetto's gate. And then, with tears streaming down his cheeks for the loss of the synagogue, the homes of his people, and a way of life that would be no more, he spoke the holy words of justice, “בשם הא בשם האל."

“In God's name,” the rabbi pronounced. And he extended the burning tip against the drenched fabric of his balled-up bedroom curtains. In seconds, the roaring fire exploded with a thunderous shudder into a thick wall of red flames and black smoke that sent the Jews fleeing out the outer door which they locked behind them. Climbing from the hidden tunnel's exit, the straggling line of Jews clambered with their few possessions up the rocky face of Pitigliano's base toward the bridge from which they could more easily make their way from the burning ghetto. “Hurry,” called Rosetta, “We will be safe once we are on the bridge.” It seemed the oracle's knowledge hadn't divulged to her everything.

***

Looking across at Pitigliano through his field glasses, Aldo gasped again. “I don't understand, there are people mounting the bridge—coming from beneath the bridge. And there is smoke. From where?”

Giuliana preemptively snatched the binoculars from Aldo, forcing them tighter to fit her face. “My God,” she said focusing on the thin straggle forming into a cluster at the top of the bridge. “They are Jews from the ghetto. They have left the ghetto. It is on fire! I can see the rabbi is carrying the Torah scrolls! And… and my *nonna*... Rosetta! Rosetta is with them!” Then, with a second gasp,

"And the Monk! My God, Aldo… the traitor is on the bridge in their midst!"

Suddenly, from behind them, came the voice they had been awaiting for the last hours. Sergio was running toward the group, drenched in sweat, his ancient horse's reins thrown to the side in the bushes.

"The box! The detonator box!" he yelled. "It is time! It is late! The bridge must come down now! The American planes are on their way. Bring me the box to blow the bridge!"

And from the shadows behind him, Rebekah's blue eyes found her cousin and her cheeks began to warm.

The partisans could sense them even before the low grumble of American planes could be identified as bulky fortresses carrying destruction. Now, over the pastoral undulations of Italy's Tuscan hills, slowly climbing the sky from behind the dark line of trees in the distance, the bombers seemed to gain speed and like black fowl bent on devouring ancient Pitigliano, they identified their prey.

Sergio's late arrival had placed the whole of the partisans' carefully-timed plan in question. With the bridge still intact, he realized the Germans might very well find a way to evacuate safely. Now the scene through the binoculars of dozens of Jews streaming from beneath the walls onto the carefully-mined bridge had thrown all into chaos.

"Get back! Giuliana, get out of the way!" Sergio's panic lifted his voice like a bawling child's, forcing it both deeper and higher than normal. Giuliana had swung back from straining to see the fleeing Jews and now desperately placed herself between Sergio and the box to which he had the key and the command to explode the stone structure.

"It is your grandmother!" she screamed. "Rosetta is on the bridge! And all the Jews of the ghetto! They are out on the bridge! You cannot bring it down! You must wait!" She stared at him. And Sergio took a menacing step toward her, his eyes narrow and alien.

Giuliana's dread swelled with the incoming roar overhead. "Choose, Sergio! Is it innocent people you are willing to murder? Will you kill Rosetta too? Choose! Offer mercy, my love!"

For a moment, Sergio hesitated, gazing at the black line of people on the bridge, searching Giuliana's face as if she were a stranger from a planet he had once known.

On the bridge, their upturned faces now visible, necks craned toward the bombers bearing down on the city, the Jews were in stampede. In a moment that seemed to extend to hours, Sergio's lips silently moved to form the word, "Nonna." If it had been a cry, it might have been heard in heaven. But from beside him, thin white arms abruptly spun him around.

"Do as you are commanded," Rebekah said, staring him full in the face. "Blow up the bridge!" And without another word, Sergio bent down, quickly entered the key, and pushed the plunger. The noise was deafening.

The roar of the American planes tore at the air as the B-17 ground attack bombers raced in, lifting from the valley to spill destruction from just over the cathedral's spire. Blue clouds and fire erupted from behind the aqueduct, and explosions crumbled one side of the ancient Orsini fortress where stone blocks the size of cars catapulted over the walls and disintegrated as they bounced down the tufa mountain in torrents of dust.

The partisans on the hill cowered with their heads covered as the bombers came again and twice more in waves of four that in an hour seemed to deplete the thirst for destruction. With bomb bays emptied of tons of ordnance, explosions continued to erupt within the palace courtyard and across the elegant terraces of the town long after the planes had vanished into the morning haze.

For a long time after the bombs were dropped, the sound of bursting tufa walls could be heard on the hill where the partisans now stood astonished. Twelve centuries the town had withstood its enemies. Now it burned into rubble in as many minutes.

But the bridge still stood.

With the last of the bombers' growls receding into the distance, the remaining dark figures who had knelt in terror on the bridge floor now got up and ran into the fields for cover and the anonymity of the forests. But the towering arches of the expanse stood untouched, flouting their disrespect while Sergio gazed in disbelief as if the entire bridge were an apparition that should have disappeared.

"I don't understand," is all he could say. Even the partisans who had crouched beside him during the bombardment, realized Sergio had failed in his mission. Whether Germans had been trapped or Jews saved was still unclear, but one thing was obvious—the partisans' proud task had failed. Slowly, the men clustered around him got up, gathered their canteens and hunting rifles, and faded into the trees, throwing glances of exasperation toward the one they'd allowed to lead them. Rough men like these wouldn't forget easily.

Then, only the three of them remained. Beside Sergio, Rebekah stood calmly, her head tilted slightly to the side like an artist who wishes to evaluate her work. And on the far side of the detonator box, was Giuliana. Dust, dirt, and sweat covering her face, her partisan's jacket grey with river dirt, she stood holding the wires she had ripped from the box as Sergio forced down the plunger.

"It is you who made the choice," said Rebekah to Giuliana. She smiled at her cousin with a kind of pity. "It was the wrong one."

Giuliana could hear the sporadic gunfire and intermittent explosions that continued to come from Pitigliano. Now added to it, were voices and crying, the wails and screams of residents who had survived and had begun to emerge onto their ruined precipice. And yet the only sound that touched her was that of Sergio's sobs.

Rebekah wasn't all right. Nor all wrong. Giuliana watched as the strong man she loved wept with humiliation and weakness, blending the opposite failures to comrades and country with that of his disloyalty to his family and hapless innocents—and Giuliana now guessed, to her as well. And she watched as he seemed to somehow evaporate before her, diminishing in stature as he dropped to his knees, a boy now, shamed and outcast, stood over by two powerful women—whose very ascent had brought him to this. And Giuliana wondered as she gently laid down the torn wires, at the years it took to make a man, and how fragile that monument to strength and bravura could be—how her love for him, as she felt it too recede, was ephemeral as well.

Giuliana now became aware of the sounds of "tsking" nearby, and lifted her gaze to see Rebekah slowly shaking her head with a kind of arch derision. "Your bleeding heart will be your downfall, cousin," she said in a hushed voice.

"You might have had him if you'd let him be a hero—taught him the waste in sympathy and the stupidity of second thoughts. Now he's really no good to you or me, is he… is he, cousin?" She lifted a blonde curl behind her ear and smiled. "But he was really mine in the end, wasn't he, Giuliana. You have to admit that. He didn't save the Jews nor was he touched by your sticky family loyalty." Here, she smiled with the long-suffering sigh of one exasperated by inefficiency or incompetency. "Altruism? Is that what you were hoping for? But for whom?" And she began to laugh. "Just remember, he pushed the plunger, didn't he? He pushed it."

Rebekah let the thought settle in. And then, like a parasite abandoning its host after it has sucked away its life-giving juice, she turned and walked toward the skeletal horse chewing obliviously in a stand of trees. She mounted him and pulled the animal toward Giuliana.

"Oh, and one thing before I go, I have always wanted to thank you for sharing your mittens with me in the cave the night we first came to Pitigliano. Your fingers were cold. I wouldn't have done it. But I bear you neither great good will for it nor misfortune." Rebekah looked down at Pitigliano, now incongruously drenched in brilliant sunshine, turning the blue plumes spilling from inside its walls to a Renaissance aquarelle.

"I likely will not meet you again, cousin," she said. "I have what I need and will only find you if I need more… or if, of course, our wills collide. But of that I doubt. You have become stronger, it is true. But my source of strength is depthless… and it is… eternal." She smiled down at Giuliana, then suddenly bent forward and whispered, "Oh, yes, and… good luck in this war. You Jews will need it." With that, and a peal of laughter, Rebekah turned the horse's head and led it into the forest, quickly covered by the darkness that would remain there even as the sun rose.

Giuliana dropped her head back and closed her eyes, steadying herself against a thin sapling. The only other sentient creature in the little clearing remained still, Sergio's shoulders offering an occasional shudder of what she guessed was remorse. How she had relied on him. How moral a man he had seemed—rather like Nathan, her father, she'd thought. But morality, Giuliana now understood, was only proven by the choices one makes. And she could not forgive Sergio for his choice to murder his grandmother and a stream of the helpless on the dubious orders of a faraway commander. Nor could she respect a man who had succumbed to the power of a blonde enchantress.

Giuliana stood looking at him for a long time, then picked up a dirty blanket one of the partisans had left and draped it across Sergio's shoulders. He didn't move from the pitiful mound his body made in the dirt. Then, with one look back at the smoldering town and not a word to what was left of the man she had loved, she left the clearing. Rosetta and the refugees from Pitigliano would be somewhere not far. She would find them, join them. She, in fact, had become one of them.

Yet she felt stronger than she ever had before. Sweaty and dirt-caked from days as a warrior against a treacherous enemy, she now knew that evil resided on both sides of this hellish line. Internal, foreign, familial, and even within one's own heart, battles could be won or lost. And Giuliana felt she had found the tools to engage such a fight. She fingered the shards of her father's tiny ruined vase collected in her pocket and smiled at the other necessity she had discovered—her own intangible, but vital, moral compass. Perhaps her strength could be found even beyond that of the little vase.

And then, just as she turned to leave the clearing, Giuliana felt a most unusual sensation. A fluttering, a kind of tumble in her mid-section. It was as if something had stirred there. She put her hand across her belly and again came the not unpleasant feeling of—something awakening. But she needed to find Rosetta. Giuliana had not eaten in many hours—perhaps—perhaps that was all it was. She would ask Rosetta.

Chapter 45

Boston 1975

She drifted this way and that. Thoughts, like clouds, carrying her between mountains, across open meadows, and then beneath the earth that both boiled like fire and caressed her in air as cool as water. And like thoughts or clouds, time passed, transmuting into other forms, offering indistinct meanings, its trajectory a jagged careen of her past and this present—and only the knowledge of her own death a certainty.

To one day die here or in the country of her birth had been a decision Giuliana had dispassionately made, knowing that either course would be the loss of something she held dear. Yet there was this one thing she had not counted on—though it was the ever-present thing. It was the mysterious, awful, omnipresent evil that had always been near, threatening, growing, receding at times, but returning in one guise or another. Had it followed her here, or simply never left?

She turned restlessly in her bed. Pale, her skin shrunken now, Giuliana felt her nurse, a senior citizen herself, appraise the significance of the movement in the bed, then assured it was but a simple stir, drift back to sleep. For a moment, Giuliana wondered what an observer would see among the light piles of cloth.

Though she looked a generation younger, she felt she was old. She had lived a thousand years, she guessed, each minute now as valuable as gold, each of her memories tied to another one like royal pack animals who carried treasures in orderly succession, only now and then confusing themselves on the trail.

The trail—ah yes—the trail. But which one would she take now? Into which store of memories would she dig? Which one would offer safety from the glances of eyes that bore her ill will? For, in truth, each route of her life had had watchers, eyes that bored or pierced, stares that taunted her even when she slept.

But the trail that called her now was one at the base of Pitigliano, the city of her youth, the one filled with loss, war, and so many deaths. From here in Boston, so far in both distance and time, she could watch the players in her life; watch them make choices that were obviously wrong; watch them succumb to jealousy; watch them give up treasures without price; watch them as heroic or craven actors play across her life's stage. And she had been but another character shuffling back and forth across the boards, weaving hearsay and truth, magic and reality, never sure when to embrace joy or when to flee evil.

And why not watch the play one more time, choosing neither to be heroine nor villain—but rather like the vacant eyes that lined Etruscan tombs, a voyeur from afar.

Chapter 46

Italy September 1944

1944 was already one of the coldest on record. Though it was only fall, the layers of rags most Italians were now wearing did little to keep their scrawny bodies warm. When away from the carefully preserved fire, moving was the only way to keep vulnerable digits from slowly losing their color and becoming numb from the cold. But without proper nutrition, the slightest stir brought pain to every joint and muscle. It was as if even one's blood ran cold.

Though it seemed the war that had enveloped Europe and much of the rest of the world was about to burn itself out, here in Italy, the German presence had become even more tenacious, more vicious. After the Allies' spring landing in Normandy, when so many of the American soldiers had been pulled from Italy's boot-shaped peninsula to fight in France, the Germans seemed to make a point of how tightly they could squeeze what was left of the weary Italians.

It had been four months since the Americans had offered a few sorties and much destruction to Pitigliano. Now, after the debacle of the partisan effort there, Il Buio had shifted his efforts to Orvieto, where he found the volunteers more dependable. But against the ever-more-oppressive German troop presence, guns good for rabbits and a few cylinders of dynamite were no match for an enemy that had felt itself poked in the eye and didn't like it.

"Things will be worse now, I think," said Rosetta to Giuliana who, chap-cheeked, had just ducked through the rough door. The old woman rarely left what appeared to be a tiny campsite built deep inside one of the abandoned tufa caves at the base of Pitigliano. Her face, like that of many Italians huddled for hours a day in cramped quarters near a stoked fire, seemed to be made of charcoal-stained leather, its lines etched deeply with soot. With rheumy, red-rimmed eyes and permanent coughs, clutches of peasants huddled in such ancient rooms. They had largely left the countryside to the remnants of the Italian Fascist Army, which in the last months seemed to have decided that a civil war against rural partisans they called communists might save them from the yet more savage revenge being taken on Italy and Italians by the entrenched Germans. From the trucks rumbling the rutted Tuscan roads now filled with Italian Fascist deserters and prisoners of war bound for camps in Germany, it would seem that the SS were not in a forgiving mood.

Before she began to make some tea, Giuliana pulled one of the ragged scarves from around her neck and wrapped it around the ankles and feet of Rosetta. "Do you feel that warmth? I will make toast from your toes!" she smiled, kissing the top of Rosetta's kerchiefed head. "And then, even though it is cold, maybe you will walk with me a way to meet some new travelers."

Sergio's plundered storage cave was at the base of the hard-scrabble circuit winding its way around the base of the ruined town, and it, like many of the other cavernous "tool-repositories" now lay empty. The years of pilfered antiquities Sergio had cached and treasured were gone. Now, when they ventured from their little cave, Rosetta always took another route, telling Giuliana she couldn't bear to pass Sergio's "museum," seeing that its contents were no doubt now a hidden trove somewhere among the Reich's elite.

Yet, Rosetta hadn't wanted to move back to her isolated farm house. "I want to stay near to the Temple," she had told Giuliana. "The ancient tomb is a sacred place… and there, answers will come when the time is right for them." Surprised at how easily Rosetta had transitioned from rosaries to revering an ancient metal plate, Giuliana too felt safer near to the holy ground of a departed people she had come to feel were friends. It was also conveniently a place she guessed was less likely to be visited by marauding SS cadres whose morality had all but vanished. Many evenings the two women would simply enter the "temple" with no purpose other than to repose among these spirits and put away thoughts of war.

"Or shall I bring our travelers to you?" smiled Giuliana, picking up her conversation. It had been Aldo who had suggested it—"hosting the travelers." Aldo, the dependable partisan from Sovana and his ruddy-faced wife who had scrubbed Giuliana clean in their kitchen were sympathetic "helpers" on the secret highway that was spiriting Jews south and west. From village to village, tufa cavern to cave, newly clean-shaven Jews and their families were hidden and moved, fed and blessed by dozens of quiet Italians who passed them like presents to one another, accepting and relinquishing the precious gifts with taciturn nods of understanding, and not a lira changing hands. In the months since Pitigliano's ghetto had burned, its Jews and dozens of others from the north had made their way along this human chain.

"No, it is too cold for me to leave tonight," said Rosetta. "I will make some porridge for them here. I am sorry to ask you, child, but could you fetch some water at the spring below? I worry it will freeze as it comes out of the earth tonight." But Giuliana wasn't paying attention. Instead, she had stood up, her head touching the stone ceiling, and then suddenly she doubled over, retching violently beside the fire. She held her belly and looked with alarm toward Rosetta for an answer.

The old woman didn't move, but watched carefully until Giuliana had finished the coughing and had wiped her mouth with her scarf. Then Rosetta reached out an arm and said to the whimpering girl, "This is not the first time, is it? For a month or so you have been feeling sick like this?" Giuliana didn't lift her eyes. She guessed what the next question might be. Without the monthly visits to the ritual baths in the ghetto overhead she wasn't sure when her periods had ceased to come, but they had stilled—even as the odd sensations in her belly had slowly begun.

"Yes," she whispered. "It is not the first time."

Rosetta pulled Giuliana to sit beside her on the stone shelf of their earthen home. She wrapped her with her own shawl, joining them in a sisterhood that women had entered for millennia, one made of shame, of fear, of a tragic joy. She was silent for a time, and then, "It will be a child of love," she said softly against Giuliana's cheek. "In the midst of these terrible times, a new hope will be born."

But instead of a breath of calm, Giuliana bent her head to her knees and wept. With shudders and deep sobs, she told Rosetta part of the story—the part in which she believed Sergio had chosen another, her own cousin, Rebekah, and had now left, perhaps to join partisans elsewhere—likely with his new love.

Giuliana would not tell Rosetta the rest of the story—that Sergio had pushed a plunger that would have killed her or that he was not the only man Giuliana had known. For how could she describe the fear that inside her grew not the seed of a man she had loved, but the semen of Simon, an evil her body would now be forced to feed?

As Rosetta softly rocked the orphaned girl she had come to love, her right hand made the sign of the cross over the youthful head, a kind of insurance against the myriad dangers swirling around them, each of which would soon descend on the unborn soul to come. But a new danger had arisen, one the old woman could never have foreseen. And for the life of her, she could not guess how Rebekah, the wily blonde child brought to her by her confounded mother, had found Sergio and perhaps beguiled him. Yet she knew too the power of *il malocchio* and its potential to harm. Rebekah, whether of her own volition or a product of her nature, was a beautiful young *strega* with a selfish streak.

Chapter 47

"You will have to do something to earn your bread," said the old nun. Her face, which may have been gaunt since adolescence, was now a haggard skull framed by a frayed grey wimple. She was a woman as unused to smiling as she was to discussion or nuance. In blacks and whites and with a few immutable laws was how she ran the convent. Cleanliness. Work from sunrise to sunset. Pray when not occupied. Help to the stranger who comes begging at your door. And when a pale young woman came to the convent's gate for the second time, she was not turned away. Nor was she this time to be treated like a guest.

"Where have you been since last you left us… abruptly and without thanks, by the way?" asked the old abbess. She sat rolling strips of cloth into bandages that would be used for some of the dozens of injured Italians brought to the nuns during skirmishes or from the beatings that were arbitrarily administered by the occupying Germans.

Rebekah sat at one end of a long wooden bench, as if waiting for a complimentary bookend to take its place at the other side. The down-like hair that used to float about her shoulders now hung lank and thin, and her delicate features' glow had been replaced by a dry pallor through which the veins showed blue.

"I… I was in the city when the bombs came," she said in a soft voice meant to evoke pity.

"You were in the city? In Pitigliano?" said the abbess. "Nearly one hundred people died that day." She looked at Rebekah. "Were you injured?"

"Not very badly. There were many who were worse… but my back… I just cannot do heavy work for you, nor stand for long. Perhaps I could roll bandages?" Rebekah glanced at the cushion under the abbess and outside the door heard the clank of other nuns scrubbing floors and cleaning beneath kneeling benches. Yes, rolling bandages would be fine. Four months of sleeping in stalls and running from starving dogs and sexually-starved soldiers would make bandage rolling exactly what she wanted to do.

"Can you read?" asked the nun.

"Yes, I can read," said Rebekah.

The old woman was quiet for a while, then, "There was a man brought here, a military man, after the bombing. He was burned very badly, and he has not spoken since he arrived. Though he seems to be asleep, we think that he hears us… that he listens sometimes." The abbess looked up at Rebekah, assessing her from head to foot. "You can be his caretaker. Change his bandages, read to him. As soon as he can be moved, the Germans will take him back. They give us a small stipend to keep him off their hands. They don't want him to die in their custody."

Rebekah nodded. Then the abbess asked her to stand.

"How far are you along?" she asked flatly.

"What do you mean?" stared Rebekah.

"You are with child I will guess. Perhaps you already feel the movements? You are not the first such one with a secret that refuses to be kept." The old woman shoved the rolled bandages into a basket. "Pray God that its father will find his honor and will come to take you both when the time has come." Then the abbess rose with a barely obscured shrug and bid Rebekah follow her. "I will take you to the room of the injured officer. His name is Col…."

But Rebekah didn't catch her words. Instead she found herself picturing "the father" the nun had given the title. Sergio, his black curls, burnished skin, and laughing eyes—the human prize she had extracted from her rival, but the man who now had vanished to the North in shame. And then without wishing it, as if entering from a rear door, another candidate appeared in her mind's eye—the sin, the shadow that she would bar. Yet there he stood. How to know the difference between the two when the child would come? Would she dare kill the seed of one, not knowing if it were pure or already corrupt? And was she not corrupt as well? For a moment Rebekah lost herself wondering if the meld of the evil of her brother and her own would not make for a volition no other could match. In the second before the convent's sick room door opened, Rebekah pictured the eyes of such a child—made of the two of them—wide and streaming raw power. And in that moment, she felt a thrill of pride.

The door to the darkened cell rubbed along the floor as the old nun pushed it gently and pulled Rebekah toward the cot where a form lifted sheets into the shape of an invalid.

"Come here and meet the man you will care for," she said. "His name is Dietrich Hansbach. I don't know what kind of officer… enemy officer he is. A Colonel is his rank. He was brought here by one of the monks who himself was hurt. Ha… ignoramus…. The young cleric tried to pay me with a coin covered in dirt… some ancient currency he must have just dug from his garden." She emitted a sound that might have been a derisive laugh. "So here he is. Read to him. Be careful of him. Try to believe he is God's child…." And as she closed the door, she added, "Another lost soul… just as are you and me and the one you will bear yourself."

December 1944

This would be Giuliana's last group of travelers, she thought. The 10 kilometers from Pitigliano to Sorano, the descent into the valley of the Lente River to ancient Sovana, then the steady climb to San Martino sul Fiora, and another river beyond that crisscrossed the foothills of the Apennine mountains. The journey had become wrenching for her at seven months. Guiding weary Jews from the North of Italy who had escaped the cattle cars' relentless roll to concentration camps scattered from Poland to Germany itself, had left her exhausted and frightened.

So far, winter had been brutally cold, now the recent snows added to the danger. Other guides would take the refugees along the

Roman Via Clodia toward Grossetto and finally to Piombino's port and safety with a smuggled boat ride to the Isle of Elba which had been liberated in the spring by Allied troops. There it was hoped the Jews would find protection. Giuliana sometimes wondered if she should simply continue the journey with them and present herself as one of the endangered Jews. Wasn't she in fact, one? Instead, each time she had returned along the route back to Pitigliano, whimpering with cold, trembling with exhaustion, but determined to care for Rosetta, the old woman who had cared for her. She would have her child born on the soil which she now knew to be her home and remain among those others, those who lived beneath the soil, whose presence had become friends.

***

The convent bells had just finished their last full lament of the day. Evening vespers, the call to put down your work, wash your faces and hands, and join with the other half-frozen religious on your knees in the chapel had just rung. Beneath the vaulted heights that stole any hope of warmth, Rebekah could hear the shuffling feet, most of them wrapped in wool and bound with the string the nuns would use for pole beans in the spring. If there were any bean seeds—if there were a spring.

Though God's presence was supposed to offer solace and hope, it was not unusual to hear weeping at night or find a nun staring out at the stark, frozen landscape, tears running down her cheeks. These women were from all over central Italy, their families in various states of disruption and harm. Yet they had dedicated themselves to this life, where at the moment, prayer seemed no substitute for a gun or the taste of a roasted fish, or the arms of an elderly mother in a village far away.

Such depression might have gripped Rebekah as well, large now with a being who kicked and squirmed and at times seemed to claw with urgency at the prospect of being born. But instead of despair at her circumstances, Rebekah had found herself oddly preoccupied with her role of nursemaid to a deformed and debilitated invalid, an enemy occupier, who could not lift a spoon to his mouth.

"Kommst du her?" The soldier asked if she were on her way. He seemed to know the ritual now—morning removal of his bandages, the gentle washing of his face, limbs and torso, the metallic-smelling smearing of something onto his burns, and then the rebandaging with newly washed linen. It happened three times each day.

He had begun to speak the month before, at first only in German, now with a mixture of Italian and perhaps French. And he always used, *"Per favore"* and *"Bitte," "Grazie,"* and *"Danke."* Rebekah did not dislike him.

"I must take your bandages from your face now, Colonel. They are stuck a bit, so you must be patient." She bent over him, unwinding the yellow-soiled strips, holding his hairless head with one hand as she peeled off the oozing bandage. And as she leaned across him, she became aware of the back of his hand, one of the few pieces of unburned flesh on his body, as it grazed her stomach. Tentatively, he moved his hand across her swollen belly, following its contour, stopping when it might have felt a tiny foot aim for the interruption. He pressed in to feel the tight spring of her abdomen and turned his head as if to see its magical girth.

"Sei incinta?" Rebekah closed her eyes and with a smile to the obvious said, "Yes, I am pregnant." She continued her cleansing, daubing the nun's handmade soap across the forehead and stump of a nose, the scarred lips, and the unseeing eyes. And after smoothing the medicine across the remains of the soldier's face, she wrapped him again in bandages.

"When will you have this child?" asked Dieter Hansbach, again placing his hand on her stomach before she could turn to leave.

"It will be two months more," said Rebekah, wincing at having to speak of the time of dread.

"And its father? Why are you not at home with the man who made this child?" Rebekah had not heard the German speak like this before. The officer had revealed himself to be in command even if bound to his bed.

"He is dead," she said flatly, and turned to go.

"Wait a moment, fraulein. *Kommst her*." Rebekah set the bowl of water down and came beside the Colonel. He reached his hand again for her belly and let it lie there as the life inside turned itself once, then seemed to drift off to sleep.

"When I leave here, you will come with me. You have been good to me. You have kept me from dying. I shall do the same for you and this child." His voice was guttural from disuse, but his hand lingered almost lovingly on Rebekah's belly.

"Do you understand what I am saying? Italy will be no more at the end of this war. There will be famine and desperation throughout the country… if there is a country at all. Germany will have won. Bent, yes, but we will be victors. Your kind spirit should not go without gratitude." He patted her stomach once, then let his hand fall. Exhausted with his effort, he quickly gave in to sleep.

Yet Rebekah had seen that he was growing stronger and that his burns were healing. And she wondered if when the time came, such a new opportunity was not the best offer she would have. Then the irony of it all made her laugh out loud. Here was someone who offered her the gift of freedom from misery, an escape from her past. And she had not even needed to use her powers, nor had they risen up to be used. Indeed, here was a man who would always be immune to *il malocchio*. Here was a man with no eyes to be enchanted.

Chapter 48

February 1945

The baby had been born just as Giuliana had wanted, in the cavernous "temple" that she and Rosetta believed to be a kind of holy place. With folded clothes beneath her and candles that illuminated the radiant walls, Giuliana imagined herself attended by an audience of ancient well-wishers, draped in garlands, with wine held high for toasting. And as the silky little life emerged, she felt the trepidations of its beginnings fade. Rosetta had blessed the child with holy water and a touch to its little hand of the inscribed metallic oval discovered here. With these acts, she invoked not only the Trinity of her youth, but the other gods of this land, those who passed their spiritual torches to one another across the ages. Giuliana didn't know any prayers for the birth of a Jewish child—or even one who was half-Jewish—but as she cradled her swaddled baby, in her parents' name, she offered one she'd made up herself.

March, 1945

"Rosetta!" Giuliana's headscarf was pulled off as she ducked into the crowded lower cave where Rosetta and the baby were surrounded by four forlorn Jews who had been brought there the night before. Giuliana ignored the "travelers" and threw herself beside Rosetta and the month-old infant, pulling out her breast and gathering the tiny child to her.

With a cold kiss to the baby's forehead, she turned her back on the huddle of hungry refugees. "We must move these people now," she whispered to Rosetta urgently. "Germans are everywhere.

Somehow, they have infiltrated or tortured others to know the routes we make. They have followed the paths of these people and have executed their guides. Soon they will be here."

She gazed at her child snuggled against her. "Perhaps the SS were following me. I must get these four away from the caverns… and you must hide this little angel…." Again, she looked at the soft skin of the child at her nipple and listened to the sounds of suckling that were so similar to the lambs she had loved on the farm. She stroked the tiny round head with the dainty pink shells that turned into ears, and felt the joy in knowing that her own body had produced this masterpiece. It would have been impossible, Giuliana reasoned, for a child so perfect to have been created from anything but love. Surely this was Sergio's *capolavoro,* his masterpiece, as well. She let her fingers trace the tiny nose and soft cheeks that grew pink in feeding. This baby was her destiny, she smiled to herself. All of the questions she had had about how to grow up, how to proceed in life without a parent's protection—had dissolved with this miracle of creation. There was hope for a future from the current madness in the very fragrance of this child.

"Please take care of this precious bundle," she said to Rosetta, gently lifting the baby from her breast. She kissed its wet lips, and whispered, "I will be back. I will always come back for you."

And with that, Giuliana gathered the cluster of Jews and their packs of rags and herded them out of the cave.

***

It hadn't taken long.

Eleven hours later, standing in the cold of a railway terminal in Grosseto, Giuliana, the Jews in her care, dozens of sympathetic Italians and other fleeing refugees were on their way to Trieste and the storied Risiera di San Sabba, a rice mill turned concentration camp the Germans used to exterminate Italians. Intercepted along a tortuous rocky path, the elderly refugees had been easy prey for the SS bullies, who forced the Jews like animals into trucks, administering indiscriminate blows with clubs or whips where they could. There was nothing Giuliana had been able to do—and the bloody cut along her jaw was the proof.

In one way or another, each of these Italians, Jews, or other "undesirables" had crossed a German by an act of aggression, of sabotage, the stealing of a morsel of food, a random glance, or the simple act of wishing to live. Now upright citizens and thieves alike would lose their humanity as numbers replaced names and a bullet to the head would serve as a gravestone.

On the teeming platform where signs heralded trains heading to Rome and Naples, Germans paraded back and forth in front of a dozen slump-shouldered groups, yelling orders and seeming to delight in the obscenity of their own voices. Frequently, a pack of shuffling prisoners would be herded like sheep from one end of the tramway to the other, opportunities for rifle butts to be shoved into ribs and slow women to be knocked to the ground. There was noise everywhere, and smoke and rumbling tracks and engines that thundered, and confusion and disbelief.

Giuliana, her dress wet with milk that had yet to be drunk, stood protectively before a crowd of Jews who seemed unable to lift their eyes from the fetid platform. Occasionally, an official would appear from a large car or a military vehicle, and a way would open in the crowd accompanied by heels slamming together and straight arms shooting wickedly skyward. Amidst the noise and churning chaos, she searched for someone in authority. Someone who could give orders to the strutting SS troops that deals could be made—favors done—if only these few souls could be returned.

Then suddenly, the crowd seemed to part and a car drove nearly onto the platform. It was from the grand, grey-polished touring car that a military officer slowly emerged. He was clearly a dignitary requiring special attention. He wore dark glasses and moved with such deliberation that it could be guessed he was in pain. He wore a uniform that appeared too large for him but was covered with dozens of medals and with shining epaulettes. The officer gingerly moved with his cane to a wheelchair that had been pulled from the back of the sedan. He and the entourage of assistants seemed readying themselves to board a special train. And then from inside the car, another figure emerged.

As Giuliana watched from the grey and brown mound of huddled Jews on their way to extermination, a beautiful, blonde woman stepped from the car onto the running board. Rebekah's hair floated about her shoulders and above her slim waist she seemed fuller busted than Giuliana had remembered—but no less beautiful. No less in control.

It had been almost a year since she had seen her cousin on the hill overlooking Pitigliano when Rebekah had said they may not meet again. And now it was no doubt true. Somehow it always seemed that Rebekah found the way of winning—parents who lived, the love of Sergio, survival in a world that had erupted in flames. And now, in a clean dress and with rosy cheeks, she had again floated free of the brutal misery and death that awaited her cousin.

No, thought Giuliana, just as Rebekah had said, she would not again see this kin of her childhood, this enigma—nor Rosetta—nor Sergio or Simon— nor the one thing that meant her life had had value, the tiny baby alone in a cave.

So quickly it had all passed. Her life with her father, her love of a man, her understanding of her own strength. And now clearly, she saw how paths perversely divide. How in the end, it was evil that triumphed and the powers of good that fell impotent.

And try as she may to fix Rebekah with a gaze that would let her know the universe might hold other powers of righteousness—Giuliana's eyes were simply too filled with tears to try.

Chapter 49

Late May 1945

"No, no… Torni tra una settimana.... Torni tra due! Per adesso, dacci solo cibo e dei vestiti. Dacci latte per i bambini. Loro sono solo piccoli. Abbiamo bisogno di tempo prepararli. Ti ringraziamo... solo un po' di tempo in piu."

"No, no… You come back in a week. Come in two! For now, give us only food and some clothing. Give us milk for the children. They are only little. We need time to prepare them. We thank you…. We thank you… only a little time more."

The abbess of the convent was surrounded by men and a few women in khaki fatigues. Unlike the others, the Italian Fascists, the Germans, the grubby partisans, these people did not carry guns. But they spoke urgently to each other, writing things down, preemptively opening doors, going up and down halls, surveying the convent with a kindly intrusion which was disorienting for the old nun.

For her and for the rest of Italy, the war had officially ended. In early May, the Germans had retreated or been swept up as prisoners from the farmlands and cities of Toscana. And on their heels had come the jockeying for leadership, the discredited public announcements, the rumors and confusion that was spreading across Italy's midlands. Replacing the national rebellion against the German occupation which had united all Italians, now villagers saw each other as rivals for handouts from the Allied liberators or as competitors for the temporary jobs they offered. But mostly for food. And there was so little.

As she walked among the milling group of military personnel, the abbess was followed by another group—small children of two and three years whose spit and tear-stained faces were blotted against her habit. There were others, older ones, brought here by widows who could only feed the smaller mouths, and the ones who stood alone in corners, runaways from the famine that had plagued the winter and the misery of the hovels they'd called home.

The thrifty nuns had canned and smoked and salted food for their own sustenance for years. They had shared their meager storage with the children brought to them, but the last months of the war, and strangely, even more so with its end, had brought even the convent to desperation. And though it all seemed to be coming too soon, now, these highly organized caravans of fast-speaking foreigners—Americans, the nun thought—were here offering a solution, a Christian hand of help.

An Italian translator also wearing the khaki uniform of authority came into her office with a large notebook in her hands. Asking the abbess to sit down across from a man in his forties who had already made himself comfortable in her office, the woman began to ask questions and write their answers in her book.

"How many children do you have now at the convent? And their ages…" she asked. The abbess slowly pulled her own notebook from her desk and examined the list. Though these people seemed benign, everything was happening so fast. The years of occupation had taught her to be cautious of people in drab uniforms and with notebooks.

From the convent's older pages where names were entered once or twice a year to the recent entries when it was noted that three or four children had been deposited with the nuns each week, she began to name the child, give the age, and the length of time he or she had spent at what had become the region's de facto orphanage. Looking up at last, after the lines of names had blurred, her eyes were aching and her old heart was feeling broken, she said, "We have a total of 83 children who range in age from 17 years to 8 months."

The translator looked up too. Though neither of them had ever given birth, their eyes met as each of them tried to force down the maternal feelings that united them in sorrow for the frightened, hungry children and the parents who had lost the only things they could have truly called their own.

The woman in the khaki uniform took a breath, closed her eyes, and resumed the official tone she had managed earlier. "The Red Cross Field Officer for Central Italy in collaboration with the United States' Fifth Army Division has directed me to tell you that we can evacuate 50 of the children you are caring for here. The children, in a humanitarian gesture, will be evacuated to the United States where, given that they have no responsible relatives here in Italy, they will be placed for adoption with couples and families who will be able to give them proper care." She turned and looked through the open door at the tumble of dirty children who had accumulated around the door—scratching at the ubiquitous lice, sucking a finger or two for comfort, or rocking a child smaller than themselves. Then she closed her eyes and silently wept.

The abbess nodded her head. "Give me food for them first and two days to make them ready," she said. In fact, she would need two days to say goodbye to children she had come to love and to grapple with the selections that should only be made by God.

And then the man who had remained quiet stood up. "Sister, may I ask a question privately?" he said in Italian. The translator looked up surprised, then in some confusion, excused herself and left the room.

"My name is Major Charles Burke. I work with the Red Cross in this… this difficult job of bringing assistance to those impacted by war. I wish that we could take all of the children. I am not without sympathy… nor gratitude for what you have done. You have made life possible for so many children here. I even saw that you have tiny babies… babies without mothers at that age. I marvel that they have survived."

He stopped speaking and the abbess realized he was waiting for some kind of explanation. "The two babies here come from different circumstances, if I can be frank. The one was left here by a woman we had sheltered, but who left us… and has, I am afraid, retreated with a member of the German occupiers when they left. The other one was brought to us by a grandmother whose granddaughter was arrested as she tried to help fleeing Jews. She was apparently sent to a camp somewhere to the north… the one in which the Germans exterminated Italians on their own soil." The abbess looked the man fully in the face, assessing how much he wanted to know and why. "Another woman here had a newborn and she has suckled the two infants the last months."

The man stood slightly stooped, his head bowed and rocking slowly back and forth. Then he took a breath and began to blink his eyes in the way people do when they have made a decision. "I once had two babies too," he said, raising his eyes to the abbess. "My wife and I had two little twins… beautiful, beautiful twins. But, a house fire…." He stopped, overcome for a moment. "They were just six months old, about the age of these two little babies here… these beautiful babies here."

Then he came around the abbess' desk and knelt down beside her. "Will you give me your blessing, Sister? A blessing. And will you put those two children on the list for adoption?"

June 1945

Scraping his way along the tarmac with a wooden cane, a blonde, but otherwise nondescript man in a black cassock, shuffled his way forward behind the other passengers preparing to board an American transport plane. Around his neck hung a small placard bearing a tiny Stars and Stripes emblem and on it was written:

Religious Evacuees to United States of America Passenger Manifest:

Name: Brother Paolo Ricci
Age: 24
Religion: Catholic
Rationale for evacuation: Italian non-combatant tortured by German occupiers.
Sponsor: Diocese of Boston, Massachusetts

The only thing that might have seemed unusual about the slightly haggard young cleric was that in spite of his disability, he carried a valise that appeared inordinately heavy. Heavy enough to contain rocks, another evacuee quipped. Or urns. Or vases. Or delicate statues made of bronze.

Chapter 50

Boston, October 1975

The taxi finally crept into line behind the others belching exhaust beneath the portico of Logan's International Terminal. Contending with ripped-apart streets, detours, delivery people who jammed the streets, and most of Boston's commuters seemingly primed and ready for a good fist fight had left Carlo too in a black and panicked mood.

"We should have left an hour earlier!" he fumed to Sylvie. "Suddenly, you're into long good-byes. We should have checked-in last night!" Carlo began fumbling with the door handle while simultaneously throwing some too large bills at the cabbie. "Get your suitcase! We're going to have to run if we want to be on the plane to Rome!"

His sister turned a languid look at the fulminating Carlo, then seeped out of the car and took her valise. "We'll make it," she said with a sigh. "There are always ways...."

Carlo was already striding through the door of the terminal with his own luggage and another valise stuffed with his aunt's nightgown, slippers, hairbrush, including a separate cloth pouch holding what he guessed were favorite trinkets—little touchstone souvenirs she had carried for good luck. Maybe one of them would be the "magic" conduit the old priest said certain village women or superstitious clerics could use to lift the "curse" on the old woman. Carlo was beyond skeptical of the whole thing—the absurdity of evil eyes, lucky pottery, Italian voodoo chants that supposedly could lift illness from an ailing senior across an ocean. He felt deeply foolish, embarrassed at his own transatlantic leap of belief.

And yet—and yet—a dying old woman lay in his house with only one proffered explanation as to why.

The crowds were churning along the concourse of Terminal E. Like a luggage-dragging city fleeing from gate to gate, hopeful passengers dodged in and out and between one another as if their ticket counter target would provide protection from the hounding hordes behind. Carlo led the way, a broken-field runner on a mission.

Sylvie found herself so distracted by the newly installed shops and food vendors, the art exhibits and posters advertising everything and anything Boston had to offer that she was barely keeping her galloping brother in sight. But while she was jostled from time to time by a suitcase or an arrogant shoulder, she was aware of another physical intrusion. The closer they came to the International Departure gate, the stronger the odd sensation in her hands became. Something almost electric. Something like the hum a transformer made, but now its current seemed to run through her whole body.

Carlo had finally come to a stop. He was beaded with sweat, and the normally fastidious broker wore wrinkles across his forehead that matched those of his rumpled clothes. "Ok, ok, they're getting ready to board now," he panted. "All they have to do is disembark the arriving Italians and let us get on." He fumbled in his pockets and began arranging the tickets to Rome and the next legs to Florence and by car, to Pitigliano.

"I'm going to sit down 'till then," said Sylvie. No seats were available but she found a pillar to slump against on a ledge beside a broad window. She noticed the vague electric tingle had revved up a notch or two as she gazed out at the huge silver plane parked next to her vantage point. She could even see the Italian passengers inching down the inside aisles of the jet—actually follow a disembarking individual from one round porthole to the next. And then one of them caught her eye.

The woman was impossible to miss, even from Sylvie's distant position. As passengers slowed to halts near each tiny window, the woman would touch her hair or readjust a fur that was draped across her shoulders. What must have been diamonds sparkled from her ears. And though older, she was beautiful. Sylvie saw more than one man wait to enter the file, giving his place to this elegant woman who seemed too good for the likes of Boston, Sylvie thought. Yes, perhaps a Roman film star or the mistress of a head of state. Soon this figure would be coming down the narrow hall and into the ticket area, and Sylvie didn't want to miss her entrance.

Yet as she tried to rise, she realized the "current" she had felt earlier had begun to affect her lower limbs. With each step, an unpleasant sizzle traveled along her ankles and into her thighs. As she made her way through the crowd, Carlo suddenly seemed very far away. And then, as she tried to focus what was becoming a kind of tunnel vision, she realized that the Italian passengers had already stepped from the plane and that the sophisticated goddess she'd been hoping to glimpse was standing directly in front of Carlo and that together, they were involved in a conversation.

Sylvie began to push her way through the waiting passengers. How would Carlo know such a woman? Why would she deign to speak to any of the short-tempered passengers, much less to Carlo? It was only when Sylvie was feet away that the woman shifted her gaze. Sylvie thought she saw her brother visibly slump, as if a plug had been pulled. And then the woman's ice-blue eyes found Sylvie.

Immediately, she could feel the vibrating hum surge. Now the current came in pulsing roars that forced her to gasp for breath. The woman didn't change her regard, but said to Sylvie in an accented voice that was both quiet and clear, "You look familiar. Have we once known each other?"

Then receiving no response, the woman lifted her chin, turned away as if her momentary pause had been an ill-thought waste of time, and proceeded down the concourse as the crowds parted before her.

Sylvie stared after her, but already she'd begun to feel her breath come more easily. "Who was that, Carlo? She stopped to talk to you. Why? How do you know a woman like that?"

Carlo put his hand to his head. He was red with a blush he had not worn since grade school. With a sigh of recovery, he said, "I don't know her. She was just walking by, coming off the plane, when she turned, looked at me hard, then she said, "I have something I must ask you. Maybe you will know the answer." Carlo began to laugh.

"What did she ask you? And why you?"

"She asked me if I knew anything about Etruscan art. She said something about an exhibition here. And a lecture. Said she had to be there."

"But why would she choose you to ask, Carlo?" Sylvie asked. "You don't look like an archaeologist…." Then she stopped and turned to stare at Carlo. "But there is an exhibit here. The poster…. We passed it in the main concourse. At the university. About Etruscan art. Yes, and a lecture… by, wait… by a Professor Sergio somebody."

Carlo stood staring at his sister. The line had begun to move. Carlo let them pass, seeming to silently ignore their *sotto voce* curses. "I want to go to the lecture," said Sylvie flatly. She looked him full in the face, a peer, not an adversary. The electrical "transmissions" along her arms and legs had stopped and she felt alert and sure. "I don't want to go to Italy right now," she said with an assurance that was not confrontational, but which seemed confident of its rightness. "I want to go… to the lecture." And then even Sylvie laughed out loud. It all seemed absurd. She had no idea why, but there was no question where she belonged.

Carlo had joined in with a head-wagging chuckle, and then a full-out laugh. The tickets would need to be turned in. Luggage retrieved if they could. But in some way he didn't understand, he knew Sylvie was right. "Well… all right. Turn these tickets in then… for another trip… to Florida? Maybe take Zia too, and that will get her well." He stared at his sister with a goofy smile, barely believing what he was saying.

It wasn't until a quick trip to the men's room before the taxi home, that Carlo had opened his aunt's small valise to see if he'd left some alarm clock running, or a battery had gotten turned on. The thing had been vibrating or humming since he was in line to embark. Now, pushing aside the thick cotton gown and worn slippers, he saw the faded fabric of the souvenir pouch, so old, it seemed covered with dust. From within, it quietly emitted a low frequency he couldn't identify. And it glowed. Odd for a flashlight, thought Carlo. Then he pulled apart the little draw-string opening, reached his hand inside and pulling it out, found himself staring at a luminous artifact lying in his palm—a tiny vase, glued together from fragments, that appeared to be trembling. Snickering at the things an old woman would keep, Carlo shoved the cheap, probably Hong Kong-made pseudo-urn toy back into the pouch, and decided he and Sylvie could verifiably use a drink.

Chapter 51

"I don't remember much," said Carlo taking a deep swallow from the glass of scotch. Sylvie sat beside him in the chilly airport bar, both justifying the hard liquor after the bureaucracy of cancelling their flights to Rome.

"Remember, I was only five or six." He glanced up, surprised she was still listening. A conversation like this with his sister was a rarity, even an aberration in the tense relationship that had evolved between the two of them through the years. In so many ways, she didn't feel like a sister at all.

"You were lucky. Italy in the summers..." she said, dragging at a cigarette, staring at it, then stubbing it out next to the others in the tray. "I guess I was still with Aunt... what was her name? The one in Bunker Hill who took in boarders. The one whose husband would backhand her on Saturday nights. I stayed there 'till I was ten, then added a few other 'mothers' or 'aunts' after that...." Sylvie moved a little phalanx of cocktail peanuts into a flank position on the Formica. "Why did your fosters send you to Italy?" she asked. "They must have been rich, I guess."

Carlo didn't smoke, but reached over and pulled one from her pack, and lighting it, said, "Everything is confused now in my mind.... The Burkes, who adopted us from Italy, had already died, three or four years after we came. The car crash... it messed everything up. I was sent to Mrs. Burke's mother and you went to Mr. Burke's sister. It was whoever was willing to take on a toddler who wasn't their own. Luck of the draw. A judge's call." Carlo looked over at Sylvie who was staring at him with something he rarely saw, a look of sadness. And he said what was true, "I missed you."

For the first time since childhood, they gently shoved at each other's shoulders, bashfully staring at their hands, and were glad they were in the same room.

"I don't remember too much about those trips to Italy," said Carlo. "Grandmother Burke had somehow contacted the orphanage and gotten the name of the woman who had brought us there. I guess she was willing for me to visit. I called her Nonna, grandmother. Rosa… Rosina, maybe? Anyway, old Mrs. Burke always said it was important to smell your roots. So, for about three years I went there in the summers, until Mrs. Burke died. Then, like you, I began the round of foster homes… miserable, good, shitty… nothing that felt the way it should."

"What was it like in Italy," asked Sylvie. Then quietly, "I wish I could have gone too."

"From what I can remember, there were women everywhere in that tiny house," laughed Carlo. "Nonna… but a couple of aunties too. There was Zia Giuliana and another woman, older, Zia Tati, I think, who lived there. And always women who came to talk with Nonna… Rosetta, that was it. And Giuliana. Those women were like, like pilgrims or something, always saying rosaries and chanting in the back room. I never knew why they were there."

Then he turned to her. "It's kind of a miracle that Aunt Giuliana contacted us. I would have forgotten her name if she hadn't gotten that letter through. I still don't understand why she thought it was so important to come. She was a peripheral figure in the house… always out somewhere, coming back dirty… like she'd been digging in dirt."

"I'm glad she did, Carlo," said Sylvie. "I like her. She's no longer young and she is very sick, but I feel something. I can't explain it to you. It's as if I have known her. Even when I sit in her room and she's sleeping. I think she wants to tell me something."

As they rose, Carlo put his arm around this girl whom he barely knew though they had shared a house for the last five years. "Let's go back there then… see if Zia Giuliana has something up her

Italian sleeve. And let's pray that I can find another priest who can use some of her night clothes or souvenirs to turn the tide."

Sylvie smiled at him. "And while we're at it, let me make a reservation for that lecture. Maybe we can see the mysterious, fancy lady who singled you out of the crowd."

Chapter 52

"Who is it?! Stay where you are! The police have already been called!" The on-duty nurse was a tough Irishwoman who seemed used to break-ins and could handle things even if the police never showed up.

"It's us, Helen!" yelled Carlo up the stairs. "Missed our plane to Rome!" He pocketed his key and jerked the luggage into the downstairs hall. Sylvie preferred to bounce hers up the steps and onto the stoop where she sat on the valise for a welcome-home smoke.

"Ah, missed it, did you? Maybe just as well. Those things crash all the time. You might a' missed your own death." The nurse came down the steps still looking around as if to make sure Carlo wasn't an imposter.

"How is my aunt?" he said, ignoring the macabre suggestion offered by Helen, who, he guessed, had chosen her profession to coincide with a certain preoccupation with extinctions. Carlo picked up the pile of mail that had been delivered that morning, mostly to sidetrack any further discussion about crashing planes, but noting an opened yellow telegram lying on top. He would check on his aunt for himself.

"Well, you are a jammy person, I would say." Helen's brogue was salted with Irish slang that Carlo mostly passed on. To ask for interpretations meant an extended conversation.

"You are one lucky man, I do believe," she translated, coming alongside him and jabbing her finger at the mail. "I took the liberty of opening… not your mail… mind you, but that telegram. In my experience they are always bad news, and it's no help to keep yourself blind. I needed to know what it contained to tell you when you called, don't you see?"

Carlo looked at her from the corner of his eye with exasperation. "You should not have opened that, Helen."

"Wait till you know what it says, and you could already have booked your flight back home," she retorted. Then she continued without looking at him, "The woman… a Rosetta somebody… the one you was going to visit to get help with the lady upstairs, is dead. Died suddenly it says. But says she's still going to get her award or something."

Carlo turned to her and said, "Go back upstairs to my aunt. That is your place and that is where you should stay." Sylvie had come in to hear the last part of the conversation and he nodded to her to come into the sitting room to read the telegram.

His hands were trembling slightly as he spread out the paper.

We regret to inform you that Rosetta Portini died yesterday at her home outside the town of Pitigliano. Stop.
We understand that she was preparing to welcome you to her home. Stop.
Please inform her granddaughter, Giuliana Ferraro. Stop.
The Ministry indicates that the ceremony honoring them for their achievements will continue in Rome January 30th with Signora Ferraro and, posthumously, Signora Portini. Stop.

"I am thoroughly confused," said Sylvie. "So, the woman you visited as a child, the one you thought knew the old ways, the old superstitions, and with a piece of clothing could lift a curse… is dead! We would have traveled all the way there, only to have found she had died?" As if echoing Helen, Sylvie's usual sarcasm had blossomed. The underlying effect was that people would do anything, even die, just to inconvenience her. Yet she didn't leave the room. She had become interested, seemingly invested in the old woman upstairs, and for the first time Carlo could remember, she apologized.

"I'm sorry. She was our grandmother. I am sorry. She sounded like she was a lovely old woman. But I don't understand any of this.

I had the impression these were peasant women, Carlo. Now it says they're being honored for something in a ceremony in Rome?"

"They were peasants," he said. "Living in a tiny house on a scrap of land. But I don't know everything, I guess. What the hell, I was a tiny boy. Maybe land has become valuable, maybe they're big-time developers? All I remember is from a quarter century ago. Now one is dead and the other…." Carlo looked up, then said, "We need to be upstairs."

First Carlo, then Sylvie entered the room. The late afternoon had turned the narrow space to grey, as if a film lay across the bed and the heavy furniture, purging its color, robbing those inside of life.

Carlo could make out Helen sitting in a chair against the wall, her arms folded like a pouting teen. On the bed, the outline of a woman was discernible beneath a light sheet. And against the other wall, Carlo caught the shape of two unfamiliar forms—a pair of men's shoes at the end of two legs of trousers. Involuntarily, he jumped back and reached for the light switch.

"I wouldn't do that. It will disturb the patient," came a thick male voice. But Carlo switched it on anyway. Father Paolo slowly rose and lowered his lids against the glare.

"What the hell are you doing here?" said Carlo, nearly coming at him. He looked from the priest to Helen, who was on her feet now as well. "Who told you you could admit anyone to my home… especially one who was supposed to be halfway dead?"

Helen was angry. "You can't talk to a man of God that way, Mr. Carlo. I don't care who's payin' me fee, you can stick it up your ass. Besides, you never told me the Church and its Holy Ministries is off limits in this here house." She was standing protectively beside the woman in the bed. Then the priest, apparently miraculously recovered from the sudden heart ailment he had suffered, moved to the other side of Giuliana—no longer the avuncular "amico" of his first visit with Carlo.

"This house is not a safe place, young man. I can attest to that by what happened to your aunt… and what happened to me." He let his glance drift to Sylvie. "There is an evil here which will soon be unleashed. Your aunt is in grave danger." Here, he paused and darted a look toward Helen. "Without an item that will conduct and contain this calamity, no exorcism can be counted on now. Have you, by chance, found such an item… of the kind I mentioned before?"

"Get out of this house… this "contaminated" house, Father. Aren't you afraid you'll catch something again?" Carlo was as angry as he had ever been. "And no, I have no trinkets for you to dangle over somebody's head, then probably pocket and sell. I don't know what your game is, but you'll play it away from here!"

And then a slight sound and a movement near the door distracted each of them. Sylvie stood near the entrance with her eyes closed, but her arms open, palms facing upward. One hand seemed to reach toward the woman in the bed, the other toward the small rocking chair near the door that rhythmically, was beginning to move back and forth.

Helen frantically crossed herself, howling, "Holy Mary, Mother of God…." And Paolo grasped at the bed, looking as if he might fall.

The only figure in the room who remained peaceful was the old woman, who, if anyone could have seen, had once again lifted a long, tapered finger in the direction of the chair.

Carlo glanced at his sister, standing strangely quiet beside the fragile piece of furniture in its violent arc, then he grabbed Helen's arm and shoved her toward the door. Paolo too, now backed his way past Carlo. With the crucifix from around his neck pointed at Sylvie, the priest mouthed what might have been prayers, or thought Carlo—blasphemous curses he used to frighten demons or parishioners not bending to coercion.

But as the cleric came even with the girl, suddenly, the frantic sweep of the chair ceased. Paolo seemed unable to move and the chair slowly creaked to a stop before him. Sylvie dropped her hands and turned to stare directly into Paolo's face. It was as if any volition had been swept away, and like a specimen with a pin through its chest, he was held for examination. Only when Sylvie turned her head, did Paolo, with the crucifix still clutched in his fingers, appear released to react. With a gasp of pain, he covered his eyes and lurched toward the door. Then not realizing that the little chair was in his path, he crashed over its wooden runners and onto the floor of the hall. Humiliation and Italian fury could be heard down the stairs and even after the front door was slammed. Carlo guessed the dismissed Helen would somewhere be offering a shot of eucharistic Jameson to ease his pain.

Chapter 53

Carlo assured himself that his aunt was none the worse from the visit of the priest whom he himself had once called for help, nor from the ministrations of the nosey Irish nurse. As far as he could guess, the priest's mission to his aunt's sick bed had something to do with little tchotchkes the cleric thought she kept somewhere. If he'd seen the patched souvenir vase inside the little pouch, as Carlo had, he was sure there'd have been disappointment.

His head throbbing, Carlo had left Sylvie with his aunt, the two of them in the darkened room, holding hands in some kind of growing devotion he couldn't figure out. For the moment, he'd decided to put off a discussion about what the hell had just happened. Between his aunt, the priest, and now magically bouncing chairs, he wondered if he were losing his mind.

Carlo unpacked just the necessities, left the rest of the luggage strewn at the foot of the stairs and with a stack of mail with which to reground himself, though it was only late afternoon, he headed up to bed. In fact, he was back where he'd started with the dilemma of his aunt's sickness. But what he had seen in the room where a chair seemed to rock on command suggested the terrain had changed. For now, though he and Sylvie had passed one another in the hall, the phenomenon that seemed worthy of a bad movie had left him incapable of deciding if any explanation would add up.

In the haven of his bedroom, Carlo felt too tired to even put on his pajamas. He poured himself a glass of wine, then let himself down into a new Eames chair he'd bought as an antidote to the rest of the furniture in the house. It felt hard and cold and he wished for one of the overstuffed 1930s armchairs downstairs. But the white leather would do while he glanced at the mail and rolled the slightly sour Chianti around in his mouth, his bed and oblivion calling to him steps away.

Amazed at how many grocery coupons could be stuffed into one envelope; how attorneys lurked in the mail hoping for an injury they could blame on someone else; and how just when you thought all the bills were paid, the insurance and tax assessment chits arrived, he pulled another more interesting envelope from the pile.

It was of thick, vellum paper, one not addressed to him, but "in care" of him to "Signora Ferraro." And it was bizarrely sent from the Ministry of Culture in Rome. Carlo could feel his wave of sleepiness dissipate as he unabashedly slit open the envelope and stared at the seals beside the letter's signatures. With wide-eyed curiosity, he only hoped he could parse out its Italian-written content.

Signora Giuliana Ferrero e Signora Rosetta Portini,

Anticipiamo il vostro arrivo in Roma per la cerimonia per onorare la creazione del vostro museo in Pitigliano. Anche noi vi onoriamo per il vostro dono sorprendente ala Repubblica d'Italia, "Il Fegato di Pitigliano."

I vostri contributi archeologichi ala paese sono immensi.

E' qui confermato che riceverete L'Ordire al Merito della Repubblica nel Collegio Romano Palace, gennaio 15, 1976

Con gratitudine del intero paese,

Federico Batelli, Ministerio di Cultura
Cardinale Giancarlo Franci
Professore Anzio Attasi, Universita' di Roma

Carlo was wide awake now. There were a few words he didn't understand, but most of it, if he read out loud, was clear. Nothing about this letter fit the images he had of the peasant women on the little farm of his youth. The letter was from the Ministry of Culture in Rome, for god's sake. Zia Giuliana and his grandmother, Rosetta, were said to have started a museum! They seemed to have become archaeologists? He read the letter again. They had made a gift to the country of something—a "*fegato,*" that he would have to look up. And now they were receiving some amazing Order of Merit presented by Cardinals and Professors and Ministers in Rome. Why hadn't he known something like this about these women? As far as he knew, neither of them had even gone to school. Then remembering the telegram, he realized that only one woman remained—the one upstairs, and her future was far from certain. Carlo was struck with a deep sadness that in the years he and his sister had bounced from foster homes to their own preoccupations with trying to grow up, they had missed out on lives that held wonderful secrets. Remembering for a moment, the moving chair, he amended his thought to simply, "secrets," wonderful, and perhaps otherwise.

Carlo shifted himself from the chair to the bed and pulled an old quilt around his neck. He would try to contact the Ministry tomorrow to appraise them of the changes in the health of his aunt and grandmother; someone must have told them his aunt would be visiting in the States. He wanted to find out more about this honor, this museum, their gift. But for now, all he heard was the faraway chime of a church bell, a signal to his brain that this day was at last over, and that he could give in to sleep. He really had no choice.

***

Hours had passed and night had quieted the stores and traffic of the North End. A few deep-throated bells again pealed the hour, a carryover from the churches across Europe that would give a quiet chirp in the middle of the night. The mostly Italian neighborhood found it comforting—as apparently did the old woman lying in the bed in Carlo's house. As the bell rang twice in the darkened room next to where he slept, Giuliana slowly turned her head and opened her eyes, smiling when she saw that it was the young woman who sat beside her, and touched when she realized the girl held her own wrinkled hand in hers.

"*Dormi*?" she asked, first in Italian, then "Are you sleeping?" With a tiny jerk, Sylvie's head quickly rose and she leaned in to the woman. "No… no, I wasn't asleep. It was a long day. But I see you aren't asleep now either."

Giuliana let her eyes linger on the grown-up girl, in whose face she thought she saw the vestiges of early youth, perhaps the contour of the child's face, a nose that had not so long ago been turned up and pink. In her mind, she removed years and inches, imagining Sylvie as a sprite who skipped and stammered, who once suckled and cried, and who had been held, she hoped by someone who loved her.

"I would like to tell you some things," said Giuliana, letting her own thin fingers explore the swells and crevices of Sylvie's hand. "Do you want to sleep, or have you a moment to listen? A life goes by so quickly," she whispered. "Like pages that are read and not remembered—only a chapter or a character here or there to recall." She closed her eyes and when she opened them, they searched the ceiling as if trying to organize a picture book whose captions she would soon recall. "I would like to tell you about how I lost my baby," she said, "… and yet have watched her ever since."

March 1945

Giuliana didn't know how long she had been on the train. Stinking with sweat and fear and people who had defecated on themselves and urinated where they stood, the darkness had hidden some of the humiliation, but the feeling of suffocation in the putrid air was only worsened by the dark.

It had taken a day and half a night for the decrepit line of cattle cars to make its way from Grosseto in Italy's heart, north to Trieste. Stopping along the way for more prisoners to be shoved into the gasping, heaving stalks of humanity already in a car, the trip had accumulated Slovaks and Czechs, Jews, and Italian partisans who were now simply expendable fodder, walking repositories of the gold and silver the SS would soon pry from their bodies.

When Giuliana and the others had finally been spilled from the train, it was dark and along the northern Italian coast, freezing with wind-blown rain. Yet, the SS troops were energized. Like spoiled children used to getting daily gifts, they pushed and shoved, bullied and cursed the "presents" the train had brought them. As if selecting the wanted versus unwanted bounty, the prisoners were herded from an open yard either to the right or left of a massive brick structure that with its thrusting tower looked like a giant's chimney. None of the prisoners knew then that the "smoke stack" of Risiera di San Sabba, a late 19th century former mill, was being used for that very function—a chimney up which went the smoky fragments of the cremated prisoners below.

Giuliana was not forced left into the holding cells of those who would be exterminated within the next few hours or days. Instead, along with others who seemed healthy or were wearing clothes that suggested some wealth, she was prodded into the central holding space behind the great tower, behind the crematorium that was kept alight day and night.

The sounds were overwhelming. Crying and shouting, the unloading vans, the boxcars that lumbered on aching wheels throughout the night, and the low thunder of heated air as it vibrated inside the tower. Only once did she look up through the smoke and the hands thrust heavenward and the muzzles of rifles and her own sodden hair toward a sky where raindrops were colored fuchsia, and the plumes of roiling smoke made her think not of death, but for a moment, of the sea at sunset. And of friends who might be dancing in a festive place, a tomb beneath the earth... and of her child with its rosebud lips. And Giuliana in that moment believed she would survive.

She was taken first to one of the cells, small rooms that once held rice—no bigger than a cow stall and without a window or a shaft for air. For a month her days were spent in the yard pulling to the crematorium people who had been either shot or bludgeoned to death. Nights she curled in the corners of the tiny cell with neither blanket nor padding, with only the bony shoulders of another prisoner upon which to lay her head. She had at first tried counting the people whose ankles she held as she bumped their bodies across the graveled yard, but she stopped counting at three hundred. Like her, they already had numbers, they didn't need one of hers.

In the prison, it had become impossible to know how things were on the outside—how the war was going—if the Americans and British and the Canadians and others who had promised they could win, were in fact besting the Germans. Here, time mattered little, and yet it was everything. So many could die in so short a time.

But little things seemed to suggest that changes were occurring. Slowly, after months, Giuliana noted that the guards seemed particularly on edge. She had seen them eating prisoners' rations as if their own were growing scarce. The Italians passed the nugget of information among themselves. It gave them hope. But other things frightened them more. Increasingly, like insolent bullies trying to outdo each other with cruel bravado, prisoners were subjected to humiliations even on their way to an execution minutes away. Any inhibitions about taking the lowest ground had given way; beatings and overt torture had increased. But occasionally, even a satan could not perceive the horror.

In her final month at the Risiera, a guard had come into Giuliana's cell. It was the middle of the night and his flashlight had had to search back and forth among the limbs and thin faces of those who now slept there. Pulled roughly from the scramble of bones and flesh, Giuliana was taken to the third floor of the building—a place from which female prisoners often didn't return—and when they did, their eyes were empty. They might have been dead.

"You will be the night nurse," one of the SS had told her. "We've got babies here... five... a dozen? Keep them fed so they don't bawl...." She didn't understand. In this division of hell, a concern for babies was an aberration; their lives an anomaly. She

would later learn that some were kept alive to be adopted by barren German women, others for "scientific experiments" to benefit the race of Titans the Germans planned to build. But for at least a few hours a day, she believed she would touch life. She would feel the softness of new skin and feel the warmth of little bodies—like the one she had loved for what was too short a time. She would survive, Giuliana thought again. And she would one day find her child.

It was a week later that he had seized her, she remembered. The visiting SS Commandant who had given her the first coffee she had tasted in years, who told her she worked too hard and had offered her a chair—the Nazi who had then raped her with his hand and the point of his gun and a member that was even more cruel. And who then had told her to change the diapers on the stinking Jew babies. And to kill them before dawn the next day.

Boston October 1975

Sylvie felt as if her own life had stopped. She watched in the yellow light of the old lamp as the years had been excavated by a woman who had chosen not to die— though why Sylvie couldn't know.

"When I took the stick," said Giuliana, her eyes very far away, "... after four weeks... maybe five, and found the opening and destroyed what the German had placed there, the bit of flesh that was trying to grow inside of me, I offered up that little soul as a sister or a brother to all the others I had been made to kill. I prayed its spirit would be joyful, to not have to live and then to die from hate. And as I did this deed, as I had with the little babies on the third floor, I thought of my own living child. The one I had suckled, the little one I prayed had lived. The one who would need the only thing I had to give, a love that will never die."

Chapter 54

"Excellent. Thank you. We will pick them up at the window." Carlo heard Sylvie's voice finishing a call, though at the moment he was still too sleepy to fathom what she would be picking up.

"There are two of them. Two lectures!" she beamed, turning toward the shuffling figure coming in the kitchen. "And we can go to both." Satisfied with herself, she stood a tall box of Wheaties in front of Carlo, poured him a cup of coffee, and actually slid the cream near it.

"What?" The too-early sunshine was hurting his eyes and he could only listen keeping them closed.

"The Etruscan exhibition. The one the gorgeous model-lady is going to. Remember, the fancy lady with the fur who sought you out for conversation at the airport? The exhibition at the Peabody Museum… on the Harvard campus?"

Everything was a fog from yesterday, but it was clearing, making Carlo want to go back to bed. "Right, the lecture," he said, sipping his coffee. "Tonight?"

"It's tonight and then tomorrow. They say the lecturer, a Professor from Sweden, will take people through a different kind of exhibition on the second night. It's a recreation of an actual tomb."

Carlo swallowed his coffee, the first Sylvie had ever made him. He didn't realize she took it so strong. "Did you stay up late with Zia Giuliana?" Carlo didn't want to think about tombs right now. At this hour, the rocking chair could wait too. "I heard voices, I thought."

Sylvie's back was to him and she didn't turn around, only stirring a tea that contained nothing but tea. Carlo tried to organize his thoughts. "Sylvie, did you tell Zia Giuliana about Rosetta? Hell, we don't know anything about arrangements…. Sylvie?"

"I think she already knew," his sister said, gazing out the window. "Nobody told her, but I feel like she already knew." Then she turned to face Carlo, and he saw that thoughts of the exhibit had been put aside.

"Did you know she had been in a concentration camp?" she said. "Did you know that she had had a child?"

Carlo spread his arms straight along the counter. "What! No, I have never heard that. What are you saying? A concentration camp? She's Italian… not Jewish."

"She's both," said Sylvie. "And more."

Carlo rubbed his head, swigging at coffee that was bitter and black. "You're saying that the little Italian auntie, the one, who with Rosetta, would cross herself a hundred times a day and keep a votive candle in every nook of their little house… was Jewish?" He swung around. "And a child? There was never a child when I was in Italy."

"She was a Jew who had had to blend in during the war. It probably saved her life. Until the SS got her." Sylvie went silent for a beat, then, "After that, she saved her own life… at least the visible part." They were both quiet, waiting for the strangeness of talking to each other as peers to abate and for Carlo to begin consideration of the new persona in the room overhead. Other questions hung in the air between them—the chair, the earlier incapacity of Paolo—but neither were ready yet to explore their answers.

"But…" said Sylvie gathering up both Carlo's empty cup and the untouched cream and willfully changing the subject, "I found out something about the award she and Rosetta are… were… are to receive. Your aunt had become an archaeologist after the war. I guess not the university kind, but sort of a practicing amateur who discovered all kinds of amazing things. Even grandmother Rosetta made some discoveries that professors and scholars are still studying. And, a museum, their museum, is there now in Pitigliano, where you went to visit as a kid."

Carlo looked up, grateful for a turn from concentration camps to museums. "Right, in Pitigliano… although their house was in the countryside nearby." Carlo was thinking, his eyes glancing from one corner of the ceiling to the other. "You know, the letter from the Ministry said something about the… what was that word… *fugo, fago…* of Pitigliano? Let me go see what they've donated that is so freaking important." He jumped up and came back from the living room with a worn Italian dictionary left in a box of books inherited after the death of their father. "Let's see, here's the Ministry letter. And the word is… "*fegato,*" the *Fegato di Pitigliano*." He thumbed back and forth in the dictionary, checking the spelling against that in the letter. And then Carlo burst into laughter. "It's a liver! A *fegato*! A weird body part, if I ever heard of one!" He and Sylvie giggled for a time about whether the liver had been mummified or fried up with flour, and then embarrassed, they became serious, each reflecting on the import of the women's accomplishments—and the strange things that had happened in their home since Giuliana arrived. Eventually, seeing that his sister had grown suddenly pensive, Carlo opened his mouth to ask about what he had avoided all morning—the wildly rocking chair and Sylvie's role in making it move. But before he could, she turned to him and said, "A jealous eye can see from a far country to this, Carlo. We must be very careful. But help may come."

He stood staring at her for a moment. No longer the sarcastic, lost post-adolescent from a month ago, Sylvie seemed now a mystic who prophesized with knowledge of things beyond his understanding. Somehow this new version almost frightened him.

"What time is the lecture?" asked Carlo, pivoting from talk of jealous eyes and the silence that dropped between them. "Write down when we should leave, and I'll make arrangements for a cab." Carlo headed for the stairs. "I don't care if the sun is up. I'm going back to bed." As an afterthought, he called over his shoulder, "We'll have to find another sitter for tonight."

***

Giuliana had awakened with a start. She believed it was morning, though with the heavy drapes pulled shut, it was hard to tell. It was the fourth or fifth time she had found herself looking out into dark space where little white motes floated in and out like stars. After the middle-of-the-night talk with Sylvie, it seemed the long-playing record of her life had slowed down. She'd recounted the horrors of the Risiera to the young woman, but the "disk" hadn't stopped turning. Now, each time she'd awakened, her life was further along, and she wished Sylvie were still sitting beside her to listen. Giuliana had shared the worst parts, but there had been many years since, and though each of them was scarred by what had happened at the mill, she decided now to just observe and whenever possible, find some joy in the revolving scenes her memory served up. But even the first one was not one to be savored, and she turned her head against the pillow, unsuccessfully commanding it to stop.

Pitigliano 1946

"The child is gone, my dear. It is better. Your baby is one of the lucky ones. Do you really think an infant would prefer to eat cooked roots and broth from the hooves of horses?" The old nun lay on a kind of reclining bed, an iron contraption with wheels that allowed travel or napping, and from which she still oversaw the convent's diminishing cadre of sisters. For them, donations came as the gleaned residue of a peasant's paltry harvest or the remains of a basket of food from a charity across the sea.

"What could you offer a child now?" said the nun. "Though the war is over, you are a woman alone. The earth gives us little. Would you shelter it in a bombed-out building or a cave? No, my dear, your child will have found a home in America... where she grows fat on meat. You must not blame old Rosetta. She had a hard choice." The nun retreated into the blankets around her neck, an amphibian wishing to hibernate.

Still in her twenties, Giuliana's hair had streaks of white. She had not seen herself in a mirror in nearly a year, but her fingers could trace the bones of her face and feel teeth that shifted in their sockets. As she stood beside the old nun, a supplicant begging for her own child, she knew the rice mill's ravages had marked her... and not only her body. Of the 4,000 who had been murdered there, she had been one who was spared. And somehow that fact alone, made her wish to be with them.

It had taken her months to find her way back to this part of the countryside. Italy was destroyed, and bands of people, like wild dogs, roamed the cities, preying on each other, learning to lie and steal, to break every commandment they had been taught as children. And so too, Giuliana. For a half loaf of bread, she had opened her legs on a bed of straw; for a few carrots she had knelt. She'd bathed in the street with other beggars in the rain, and she'd taken shoes from a woman who'd died alone in a field. She knew without doubt that what the nun said was true. She was not fit to raise her child. Hadn't she performed the ultimate sin against others? But still, from afar, she would like to watch.

"You are right, Sister. But can you tell me to what city the baby was taken? Do you know the name of the person who took her? I promise I will not try to steal her back. I only would like to write to her. No... no, I would not do that. I would only like to know that she is... growing."

The nun seemed to stifle a laugh. "Do you think it is so easy?" she said. "The baby was taken a thousand miles away." Yet her hand reached out and took the thin one of Giuliana. She looked at it, turned it over, then shaking her head, said, "Young woman... poor woman, your hands tell me much... and your face." She broke off her thought and stared through the peaked window at the dried fields stretching toward the sunset.

"I believe I know the name of the person who wanted your child. It is actually not permitted for me to say it. But he seemed so eager... so eager, that he wanted two babies. Let me think what I must do. In the meantime, you must think of what you will do.

Something that is not sinful, my child. You must think of what you can do for this poor country," and looking at the emptiness in Giuliana's eyes, "...what you must do to regain your soul."

And over the next years, she had regained it to a certain extent, she thought. She had forgiven Rosetta for making a decision that had perhaps saved her child's life. And at least superficially, she now led a life that appeared normal in these postwar abnormal times. Rosetta had survived the war, though she was often sick and required long stays in bed. But life in the little house had somehow shifted into its former pattern—feeding the little animals that one by one had come to live in the stable, bartering in the weekly market with farmers whose harvests were now big enough to trade, kneading bread, washing clothes, saying her Hebrew prayers alongside those of the Roman Catholic church, and once again, welcoming the women who came to the little house for the removal of spells and curses that even the war hadn't squashed. In the quiet of the long winter evenings, Giuliana had pieced together the fragments of the little vase, which though it still grew warm in her hands, she never used. It was for her now, only a touchstone from her childhood with her parents, but one which she believed carried the memory of both evil and a justice that still frightened her.

"Giuliana," Rosetta had said one day, "We have not spoken of it in a long time, but you see the women come visiting again. They have their few lira and their worries, which when I remove the Evil Eye benefits us both. You could do as I do. I know of your gifts... greater ones than mine... and it would help us to eat, maybe even to prosper."

Giuliana stood up, finding her heart pounding. "No, no, Rosetta. No more." And she had abruptly left the old woman standing in the kitchen and gone to the one place that offered a place of solace... the "temple" beneath Pitigliano's plateau.

It was here that Rosetta had found the metal liver which now lay wrapped in bed clothes beneath her bed. And here that Giuliana's father had discovered the tiny vase whose touch transmitted a power that confounded her. Evil had visited this tomb it was true, but Nathan's presence remained and that of her mother as well, surrounded by the feeling that others in this tufa cavern were just and strong and were advocates for the plan she felt evolving.

Giuliana had decided to make a museum. It had been Sergio's dream. And now, without him, she dreamt it too. Though his cherished excavated artifacts had been stolen and dispersed, the beautiful pots and urns and statuary that she had glimpsed in this cave alone would fill a small building dedicated to the Etruscans' lives and deaths.

And so, she had begun, working quietly, never bringing her artifacts out of the cave, but secreting them in one of the hidden rooms. She worked behind a locked door, a flashlight or a few tiny candles illuminating her delicate extractions. And it was often then that she thought of Sergio. She could hear his instructions to go slowly, to avoid a removal until all the dirt was brushed away. Like him, she constantly referred to texts on shape and design, poring over the three archaeology books that remained with her from their work together on the tombs in the hills.

She thought of his respect for the people of this culture and desire to show the world the great beauty of their civilization—and she thought of his body, the long limbs that had glistened in the candlelight, and the lips that knew every part of her. And each time, she would wonder if the child who now grew in a country she would never know, was the product of this man she had loved or of another. And in the end, as she went back to smoothing away the dirt from a vase, she decided it wasn't important. Sergio had disappeared, and her child gone too. How appropriate that her own life as well was being lived unseen and apart.

Chapter 55

Boston 1975

"I hope the lectern isn't too high, Professor." The Peabody's curator for Ancient Civilizations scurried from the back of the auditorium toward the stage, followed by two eager Anthropology graduate students holding clipboards as if auditioning for stenography work. The silver-haired gentleman on the stage was dressed in a rumpled suit, but his erect bearing gave it the look of an elegant period costume.

Doctor Sergio Portini walked back and forth on the stage, gazing up into the tiered seating and at the backdrop upon which he would project his slides. "It is perfect," he said. "Not too high nor too low. And I apologize that I am somewhat late—the airlines' strike. It always happens," he laughed pleasantly. "I would have liked to have been here two days ago." He came forward to greet the curator and to be admired by her minions.

The Geology Hall was daunting, but impressive in the way of a Smithsonian-era building. Built on the Harvard campus in 1866 and now holding over a million items, the Peabody's five stories of smooth red brick were filled with artifacts of the Americas, but curators hoped to bring in more exhibitions from ancient civilizations less known. The new Etruscan exhibit would be proudly promoted both here and around the world. Sergio Portini's international aura would be a vaunted perk.

"We cannot express how delighted we are to present your work and display the wonderful pieces you have sent, Professor Portini. Your contributions to the understanding of this civilization are unprecedented in Etruscan/Greek studies. And you will convey our gratitude to the University of Stockholm as well? Tonight will be an event to be remembered."

Sergio bowed a kind of old-world acceptance of the praise. It was far from the first time he had received such plaudits. In his office in Sweden, the shelves were dotted with awards and prizes for his work. Though the crown of dark curls that so long ago had reminded Giuliana of an Etruscan reveler was now a no-nonsense Nordic crop, many other mannerisms had remained as Sergio climbed the ranks of academia. Even now he would chuckle at how the Swedes, who four decades ago had taken in the fleeing Italian partisan, would brace themselves when he offered an Italian embrace; how his Tuscan passion for archaeology, which seemed to have charmed the university into letting him study in Stockholm's elite department, still made Swedish colleagues blush. Now he guessed he was more Swedish than Italian—though it was still to the ancient people of Italy that his heart belonged.

"Good, that is very good. I am glad the hall is acceptable," said the curator. "But now I must show you what we have created as the *piece de resistance* to the exhibition." She gingerly touched his elbow to point the direction from the stage toward another wing. "After people will have walked through the displays of artifacts, the space will open into a reproduction of an underground Etruscan necropolis. From your wonderful photographs and diagrams, we have recreated the exact wall paintings and the precise layout of several complex chamber tombs. There are several side rooms as you've described in your writings."

"Ah… I will be most happy to see what you have done." But as they chatted their way up the aisle, Sergio suddenly came to a stop, causing the curator to stumble and actually grasp his arm for support.

"Professor, excuse me. I must have tripped." But Sergio's attention had turned to the rear of the auditorium, where they both could now see a stunning woman in pale blue stepping from beneath the balcony's shadow and into the stage's glow. She was tall and slim, with smooth skin and golden hair swept up into a coil on one side. Her eyes were dancing with delight and her arms were open wide. *"Il mio sogno e' diventato realita',"* she said advancing toward them, her slight limp rekindling a memory. And Sergio stood without moving, recognizing with something akin to shame, that his own fantasy was walking toward him down the aisle.

Rebekah embraced Sergio in a warm, though public way in front of the curator. But amid the perfunctory English platitudes and Italian exclamations, she pressed an address into his hand, whispering conspiratorially that she would be at the Hawthorne—a darkly intimate bar, waiting for him in one hour. She had come so far, she said, and she couldn't wait to see him again.

Sergio realized that the curator, as he suddenly explained the necessity of excusing himself for a few hours, was taken aback. It seemed a dozen technicians were still busily at work, meticulously recreating the tombs for the exhibition and needed his approval as they completed the intricate paintings and designs. She had scheduled several media interviews and the television people wanted his thoughts on modern archaeology. Yet, Sergio felt unable to counter the overwhelming compulsion to meet with the woman who had so changed the course of his life. Ashamed, curious—and filled with a desire that he couldn't explain.

Forty minutes later, having hesitated at the bar's door just to observe from afar the aura that still seemed to surround Rebekah, Sergio approached, then settled into the green leather booth beside her. He felt as expectant about what was to happen as he was when the top stone was lifted from a tomb. In many ways, this rendezvous would be stepping back into his own ancient past.

"I would have recognized you, even if you hadn't called my name," said Sergio, looking at the luminous face and coiffed hair. He marveled, "You have amazingly not changed from… our other days." Rebekah's fragrance was light and suggested to him rain and tinted leaves, and he saw that her hands were not those of one who used them for work. But as always, it was her eyes which pulled him. Within a circle of black, clear blue faded to crystalline near the wide ebony iris. They moved and darted, shadowed one minute with thick lashes, other times floating orbs in brilliant white.

"And you have changed but little," she smiled, only laughing when she touched his hair. "You look very intelligent!" She sipped a glass of late afternoon champagne and adjusted herself slightly nearer him.

"But do you live here now?" asked Sergio. "To find the girl from Toscana, from the time when life was so hard, now transported around the globe… it is extraordinary."

She smiled again, and gazed at him from beneath her lashes. "Extraordinary? No, not really. And no, I do not live here. I live in Berlin. Italy? Now I only go to Milan." Rebekah shifted herself slightly nearer to Sergio. "I found some luck in Germany… well, after the hell of the war's end anyway. That bad time finished and somehow, I don't know… I found my place."

"And your place? What profession did you choose?" It was clear that Rebekah was not one who had spent much time impoverished, and as he asked, Sergio momentarily wondered if an answer would be honest.

"I became a fashion designer," said Rebekah. "I am founder of Berlin's Haus von Savoyen— and several other design groups now." She shrugged with an unconvincing humility. It seemed that Rebekah was all that she appeared, rich and powerful. But then, Sergio reminded himself that she had always been powerful, even at her most vulnerable.

"Ah, what a good life! I am happy for you. And you are, of course, very clever to have earned such success. You are then perhaps here on business for your clothing?"

She looked surprised, perhaps a little hurt. "Why, no, Sergio. I am here to see you."

"Me?" He swallowed his drink. "You have come to the States to see an exhibition of Etruscan pieces?"

"No, my dear. I have come to see you. I have thought about you… us… through these years. Is it not strange that such a little time, such an intense time as we had together should have never left its hold on me? I wonder if you remember it as I do?" She lifted her eyes to his, wide and wondering, seeming to need his assurance.

Sergio suddenly was aware of something he had not experienced in many years. He was a working professor without time for romance or stirrings prompted by students or colleagues who would stand a few inches too near. Yet, as if only minutes and not decades had passed, he felt himself hungry once again for the feel and taste of the woman beside him. But on this afternoon, he said, "I remember. But old memories must be forsworn for present responsibilities." He laughed at his own pompousness.

"Rebekah, I am flattered that you say you have come to visit my exhibition… and me. But for now, I must concentrate on what this evening holds… what I must present." He reached over and pulled her hand to his lips. "I am flattered." Then standing with money ready for the bill, he said, "But perhaps we shall have a dinner with the curators and director this evening. You will be my guest. For now, I must leave and return to the museum."

Rebekah's smile remained, but her eyes had altered. "Of course, a dinner. Why not." She pulled her pale fur around her shoulders. "Perhaps you will be inviting another colleague as well? A very minor one, I understand, but then again…."

"A colleague? Who would that be?" he said counting out some bills.

"Why Giuliana Ferraro, of course. Certainly, you have heard that the little '*archeologista*' is receiving a Ministerial award for her new museum?" Rebekah couldn't contain her laugh. "I understand she is visiting in the area… But I believe too, she is not well. Not very well at all."

Chapter 56

The agency had declined to send out another nursing assistant after Helen had described all manner of abusive and even occult practices going on in the Burke house, and Carlo had had to scramble to find a second company that could send a sitter for the evening. After a quick interview with the eager young nursing student they sent, he was satisfied that the 20-year-old earning side money while she babysat sleeping oldsters, would do. She was pleasant, alert and nothing at all like Helen. He'd left her with instructions to stay in the room with his aunt and nothing more. Particularly, not to touch the mail.

An hour later, Carlo and Sylvie were finding that the Harvard campus in Cambridge felt to them like another country. Used to their own North End turf or for Carlo, Back Bay and North Station pub-crawl real estate, the wide greens, steepled halls, and entry gates that curled like iron embroidery all reminded him of an American History class he'd taken. He could easily have been persuaded that a founding father in white stockings would ease a carriage into a parking spot between a motor scooter and a car. It was beautiful here, but it certainly wasn't home.

"There it is!" said Sylvie. "The huge brick building that looks... angry." The two walked quickly toward the Peabody. Looming tall, and despite the festive posters of painted Etruscan figures waving from its façade, it managed to glower at the dozens of people climbing its entry stairs.

"I'm glad we got here early, that way we'll have time to see the exhibition before he begins talking," said Sylvie. She actually slipped her arm beneath Carlo's elbow. "I wish Zia Giuliana were able to come. She could have spoken to the lecturer... or even given the lecture, I'll bet!" Carlo smiled, feeling like a father whose wayward offspring has suddenly won an academic prize. Sylvie and Ancient History? An odd pairing, he thought glancing at her. But then, everything of late was odd.

They slowed as they walked through the double entry foyer, noting how the ceiling heights grew taller as they progressed toward a central rotunda. Here, beneath a cream-colored dome, complete with marble-fluted columns, arches and groins, the crowd slowly circled, then mounted like royalty themselves the two sets of granite stairs which led upwards to a balcony and to the theatre-like hall inside. It was as close to a palace as either of them had been.

Along the upstairs galleries were displays of massive Etruscan vases brilliantly lit to illuminate their ruddy oranges, reds and the lustrous blacks. A few sarcophagi, whose nearly life-size reclining figures seemed to make a few viewers start, appeared to be enjoying the spotlights aimed at their painted faces. Men and women in suits and cocktail dresses sipped prosecco and nibbled at hors d'oeuvres, almost inviting the Etruscans to pop out of their displays and join them.

Then as the food and drink disappeared, the scholars and erudite public filtered into the large, tiered lecture hall where on either side of the podium hung swags of crimson cloth hemmed with a Greek key design, and before them, students from the Drama Department danced in short tunics and cloaks. "I can't believe this!" whispered Sylvie. "Is this what college is all about?" A mixture of derision and envy filled her voice, but it was clear everyone was enthralled.

Carlo and Sylvie were seated to the left on the first of several elevations. Behind them, three more tiers rose toward the ceiling; in front was the orchestra level. It seemed that the middle-aged woman, the apparent organizer of the lecture and exhibition, who had now taken the podium for introductions, was going to make the most of it. After her fifth round of thank-yous to Board Members and patrons, the audience was beginning to amuse itself by studying the chandeliers, the air vents, and their neighbors. And that's when Sylvie saw the woman from the airport.

"Carlo, look over there. There she is. Look at her!" The stage-whisper turned the head of the woman on her right, who indeed did begin to stare at Rebekah. "She must be royalty or something…" hissed Sylvie. The woman beside her turned, smiled confidentially, and said, "Not royalty exactly, but the head of Europe's largest fashion house. Richer than a royal."

Then the lights went down, and Sergio, elegant in a tuxedo, strode onto the stage. Later, Sylvie would have a hard time describing what specifics he had given, what details he had emphasized, but the tale of a civilization that had found joy and bounty in its love of art and commerce enthralled her. It was as if, she said later, she had walked into a room and known everyone there—like they'd been waiting for her— these Etruscans with the smothered smiles.

"I must speak to him, Carlo," she said when the house lights came up. "Let's go down. I want to tell him how much I loved this lecture."

"All right, but wait until the crowd thins. If you're the last one, he'll have more time to talk to you." Carlo hoped she would lose some of her overt enthusiasm after the delay. In the meantime, he began to scan the departing crowd for the elegant woman who had dressed in white like an angel.

At last, the final group of well-wishers and admirers who had engaged Sergio for a full half hour stepped aside, and Sylvie walked forward to speak. Except she didn't. She simply blushed, executed a kind of curtsy Carlo had never seen, and tongue-tied, she fairly ogled the professor. Carlo extended his hand, glancing at his sister to see if she was about to faint. "My name is Carlo Burke, Professor Portini. I am a businessman here in Boston. My sister, Sylvia, was much moved by your lecture… and the pieces of Etruscan work you have brought."

"Ah, thank you so much," Sergio said, looking weary and pleased. "Are you a student of archaeology, Signorina?" Sylvie blushed again, but managed to say that she was not… not yet.

"Well, then I can recommend it as a course of study. You will find the past is filled with wonderful things... with magic," he laughed genially.

And in that instant, Carlo recalled the moving chair, his aunt, and the news he had received in the Ministry's letter, that Giuliana too was an archaeologist—with a museum! "Professor, perhaps my sister comes by her interest genetically!" It was a humorous inclusion, he hoped would impress the lecturer. "My aunt is also an archaeologist, I believe. She has opened her own museum in Italy only recently. I understand she will receive some prize for it. Perhaps this is a familial interest that your lecture has awakened." Carlo shrugged disparagingly at his own guess and little joke, but Professor Portini was not smiling.

"Your aunt? Where is this museum she has made? She is American?" The ushers were picking up discarded programs and forced the group to retreat up onto the stage.

"No, no, my aunt is actually from Italy... from a small town called Pitigliano. She created a museum there. I believe it displays items from the area. Anyway, it is to be recognized by the Italian Ministry of Culture." Carlo saw the pallor that swept across the Professor, but he continued with what he thought might be amusing in case he had somehow offended the man before him.

"Anyway, she and my grandmother will donate to Italy one thing they found. It's very odd. I frankly can't picture it myself. But it's a... a liver! A '*fegato*' I believe it's called." Carlo sniffed a laugh. "Did the Etruscans mummify organs? I don't know, but the Italian government seems impressed." Carlo wanted to flee. The Professor stood staring at him with his mouth ajar. Clearly, Carlo was rambling himself into some hole, while Sylvie stood beside him, a statue without a tongue.

"*Il fegato*? This woman... your aunt.... She is in Italy, no?" said Sergio. "She remains in Pitigliano?" His words were husky and thick. "I cannot believe this... I...." He looked as if it were he who would faint. Carlo signaled to Sylvie to pull a chair from near the lectern.

"No, no… she is not in Italy. She is here. Here at my house, in Boston." At this, Sergio's legs seemed to give and he grasped for the chair. "Tell me, is her name… Giuliana?" Carlo and Sylvie stared at one another, then nodded, as if they had inadvertently gutted the man before them and needed to flee.

"I must meet her," said Sergio, shaking his head back and forth. "I have known her from before, she was my… my friend," he said enigmatically, setting off little alarms in the two bending over him. "Will you take me to her now?"

"Ah, ah… Professor, it is late. It is very late, and I'm sure you are tired from… from all this. And besides, my aunt is ill now. I…."

Sergio grasped Carlo by both arms, pulling himself up to look directly at him. "I must see her. Not for the museum or archaeology. But…."

And here another voice said, "You must see her for other reasons?"

They turned, each of them seeing something different: Carlo took in an elegant woman who wore expensive clothes and jewelry worth thousands, with eyes that were as captivating as her obvious wealth. Sylvie saw a woman of confidence and glamour, one she might like to model herself on. And Sergio saw before him the apotheosis of the vulnerable girl he had bedded so many years before, even as he was unfaithful to the one he loved. Now, fully evolved, Rebekah reflected in her dress and elegance the authority she wielded—through a power that stretched back to something both ancient and cruel.

"I believe we have a dinner date now, Sergio," Rebekah's voice was sweet as she ran her hand along his shoulder. Then turning to Sylvie in a soft aside, she said, "I remember seeing you yesterday at the airport. You are very pretty… and very smart. I believe I would like to teach you some things. Would you like that? I could be your friend…." Sylvie felt a surge of something like electricity bound between the two of them, stronger than the sensation she had had when the chair had begun to rock. "I… would like that," she said.

"Good," replied Rebekah. "Then I must come to visit you. What is your address?" Sylvie repeated it mechanically and Rebekah nodded. "I will come tomorrow, then."

The two men were grasping hands, nodding to one another as Rebekah pulled Sergio away. "Tomorrow," murmured Sergio beneath his breath and Carlo closed his eyes in acknowledgment.

***

And in the North End, an old woman slipped from Carlo's house, the narrow ravines of her face moistened with tears. Her course finally clear.

Chapter 57

Sergio arched his back and turned to stare at the ceiling. The position of the wood millwork shifted where it met the walls and the light fixture behaved as if it were made of warm taffy, stretching and retracting with an odd syncopation. His head, without hurting, nevertheless felt like a moving jigsaw puzzle, dislocating thoughts the moment a pattern threatened to form. What he did know was that his left arm was warm and that the woman's shoulders he cradled were warm as well.

Sergio turned slightly to look at her. Pale, firm skin that showed no sign of age, no sagging nor surgical sculpting, nothing but a body that had been exercised and massaged, moistened and probably worshipped by many. And like them, he had fallen in line—not only overcome by Rebekah's beauty, but as before when they were young, by the strength of a source that pulled him in. Had he struggled against it? He rubbed his free hand across his face. No, and that was the power. Even as every rational thought lay before him, even as he had been handed the gift of a reunion with Giuliana, he had watched the pale eyes, the faux-innocence that drove his libido, the helplessness of a woman he at any other moment would know to be filled with guile—and he had made love to Rebekah with all the passion of their last time so long ago. And it made him sick.

Sergio extracted his arm and rolled to a sitting position, staring out at the Charles River where rowers slipped by in earmuffs and gloves. At least today he would see Giuliana—the dark girl whose last touch had been to place a blanket around his shoulders the day Pitigliano was bombed. Knowing he had been unfaithful to her, she had nevertheless, performed a simple act of compassion. He wondered if there still remained any love.

The rowers had moved downriver and now only the grey ribbon dividing Cambridge from Boston rippled platinum in the late morning light. Sergio didn't notice; instead he stared at the wall, watching the years reel by.

He had left Italy as soon as he could after the debacle at Pitigliano's bridge. The Americans had taken him on for a while, then the Brits. And as reconstruction had begun, Sergio was helping with identification of treasures lifted wholesale by the Germans and needing repatriation to their native soil. A blessed Swedish archaeologist who worked beside him had seen potential in the bright young man who so loved antiquities, and as Europe's new era began, Sergio became a student at Stockholm's most respected university.

But *self*-respect was not to be found. Mornings would find him gazing in a mirror, visualizing his hands on a plunger that would have killed his grandmother, betraying his comrades through lust, failing at a mission meant to have saved Italian lives. Instead, in the end, it was Giuliana who had made a moral decision. Judged right or wrong, he knew her to have been right.

Sergio had never been back to Pitigliano. Instead, he lived a quiet, solitary life in the North. He studied ancient cultures, and he even did field work in Italian cities, but never in those near Pitigliano. Though he longed to see Rosetta again, he had not gone. Better for her and for Giuliana, he'd rationalized, that they thought him dead. And in many ways, he was. A cosmopolitan academician, at home before crowds, but when alone, empty, living a paper cutout life. Yet now, Giuliana was near and he had been overwhelmed with the need to see her, to investigate if the roots of what they had once had had survived despite the causality of its flower. There could be a chance.

But with a glance at the figure beside him, the self-loathing of so many other lonely nights washed over him. For even as he held Giuliana so tenderly in his thoughts, he betrayed her.

Then the phone rang, and Rebekah stirred, turning over so that her full breasts fell toward him, with the rose-tipped nipples he would have to reach across for the call.

"Yes? The Peabody… yes?" Though Rebekah was now awake, he kept his voice low. "Yes. Yes. There are three of them. Yes, three pillars on the left side. No, the inscriptions are not to be there, the diagrams show them to be at the back near the…. No, no that is wrong…." Sergio supported himself on his elbow, his other arm leaning against Rebekah's hip. "If this is so, what we agreed to has been constructed incorrectly," he said. "That actually will not do for the exhibition. Yes, yes, I must come…."

As he spoke, she had begun to rub the skin between his thighs, the dark hair coarse, his skin soft beneath. As the voice continued on the other end of the line, Sergio could not stop, but slowly opened his legs to her touch, feeling himself rise in her fingers, growing toward her with each stroke. "I… I… when do you need me, Dr., Dr…?" His breath was coming in short bursts and he lowered his face to her breasts, feeling their weight along his cheek and lips, the voice on the phone becoming an indistinct murmur. "Yes, I will be there," he gasped. "Yes, yes, of course, I am fine. One hour… one hour."

When they had finished, Rebekah cradled his head in her lap, wandering a finger along his chest and belly, but leaving the rest to recover. "It was long ago, wasn't it, Sergio… the first time. You had taken me from the convent, do you remember?" Through the slits of light that crisscrossed her face, Rebekah was pensive, perhaps even sad. He thought she looked as she had the night he laid her down in the abandoned cottage, an ephemeral presence against which he had felt powerless.

Rebekah's voice dropped and she seemed to enter a private reverie he was surprised she would share. "People have often said of me that they fear to look in my eyes… that there is something there that alters their volition, that gives me a power over their will." She looked down at him, and distractedly drew his finger to her lips.

"It is inconvenient sometimes, this something I do not understand. It comes over me, like a sensation that I feel when I am angry, or when someone wishes to take something from me, when I feel jealous. Even my private thoughts, I feel, are transported into my eyes." She closed them tightly and passed her hand across her brow. Then caressing his face gently, she said, "But with you it is different. I have said it before, and it is yet the same. You have the real me. I want nothing from you... and yet, of course," she whispered with a kiss, "I want everything."

***

Sergio spent the afternoon and evening without lunch or dinner. The Peabody construction crew and the curator's collaboration had, in its final design, differed monumentally from the designs he had specified for the recreation of the Etruscan tomb. Without heroic changes, he would be ridiculed by scholars everywhere, and Sergio, in shirt-sleeves and stockinged feet, found himself climbing along the scaffolding of the giant tomb, repainting inscriptions in their proper places. Thoughts of women, had, for this moment, been driven from his mind.

For her part, Rebekah had bathed and changed into a flattering daytime dress, arranged her hair, almost as if she had washed away the unguarded admissions she had made to Sergio. Yet now she became aware of a certain glittering in her field of vision, the sensation that emanated from the very thought that had propelled her from Berlin, first to Pitigliano and now to Boston, this god-forsaken city. And she looked for the scrap on which she had written an address.

The cab had pulled up in front of a turn-of-the-century brownstone in a section called the North End. It was grubby and commercial, a few parks here and there, but mostly laundromats next to pizza joints, and old men in coats talking in lawn chairs beside trash bins on every stoop. Rebekah checked the address again, loath to get out of the cab, and yet this is where Giuliana was. Giuliana with her own museum. Giuliana with the award to be presented in Rome. Giuliana, who even as Rebekah had felt Sergio abandon himself to her, knew that only his body was hers for the moment, and the rest reserved for the woman in this shabby house.

Rebekah took in a breath, closed her eyes, and extended one elegant leg from the taxi. And then abruptly pulled it in again. It seemed she wasn't the only visitor that afternoon.

The woman who walked up the stoop had on a worn green coat and a sagging cloche hat. She didn't use a cane, but it seemed she could have used one. Bent, she took one step at a time, stopping on each narrow landing to readjust her footing. When she reached the door of the building, she rang the bell, waiting politely for someone to answer. It was when she turned slightly, readjusted her hat and pulled at her coat, that Rebekah could see her profile. There was a familiarity—something from years ago. Almost involuntarily she replayed how the old woman had walked along the sidewalk, how she'd touched her hair with an annoying diffidence, how she'd lifted her chin with a certain haughtiness that Rebekah remembered—and with a gasp of recognition, she abruptly closed the door and directed the cabbie back to Cambridge. This was a woman she had not expected. Yet Giuliana remained ill—bed-bound, if she wasn't mistaken. She would still be there tomorrow. And Rebekah would return.

***

Upstairs in the brownstone, Carlo was kneeling beside Giuliana's bed, and if a human being could actually explode without making noise, Carlo's remains would have covered the walls.

"I apologize Zia. I'm going to sue somebody. My God. They're going to pay. Terrible agency, terrible!" Carlo pulled himself up to sit beside Giuliana and pat her hand. "I'm sorry. There were instructions given. She looked so goddamned smart, the little idiot. That girl would have given tea to the Ripper!" He railed in whispers to Giuliana about the new sitter who had allowed another uninvited visitor, a woman this time, to enter while he and Sylvie had been at the museum last night.

Giuliana regarded him with a bemused smile and as she listened, let her eyes drift to the little bouquets and butterflies that danced across the paper on the wall. Downstairs, unbeknownst to Carlo, the same woman in the green coat waited in the hall, chatting with Sylvie until the muffled conversation upstairs would subside.

"What did she say again?" asked Carlo. "The old lady called herself 'a friend from your hometown?'" From Pitigliano! Right! They drop in all the time. We're away for a few hours in the evening—even after I warned the sitter to just stay put—and she lets in a stranger "from your hometown!"

Giuliana had become a little stronger over the past few days. Carlo knew she'd been spending time with Sylvie, hours, in fact. They seemed to be going through Giuliana's luggage, fiddling with tiny boxes, little packets. He supposed they were examining some of the healing potions his grandmother had always had lying around. Now Giuliana stretched out a hand that felt warmer than in recent days, and said, "Be calm, my child, you may know our visitor too."

Sylvie now called to Carlo that there was someone she wished to bring up. To please check if Giuliana could see her now. Carlo lurched to the doorway to abort any confidence game being played by actors entering people's homes and masquerading as old Italian peasants. He would block a new one on the stairs. Then behind him Giuliana said, "It is all right. Let her come."

After the "visit" of the evening before, Carlo had checked that none of the valuables had disappeared, now he would check the woman herself—no doubt a clever imposter of some kind, hardly a serendipitous farmer wandering over from the old country.

After a few minutes climbing the narrow stairs, the woman entered the room, steadied by Sylvie. She was taller than most of the old ladies Carlo remembered from Italy, and in the shaded light, her features were difficult to make out.

"Look at her carefully, Carlo. Tell me if you recognize her." With effort, Giuliana had shoved herself up into a semi-sitting position. Sylvie came to her, serving as a soft pillow from behind.

Carlo skeptically scanned the woman's face. Dark skinned, white hair in a kind of finger-wave do from another century. The woman stepped toward him and smiled. For an instant there was something he recognized—a glimpse of a memory that quickly disappeared. "I knew you as a little boy," said the woman with a thick accent. And turning to Giuliana, she laughed, making a sign that Carlo had grown big.

"I am sorry," he said. "I don't know you." Carlo was still on guard. A scam would be easy to carry out on an old, sick woman and two American imbeciles. He would not play the game. "Tell me your name, maybe it will come to me."

Then Giuliana said, "Ah, you don't remember, my boy. But look carefully. She would play with you the card game… Scopa! You were quick to learn. The four of us, you, me, Nonna Rosetta…" and here, Giuliana's eyes filled with tears. "… and Zia Tanti, your great-aunt Talia." Giuliana reached her arms out to the woman in the green coat and said, "My aunt too, and my friend from the hard days when the war had ended. We were three women… two Jews and a saint… who survived."

Chapter 58

Carlo simply shook his head. He felt as if the past had been loaded onto an express train that would soon overtake his bumpy commuter locomotive. All these years with only summer memories that he had lorded over his sister, now there were actors arriving daily from Italy whom he was trying to locate on the stage.

This new aunt he could visualize only on the periphery of his childhood experiences. Zia Tanti, Talia. He tried to picture her with a different color hair, without wrinkles. She seemed to have a "city style" unlike the open, countryside demeanor of Giuliana, but she was pleasant, and it was certain that Giuliana was happy to see her.

Carlo and Sylvie decided to leave them alone for a while, as they sipped from little glasses of Chianti that Giuliana had decided she could drink. The women had reverted to Italian as the door closed, and Carlo thought he detected a kind of conspiratorial tone rise up between them. But this time, he shrugged, what an outsider might have thought a very Italian, palms-to-heaven gesture. Let the old girls chatter, he seemed to say, and he joined Sylvie downstairs for their own glasses of wine.

"I don't think the beautiful lady is going to come," said Sylvie, putting her feet up on the frayed brocade of the couch. "Last night…. Did I tell you? She was going to 'be my friend,' she said. Was going to visit us here."

Carlo stared at her blankly. "The woman in white? You invited her here?"

"She invited herself. But it's late now. I don't think she'll come." She finished the last swallow from her glass. "And the Professor? More importantly," she asked, "What about the Professor? Did you see him last night? There must have been something…very strong between him and Giuliana once." Sylvie laughed, "How romantic. Two old people, still in love." She made little smoochy noises with her mouth, and then stopped, seemingly aware that was not how she felt. "I wonder what happened back then," she said seriously. "I've never seen a man stricken like that."

"I didn't mention it to Zia Giuliana," said Carlo. "He seemed so desperate to see her. But perhaps he decided he'd made a mistake, a confusion. He is after all, a very important man." Carlo poured himself another glass of wine, then as an afterthought, did the same for Sylvie. "I'm going upstairs to shower now. Tonight is the bigger of the two museum events, right? The big reveal of the tomb. Maybe I'll ask Talia if she could stay with Giuliana. Otherwise one of us would need to stay home."

Carlo took the bottle with him upstairs, knocked, and with permission from two high-pitched voices, entered the room where Giuliana and Talia sat holding each other's hands in a kind fireman's carry of support.

"May I offer each of you a little more sustenance?" He purposefully ignored the tight looks on their faces, as he lifted the bottle high. "I am very glad that you have come all this way, Aunt Talia. Do you have other relatives in Boston that you are visiting?"

Talia glanced at Giuliana and said that she didn't, but in response to the proffered bottle, accepted a half glass of wine. "Most of my relatives are dead," she said, then quietly, "But perhaps I have others…."

"I have a question for both of you," said Carlo, not understanding her meaning and deciding to proceed. "Sylvie and I… my sister and I… must go out again tonight. It is the museum exhibition, this time open to everyone. The second night, the one where the replica of the tomb will be on display. Sylvie is very eager to see it. And of course, I will bring home all of the brochures and pictures to share with you. Perhaps when you see them, you will have ideas for your own museum at home." Carlo had no idea what he was talking about. He hadn't had a chance to sit down with Giuliana, as Sylvie had, to know anything about her "museum." "Talia, would you be willing to stay with Zia Giuliana?"

"There is no need to ask her," said Giuliana, pushing herself up to a fully seated position. "I am going with you. I long to see this Etruscan tomb."

Chapter 59

Sergio hadn't left the museum since the late afternoon and now he could glimpse people already arriving for the tomb's exposition. A custodian let him into an unused office where he was able to wash up in the private bath. Covered with little pieces of Styrofoam where he had cut out sections of the tomb's "stone" and with paint from adding "millennia" to the inscriptions' patina, he was exhausted, wishing for the minions who usually stood awaiting his slightest wish before an exhibition in Europe.

Still, the recreation here of the Etruscan sepulchers was dramatic. Walking through the completed project an hour ago, he had had the same feeling from nearly 50 years before when he had first let himself down to join Giuliana in the never-before opened tomb in the hills near Pitigliano. He hadn't been back since the war, but it was this tomb he'd chosen to reproduce. His notes—and his memory were as vivid as yesterday.

He had only finished combing his hair, hoping for a moment to slide onto a tattered, but inviting sofa for a moment when the curator knocked at the office door. "The newspaper people are here," she warbled. "Could we have you in the tomb for just a moment or two? They'd like a few photos for the Globe tomorrow morning!" The Peabody had promoted the event for months, and Sergio indeed was grateful. "I'll be down straight away," he said wearily.

***

They had come in two separate taxis, Carlo and Giuliana in one, Talia and Sylvie in the other. And from the North End to Cambridge, Carlo had barely been able to keep his eyes from his aunt. "I would barely know you," he'd said when she was wheeled from the bedroom, awaiting him to carry her down the stairs. "What did my sister do?"

Giuliana laughed, "She brushed my hair… maybe a little color here and there on my face." In fact, Sylvie had thrown herself into an emergency rehabilitation of the naturally bronze skin and wavy black hair that had received only rudimentary attention since Giuliana had fallen ill days after her arrival. Though no longer young, now she was not old. No longer frail, she appeared elegantly slim. And her eyes, framed by lashes that brushed her cheeks, danced with ebony flashes. Carlo was perplexed by her unexplained "recovery," but he was concerned it was only his intrepid aunt forcing herself to appear healthy before Talia—or simply antiquities' pull.

The taxis arrived together at the Peabody, and as Sylvie came back to stand beside Giuliana, the valet asked if her mother would like to use the ramp. For a moment, Carlo stood still beside the wheelchair, looking from one to the other, aware of how much the woman in the chair and his pretty, warm-skinned sister seemed to share more than their interest in Etruscans.

As he wheeled her toward a sloping bit of sidewalk, Giuliana only stopped him momentarily to hand a small parcel to Sylvie, placing her old hand over that of the girl and looking long into her eyes.

***

Inside, the crowd was much different from the night before. There were parents and children, college-age adults, and people who seemed to have come from pubs after a long week's work. Carlo wished that Giuliana had come as part of the more sedate group from the night before. Still, to see her out, sitting up, somehow energized by Talia's arrival and the exhibition was a delight. For the moment, at least, she reminded him of the warm, focused woman of his childhood.

"Let's wait a bit before we get on line for the tomb," said Carlo to Talia and Giuliana. "There are some amazing artifacts you might want to see first." Sylvie walked ahead, running a kind of interference for the rolling chair behind her. There were even more display cases on view than the night before.

"Yes, look at these," said Giuliana, pointing to a series of vessels with turned necks that seemed to have been pitchers or perhaps had once held lavender, gaudy roses or sage. "These are very nice examples, very nice," agreed Giuliana.

They passed on to larger vessels, then to tiny figurines the size of those filling many a Boston family's curio shelves. There were displays of Etruscan wigs; from human or horse hair, the plaits were tight extensions the ancient dead had worn for their final bacchanal, now looking like a ladies' hair salon after the ball. And case after case of funerary sculpture, a veritable post-death party season on display.

And then the foursome came to a presentation of what seemed much finer artifacts. Gold necklaces with delicate pendants, earrings set with carnelian, agate, and lapis, twisted bracelets in jeweled spirals and carved crystal rings a contemporary woman would envy. Beyond were narrow jars for perfume, painted chests, and terra cotta boxes to hold cosmetics. It was clear women of Etruria reveled in their elegance.

As they came to the next displays, Giuliana sat forward in her chair. Though the elaborate jewelry was more dramatic, here the items were both beautiful and utilitarian.

Dozens of mirrors, mirrors no bigger than a hand, were covered in carved, silvery designs on one side and polished to look like glass on the other. The engravings showed people relaxing in chairs, people with hunting bows in their hands, and people engaged in a variety of sexual stimulations. The displays even featured a clever mechanism in the middle of the room where a viewer could grasp a handle below the glass case and rotate the mirror above—looking at the carved back's design and with a turn, gazing into the reflecting surface of the front.

As the group and others stood admiring the display, Giuliana turned its handle ever so slightly, and immediately there was heard a gasp— as if someone had been painfully surprised, as if stung by a wasp, or bitten by a snake. Carlo bent to see if it were Giuliana who was ill and Sylvie turned behind her.

And there, Rebekah stood stock still, a look of surprise giving way to something Sylvie had never seen before. A powerful light outlined a circle that engulfed the top of her face—a white radiance that came from the mirror in the glass case. It was as if its reflection held Rebekah captive, a forest animal unable to move. As if a laser had been turned back on itself.

Then with a turn of the rotating handle by a visitor on the far side of the display, the light was lost, and with it, Rebekah seemed released. She looked at Sylvie for a moment, and at Carlo with a glance, and then for what seemed the time to descend into hell and return, at Giuliana—and beside her—Rebekah's own mother in the green coat.

Then she turned, and was lost into the crowd.

As they rapidly moved away and headed for the Sepulcher gallery where now the crowd was beginning to thin, each of them noticed that Giuliana seemed suddenly to have changed, to have lost the strength that had buoyed her enthusiasm earlier. Her head seemed heavy and her face was pale. But she indicated she wanted to go on to the tombs, and Talia nodded that it would be all right. The women held tightly to one another's hands, no one mentioning the encounter that left each of them shocked and trembling.

Upon entering this part of the exhibition, they almost immediately noticed that the gallery was cold. And when Sylvie complained, Giuliana muttered, "It is just as it should be. The dead don't need warmth." The gallery led visitors down a long and narrowing tunnel. As they went, the ceilings became lower and the lights were dim. Along the "path," dust or sand had been scattered, and it crunched beneath their feet and the wheels of the chair. Small lights illuminated the paintings on the walls, where nearly life-sized figures in brilliant tunics frolicked with garlands, conjoining them in a dance or sprawling them in amorous entanglements on chaises or a lawn.

It seemed that most of the visitors had left the tomb's interior now, heading for another of the little dance presentations in the cavernous rotunda. Now, only their voices could be heard, distant and far away. "Turn this way," said Giuliana, extending her arm weakly toward a darkened passage the group had almost passed. The temperature seemed to have dropped even more and the four of them had the sensation that there were still other rooms off of this forgotten passage.

"I'm not sure we are going the right way," said Carlo, a note of concern entering his voice. Then Talia took his arm, asking if she could find a place to sit. It was a longer exhibition than she had expected. In the bluish light, Carlo turned questioningly to Sylvie. Two old women—and they all seemed to be lost beneath the earth.

"I think we should turn around now," said Carlo. "Too much going on…." But Giuliana held up her hand and stopped him. "Not yet."

He hesitated for a moment. As the man, Carlo felt responsible for everyone. "I'll take Talia," said Carlo to his sister. "Do not be long here. I'm not sure Giuliana is feeling well." And he kissed his aunt and turned Talia back around the way they'd come.

It was then that Giuliana said quietly to Sylvie, "Take out the pouch… and take out what is in it as well."

Chapter 60

As the gala opening of the Etruscan exhibition wound down and the dancers had slipped away, clusters of viewers still lingered in the towering rotunda. Finding friends or in one of the cultural groups that had arrived together, they chatted about interests in ancient cultures or about the next football game at Harvard's stadium. They were intellectuals, academics, doctors and business people, as well as children whose parents had treated the exhibit like a trip to Disney.

Rebekah had fled from the dimly lit gallery of mirrors into the illumination of the entry hall, her head hurting and her eyes on fire. What had happened in the darkened chamber, she wasn't sure. All she could remember exactly was the surprise of seeing Giuliana. Giuliana in a chair, beautiful. Somehow charmed Giuliana, who despite Rebekah's own accomplishments and lauded glamor, in a way she couldn't explain, was still the superior one, the one who survived with not guile, but grace. She had willed her to have been more ill.

Rebekah hurried to the ladies' room, her hand shielding her aching eyes, when she heard a woman's stage whisper behind her say, "Is that Rebekah Hansbach? The founder of the Haus von Savoyen?" Other voices agreed that it was, remarking she was more gorgeous than in photos and that the tailored suit must be the latest from the continent. Rebekah reached the ladies' room door, but once inside, the women aligned along the sinks began whispering to one another, and a particularly bold one commenced a conversation about how much she was influenced by Rebekah and her fashion house creations—and wouldn't Rebekah like to give them all some hints as to next year's trends?

Americans! Rebekah turned her back on them and fairly ran back toward the exhibits. Sergio was here somewhere. Sergio and peace. And Giuliana.

Inside the tunnel that led into the tomb, she found a ledge and eased herself down onto it. Her eyes were refocusing in the softer light and taking out her compact to see if her makeup were disturbed, two small, clipped-together pieces of paper fell to the floor—the two scraps that had brought her here.

She picked them up. The first, Rebekah had seen tacked to the wall of a coffee house she'd randomly happened into in Berlin. It had sent her heart racing. A small flyer announcing the opening of a "boutique" museum in Italy—probably sent out to libraries all over the continent. It was haphazardly stuck to the wall in the German capital. An Etruscan museum, it said. Purportedly featuring a never-before-seen artifact from the tombs of Toscana, the museum had been created in the "*charming, 13th century town of Pitigliano—under the auspices of a Signora Giuliana Ferrero.*" Rebekah had stood staring at it until an employee came to ask if he could help her. She didn't need his help, she'd said. For, in fact, as the redness had engulfed her, Rebekah smiled that wherever Giuliana was, she would know that Rebekah had been watching.

The second clipping was from the newspaper, Der Spiegel some two weeks later. It announced that "*Herr Doktor Sergio Portini of the University of Stockholm will be the honored speaker at the Peabody Museum in Boston as he presents his Opus Magnus on Etruscan Civilization.*" Rebekah had gazed at the photo noting how the years had changed the color of Sergio's hair, but not his dark eyes and earnest expression. The innocence still remained. All these years, and she had never known where he had gone.

She had made the travel reservations that very afternoon. She hadn't seen Giuliana in almost 30 years—and why would she want to? Poor thing, Rebekah had thought with a smile, her cousin only remained a pathetic Jewish farm girl. Yet here was Giuliana now—about to become famous—with a museum. Oh, well, Rebekah had sighed, the little archaeologist might very well be coming down with something—some illness—from which it might be very difficult to recover. Then after Rebekah had read the brochure again, she'd added to her busy itinerary a junket to Pitigliano. A lifetime had passed since there'd been a reason to go. Now, she might like to assess the damage that a surprise flood at the little museum would likely be causing.

Of course, a second reservation would need to be made for a rendezvous in Boston. A more-than-chance meeting at a grand exhibition would be the very thing Rebekah really wanted to happen. Yes, Sergio might have her on his mind at this very minute. Perhaps thinking of her now—and of nobody else.

A week later, Rosetta had come to the door, Rebekah remembered, blinking and trying to understand what a tall, sophisticated woman was doing on her Pitigliano doorstep. The house was in disrepair and smelt of leaks and mildewed wood, but the old woman who seemed nearly blind, had understood Rebekah was someone who had lived in the area 30 years before, and she had invited her in. "Were you here during the war?" asked Rosetta. "Did you live on one of the farms? Did you see how the city was bombed?"

Rebekah wanted to know if any of the other people of the area were still nearby—people her own age. She said she had remembered one or two, a boy named Sergio, and a girl. Wasn't there a girl who had lived here with Rosetta?

The old woman had grown quiet, running her fingers along a rosary she kept wrapped around her wrist. Now, she shoved herself up from a sagging settee and felt along the furniture to a shelf from which she lifted a small bottle. She turned back to Rebekah and said, "I believe I know you. But the one you're looking for is not here…."

"Where is Giuliana?" said Rebekah, stepping closer. "I need to see her."

"Gone to America. To the city of Boston!" Rosetta croaked with a triumph of recognition. And with that, the old woman made the sign of the cross and hurled a spray of holy water at the designer dress before her, spattering Rebekah's arms with droplets that began to sizzle.

Rebekah wiped the water from her arms and gazing at the old woman, softly said, "Still, I see you… don't I, Rosetta. I look at you and see." The old woman's chest had begun to heave. And finding nothing to support her, she dropped heavily to the floor.

***

Talia and the neighbors of the countryside buried Rosetta with no delay on the land where she had lived. Where the three women had spent the last decades together. Where a niece and her aunt had found haven and lives being both who they pretended to be and who they were.

And then Talia had put on her green coat and headed for Boston, guessing that "il malocchio" had crossed an ocean.

Chapter 61

Though Sylvie knew herself to be in a museum, it was as if the atmosphere in the "tomb" had become heavy and moist; as if the smell of earth were about them. Sylvie looked down at Giuliana, who had directed them into a small room where a bank of seats circled three painted walls. In the dim light, Giuliana seemed serene now, washed of age and the sickness which had kept her weak. "What do you feel here?" she asked Sylvie. "Are you frightened?"

Sylvie let her gaze flow along the walls, where despite the gloom, the faces of the figures seemed animated and friendly. "No. No, I'm not frightened. We are in a museum. If we were beneath the earth, perhaps it would be different…." She smiled at Giuliana. "But, in fact, I don't feel frightened. Even if I pretend we are beneath the ground, it feels peaceful and warm here."

"The earth is welcoming. It holds both the end of things and their beginnings; their decay and the nourishment for renewal." Then Giuliana paused and said, "Where were you begun, my dear?"

Sylvie looked at her abruptly. She wasn't sure why they were sitting here together, as if waiting for something to happen, something for which she now clutched the souvenir vase that Giuliana had handed to her. But she hadn't anticipated such a personal question.

"What do you mean? Begun? How?"

Giuliana reached over and lifted Sylvie's chin slightly. "Where were you conceived? And born? I saw Carlo when he was a little boy, but never you there."

Sylvie shook her head. As always when such questions arose with peers, she found a reason to excuse herself and avoid the absence of answers. "I was adopted. Carlo too, of course… from Italy. But when the people who took us died, I was sent to different homes, many. To answer you honestly…" she turned to Giuliana, "I don't know who my parents were. Certainly not where I was conceived."

Giuliana smiled. "I have always believed something. I believe it is true. That all things remember their beginnings, the earth, yes, and the air, and the season, and the scent of their beginnings. If this were six meters beneath the floor of a forest, would you wish to flee? If you were alone in this room… with only the revelers on the walls around you, would you run?"

Sylvie didn't understand Giuliana's questions, but despite their strangeness, she reached out to touch the walls, and smell the air, and oddly, to feel as if the very room were holding her in an embrace. And she noticed that in her hand, the little vase was beginning to glow.

"It was here that you were conceived," said Giuliana in a whisper. "This room… but the real one, in Pitigliano… on a night when I was alone and…. My dear child, I am your mother. I am the one who was forced to leave you in the cave as the war came. You are my only child, my beautiful daughter. And you see, even the little vase, knows it to be true."

They laughed between the tears. Giuliana reached her arms out to Sylvie, who fell to her knees and buried her face against her. "Mother." She repeated the word again, then again. "You are my… my own mother?" They touched each other's faces, now without embarrassment or a sidelong glance of scrutiny. They looked for cowlicks and the shape of nostrils, at nailbeds and eyebrow's arch. Each little similarity, a document of the bloodline they shared.

And then Sylvie sat forward, taking her mother's hands and saying, "Then you can tell me too… who is my father? Will you tell me?

"*Devi essere specifico.*" The voice from the passageway was taunting, carrying the cold insult in both languages. "It could have been anybody," said Rebekah, standing in the doorway.

"Why do you think one man's sperm is better than the next? Try something from one, try something from another…." Rebekah gave a low laugh as she stood silhouetted in the scanty light. Only her eyes sparkled.

Sylvie was transfixed, uncomprehending that these two very different people could have known one another, but sensing that the stakes were very high. And she felt Giuliana's hand reach out to cover her own, the one in which the little vase was beginning to pulse.

"Ah yes, sometimes holy men are in the mood for recreation too, aren't they, Giuliana. Playing in the dirt with your ancients or simply playing *with dirt who wears a cleric's collar*... you have had both. And maybe this little girl here is not who you think she is..." Rebekah's eyes were glowing with a white heat that seemed to tremble the air. And as Sylvie rose, the piercing light found its mark on the dark brow of Giuliana.

Sylvie felt her mother slump against her, yet still she held her hand. And with a terrifying wave that rolled from their shared clasp, through her arm and into her eyes, Sylvie felt a kind of electric discharge that staggered her. With the sensation of a lightning strike, from her own pupils had come an ejaculation of power for which there was no understanding. And gasping, she let the little vase fall back into Giuliana's lap.

The sound of running feet was coming closer down the corridor. Rebekah had crumbled to the floor with the odor of what the museum guards would describe as "something burnt."

Sylvie later said that she thought perhaps some electrical discharge had gone off in the tomb's display. The emergency workers could see that her mother in the wheelchair had seemed stunned, and she herself could remember nothing except a terrible flash of light. The health team had wheeled Giuliana and taken Sylvie away while they worked to revive the important foreign businesswoman who had been struck by some arc of electricity.

***

Carlo had come from an anteroom where he'd sat with Talia as the sirens wailed, and EMT workers scrambled down the now blocked-off hallway of the Etruscan exhibition. Though the majority of visitors had left before the unexplained accident, museum officials and guards now remained to discuss the wonderful reception the exhibition had been having, which now was likely a catastrophe. A visitor's near-electrocution would not be a convivial invitation to the Peabody's hallowed halls.

Sergio, in one corner of the rotunda, remained surrounded by technicians who were trying to explain what they thought might have occurred. Old circuitry? A lightning strike? Nor did anyone know who or exactly how many had been injured. Certainly, one woman "was down." That's all that was certain.

For the last hour, Carlo had been searching through the exhibits and the diminishing crowd for Sylvie and Giuliana. He'd inquired if they had been taken to a hospital and he had missed them in the confusion, but received no answer. But now a familiar toss of black hair caught his eye, and Carlo saw his sister standing near a woman in a dark dress, a slender woman with an elegant tilt to her head. Nearly hidden by an arching vault, he ran to them, stupidly gazing from one to the other as they stood hand in hand, their eyes wide, perhaps a bit dazed, yet smiling. And in that moment, for him, their relationship suddenly became clear. Carlo could barely catch his breath. "Giuliana, you are…. You are standing. You are… better? You are not injured?"

She nodded, grazing his face with her fingertips. She was as he'd remembered her when he was a child, quiet, strong, peaceful. "Together… you two. Together, one would think that you are a… a mother… and a daughter," he ventured. Carlo felt the tears begin down his cheeks as Giuliana nodded, saying, "It is true, my boy." He took a step back, then forward seeking her arms.

"It is true? And I… then I belong as well. As with my sister… I belong to you too. Mother. Not Zia… but…." And Giuliana turned from Sylvie and placed both of her hands to cradle his cheeks and said, "Dear Carlo… my Carlo. I must tell you…. I have had but a single child."

A rustle went through the people remaining in the rotunda as the emergency workers rolled a figure from the exhibition's sepulcher toward the waiting ambulance. Now the few staring patrons, too curious to have left earlier, felt themselves satisfied and turned to go. Officials also exited the rotunda, leaving several security guards who busied themselves with doors, alarms, and various telephone codes.

Only one figure remained. A man in a suit who stood transfixed by the woman he saw standing in a dark dress on the far side of the room. He may have willed it, but she slowly turned to return his gaze.

Giuliana let her arm fall from Carlo's shoulder, and with a benevolent gaze at Sylvie, opened the girl's hand and again, placed the little vase inside. Then slowly, but straight and tall, she walked toward the man, stopping only when she had found the center beneath the great bell-shaped dome above. He smiled at her, shy, hesitant, pleading for her agreement from the far side of the hall, then he joined her, reaching out his two hands to grasp the two of hers—perhaps not yet fully realizing that she had completed the first dream he had dreamt in Pitigliano.

"It has been… a lifetime," whispered Sergio, letting his eyes explore the contours of her face with its tracery of tiny lines that he thought designed by a master. "The years have been kind to you, Giuliana. You are beautiful. You remain beautiful. To have found you here…." His words trailed away with a shake of his head and eyes that closed with realization. Yet even as Sergio stood touching the woman he had loved above any other, he was not naïve. And her life's other actors had no doubt changed her, the years alone altering both of them in ways that were not only physical.

"A lifetime, yes," she spoke softly. "Perhaps more than one. We have both lived through much." Then Giuliana pulled back slightly and smiled at him with tenderness touched with the irony the years had bestowed. "Would you walk with me into the tomb, Sergio? Is there time? It is breathtaking. Unless one has been there, they could not know how carefully you have brought the real one back to life."

Sergio felt a small tear open in his chest—a feeling that this warmly tangible memory of love would likely remain just that. Giuliana seemed warm, but tentative, gently friendly, but fully realized on her own terms. He guessed that they would resume a relationship built on scholarly details and discussions of pottery shards, and simply step over what had for him quietly animated his impoverished personal life and his, now likely unrealistic dreams of one day loving Giuliana again. How foolish of him—a man in the last quarter of his life. What had he been thinking? Nothing remains the same, he reminded himself. Only his own faithlessness.

Preoccupied with baseball scores and oblivious of the softly lit exhibition down the corridor, a couple of guards stood near the door as Giuliana turned to Sylvie and Carlo standing together in the alcove across the rotunda. She blew a kiss to the pair who watched in confusion, then with her arm in Sergio's entered the long passage of the tomb.

"So many hours here," she said softly. "Do you remember how cold it became in the fall? All of that ancient powder and humus we must have inhaled."

He smiled at her, their feet scraping the dirt with a familiar cadence. "Your fingers would be blue when we pulled you up," he said. "But your little hips and shoulders were perfect for the aperture we'd cut. The pieces could not have been retrieved if not for you…."

Giuliana tilted her head briefly against his shoulder. "Is this the room that you broke into that winter?" She stopped, pulling him gently into what looked like a white-washed room with reds and ochres, blues and green garlands painted along the walls. Sergio laughed. "Yes! But it wouldn't have done to show how I entered it, would it? Or why we were digging in the winter…. People don't want to remember the war…." He grew quiet as he gazed at the ceiling where he had let himself down to Giuliana. Yet, both of them were remembering what had happened next.

She sat down on the banquette, the facsimile of what they both had thought of as a marriage bed. And Sergio, hesitantly, sat beside her.

"Yes, the war," she said looking around. "Later, the guns were put in that corner, weren't they? And the straw over there... surrounding the cartridges...." Giuliana sighed and leaned her head against a painted bacchanal. "So many people died, and yet from here, parts of it seem like a play, a pantomime we children learned the words to without understanding why we'd been cast in our roles. We were children, Sergio, weren't we, tasked with decisions meant for Solomons—some of us making decisions to dance with devils; I danced with them. Did you know that?"

Sergio wasn't sure what she could mean. It was he, wasn't it, who had failed—failed each of the people he loved and wished to serve. Giuliana had been the only one who had been courageous even as he'd fled with his ruined soul. And he knew that as he faced her now, he remained capable of the same sin of duplicity.

He reached across to her, almost to steady himself from his shame, but she took his hand in both of hers. "We have both done many things, dear Sergio, things that have hurt, that have harmed, yes, even unspeakable and selfish things. Yet forgiveness must come from God. It is not for you or me to seek it elsewhere. The things we have done, or haven't done, should be left here—below, in the keeping of the ancient ones—buried or at least walled away, in a place where recriminations and regrets and remorse will be left in the keeping of the dead."

He didn't know that his cheeks were wet with tears, only that Giuliana's fingers caressed his back and that with each touch he felt something lost, regained.

"I share with you my sins, Sergio, and you acknowledge yours. In this place, then, they will be left." She took a long breath and pressed their shared clasp to her chest. "You pushed a plunger that would have killed those you love. And you had been unfaithful to me," she said. She gazed into Sergio's eyes as he wept silently the years of self-loathing, the years of waste.

"And like another woman of my family who gave away her children, I have taken lives to save my own… the lives of babies… who barely knew life." She stopped as if her breath would no longer come. And then, "We are not without blemish, Sergio. Nor Simon, nor Rebekah, nor even the gentle soul of Rosetta. But self-hatred, as with a fine silver mirror, must now be turned away."

Giuliana put her fingers against his cheek and lifted his head to gaze at the illuminated figures surrounding them. "Perhaps it is for us the way it is for those here on these walls, where time was suspended, where life came and went above them, but the most vibrant part of their lives remained suspended here, the nucleus, the treasure, its living heart. Perhaps this is how it is for us, dear man, walled off, encapsulated, preserved just as it was. Perhaps now we breathe the breath of life to it again. Perhaps we start once more…."

Chapter 62

The pale blue room was quiet except for the electric lungs that pushed and pulled air into and from the inert woman in the bed. In the private space in the Intensive Care Unit of Boston's Massachusetts General Hospital, where the rooms lined up facing the nursing station, their glass walls allowing easy monitoring without a nurse having to actually rise, two women existed. One did it without moving, without conscious involvement in the endeavor. The other did it without her own consent, preferring perhaps to have never existed at all.

It had seemed such a long time to Talia—living. Trying sometimes to make it seem worth the effort, other times, knowing it was not. There had been the years, the early years with Enrico, when the handsome military man had courted her, when she saw the future—mothering a family, lighting candles on Shabbat. She had felt spoiled by him and others suitors too, and deserving of what good things life would bring. In the end, what a joke it had all been.

Talia moved to look at Rebekah. Feeling neither remorse nor maternal love, she perfunctorily touched the sheet that covered her daughter, wondering if Rebekah had ever felt such things herself.

Yet, it hadn't all been the fault of this woman, probably dying beside her. It was her own, wasn't it? Talia's own deal, her mother's deal too, their acceptance of the terms that gave to a Presence mightier than their own will, the dead first-born child—and in Talia's case, the "use" of any others. And how the Dybbuk had played with them, the pitiable children who had been assigned before their births. Simon, who found only lies to form his words and acts, and Rebekah, whose jealous Possessor wanted everything for itself.

Talia felt grateful that Rebekah had not born a child—that Simon had not fathered one—for no doubt, they too would be claimed by the Jewish demon who jealously could not be sated. Now, it was time. Long past. She could feel the peace near that she had so long anticipated. She closed her eyes and mentally smiled at Enrico. She knew he would approve.

Talia lifted her head to glance in the direction of the nurse's station where the change of shifts had the white-garbed women gossiping and applying fresh lip-stick to begin their eight-hour night. She looked at Rebekah, who had gained so much material wealth, yet was still but a piece of chattel, and blessed her with a Jewish prayer and the sign of the Cross above her head.

Then quietly, Talia took the instrument from her purse, and in movements that were as strong and swift as any selfish ones she'd made to save her own life from drowning, she opened the throat of her daughter and with a deeper cut, her own as well.

Chapter 63

Carlo pulled on a sweater and curled a muffler around his neck. He had been in bed. Several nights he had actually tried the bed, even closed his eyes from time to time. But sleep had lost its friendliness and was avoiding any efforts Carlo made to seek it out.

Instead, since the last night of the Etruscan exhibition, a steady stream of people had called—Italians from the consulate, Germans from theirs, policemen, detectives, all wanting to know connections Carlo and Sylvie had had to the dead woman and the woman in the green coat who killed her.

He guessed he might have found an hour or two of rest on at least a few of the nights if it hadn't been for the other thought that after so many years had now formed itself into a physical longing to know. Now it seemed the most important thing. Who might his own mother have been? And his father? Sylvie had found hers. But Carlo remained an orphan.

He stepped out onto the front stoop. It was chilly, but the wind hadn't kicked up yet. The park across the street looked deserted this time of night. Maybe he would walk a little, let his mind settle, look at some trees, just not ruminate on questions for which there were no answers.

Carlo glanced up and down the empty street. It mattered little which direction to take. Kind of like his life at the moment, he shrugged. Once so orderly, now he felt questions speckled every aspect of who he was. That was the question, though, wasn't it? Who the hell was he? Who was he meant to have become?

He stepped down onto the stoop, plunging his hands deep in his pockets for warmth, and was surprised when his fingers felt the outline of something rounded and rough. Something Sylvie had pressed into his hands as she boarded the plane to Italy with her mother.

The little urn. The little tchotchke the two women seemed to have traded back and forth. Funny how folks get hung up on keepsakes, he thought. Little throwbacks to some now forgotten memory. He'd stick it on a bookshelf somewhere. Let it go on crumbling and forgotten… alone. He couldn't help but feel a kinship.

As he crossed to the far side of the street where it felt colder in the deeper shadows of the trees, Carlo heard someone call his name. He looked back and forth, toward the empty sidewalks and through the oaks. He didn't notice until then that there was someone sitting very still on a bench just to the left. The man was dressed in a black coat with a wide-brimmed, homburg-like hat pulled low on his face, perhaps for warmth. He had one arm lying along the top of the bench and looked at ease with his legs casually crossed.

"Carlo? Carlo, why don't you come join me?" The man was familiar in some way, but he sat shaded from the street's light by a large branch, and at first it wasn't clear to Carlo if he knew him or not.

But as he approached, he saw exactly who it was. The priest. The intrusive priest he had called what seemed years ago, but was only weeks, to try to exorcise something devilish from his aunt. Carlo really wanted nothing to do with this cleric who had later entered his home, only invited by an irresponsible old sitter. It seemed the priest may have had something else unscrupulous on his agenda. Carlo wasn't sure, and he didn't want to know now.

"What do you want?" said Carlo without moving.

"I'd like you to sit down with me for a few minutes," said Father Paolo.

"Why?"

"Come, come, Carlo. There can be no harm. I may have something you would want to hear."

"I don't want to hear anything from you. My aunt is better, she has returned to Europe. We have nothing to talk about," said Carlo, pulling the muffler more tightly around his neck.

Then the priest leaned forward and patted the bench beside him. "Let me tell you a story, Carlo… of a family, a very complicated story. It's about Jews and Christians and war and love… and death…. And even about orphans." The old priest smiled up at him. "You'll want to know. I'm sure you will."

As Carlo took a tentative step toward the bench, the priest looked up and said quietly, "Sit, my son."

Then he added with a glance from the blue eyes beneath his brows, "Of course, of some things, we can never, ever be sure, can we, son? My son… Carlo."

The younger man stood for a moment, watching the smile that slowly formed along the priest's lips, hearing the echo of words he had so longed to hear, "Son. *My* son."

The leaves shifted as Carlo took another step, and then a fresh wind blew across his face, cool, liquid-like, new air that washed the moment.

An egg. A sperm. A "son?" Carlo slowly smiled back at the priest. Then he laughed out loud. Of "some things" he could feel very sure. And plunging his hands deeper into his pockets, he turned his back on the old man, alone in the dark, and strode off toward the lights on Boylston Street to resume his life and have a drink with a red-haired barmaid who'd never even heard of grappa—suddenly grateful for the odd warmth that seemed to be coming from the little urn deep inside his pocket.

About the Author

Marina Brown was born in Indianapolis. She has written for newspapers and magazines for the last twenty years: the St. Petersburg Times, the Tallahassee Democrat, Florida Design, Dance Magazine among them. She is the recipient of numerous writing awards, including First Places in the Porter Fleming Short Story Contest, Second Place in the Lorian Hemingway Contest for Short Stories, First Place in the Red Hills Poetry Contest, the 2013 and 2017 Florida Authors and Publishers Gold Medal Awards in Adult Fiction for both her debut novel, *Land Without Mirrors* and for *Lisbeth*. Most recently she received an FAPA Silver Medal for her poetry collection, *The Leaf Does Not Believe It Will Fall.*

Brown is a former professional ballet dancer, a sailor, a watercolorist, a cellist and a traveler. She lives in Tallahassee, Florida.

Contact Marina Brown at mcdb100@comcast.net or through Marina Brown Author on Facebook for signings, readings, or book club appearances

Available on Amazon

"Can I feel my fingertips? Am I one of them now?"

Brown's Gold Medal-winning, debut novel is set on an exotic Caribbean island inhabited solely by exiled lepers and their caregivers. Here, a sinister priest, an enigmatic nun, and a troubled doctor engage in a dangerous struggle for power, as three youths yearn for a different life, wondering if they too are diseased.

Even as the intense search for a cure for leprosy washes throughout the tale, *Land Without Mirrors* is at heart a love story—mothers for their children; men for power and fame; and a sweet first love that grows to maturity.

Available on Amazon

"There's killin' goin' on tonight..." Lisbeth wept. And in response to the young man's surprise, she whispered, "I think I killed my father... and my father has certainly killed me."

So begins the intriguing Gothic saga that leaps time and place as two families - one black, one white - discover their shared need for retribution and their capacity for fidelity and love.

Now forty years after the hurricane that destroyed the house where Lisbeth was exiled and died, her daughter, Claire finds herself compelled to bring it back to life. But the past and its evils are awakened as the ruins are disturbed, laying bare the sins of a time when Jim Crow ruled the South, when depravity took place behind lace curtains, and when interracial love could get you killed.

Available on Amazon

Southern Literary Review Editor, Donna Meredith writes, “This is an award-winning collection of poetry in language so lush and musical it dances across the pages. It offers a profound insight into the meaning of life in a symphony of sound and a kaleidoscope of colors.”

“These are gorgeous poems that turn into head-swiveling moments of truth.” Phyliss Leichester, author and poet, U.K.

“Brown conducts the moments of everyday life, rich with love and imagination.” Josephine Yu, author of *Prayer Book of the Anxious.*

The Leaf Does Not Believe It Will Fall won the 2019 Florida Authors and Publishers Association Silver Medal for Poetry.

Available on Amazon

A poignant glimpse at this side of the tarmac where travelers leave something of themselves—fragments of living, wishes, hopes, and losses. Here is a collection of Airport characters we've each passed, but never noticed, all captured in stories and vignettes during a week of dawn to dusk encounters. Brown's charcoal sketches help bring them to life.

Made in the USA
Middletown, DE
20 June 2020